THE LOST
REFLECTION

Unleashing the darkest legend of New Orleans

BRUCE T. JONES

NEW YORK
VIRGINIA

The Lost Reflection
by Bruce Jones

Published by

köehlerbooks™
an imprint of Morgan James Publishing

5 Penn Plaza, 23rd floor
c/o Morgan James Publishing
New York, NY 10001
212-574-7939
www.koehlerbooks.com

Publisher
John Köehler

Executive Editor
Joe Coccaro

Habitat
for Humanity®
Peninsula and
Greater Williamsburg
Building Partner

In an effort to support local communities, raise awareness and funds, Morgan James Publishing donates a percentage of all book sales for the life of each book to Habitat for Humanity Peninsula and Greater Williamsburg.
Get involved today, visit www.MorganJamesBuilds.com

Without the following individuals
this novel would be but a memory of never was.

For the creativity and the life given, I thank God.

For unconditional love and patience:
Tracy, Andrew, Mallorie, Ryan, and Ali

For parents, sister, and the entire Jones/Cole clan
who have filled my life with love

For all I have had the honor of calling friends

For publishing and editing me into reality:
John Köehler, Joe Coccaro, and Cheryl Ross

and my inspiration Dr. Jack Eli Cole, Sr.

The journey has just begun.

Throughout our lives we take our reflection for granted,
some more than others.
We wake up and stare, or perhaps merely glance into
the mirror, knowing the face we see
is the same as yesterday and the day before.
Aging slowly with time, reflecting pride or shame,
happiness or sadness,
many times not the person we want to see.
Some have the power to change their reflection,
most do not.
There is no hiding from the truth reflected,
but can you change it?
What would you give to see that familiar face again,
the one that has been lost forever?

CHAPTER 1

THE NIGHT AIR in Jackson Square clung like a warm and soggy wool blanket—just another August night in the French Quarter. The spicy aroma of Cajun cooking permeated as tourists blended with the vast assortment of locals crowding the marketplace. Deep, earthy blues from a nearby restaurant reverberated off the historic walls of the surrounding structures. Saint Louis Cathedral, the oldest Catholic Church in the country, vigilantly towered over the square. Dim gas-glow flames scintillated from the street lanterns and buildings, scarcely illuminating the carnival atmosphere. Musicians, artists, and gypsies all worked their crafts to the delight of the nightly gatherers.

Stella LaRue was the oldest and wisest of the gypsy fortune tellers, a throwback to the classic gypsies in Lon Chaney movies of a bygone era. Stella was old, exactly how old nobody knew. An advancing kyphosis had given her a pronounced hump on her back. Crystal-blue eyes, so clear you would swear you could see right through them, highlighted her weathered cinnamon-brown face. Gray hair, tightly pulled back, framed her bandana-covered head. Jewelry excessively draped her neck and wrists. Most of it was worthless, but not to Stella. She valued it all with great reverence. Her mismatched, bright, layered, oversized clothes stated simply that she was a fashion maven.

She did not waste her talents on the typical tourists. Leaving them to her brethren fortune tellers, Stella would wait, biding her time for the *one* to approach her. If she sensed there was something of value to share with this person, she would offer them her unique insight.

Even though the square was crowded with tourists, she felt no calling strong enough to make a little cash. She sat at her table and watched in amusement as many of the other girls worked their craft. They were indeed "working" the crowd, a skill she had taught most of them. Although the majority had never developed the gift Stella possessed, they were all good at mixing a little truth with a healthy dose of bullshit. Occasionally, Stella would casually eavesdrop, forcing herself to conceal a smile of amusement when she heard a good whopper.

Stella believed in hope and promise, not gloom and despair. Tap dancing around bad fortunes most of the time, she offered only a glimpse of potential tragedy. "What good is it to tell someone they are going to die tomorrow?" she would say. "Better to tell them that a loved one is about to suffer a great tragedy, show love to all near and dear. Tell them only a half-truth, for it's never wise to share all of life's mysteries." Stella could sense bad karma like a mouthful of sour milk. Her purpose, she believed, was to set things right. And that is exactly what she did, masterfully blending truth and fiction. In the end, her message remained an undying constant. Love for another, yourself, the planet, it did not matter. Love conquers all.

Tonight was slow. There were no spiritual emergencies looming from any of these walking, talking specimens of sociologically decaying humans. Although it was a quiet night, Stella felt there was an ill cast to the moon, but the where or why had not become apparent. Imminently, this was about to change.

"Good evening, Madame Stella," a young woman purred in a deep velvety voice as she approached.

"Good evenin' to you, Lady Isabelle," came a raspy, smoking-induced reply.

The old woman was seated at a rickety fold-up card table with mismatched chairs, appearing to be salvaged from the Salvation

Army dumpster. On the table was a deck of Tarot cards and a crystal ball concealed by a blue velvet cover.

Accentuated by brilliant cobalt eyes, Isabelle's face was hauntingly flawless. Her black hair spiraled down just past her bare shoulders, contrasting against her moonlight-white skin. Tall and slender, she made her routine nightly rounds dressed in low-cut, lacy black attire, crippling the resistance of passing men regardless of female companionship.

It was ten o'clock, and like most nights, Lady Isabelle was on the prowl, constantly searching for fresh meat. As fate dictated, she was the anointed leader of the modern cult of vampire wanna be's inhabiting New Orleans. As the stories of vampirism traveled throughout the country, many wayward souls found the city's dark heritage created an ideal home. This modern-day cult consisted of the classic coffin-by-day-blood-drinker-by-night types, sexual predators, and mindfuckers. But they all shared one common thread: Lady Isabelle was their leader. Her mysterious persona, sex appeal, and gothic style made her matriarch of this bizarre cult of misfits. Her orgasmic consumption of blood was legendary amongst the clan of the "living dead."

"It looks like a slow night," Isabelle began.

"It's been steady 'ere, but I've got dis uneasy feeling 'bout the spirit ways tonight. I've been keepin' away from d'ose people," Stella reported as she thumbed in the direction of the tourists littering the square. "I'm jus' sittin' 'ere listenin' to da wind, what little dere is." Listening to the wind, as Stella put it, was her unique way of connecting with her karma. She claimed that she could hear voices calling, telling of things to be and things that had passed, all carried on the soft, gentle breeze that occasionally caressed her senses.

Periodically, the local police would visit Stella concerning unsolved crimes or missing persons. She would provide them with insight as to what had occurred, but often those clues were jumbled by insensible rantings and ravings from the spirit world. Stella was unable to interpret her messages, as she was in a transient state, totally unaware of the words flowing from her mouth. She existed somewhere between the world of the living and the dead and had no memory of these sessions. Only when the messages were comprehensible and clear did the police find her helpful. Although somewhat inconsistent, her gift was known to many.

"Lord, child, sit down," Stella exclaimed, alarmed by a sudden revelation. "It's you."

"What do you mean, it's me?" Isabelle replied, unaware of Stella's sudden premonition.

"I've been feelin' something foul in da wind. Felt it dis morning when I got up. Been feelin' it all day. Now 'ere you are and it's plain as the black on your dress. It's you! I can feel it."

Having known Isabelle for many years through frequent nightly visits, they had grown close. Often, the wise gypsy would give stern advice, as one would their child. Like any daughter, Isabelle would choose to ignore or heed the advice. The tone of the warning, along with the belief the old lady's craft was authentic, instantly sparked Isabelle's curiosity.

"What is it? Can you tell me?"

"I don' know. Maybe Kahlea can say." Kahlea, Stella's crystal ball, was her link to the spirit world. But unlike most portals, Kahlea worked, or at least Stella believed so. Whether the globe was indeed a medium, or in fact it was merely her psychic abilities, through Kahlea Stella witnessed glimpses of the future.

Isabelle did as instructed, sitting and pulling her chair close. Stella began caressing the ball with slow, intimate strokes. Kahlea suddenly developed a steamy condensation from within. Swirling cloud patterns flowed in a clockwise motion, intermittently mixed with dark abstract images that hovered against the current. "I see a man."

Isabelle inched forward, attempting to discern the strange images being interpreted. "He comes like a storm. Misery and great danger surround his existence." The patterns intensified and began to change hues. "I see evil, a great evil rising from da past. It clouds all our futures. Dere is so much death." Stella paused and reflected. Unwillingly entangled, she fell deeper within the globe.

Genuine concern inched across Isabelle's face. Never had Stella sounded such an alarm, or steered her down the wrong path. "Much remains unclear," the old lady continued in a mesmerized tone. "There is great conflict wit'in dis man."

Abruptly, the fog within the ball dissipated, transferring its energy to Stella's eyes. Her once crystal-blue eyes quickly turned opaque gray, blinding her. Fear welled up in the old woman. "Flee 'ere child. Dere is much danger."

"Ohhh," Stella moaned woefully as she glanced up searching, unable to make out the silhouette of the familiar woman before her. "Kahlea has lost her sight. Some evil from beyond has blinded us. Never before as dis 'appened," Stella wailed, confused, but not panicked by this anomaly. Isabelle remained transfixed on Kahlea, waiting for the globe to once again burst to life and reveal a sign or restore Stella's sight. Neither happened.

The gateway to an ancient evil had been breached and unexpectedly terminated. The evil had indeed blinded Kahlea and Stella. The danger of dwelling in the spirit world is never knowing who will awaken to answer the call of the medium. All of her long life, Stella had encountered spirits of many types, their triumphs and miseries, all laid out within the reaches of her enlightened mind. Even the most sinister of the spirit world could be tamed by her compassion. But the source from which this message came was not to be interpreted, communicated, or reasoned with. Its sole purpose was to forewarn of the unleashing of a great evil to come.

Stella sat in despair. The frightful calamity foretold paled in nature to the violent disruption from the message. Her eyes painstakingly began to clear as she continued to stare at the blurry silhouette before her. Isabelle's fine details remained shrouded in haze. "I fear Kahlea 'as been injured. I must take 'er 'ome now," Stella said as she rose and steadied herself against the table.

"But Stella, what does all this mean?"

"It means, child, you must leave dis place. Leave now and don' return any time soon. Your future remains unclear, but dis man, if you stay, his pain you will endure. You must leave. Dat is the only way."

"I can't leave here, this is my home," Isabelle proclaimed boldly. "Besides, I have many friends here who will protect me."

"I fear dat will not be enough. Dis man brings death to us all. Who lives or dies? Dat vision is lost. I don't know your part, but if you stay, you will be consumed in dis, dat much is certain," Stella lectured as she hurriedly gathered her belongings from the table. "Listen to me," she said, pointing a crooked finger, "I know your people will try to take care of you. I know you believe you 'ave to stay, but please leave. Do dis for ol' Stella."

"I promise I will be careful." Taking the old lady's hand into her own, she gazed about the only city she had ever known. "You know I have nowhere else to go. Besides, traveling for my kind is not as simple as packing a suitcase."

"Your kind," Stella huffed, "I been tellin' you for years 'oney, you need new friends. Good people. D'ose people ain't doin' nothin' but bringin' you down baby."

"I am one of those people," Isabelle proclaimed stubbornly. "I know you think I can just change my ways, but you are wrong. I am what I am, and no desire to change will ever alter that."

"And so it is," Stella sighed, gazed up to the heavens, then back to Isabelle. "We are what we are, and dere's no denyin' dat. I know you 'ave no faith, but I pray, God be wit' you." With that, Stella broke hold of Isabelle's hand and finished packing her belongings into a worn tapestry bag.

Isabelle stood and watched Stella clumsily disappear around the corner. Silently, she contemplated the dire warning. But no man controlled her destiny. And after all, it was only one man. Besides, Stella did not know everything. She had never seen or believed in Isabelle's peculiar circumstances. With the old gypsy gone, Isabelle scoffed defiantly, "What do you know of my kind?"

CHAPTER 2

STARING OUT THE window of the Boeing 757, daydreams occupy my thoughts, which permits me a temporary disconnect from the intensity of life. On the plane there are no bullets, bombs, or assassins. Thanks to the castrations of homeland security, my fellow passengers are relatively harmless and rather boring. Lost in a daydream, I am shielded from meaningless encounters.

My profession demands I travel frequently, leaving no real home, few true friends, and certainly no serious romantic relationship. It was not like I did not try once, years ago. After that debacle, the notion of being attached to one woman became somewhat unappealing. Years passed, and I found the energy required for a relationship was better spent in other directions.

New York was the perfect fit for my lifestyle. I was raised in the city by my Aunt Rena. She was a large, robust woman with a heavy Romanian accent and a smile for everyone she met. Her size was only surpassed by her love of life.

Having no memory of my parents, who were killed during the early years of the Cold War, Rena filled in filtered details as she saw fit. According to Rena, I was smuggled out, only an infant, as

Communism began sweeping Eastern Europe. Vague details and general descriptions were the shallow roots I possessed. My family history, as well as half of the Romanian population, were destroyed during the war. Sadly, Rena and I were the only survivors of our family.

As a young adult, my interest led me to study computer technology at the University of Virginia. Thanks to Uncle Sam, I became a spook before finishing my degree. My forte with data encryption and foreign languages launched a career neither envisioned nor desired. It went like this: a mundane dinner meeting with the dean of computer sciences, two-hour limo ride to Washington, sign your name on the dotted line, handshake, and bam, I was a spook. For a financially crippled junior in college, that kind of money was impossible to refuse. Oddly enough, I never stepped foot on campus again, but magically a degree appeared about a year later. CIA magic.

And like the waves of the ocean, the magic never stopped. Computer geek extraordinaire, to field agent, to assassin—how does that happen? It was *kind of* a subtle thing. Subtle like a charging bull. If I knew what they had in mind for me, I would have bolted out the door and sprinted all the way back to UVA. One day while deciphering codes, a coworker suggested we go down to the pistol range to blow off some steam. Having done this on many occasions, he assured me I would love it. I had never even held a gun before, but after six hours of encryption, the thought of shooting something sounded appealing.

Appeal turned to love, then obsession. I could not get enough of the cold steely grip, the testosterone-pumping action of squeezing the trigger, the buck of the recoil, the smell of spent powder, and sound of the bullet singeing the air it dissected. In short order, I graduated to assault rifles. I made new friends there, very intense friends. They enjoyed sharing many aspects of their unique training in which I always participated, as a tagalong, so to speak. Now my daily regiment consisted of training—hand-to-hand combat, tactical assault, explosive devices, and occasionally computer work. Oddly, I never put two and two together until it was too late.

My first mission was rather simple. Sneak into the former Soviet Union, hack into an army general's computer, download a variety of top secret files, and get back home alive. Yep, piece of cake. Perhaps it was time to reconsider that sprint back to UVA. But in a bizarre way, the danger beckoned me.

Spencer and Davis, two cowboys that had been thrown off the bull a few times too many, were in charge of the mission. The mission was a huge success, except Spencer got shot, Davis killed, and I had to waste two border guards crossing back into West Germany. Lesson seventy-eight—we were all expendable. The death of Buck Davis passed without notice. After all, we were on a mission that theoretically never happened. Quite frankly, we were not all expected to return.

Pulling the trigger on those guards was simple. It was live or die, and at age twenty-four I was not ready to check out just yet. Remorseless—that pretty much summed up my complete lack of emotion. A weaker man would have felt the pain, been concerned by the disconnect, but not me. Neptune became my code name. I was cold, hard, and distant as the sea. There was no funeral for Brian Denman, computer geek.

Never being privy to purpose, the less asked, the easier my job. Europe, Asia, South America, the Middle East, and all the shitholes in between became my playground. Years faded to decades. At the end, two years in Colombia convinced me enough was enough. Those fuckers were the craziest bastards I had ever run into. Sure, suicidal radical Muslims were crazy fucks, but they were no match for coked-up, drug-running cowboys. Not humanely killing people, but butchering and mutilating, they were the icing on the cake of lunacy. Not for any particular cause or shock value to a global audience, it was just good, old-fashioned fun, Colombian style.

After twenty years of service to my country, I quit for opportunities in the private sector. Politicians and the wealthy were always in need of my special talents. People with connections, power, and big checkbooks became my new employers. Some jobs were legitimate, others well, they legitimately paid well. The beauty was I now had the ability to pick and choose my assignments. Once again, my lack of conscience served as my capitalistic guide.

It was through this new career path that I met Phillip Wilder. Phillip was the owner and publisher of Urban Legends Weekly tabloid. Urban Legends was geared for a younger, hipper audience. On occasions, Phillip paid me dearly to unravel rumored stories involving drug companies and their dangerous products. When subpoenas and grand jury inquisitions failed to get results, I was called in to apply more persuasive methods. It got ugly from time to time, but I always got results and was rewarded appropriately. In finality, a greater good was served. Phillip got one hell of a scoop, and I stayed gainfully employed and more important, compensated.

Occasionally, work proved to be entertaining—secrets of Hollywood stars, politicians and hookers, hell any public figure, and a rumor of misfortune that sold papers. True, I loved the added income, but more so it had become a favorite pastime, knocking down the high and mighty a notch or two. Especially the hypocrites.

***

A sudden violent drop in altitude jolted me from my reverie. Glancing out the window, I refocused my attention on the horizon. Once towering cotton cumulus clouds had darkened as the afternoon sun brewed up a powerful storm over the Gulf of Mexico. With each passing minute, the clouds swelled with moisture, and flashes of light announced the ensuing rodeo ride. As playful as a jeep traveling down mortar-shelled roads, our plane bounded through layers of unseen turbulence to the delight of nobody but me. Imaginary symphonies trumpeted Wagner's *Ride of the Valkyries*, announcing my imminent approach. Sensing fear in the air, I suppressed an amused grin.

Brilliant streaks of lightning were followed by another substantial drop in altitude, the sort that catapult the stomach up your throat. We were descending into the storm on our final approach. A white-knuckled, double-fisted grip was attached to a rather attractive blonde who had been seated next to me since our departure from LA. Lost in my own world of self-absorption, I had completely tuned out the existence of anyone seated next to me. Now as the flight neared conclusion, I honed in on the most delectable pair of drumsticks I had seen in a long time. A slit in her short knit skirt revealed enough of her perfectly toned and tanned thighs to cause turbulence of a different nature. And yes, you might know it, those legs traversed past succulent sculpted calves all the way down to a pair of black leather pumps. White knuckles packed my one true weakness: drop-dead legs.

Had we been in a restaurant, a department store, a park, or any-where other than a plane, I would have succumbed to my weakness and made an attempt to connect with this leggy babe. But we were on a plane. I made that mistake once, years ago. It nearly cost me my life. Hence, golden rule number one.

Appearing reasonably distraught from the turbulence, I con-cluded she was near barf mode. Or was it mere theatrics to draw me into conversation to be followed by dinner and attempted murder for dessert? Paranoid? It mattered not. Rules are rules. Regardless of her wavy, sandy-blond hair appearing to have the texture of silk, draping neatly to her shoulders, and those full, moist, inviting lips framed by flawless skin, rule number one is never broken. Certainly those sparkling chestnut-hazel eyes would not sway my resolve, but damn those legs! I wondered if the shrinks back at the CIA had a name for my paranoia. Ever since the incident, chance encounters on airplanes were taboo. No more airplane buddies. Period.

Deciding to be the "good guy," I attempted to help her. "Try to relax. It is far safer up here than it is down there." She acknowledged me with a nervous smile. "You must not fly often."

"It's the first time in over five years," she replied tensely.

"Up until the storm I would have taken you for a frequent flyer." Any statement affording distraction would hopefully help her refrain from singing into the airsick bag.

"Why is that?"

Stupid, offbeat, or humorous statements usually work the best. Her death grip on the armrest eased, relaxing the swollen veins in her hands ever so slightly. Enemy operatives are skilled in faking these reactions to initiate conversations. I was not buying into this damsel in distress, not yet.

"Well, I do not wish to offend or embarrass you, but I find you very attractive. It has been my experience that women like you, that look like you, traveling from LA for whatever purpose, usually have a lifestyle that affords frequent travel."

"Is that all?"

"No. I also noticed you don't have a wedding ring. But I am will-ing to bet you are married or were married. Judging from your tan, you spend time outdoors, and legs that exceptional," I said as my eyes wandered south, "do not happen by accident."

She absorbed my observations in brief silence as a smirk curled up from the corner of her mouth. "Wow, and to think I thought your head was crazy glued to the window the entire flight. I've often wondered what goes through people's minds when they sit in isolation for hours. In your case, now I know. How long did it take you to assimilate your observations, detective? Did you do it on the fly?"

"I am not a detective, but I must confess, I saw the reflection of your legs in the window the moment you sat down. The rest of it was right off the cuff. My line of work requires me to analyze people and situations and preemptively remove threats which might prove harmful."

She appeared perplexed.

"I hope I did not embarrass you, but I do not waste time with bullshit. I tell people what I am thinking whether they like it or not. Honesty is rarely pleasant. And my name is Brian, unless you prefer to call me detective. I have answered to worse."

She held out a well-manicured hand. "Okay, Brian, Mister Straight Shooter, I am Samantha."

I had never been one to shake the hand of women. I took her hand and kissed it softly. Her skin was lightly fragranced and smooth as chiffon. Her reaction was not uninviting. "It is my pleasure to meet you. So how did I do?"

The sensation of my lips on her hand appeared to rattle her calculating demeanor as she appeared to count off an imaginary checklist before answering.

"I have always hated flying and prefer to drive just about anywhere. I have been separated from my husband for more than a year, live in Beverly Hills, and love tennis and running. So all in all you are pretty much on the mark."

I grinned at my accuracy.

"So what is your story, Brian? Are you always this brutally charming?"

"Handshakes are for guys. This is how I greet every woman I meet."

"Darn, for a minute I thought I was getting some special treatment. That was the first kiss of any type since my husband left. And I'm not sure why, but the kiss reminded me it might be nice to enjoy the company of a man for a change."

"The company of a man? That sounds like an open-ended proposition."

A sudden drop in altitude instantly diverted her attention as Samantha redoubled her grip on the armrest. I lightly touched her hand reassuringly. She looked at my hand on hers and then back to me nervously. "I have flown most of my life. This little turbulence is nothing. Try to relax."

She loosened her grip ever so slightly and forced a smile. "Easy for you to say." Gazing intently into each other's eyes, that rare, silent, concise moment transpired when energy between two people connect, where all that exists are two naked spirits fully exploring each other's being. It happens in a flash, then bam, the moment is gone.

Simultaneously we snapped our attentions forward. She felt it too.

Frightened by a sensation she could not perceive, "I can't believe myself," she said, blushing, continuing to stare at the seat in front of her. "I have known you all of five minutes and I'm ready to ..."

"Ready to what?"

"Nothing. It's just ever since my husband decided he needed to be married to a twenty-one year-old Laker cheerleader with fake boobs, I've lived like a nun."

"Relax, Sister Samantha. Your virtue is safe with me."

Samantha felt compelled to explain, to justify her newly discovered desire to be free. Unwilling to leave the safe harbor the headrest granted, she talked to the seat in front of her. "I was so angry with all men. I just wanted all of you to go away. It is going on two years, and he is out having all the fun while I continue to live in our home, thinking he will come back. Kind of pathetic, don't you think?"

"You do realize you are thinking out loud."

"Too much information?"

"No, but I usually do not meet many women that open up quite as quickly as you. To answer your question, no, it is not pathetic. Not if you truly loved him. But it can be difficult to diagnose the difference between true love and love of a lifestyle. I know too many women that could not tell you the difference if you held a gun to their head. But take away their lifestyle and they know the difference instantly. Sadly, going from riches to rags, most will not even make the effort to stomach it. The lifestyle goes away and so do they. That is what I consider truly pathetic."

Samantha turned to me, waiting for more of my self-guided wisdom. This situation was getting out of hand. Her mesmerizing eyes glistened with sadness, reflecting pain. She glanced down at the floor momentarily, then back to me uneasily. Embarrassment and confusion resided within her eyes and were on the verge of spilling out all over me. I had never experienced such emotion merely looking into a woman's eyes. Emotional thoughts, me? There was no way. Time to suppress that shit. She was not allowed anywhere near my inner thoughts, although she was clearly inching along that barbed-wire fence. Keep talking. Make something up! I broke eye contact and filled my head with another look at her legs.

"I'm up here," she said timidly, managing a quirky smile.

"Busted!" I said. "It is easy to confuse love for a person with everything that person brings to your life—cars, homes, money, fame, or even simple companionship. I am willing to bet you had it all." She nodded affirmatively. "That is nothing but easy love, if you ask me. Could you have stayed in love if he lost it all?"

Samantha looked as if she was waiting for me to continue, but then responded, "I could have."

"Sorry if I seem a little cynical, but what little true love I've witnessed is where the greatest asset is each other. The people who have it all rely on all the wrong things. I believe wealth corrupts our ability and clouds our judgment when it comes to understanding the most basic human need—love."

"What do you do that affords you all this insight? What makes you such an expert on the subject?"

"I am an outsider looking in, an armchair quarterback. It is easy to analyze the game when you are on the sidelines. And that is all you get to know about me."

"You sound like a man who is hiding or ashamed of something." Samantha's demeanor flipped like a bad comb-over on a windy day. Unintentionally, I had insulted her way of life. On an offensive, she released the armrest, no longer paying attention to the turbulence which had intensified.

Not wanting to answer, I remained silent, sensing a growing connection on an undefinable level. Regretfully, approaching New

Orleans I found myself wishing this conversation started long before it did.

"Are you married, Brian, or have you been?" she asked insistently, arms crossed, trespassing on my thoughts and ignoring my insistence on personal privacy.

I sighed. Not an irritated sigh, but one of an unrelenting conviction succumbing to a weakness unfamiliar to me. "My job does not permit it." There was an unintended sadness in my tone.

"Oh my gosh. Are you a priest?"

"As many confessions as I have heard, one might think so. But no. Love in my line of work is just not an option." I paused to reflect on the very career that led to a life of shallow relationships. It was not that I enjoyed or disliked what some might call shallow, it was just the life that went with the territory.

My melancholy tone sparked sympathy. Again, my silence was invaded by her inquisitiveness. "So, if you are going to shut me out before we have a chance to get started, I feel you owe me an explanation." Her infectious smile weakened my ironclad defenses.

" Well, honey, if it will make our divorce less painful then I shall illuminate. I was in love once years ago. Ever seen a skyscraper collapse? That is the scale of how it ended. My job requires me to pick up and leave at the ring of a phone. It is dangerous, to the degree that one day I probably will not return home. It is much easier to have short, insignificant relationships rather than meaningful ones that crush two people in the end."

Her eyes would not release me. Unforeseen guilt forced me to turn away once more. I could not remember the last time I lost a staring contest. She shifted in her seat, revealing more of those tantalizing legs. Way too much, I thought, as a new discomfort stirred. She followed my gaze down to the object of my attention. "Stay with me up here, Brian." Damn, she was good. My concrete wall of resolve just suffered a major assault vis-à-vis my pathetic psychosexual fetish. Apparently my opponent was readily equipped with a lethal arsenal, hellbent on ruining what was once a damned good disciplined soldier.

"So why don't you just quit?" she asked point-blank. "If you met the right person, I would think love would be so much more fulfilling than any career."

I dared not tell her I did exactly that, the quitting part, almost twenty years ago. Talk about lame excuses, but that was all I had. I had never really thought about the concept of relationships after I retired. I kept on just getting on. "How would I know it was love? And love takes time and commitment. Look where it got you. You thought your husband loved you and it would last forever. Did you give up a career for him? Friends? Don't you have regrets?"

"Touché," she sighed. "But for fourteen years, I thought it was the right thing. Up until he left, I had no regrets about my marriage. Then one day he decided he wanted more than I could provide. I have spent many a sleepless night wondering what went wrong. The man I once loved, I now despise. The pain at times has been unbearable.

"As much as I loathe Mike now, as much as it still hurts like hell, I would never wish those years away. There is no promise love will last forever. Everything has an end. He was part of the life that made me who I am today. Thanks to him, we are having this conversation."

Okay, she had a small point. But I was compelled to justify myself. "I did not want my relationship to end either, but it did. So I entrenched myself in my work, never making time to get involved again. Maybe I miss it, from time to time, but love is one thing that cannot be controlled, and I am an in-control type of guy."

"Your attitude makes it hard for a girl to think she might have a chance."

"We were doomed from hello."

Samantha leaned toward me, akin to an attorney leaning over the jury box, prepared for the case-winning rebuttal. "Brian, you have made me feel ... so unexpectedly ... emotions I thought were lost. The least you can do is tell me why."

"Fair enough." I conceded to the desire in her eyes. "About twenty-five years ago, I met a woman like you on a flight—intelligent, witty, and good looking. We hit it off and one thing led to another, dinner, drinks, her place ... then boom! She put a bullet in my head. Since then, no more friendly skies. It turned out she was not just your garden-variety psycho bitch. She was a hitter. She sat right beside me, just like you, played mindfuck, then put a bullet right here." I pointed to the faint scar. "Thus the golden rule. End of story."

"Oh my gosh. Twenty-five years ago? I would think you should have gotten over it by now." A covert yet obvious smirk telegraphed her belief that I survived, thus I should put on my big-boy underwear and get on with life.

"I have, thank you very much." I protested, retreating against the window. What the hell did she know. I bet she had never been shot. "It just so happens I choose not to include anyone I have met on a plane in my post-flight itinerary." My thoughts became random and disorganized. "That woman was not the only person who would like to clock me out permanently. I know too many dirty little secrets about influential people. If I were to ever write a book, a tell-all, people would go to jail, get divorced, or have their lives totally screwed up."

"If that were the case, why aren't you living on a secluded island? Why only single out women on a plane?" Our conversation was interrupted by the standard tray table and seat upright announcement.

After a moment, Samantha broke the silence. "Brian, I want more."

"I am sorry, Samantha, this is all there is. If circumstances were different, I would ..."

"Brian," she began patronizingly.

I flashed back to my childhood. "Brian," Aunt Rena's parental lectures always began in the same tone.

"I like your straight-forward honesty, it is so refreshing. You have made me feel a bit adventurous, maybe even mischievous. But regardless of your reasons, please have dinner with me. I promise not to broach any topic you don't want to discuss."

I started to shake my head, signaling a silent rejection. Samantha intercepted my response and placed her hand on my leg. She smiled devilishly. "I promise, I won't try to kill you."

I flashed an awkward smile, but still found no words to respond. I had to turn her down, but did not want to. She turned to me once again, affording an excessive view of her legs, which I believe she did intentionally. She watched as my gaze returned to the objects of my weakness. I was on the ropes, and she damn well knew it. Unfortunately the inner boy had already left the plane and was headed for the nearest hotel room.

Samantha waited for a reply. Her expression telegraphed the Ironclad was sinking. "If it would help ease your suspicions, I am willing to submit to a strip search before dinner, to ensure I am un-armed," she whispered in my ear.

The clicking of seat belts announced our arrival. As we stood to deplane, Samantha turned, our faces closer than they had been the entire flight. She took advantage of the moment and gave me a quick kiss on the cheek. "Sorry, that's just a girl thing, I didn't mean anything by it," she giggled. She turned, leaving me lockjawed and astonished.

***

Samantha walked briskly up the jetway, her smile fading, not looking to see if I followed. "What in the hell did I just do?" she murmured.

Spotting her sister, waving comically in the baggage claim area, Samantha picked up the pace. Hugging her sister, she handed the baggage claim stubs to Dana. "I have to pee, watch for my bags." Practically running, Samantha bolted for the restroom.

In the secluded safety of the restroom, she splashed her face with cold water. "To hell with the makeup," she fussed loud enough to be heard.

She dried her face and stared into the mirror. "Samantha Allen, what have you done?"

CHAPTER 3

SAMANTHA VANISHED LIKE a federal witness in a mafia investigation. At the end of the jetway I checked to the right and left. She was gone and I found myself completely dismayed. Justin, my personal assistant back home, shipped my clothes and personal effects to wherever work dictated. With no luggage arriving, I intentionally made a pass by the baggage carrousel in hopes of seeing Samantha. Disappointed, I turned toward the ground transportation doors.

"Who left the freakin' sauna on?" I protested once outside. Looking forward to an air-conditioned ride, I sadly discovered the AC in my yellow chariot was fried. The thirty-minute ride to the French Quarter was bumpy and smelly. Closing my eyes, it reminded me of those fond afternoons on the back roads of Colombia.

"Best get used to it, boss, ain't much AC in the Quarta," the cabbie informed me. It was impossible to determine whether the odor was from Dujour, the hack, or residual man funk from previous passengers. My bet was all of the above. Beads, various trinkets of jewelry, and several voodoo dolls adorned Dujour's cab. He was heavyset, black as night, and had a thick Creole accent. He maintained a perpetual smile no matter the conversation. Unattended bullets of perspiration sprinkled his smooth forehead.

Needing a distraction, my thoughts turned to Samantha. Before dinner I could have a full background check through an illegal back-door access I maintained in the CIA database. If she was dirty, it would prove quite entertaining to chop down the obvious skill and talents she possessed. Scenarios were racing through my mind. I had made a career of breaking opponents, but Samantha could prove to be the most enjoyable.

"Looks like da rain be comin' soon," Dujour remarked, breaking the silence.

"Yes, we flew through some of it on the way in, made for a bumpy ride," I deadpanned. *Not as bone-jarring as this cab ride*, I thought. "You here to play or work, mon?" Dujour interrupted again.

"All work." I considered the possibility of Samantha's self-imposed strip search.

"Betta take time to enjoy Nawlens while you's here mon. Da Big Easy don't take kind to folks who work for da mon all da time."

"Thank you, Dujour. I will keep that in mind."

"Da Mon" would be Phillip Wilder. Anyone who knew Phillip knew his zest for life. Phillip made millions with the Baby Boomers, Generations X and Y, and just about anybody who could not resist the hottest news with an up-yours attitude in his Urban Legends Weekly, a spin-off publication from his old man's tabloid empire. When he got a whiff of dirty laundry and conventional methods of investigation proved fruitless, I was called in.

Intimidation, threats, and on occasion, more persuasive actions were all tools of my trade. I was good at my job, thanks to the CIA. More important to Phillip than the execution of assignments, I never left tracks. Was my work illegal? It depended on which side of the gun you were standing. That is how good old Uncle Sam explained it. People died back in the day, it was the nature of the business. Call me a cold-hearted killer, I would not disagree. The only people that seemed to mind were my targets, and they did not complain for long.

After twenty-five years, I retired with a less than generous government pension. But then there was my discretionary retirement fund, somewhere in the neighborhood of fifteen million dollars generously donated by dead Colombian druglords who no longer required liquid assets. What was I supposed to do with all of that cash? Our government could never confess to sanctioned assassinations, firebombing coke plants, or depositing large sums of illegally obtained funds. They never asked, I never told. Then one fine morning I woke up sweaty, dirt caked on my hands and face, mosquito bites abounding and said, "Fuck this." I quit, moved back to New York City, where several years later I met Phillip and forged the friendship which led me here.

"Here we are, mon. Welcome to da French Quarta," Dujour announced. He wheeled onto Toulouse Street. Daydreaming, I had not paid attention to where we were going, which was completely out of character in a strange city. The cab skidded up to the Maison Dupuy. "Here you go mon, dis be your new home. It's nice and quiet down this end of da Quarta. Not too loud at night, not too close to da spirit yard eida."

"Spirit yard?" I questioned my smelly friend.

"Yeah, mon, spirit yard. You know da Quarta be filled wit ghost and all kind o' unnatural tings. Tings dat come out at night. Evil tings. You watch yo back after da sun go down, don't be walkin' round da empty streets. Be wit friends, in da night."

To be certain, Dujour drank more than his fair share of the spirit water, so there was no telling what he experienced during his altered states of sobriety. "How much I owe you, Dujour?"

"Seventeen-fifty."

Digging in my pocket, I extracted a couple of warm, damp twenties, the heat and humidity already working their magic. "Keep the change." I figured he could use the extra money to buy some soap, although realistically it would wind up in the bottom of a glass. Dujour thanked me and sped off as if he had just completed a pit stop. Standing on pavement hot as a three-alarm bean-burrito fart, sweat rolled down my back. Welcome to the French Quarter indeed!

CHAPTER 4

IT WAS WELL past four, and the afternoon heat had success-fully drained my energy to the point that a power nap was in order. However, this being my first trip to Nawlens as Dujour enunciated, why bother? Undoubtedly, Phillip would be ready for me to start right away. Any free time would be before dinner. Better to freshen up and scope out the town. The mere thought of dinner reminded me that I had not eaten all day, ushering a well-timed rumble in my stomach accentuating the notion.

Étouffée, gumbo, or perhaps jambalaya. Where to start? I had seen the likes on menus in various cities around the world, but fig-ured it would be better to enjoy it, prepared by the people who made it legendary. Why go to France and eat Italian? All things in proper order, first I needed to check in.

I was cheerfully greeted at the front desk by Renaldo, a young man in his mid-twenties, most likely Cuban. He was clean-cut, pressed, well-manicured, and accented his style with tasteful jew-elry. The front desk was clean and organized with every scrap of paper, pens, and paper clips put in their appropriate place. Renaldo was a man of detail.

"Good afternoon, and welcome to the Maison Dupuy, Mr. ...?" he prompted, raising a tweezed eyebrow with a polished smile.

"Denman. Brian Denman."

With swift strokes of the keyboard, Renaldo expeditiously found my reservation. "I see you will be staying with us for several weeks. Excellent. I have you booked with deluxe accommodations, balcony overlooking Toulouse Street," he exclaimed, flashing a broad, pearly white smile as he continued stroking the keyboard. "What brings you to the Big Easy, Mr. Denman?"

"Business. Research business."

"Excellent. And this is your first stay with us?"

"First trip to New Orleans."

"Then we will do everything possible to ensure New Orleans becomes a favorite destination. If there is anything you desire, I or my staff will gladly provide assistance." Renaldo swiped a blank keycard and extended his hand. "Will you be needing additional keys?" Renaldo sported the secret-man smirk insinuating female companionship.

"No, thank you." Leaning in close and speaking softly, I proceeded to elucidate my special needs. "Renaldo, there may be an instance where I would require special assistance. It may occur at odd hours or during inclement weather. It would not involve activities leading to incarceration, but might require solicitation from other ... less scrupulous individuals. I need a go-to guy, someone that I can count on. Know what I mean? If you know where I can find such a person, let's just say the job pays well." Extending a crisp, folded thousand dollar bill, no further clarification was needed. It was standard operation to get acquainted with a staffer at the hotel where I stayed. It came in rather handy more than once over the years. I paid well to ensure full attention.

Renaldo's eyes grew wide. "There's no need to look far, Mr. Denman. I pride myself on the ability to cater to my guest's needs, whatever they be." Looking from side to side to ensure our privacy, his hand latched onto the bill, attempting to claim his gratuity. Refusing to release my control, his attempt to extract the bill met firm resistance.

"Renaldo, our business is strictly confidential. If I call you at four in the morning, I have to know you can be counted on."

"In Havana, those born without anything learn how to take care of themselves at an early age. If you wanted a better life, you learned how to do … things," Renaldo explained with a mischievous grin. "As I said, Mr. Denman, I am your man."

"Outstanding! For now, nobody knows I am here, so if anyone were to show up inquiring, notify me immediately. If I am expecting someone, you will know prior to their arrival. No visitors, no phone calls. I do not care if George fucking Bush shows up, you do not know me. Clear?"

"As crystal."

"Should anyone inquire, send them away," I instructed, handing a card with a cell number on it, "then call me, even if you have not seen me in several days, even if I have checked out. If you are not on duty, the other desk clerks are to alert you immediately. They will not know or attempt to contact me. It is imperative the staff understands the rules."

"Got it," Renaldo responded quickly, removing the bill from my hand on cue as I released my grip.

"If you see me in the lobby, please do not acknowledge my name in the presence of others. I prefer my face to not have a name at-tached to it. Now, if you will give me my key, I think we're done."

"Absolutely, sir," Renaldo snapped accentuating the *sir*. "Room 306. The elevators just down the hall, on the left." Being part of a potentially mysterious, unscrupulous deed was a head trip for any willing participant, and Renaldo was a player. Most assuredly he would be up to a task or two. Hell, if nothing cropped up, I could contrive a job for the sake of his adventurous spirit.

I headed through the quaint compact lobby, checking out the layout on the way to the vacant elevator. The elevator doors closed slowly. The old car creaked and groaned as it sluggishly lifted. Old elevators had a certain mystique to them you just did not find in the newer ones. I enjoyed watching people react to the creaks and moans or sudden jolts they often provided. The doors strained to open as slowly as they had closed. My room was three doors down to the right. I opened the door, slid my bag in, and took a quick tour of the third floor. Long hallways with intermittent left turns wrapped around a garden courtyard below. Eventually the hall led me back to my starting point. This would work out well in the event of an un-expected departure. There were several exits around the corridors, plus the elevator, and a balcony in my room. An abundance of escape routes was always welcomed. I spent the next thirty minutes going up and down the stairs, checking out all of the exits and secluded locations in the hotel. In years past, on occasions when the action got dicey with the local police or associates of governments I had pissed off, emergency exits were vital to my survival. Too many comrades without exit strategies had been killed over the years.

CHAPTER 5

I SET MY course for the door, out into the balmy afternoon sauna. Although the day had grown long, it did not feel as though it had cooled one degree. It was not difficult to plot my direction. A block to the right was the end of the Quarter. To the left was a seemingly endless stream of houses and buildings right out of the nineteenth century. Gas fumes wafted from lanterns burning in the late afternoon sun. Walking down the cobblestone sidewalk, this city felt vaguely familiar.

I pulled my cell phone from my pocket and redialed the missed call. "You rang?"

"I'm starving, you rat bastard! Where have you been?"

"First time in the Big Easy, just beginning to feel my way around, you know? What is the word my brother?" I grabbed my shades and slid them on as the afternoon sun glared down Toulouse Street with the intensity of a halogen floodlight.

"Other than starving? I have been taking care of business."

"Taking care of business? Indeed." For Phillip that entailed women and booze. "Does this mean I am going to get pounded into submission by countless hours of bullshit tales of lustful fantasies that never happened?"

"My realities, your fantasies. And when I am done chronicling my deviant adventures, you will be up all night praying to spend just one night in my shoes, buddy boy."

"Phillip, you are my idol. So tell me, Juan of the Dons, where do you want to meet?"

"Where are you now?"

"I am on Toulouse, just about to cross over Bourbon Street."

Bourbon Street. Talk about infamous tales. Every swinging dick I knew had at least one outrageous anecdote about this place. Why did it take me sixty years to get here? Music was streaming in from all directions as the aroma of piss and beer oozed through the doors of the numerous open-air bars. To the left I heard jazz on top of jazz, mixed in with some blues from the opposite side of the street. To my right a band was ripping "Walk This Way" loud enough for Steven Tyler to hear it all the way back in Beantown. The musical smorgasbord fused in a most unexpected yet pleasing disharmony.

The late afternoon sun cast a golden glow on Bourbon Street, rendering a quaint inviting feeling. The sidewalks were crammed with a hodgepodge of shops, bars, and hotels. Weathered signs of every shape, color, and size hung over the distressed sidewalks, proudly proclaiming the establishments they adorned. And then there were the leaning balconies. No sober person would ever venture onto them. These platforms defied the laws of engineering when the clock strikes party time.

"Keep coming up Toulouse. When you get to Chartres, take a left. Down on the right about a half a block, you'll see a restaurant called The Alpine. I've already got us a table."

"Alpine? What the hell? I come all the way down here, with all of the legendary food, and the first place you take me is to a Euro dive!? I do not think so, Jack."

"Chill out, my friend. Don't get your lederhosen in a wad. All things in the universe will be righteous. Just know there is a very cold brewski waiting with your name on it," Phillip reassured.

"It had better be cold. Otherwise I may have to cap you on the spot, run up a tab, pay with your platinum card, and leave your stiff ass behind."

"Well," Phillip began, "except for the fact we are in New Orleans, that would be exactly like South Beach, if memory serves me right."

"Funny you could even remember. The last I saw of you in Miami

I did not think you would survive the night, much less remember any of the little details."

"Little details? Like a five-thousand-dollar tab?"

"Sucks being the drunken bitch." I hung up the phone and stepped up my pace.

The Alpine was hardly European cuisine at all. More like Cajun gone wild. I was all in. It would be good to see Phillip and turn my focus to business. Time to purge, cleanse, and not mention Samantha, not to Phillip, not to anyone.

Phillip was sitting in the back on the left. The tables immediately around him were empty while the remainder of the restaurant was packed. The aroma of the food immediately set me salivating. There were two beers on the table, as promised. Phillip never disappointed.

"Brian, it's great to see you! How the hell are you?" A smile exploded across his face.

"I feel like shit! You see ... I met this woman ... Samantha ... on the plane"

"Holy hell," Phillip interrupted, "you waltz in here and the first words from your mouth are about some bimbo you met on a plane? She made you feel like shit? How in the hell does that happen on a three-hour flight? Did she bone you?" Phillip shook his head in disbelief as he slid the bottle of beer over. "It's gonna take all night to work our way through this one. Sit down, drink up. The Love Doctor is in the house."

I sat in silence. It was as if the teeth of some hidden truth were gnawing into me. "It is like I got fucking T-boned by Cupid or something. I have been trying to figure this, I mean her, out since I got here. Truth is, I do not know what the fuck is going on with me."

"Maybe you're sick. Do you have a fever? Could be something you ate," Phillip asked in his cynical I-care-but-I'm-going-to-unmercifully-joke-the-hell-out-of-you smart ass manner. "Hey, might even be this deadly beaver fever I've heard was going around."

"Know where I might get a vaccination?"

"Well now that you ask, I've got the perfect prescription. We gonna take you down to Bourbon Street General Hospital tonight. I'm gonna prescribe some tequila shots chased by at least a dozen brewskies, and maybe a hot oil rubdown from Nurse Hooker. How's that sound for starters?" Phillip raised his beer bottle to the proposal. We clanked bottles and doused about half of the beer, thudding the bottles heavily on the wooden table.

"So ... how hot is she? Mile-high club hot?"

"No? Yes? Fuck, I don't know. But she is in my head and there has been no getting her out. She is attractive, not like drop-dead supermodel gorgeous. More like smokin' sexy librarian."

"Oh kinky, like MILF in the grocery store," Phillip chimed in. "I know the appeal."

"Maybe like that, but then not really. As we talked she cut right through my bullshit, reversed tactics on me, and generally unraveled me like a ball of yarn rolling down the stairs out of control with a cat in full pursuit."

"What kind of cat?" Phillip asked, ever the smart ass as he polished off his beer. I did not humor him with a reply. "That's pretty deep, Brian. A ball of string being chased by a pussy. I am completely underwhelmed. And on a plane of all places. What happened to the golden rule?" I stared at Phillip with a dumbfounded expression. "You, my friend, are in deep shit." Phillip stared, eyes gleaming. "What did you say her name was? Brenda?"

"Samantha. And it is over. Golden rule intact," I proclaimed, defiant of my mischievous thoughts.

"Ease it down, Romeo. I wouldn't bet the bank on that one. On the contrary, I'll bet you've got her name, number, and know where to find her. And judging from how ate up you appear, five thousand smackers says you will see her again."

In stone-cold silence I gave Phillip the poker face death stare, my line drawn in the sand.

"You can write the check now, unless you have cash," Phillip beamed confidently.

Considering his curious insistence, this entire Samantha scenario stunk of staged happenstance.

As the empty soldiers accumulated on the table, nighttime seeped through the windows, replacing the golden glow of the afternoon with encroaching lifeless shadows. Phillip was always on point concerning work, like Bill Clinton at an intern slumber party, but thus far had avoided any topic remotely connected to the assignment.

"So are you gonna tell me why we are here or are you going to just flap your jaw all night?"

Phillip looked at his watch. "Two hours and eight beers. Damn, I never thought you'd make it that long without asking."

"OK, this one *is* special, and I am jacked beyond words. Believe it or not, I've got a plan and that's why you've got to wait just a little longer." Phillip leaned into the table, stretching his neck in giraffe proportions. "This will require more skill than you've ever needed before, at least working for me," he said in hushed tones. "The potential downside could be cataclysmic."

Phillip had finally earned my undivided attention, work mode firing on all cylinders. "Bring it on, big boy. A job that hot is going to cost you big time," I said, sporting a cocky smile. Phillip did not smile back. "We should stop by the bank first, so you can fill out a loan application."

Phillip remained unamused. "Brian, I've gotta tell you I've considered having my head examined for even attempting to pull this stunt off. But if we can pull it off, it will be one of the biggest scoops of the decade, quite possibly the fucking century. But you must understand, if you don't feel right about it, even to the slightest degree, don't take the job," Phillip lectured, deep-rooted concern chiseled across his face.

"Geez, Phillip. Let's hear it."

"No, not yet. There's something you need to experience first."

CHAPTER 6

Our post-dinner stroll led us to Place d'Armes, now known as Jackson Square. The plaza was fronted by a wrought-iron fence encompassing the park on one side and three historic eighteenth century buildings, the Cabildo, Saint Louis Cathedral, and the Presbytere on the opposite side. The space between was filled with various street urchins selling worthless trinkets, fortune-telling gypsies, and a few performing artists, all conning the tourists for cash donations in a subdued carnival atmosphere. Weaving through the masses, we approached an eclectic assortment of people gathered on the steps leading into the park. Entire families, some with small children, some with teenagers, groups of friends, couples of assorted ages, and a few just outright-bizarre individuals completed the mixed bag of nuts. Most looked as if they had arrived from an Ozzie Osbourne concert caravan sporting dyed jet-black hair, black boots, black clothing, silver chains with excessive studding, disgusting body piercings, and unrestrained tattoos.

"I'll be right back." Phillip briskly departed in the direction of a buxom woman who seemed to be in charge of this unusual gathering. Night had wrestled control from day, humidity glared as filtered haze in the soulful presence of the moon.

"We are set to go my friend," Phillip chirped in giddy tones.

Images of this plaza from a distant era flashed as my thoughts transferred from Samantha to current circumstances. Shaking my head to clear the images, Phillip redirected my attention, "I hope you are ready for some bizarre entertainment."

"From you, I would be disappointed with anything less. So what is up with the Goonies World Tour Group?"

"Means to an end. I did this last month and haven't been able to get the damn story out of my mind since," he said as he waved his arm in the direction of the group. "I want you to experience the myth before you make any decisions."

"Damn, if that is the case, what the hell are we waiting for?"

"Ladies and gentlemen," a sinister voice interrupted "if you will all follow me, we will begin the tour." A pale, lanky man, near forty, sporting long jet-black hair, matching the color of his tight pants and ruffled shirt, led the group away from Jackson Square down a dark alley. The sudden arrival of Spookzilla captivated our group of gothoids. Walking down the street about a half a block, Lurch stopped in a doorway and stood on the elevated door stoop. "Gather around please, closely, so all can hear," he recited in a theatrical tone. His accent was definitely imported, most likely a dialect native to Chicago. While he attempted to put on a pretty good "Louziana" drawl, he could not entirely mask his Midwest roots.

He waited patiently until all complied and were listening intently. "New Orleans, in particular the French Quarter, possesses a rich history involving vampirism. Vampires, are they real, or are they just a fantasy of our sick and twisted imagination, embellished on the pages of novels over centuries of storytelling? Whichever is true, the fact remains that they have been made notoriously famous through years of cinematic magic. This in turn has led many to desire the immortality and power possessed by these creatures, and for others, the most terrifying nightmares imaginable."

Our guide's theatrical training was evident. He was captivating the crowd with every accentuated word and gesture.

"Historians have documented blood-drinking creatures such as Vlad the Impaler. His murderous deeds inspired many of the modern-day vampire tales our society craves. It was his very actions that awoke our eyes to the extreme evil men and women are capable of committing. What kind of creature was Vlad? Throughout the course of history, this question remains unproven. But his deeds of cruelty are well-documented and remain to this day a legacy of pure evil." Our guide took a dramatic pause as he glared at two chatty girls, who silenced immediately.

"And it is in history, not myth, that we look for clues of the very existence of vampires living among us today. Tonight, I will testify of historical facts. These facts, validated through court, police, and hospital records, are of a blood-drinking culture existing for centuries on these very streets. Listen to the stories, research what you wish. You will find my words true. Decide for yourself what you choose to believe. Did vampires only exist years ago or do they still roam the streets tonight?" Abruptly his speech ended as he hopped down from his perch. "Follow me," he instructed in his best sinister tone.

Walking down the dimly lit rugged streets mixed of pavement and cobblestone, our tour guide meticulously related documented tales of vampirism at pertinent locations, the first being the home of Saint Germaine. According to our guide, in 1903 a young unidentified female victim escaped his villainous schemes and reported the incident to the police. According to official reports, his seduction was initiated by partaking in a mysterious burgundy beverage. Eventually, in a sex-driven frenzy, he began to lacerate the victim and collect her blood. Surmising his intents of murder, she managed a daring escape. Before the police could arrest Saint Germaine, he mysteriously vanished forever. The search of his home revealed numerous dried pools of blood and a multitude of bottles containing a gruesome mixture of wine and blood.

I visualized his ghostly image peering back through the cloudy paned glass at his home at the corner of Ursuline and Royal. The precision of his haunting features standing in the darkened window, peering over the crowd as if searching for someone, sent a wave of the macabre. I shook off the vision and my reaction, writing it off to imagination running amuck. Time to cut back on the brew-has just a little.

As we traversed, Phillip buzzed my left ear with meaningless chatter while peculiar whispers ensconced the other. Unexplainably, my amused skepticism faded, and I became captivated by our guide's every word. I did not believe in vampires, ghosts, werewolves, or anything supernatural. Having traveled the world, I witnessed unimaginable cruelty, and in the end it was always the result of mortal men. I knew we were in the general vicinity of Bourbon Street, but this road was unnaturally quiet and unsettling, with the exception of the occasional clomping of a horse-drawn carriage. Our next stop: a second-story apartment building on Royal Street, home of the Carter brothers. Recounting the tale, in the 1930s John and Wayne Carter abducted and imprisoned victims from the city, slashing their wrists, draining and drinking their blood. Their final victim, a young girl, was able to free herself and escape during the day while the Carter brothers were away. She led the police to the apartment where three other victims were found alive. They were bound to chairs, wrists bandaged, concealing the insidious wounds. The Carter brothers had been feeding off the four victims for days. Of the four victims, the little girl had been fed on only once and thus recovered from her injuries after a brief hospitalization. Her family moved away shortly after she was released. Her whereabouts or fate remains a mystery. The adult female victim recovered from her injuries, however she chose to institutionalize herself in a state psychiatric hospital for the remainder of her life.

"Knowing the condition of present-day state psychiatric hospitals, to do this to yourself in the thirties? Her mind must have been totally fucked," Phillip whispered in an almost jovial tone.

He was loving this a bit too much, I thought. Where was this heading?

The story of the nine-year-old boy, one of the two surviving males, ended so tragically it actually wounded my spirit. According to our guide, he was treated and released to his family after being rescued. Several months later, he died in his home, consumed in a horrendous fire. The man who later turned himself in and confessed to the hideous crime was none other than the boy's father. In his confession, he stated the child returned to him was not the innocent son he had once loved, but instead, a creature of pure evil.

In an adjacent room of the Carter's apartment, the police located the bodies of seventeen other victims, drained of blood, covered in lime, stacked in a pile, all in various stages of decomposition. For their crimes, the brothers were tried, convicted, and electrocuted. Their bodies were sealed in the cement tombs for a year and one day, as was customary at the time, to speed up the decomposition of the corpses. The brothers were to be exhumed from the crypts after the year to dispose of the dusty remains. When the tombs were chiseled opened, there was no sign of either body. The sheer nature of the disappearance was considered by many to be more disturbing than the murders themselves.

"It's true, you know. I checked it out," Phillip whispered with a poke to my ribs. "And on top of that, right next to the frigging police station."

On the move once again, I considered the complexities.

"I did this tour a month ago, with four out-of-town girls I met in a bar," Phillip explained as he slapped his hand on my back.

I rolled my eyes. Here we go again, another tale of Phillip the snake charmer. I pretty much knew the story, just insert a new locale and add water.

"This one girl was totally smoking. We hit it off from the get-go, but I got shut down by her femme Nazi girlfriends before I could seal the deal. They were looking for something different to do the next night, so I wined and dined them, you know, turned on the charm and loosened 'em up. One of them was pretty intent on doing the tour, so I figured what the hell? Why not? Initially I thought it was a load of bullshit, but I played it up, like I was completely freaked out by the whole vampire thing. That was the covert plan. When my girl got spooked, she would need my protection. Pretty ingenuous, eh?"

"Frighten them into sex? Shameless."

Undeterred, Phillip chirped on. "So I pointed out the freaky people we passed on the streets saying, 'Bet he's a bloodsucker.' It really wigged her out. She stuck to me like tree sap all night. But I think I went a touch overboard. Hell, the rest of the night I could hardly take a leak without her clinging to my side."

"Barracuda, how long until you start nailing women in the hospital head trauma unit?" I joked. "And you know what comes after that? I do. It is called necrophilia! That's right, the morgue. And sadly that is where you will meet the only woman who will ever tolerate all your antics."

"Necrophilia, why not? You know, at least one time. Don't call it sick until you've tried it." Phillip laughed loud enough to turn heads.

I just shook my head. "You, my friend, are indeed a sick bastard."

"I'll bet you a G note I can pull it off again, just for instructional purposes. You can observe the master honing his craft, up-close and personal."

Our banter abruptly halted as my eyes consumed a structure worthy of the blackest nightmare. A dark, uninhabited house with a rusty, buckled tin can roof served as the focal point of our host's attention. Upon the rickety porch was a weathered and dilapidated front door, no longer capable of withstanding the assault of intruders or containing the bitter memories it once hid from the unsuspecting outside world. The paint remained peeled in large chunks around the broken window glass. Although there was no discernible wind, the ragged curtains appeared to flow from an imaginary breeze. Whether an illusion of the darkness, or result of neglect, every single tree, shrub, and plant appeared withered and lifeless surrounding this desolate structure.

"This was the house of the Carter brothers' fourth victim, Phillipe DeFond, a young man not yet twenty at the time of his abduction," our guide began in a morose tone. "With much of his blood drained, he was saved only days before perishing into darkness. It was believed he was saved just in time, affording young DeFond to return to a life of normalcy. From a family of considerable wealth, upon release from the hospital he remained under psychiatric care, hidden away from public scrutiny and attention for several years."

Our guide glared at a kid in the back of the group immersed in a cell phone conversation until he became aware of the unintended intermission, his voice silenced by the icy penetration of our irritated escort. With all attention now forward, the tale continued.

"Upon DeFond reaching adulthood, the family purchased the home standing before you. He remained here in solitude for many years, a forgotten man. It wasn't until decades later, as the home was being renovated, that a journal chronicling the life of Phillipe DeFond was discovered. It meticulously detailed every thought and evil deed by this profoundly disturbed young man."

Captain Creepster's voice grew stern, intensely punctuating the graphic verbiage to enhance his message.

"The journal was the idea of the psychologist treating DeFond following his release from captivity. DeFond chronicled an increasing occurrence of bizarre dreams involving grotesque rituals of blood consumption. The journal went on to describe the dreams in increasingly explicit and erotic details as time passed. These satanic fantasies eventually overpowered the young man until he succumbed and subsequently committed his first murder. The murder involved lavishly painting his body with the victim's blood. It was during this psychotic ritual that DeFond first consumed what was to quickly become his insatiable lust for the blood of life. The diary went on to describe another thirty-two grisly murders that transpired over the following years.

"According to the journal, the remains of bodies were dissolved in a bathtub of lye, leaving only a substance equivalent to human jello," our guide continued to explain with well-performed theatrical mannerisms. "The gooish remnants were then poured into large drums, sealed and then transported to the Mississippi River in the dark of night, at which point DeFond simply dropped the barrels into the river, eventually being swept out into the Gulf of Mexico.

"DeFond feared the police were becoming suspicious of his activities and fled New Orleans in the late 1940s. His suspicions proved to be completely unfounded. It was not until his journal was uncovered in 1949 that the police considered him a suspect in the many disappearances that transpired over the previous decade. The police found not a trace of DeFond. It was as if he completely vanished, leaving no evidence of his brutal crimes other than the journal. His journal hinted he considered relocating to Chicago, but he was never again to be found.

"In 1963, many years after the gruesome memories faded, the house eventually sold. But not one soul has ever endured living in it. 'Haunted and cursed,' all claimed it to be. In the end, the local real estate community realized it wasn't worth the effort to attempt selling the house ever again."

Our guide inched closer and spoke softly as if keeping a well-guarded secret.

"DeFond, as he perceived the police to be closing in, left one final entry in his journal before he vanished: *'I cannot explain, nor do I expect forgiveness for the crimes I have committed. I know now I must leave, never to return. Do not chance to seek me out. You will not like what I have become.'* His final entry proved to be the most unsettling, alluding to the transformation of a troubled man, evolving to a being of pure evil."

Mystically, our guide's words resounded wearily in the light breeze once more. They did not appear to come from anyone in our group, and certainly not from our guide, unless he was a gifted ventriloquist. Faintly, they wafted from the house and somberly passed overhead. I presumed everyone heard the hushed phrase repeated, "You will not like what I have become."

"Nice touch," I remarked sarcastically, loud enough for our guide to overhear.

Even with the staged theatrics, there was no doubt as to the truth of this story. I did not need Phillip to confirm the details. Confirmation came from some kind of déjà vu buried deep in my subconscious, affirming its validity. I felt connected, plugged in, as if this was part of my past. The connection was distressing, to say the least.

Phillip had drifted away. Sure as the sun rises in the east, Captain Horndog was on the prowl. He was working a pair of babes fresh off the graduation party boat. Just as I was preparing to yank him away, our tour guide ended his Q and A session and we were on the move.

Several blocks away the tour paused. Before us stood a harmless, L-shaped three-story building. A white-block exterior, topped with a slate roof, dormers, and hurricane shutters, the Old Ursuline Convent was our final stop. Completely unaware of its impending significance, I studied the innocuous structure that would forever change my life.

Our guide resumed drilling deeply into historical details, how the Church played a role in a larger legendary myth that remains to this day the root of doubt and suspicion.

"In the seventeen hundreds, malaria, various other diseases, and merely living in a city inhabited by pirates and criminals wreaked deadly havoc on the population. The Catholic Church took it upon itself to bring in young, impoverished, incarcerated women from France, with the intention of marrying the multitude of unscrupulous men residing in the city. These desperate women were to marry, bear children, and reverse a shrinking population.

"The first ship, the Pelican, arrived in New Orleans transporting ten women for the repopulation project. All of their worldly belongings, clothing, and household items, gifts from the church, were packed in crates resembling caskets. The women were to be initially housed and educated at the convent before being introduced to the city's finest gentlemen.

"Within days of the ship's arrival, residents began to vanish. Reported sightings of unfamiliar mysterious women roaming the streets at night cropped up frequently. The Casket Girls, as they became known, were blamed for the city's latest misfortunes, yet not a single one was ever caught in the act. Believing these women were related to the evil doom descending, the priests of the Church were judged to be accountable for the deadly occurrences. In most unpleasant manners, they were ordered to remove the women and the caskets with all haste. In an effort to pacify the residents, hurricane shutters were installed on the third-floor dormitory windows of the convent, sealing in the new inhabitants and their caskets, until transport could be arranged. Rumors had it, the nails and the wooden shutters securing the dormers were blessed, then submerged in holy water. The purpose of keeping people out, or whatever in, remains unclear, but the fact remains the shutters have not been opened for over two hundred years, according to all historical accounts. To this day, the actual documentation of their arrival remains, but no evidence of their departure."

I gazed up to the slate roof and dormers. Two hundred years, never opened? I could only imagine the summertime temperatures pre-air conditioning. A convent filled with sweaty nuns? Either our guide was fabricating malicious anti-Catholic rhetoric, or ...

"In New Orleans, over the past two centuries, there have been numerous suspicious deaths involving savage attacks involving blood consumption. If an investigation led to the doors of the convent, the police were refused entry. The Old Ursuline Convent is Vatican property, thus sovereign ground impervious to search warrants."

Search warrants are for pussies I mused as the story continued.

"Late in 1987, as a small group of psychology students from New York University were studying paranormal activities, the most recent recorded murders occurred. Two students were researching in the city library and stumbled across accounts of the convent. Although their research was to be specifically limited to spiritual activity in the Quarter, they decided to partake in an extracurricular surveillance on the last night of their trip.

"Armed with a video camera to capture, as one myth foretold, the Casket Girls' nightly departure from the convent, the two students filmed from the Beauregard-Keyes House across the street. Shortly after one in the morning, as their friends were unable to make contact, a search ensued. All that was found was the video camera, violently smashed into hundreds of pieces. Hours later, just after five in the morning, in the solitary beam of a police car spotlight beacon, the two coeds were found. Their naked bodies were painstakingly posed on the steps of the Chapel of the Bishops, the church adjacent to the convent. The bodies lay directly under a marble carving above the archway, in morbidly similar fashion. The carving was of two angels holding a chalice, the cup containing the blood of eternal life."

Above the door was the Latin inscription, which I read aloud. "HIC DOMUS DEI EST ET PORTA COELI." Why I knew the English translation will remain a mystery, but I shared my newfound proficiency with the group. "Here is the House of God and the Doorway to Heaven," I announced.

"So you know your Latin," our guide replied with irritation. "I was just about to cover that. Would you care to finish up here?"

I held up an insincere apologetic hand. Unconsciously having just stolen a bit of our guide's thunder, a smile crossed my face. With a roll of his eyes and a scoff, he continued.

"The coroner's report stated the women showed no sign of a struggle, induction of drugs, or blunt force trauma that would account for what he observed. The cause of death documented was directly attributed to identical lacerations in the victims' backs between the left shoulder and the spine. The victims' aortas had been manipulated to the incision. Approximately eighty percent of the victims' blood volume was missing. This anomaly, he reported, was beyond medical explanation. In the most severe cases of severed arteries, the maximum blood loss is forty-two- to forty-five percent. A disturbing footnote in the autopsy report by the coroner stated that it appeared as if the victims allowed their attackers to kill them.

"The police pressed the Church for access to the convent, but were continually denied. Unexplainably, several weeks into the investigation the case was ordered shut, a gag order issued to all parties involved. The case remains unsolved, and less than a handful of the people immediately involved with intimate knowledge exist. And of those individuals, not one has ever broken their silence. Why? Oddly enough, the physical evidence existing of vampirism has been reduced to imagination and conjecture."

Our tour guide rounded everyone back together tightly as he began to summarize our evening.

"As I promised at the outset, you have been presented historical facts. Verifiable through police, court, and newspaper records. You must now decide for yourself. Do you believe vampires exist and continue to roam these very streets tonight?" His dramatic tone became noticeably softer, as if to keep his thoughts amongst our group alone, not loud enough for the ears of what might have been lurking behind the concrete walls of the convent.

No doubt, I thought, something was hidden away, sheltered deep behind the forbidden walls.

"This concludes our tour. I will now lead you back to Jackson Square where the tour originated. Thank you again for your time and attention. If you desire to meet any modern-day vampires, they congregate at the Chamber on Toulouse Street. It opens at midnight." He pointed a crooked bone-white finger at the group. "I warn you this cult indulges in the consumption of blood and does not like outsiders. If you venture there, do so with caution. Do not go alone and do not presume they want to be your friend. Regrettably, those who have not heeded my warnings are incapable of explanation. Thank you again for your time," our host said as he turned and briskly led us to Jackson Square.

Phillip did not have to say a word—I knew the job. He wanted to know what was on the third floor of the convent. Hell, I wanted to know. I turned back and studied the ominous building shrouded in a ghostly haze as the tour paced away. I would even do this one for free, but I was not about to let Phillip get off that light. This one was going to cost him dearly.

"So what did you think?" Phillip inquired with the anxiety of a schoolboy. "A bunch of BS?"

I ignored his inquiry as our group paraded back to Jackson Square. I had a crooked smile on my face as I intentionally avoided replying to Phillip. I knew this would irk the hell out of him.

"You probably think it's all a big crock, and it might be, but it will sell a shitload of papers. I've already had my people researching every available fact, and as far as I can tell, everything on this tour, minus a few embellishments, is more or less true."

With the tour group gone, I turned away from the convent and placed my hand on his shoulder. The few minutes of quiet had given me time to reflect. "Let me tell you one thing, buddy boy, this is going to cost you more than you want to pay, and for what? If there is nothing inside, there is no story. Just a big fucking waste. If I do find something, I do not know how you'll be able to use it. Think about it. Breaking in that convent goes way beyond a simple misdemeanor. How can you write a story admitting you were complacent in violating Vatican sovereign rights?"

"See, that's why I love you Brian, you're always looking out for my best interest." Phillip cut a reassuring used-car-salesman smile. The pitch was on. "For one thing, the story is a done deal, whether contents are verified or not. Urban legends are always a great sell. I plan to run this story just the way you heard it tonight and it will sell. Part one will run after you've completed a search of the property. If you find anything, that will be part two. If you don't find a thing, the story will remain merely an urban legend, only now with national exposure. I will sell millions of papers and the Goonie tour gets thousands of new customers. Win-win for everyone. It will move right up in the annals with Big Foot and Nessie."

"Consider this, Phillip. All I have to do is break in, snap a few pictures, maybe snatch an artifact or two, and haul ass. Once the dust settles, I will be half a world away. You, on the other hand, are knowingly steering head-on into a shitstorm unlike anything you have ever sailed into. *The Da Vinci Code*—lethal monks and ancient societies guarding secrets of the Church ..." I wasn't fucking around, and Phillip knew it.

Grabbing Phillip by both shoulders, I looked him squarely in the eye. "The job is going to cost you one million dollars. Once I deliver the goods, I am out of here. You will need an impenetrable cover story and a trail back to a fictional, but believable, source that will keep the goons off you.

"I love you like the brother I never had Phillip. If the pressure gets too hot, and I believe it will, you could go to prison if you do not play this spot-on. And I will not let you sell me out for a pass. You do know what I am saying? Right?"

"I do, and believe me, Brian, I would put a gun to my head before I would ever sell you out."

"Well I guess you will finally get the opportunity to grow a big, smelly, hairy set," I said with a crooked smile. "I will start tomorrow. I want to see your plan to keep the heat off, to be sure this will not come back to burn me. Before I take the first step into that convent, I need to know how you plan to cover our tracks. Not that I doubt your ability to lie your ass off, but I want to check it out before there is no turning back."

"Deal," Phillip said with a broad smile, hand extended to seal the pact. We shook on the agreement. "It's time to celebrate," Phillip declared as he placed his hand behind my shoulder and ushered me back in the direction of Jackson Square.

We walked a few blocks and arrived at Bourbon Street. It was our usual custom to pound a few down once we had come to terms over a job.

"Tell me where you want to meet. From this point on, it is best if we do not arrive at too many places together. We will be just a couple of guys that met in a bar." I looked down Bourbon Street. "I am going this way. Call me."

"Hell, I don't know any of the bars down here."

"Write this number down." I pulled my TracFone out and flashed its number. Phillip jostled for a pen and a piece of paper. "Some newsman you are." I reached in my pocket for a pen. "Do not call my other number ever again. Delete it from your phone. I suggest you pick up a TracFone as well. Once I start, our only contact will only be initiated by me."

"Always planning in advance," Phillip observed as he scribbled the number.

"That is why I am still alive, Phillip, and plan to remain that way." Taking a few steps to the south, I stopped in my tracks and turned. "Phillip, have you taken the time to consider whatever is on the third floor was not meant to be disturbed, something far more secretive than a vampire story?"

"Such as?" Phillip asked as he was still struggling to write the number on a crumbled piece of paper.

"I don't know, Holy Grail, Arc of the Covenant, something like that."

"Talk about a far stretch of the imagination, I'll bet my last dollar you find two-hundred-year-old vampires before you find any of that mythical crap. You have seen way too many Indiana Jones movies my friend."

"Understand this, Phillip, I really do not care whether you believe Christ was the son of God, or was just an ordinary prophet, but I believe He existed. The cup of Christ, Moses, Ten Commandments, Mount Sinai, the remnants of the tablets, the Holy Crusades were not a myth. Do not readily dismiss history. I believe it is quite possible the Catholic Church might just be in possession of these items. If you had them, where would you hide them? Probably a safe place, far away from suspicion. Somewhere like a convent in New Orleans?"

Phillip started to speak, but could not assimilate his thoughts. He raised his index finger to gesture, his lips searching for vocabulary, but remained momentarily befuddled.

"Let's just say for argument's sake you are not completely off your rocker, this time. Let's say you do find a cup or an artifact to that effect. You bring me something of that magnitude, and I'll pay you ten times the amount we agreed on. How does that that float your boat, or should I say ... Arc?"

"Stealing holy artifacts will put me on an express train to Hell. I'm probably headed there anyway, but I was hoping at a slow, maybe even reversible pace."

"Come on, Brian. You won't be doing anything more unholy than the Catholics have already done and are still doing. If there are some mystical scrolls or cups or whatever in the convent, how do you think they got there in the first place? The Church stole them from somebody else, that's how. I don't think the popes who conquered Babylon went to Hell. And, if they did, you'll be in damn good company."

"Speaking of good company, make sure you find a place with really cold beer." Turning away, I smiled at the image, me and the popes ... just hanging out.

CHAPTER 7

PHILLIP INSTRUCTED ME to meet him at the Bourbon Street Blues Company, several blocks up the street from Lafitte's, where I was having a beer. I glanced around the dimly lit bar one last time and bid adieu. Nestled amongst quiet residential homes drawing near the end of the French Quarter, Lafitte's was a far cry from the mayhem ahead. Within several blocks the street was ablaze with partygoers reveling in the music, alcohol, and a sexual-frenzied atmosphere that permeated the night. Throngs of people were gathered beneath the balconies scattered above the various bars, continuing the nightly tradition of earning one's Mardi Gras beads even though it was nowhere near Mardi Gras. Practice till you get it perfect; you have to love the commitment of these people.

Looking up to the balcony observing the methodology of the bead chuckers, I spied Phillip leaning over a rail. Oblivious to my approach, with a fistful of beads, he was attempting to entice any willing, attractive female to eagerly fulfill her end of the traditional obligation. A small line was formed below the balcony of decadence. A muscle-headed bouncer nodded in the direction of the line as he chatted with a small group of pectoral-mesmerized girls. I played ignorant to his innuendos and continued toward him.

"Sorry, but you'll have to wait in the line with everyone else, chief," he instructed as he pointed with a sneer of superiority. "We're filled to capacity. Got a killer band tonight. Might be as long as an hour or so."

I slid my hand into my pocket and grabbed the pre-rolled hundreds I habitually kept on call. I conspicuously peeled off two bills and leaned a little closer to his ear. "I am supposed to meet my cousins Benjamin and Franklin here. I am running a little late as you probably might guess." I placed one hand on his shoulder and then discretely slid a couple of bills into his right hand while shaking it.

He looked down to verify the denomination and said with a smile, "My bad, bossman, didn't recognize you. They told me I should be expecting you. I'm sure you'll have no trouble finding your cousins inside. Tell Jerry at the bar, Doug said the first beer's on me."

"I appreciate that, Doug. I'm Brian. Sure I will be seeing you around."

The music was blasting and the crowd was bouncing off the walls. People were packed so tightly around the stage they resembled a work of modern art more than a crowd of drunken *So You Think You Can Dance* contestants. The outlying tables were all occupied with sharks scanning the waters. Neon lights adorned the plank walls as the smell of beer, sweat, and smoke hung heavily in the air. My shoes stuck to the floor, making me long for the dirt floors of Third World bars, where plastic people dare not tread. Scanning the crowd of inebriated patrons, I confirmed there was more than an ample supply of apparently single women available for dancing and who knows what else. Opportunity abounding, I set my sights for Phillip.

I elbowed my way through the packed sardines to the stairs. The old worn stairs creaked heavily, protesting the multitudes scuttling up and down to their destinations as I ascended to the second floor. The loft was only slightly less crowded than the first floor, the speakers crackling music from the band downstairs to a lesser degree. Off the right was a small impromptu dance floor, another bar against the back wall, and packed in the middle of the room were one too many pool tables. To the front, accessible through three open air archways was the balcony. I made a quick trip to the bar and grabbed two cold beers in hand. I twisted and snaked my way through the room, working my path to the balcony.

Phillip had not budged from his perch, leaning on the railing with his boyish smile, tossing beads to the girls below in an effort to get them to show their assets. The crowd below resembled an overcrowded pigpen at feeding time, all jockeying for position to the most suitable locale for the feast of boobage. "Missing high school a bit too much, are we?" I held the cold brewski against Phillip's neck.

"Nope, just honing my skill," he replied, not surprised by my appearance or the fact he did not see me coming. Over the years, he became accustomed to my ability to sneak up on him whenever, wherever.

"And what skill would that be?" I asked curiously, wondering what the inner boy known as Phillip had been scheming.

"Just a friendly little wager." Phillip loved to gamble on everything under the sun. He was an excellent poker player. He loved the game because he controlled his fate, for the most part. Good hand or not, he could bluff with the best of them. He loved all other sorts of gambling such as craps, the ponies, and just about anything else he could fathom a wager on. At times he would wager for the sheer thrill of chance. "Ten thousand dollars, the next car that turns the corner will be silver." The adrenaline rush of a dice roll was such a boner for him. It got his rocks off watching another man or woman tense up and sweat the uncertain outcome of what was yet to be. Bankrolled with a massive bank account, he could afford to be wrong and shrug it off.

Phillip's ego thrived on watching people wither and fold. Over the years we had done a few hundred-thousand-dollar bets and though never embracing the magnitude of those wagers, I never backed down.

"Five thousand bucks per shot. I pick the girl and you must get her to flash the goodies. If she doesn't flash, I keep picking and you keep paying until you succeed. Then we switch. We play until you cry mercy," Phillip proclaimed, sensing assured victory.

"I seem to be at somewhat of a disadvantage. You have been out here practicing—"

"Puss meat," Phillip clucked in a mocking tone.

I stared him down. "Game on, bitch!"

At times my testosterone-laced ego could get in the way—call it a suspicious lack of better judgment. This had all of the classic signs of shaping up to be one of those events. But this was New Orleans and it was boy's night out. So I might as well play the part, bid farewell to intelligence, and greet stupidity with open arms.

Within the flash of an eye I was down fifteen thousand. He chose a little old lady, properly dressed for church, a woman with her husband and kids, and a young girl about ten. His sinister laugh with each selection had me questioning what the hell were these people even doing on Bourbon Street at this hour? Two more picks and I was down twenty-five grand. Then came a small group of middle school cheerleaders, followed by an obvious butch lesbian who offered not to show her boobs but to come up on the balcony and kick my ass. It took all of approximately twenty minutes for me to be down thirty-five Gs.

"Your turn to buy. I am running out of cash," I insisted, feeling the need to break his rhythm.

"Not a problem, buddy. Are you in need of mercy yet?"

"Get my beer, bitch. I will have you crying mercy before the sun rises in the east."

"Somehow I doubt that." Phillip departed with an arrogant smile wide as the Mississippi.

I was going to have to change strategy fast before my financial clock got cleaned. Nothing usually works better than luring an opponent into a false sense of victory, just like sandbagging on the golf course. The first objective: slow down the pace and drink more. Second objective: allow him to win a lot, been there done that. Third objective: reel him back in and then take him to the cleaners.

Before Phillip had returned, a waitress appeared on the balcony.

"Can I get you anything, sweetie?"

"What is your name, darlin'?" I asked with an intentional Southern drawl.

"Debbie," she responded, flirtatious smile ablaze.

"Debbie, my name is Brian, and I desperately need your assistance."

"That's what I'm here for." Her turbo charm ignited with the scent of financial opportunity arising.

Looking out for Phillip, I reached in my pocket and pulled out two hundred dollars off the roll and placed them on her tray. "Every trip you make out here I need you to bring me two tequila shots. Have one poured about three-quarters full, and the other one full to the rim. The guy I am standing with gets the full one. Do this until the first hundred dollars runs out. The other hundred is your tip. If he is still standing after the hundred is gone, I will refill your cash. Flirt with him. I need him distracted. The more you flirt, the better your tip. If he asks where the shots are coming from, tell him you're buying. Give him some believable bullshit story. Play with him as much as you can but do not worry, I will make sure he does not give you any trouble when it is time to leave."

"And when you're both shitfaced drunk?" Her coy smile displayed confidence that she would not be worried if we did get out of hand. Rest assured the goon at the door and his clones were ready to answer the sweet damsel's call.

"If we give you any trouble, I give you my permission in advance to call your bouncers and tell them I said it was okay to beat the shit out of both of us."

"What makes you think I wouldn't beat the crap out of you myself and enjoy every minute of it?"

"Probably the fact after the first punch my incessant begging for more would allow you to see how much I enjoy it. Aside from that, your jeans are way too tight for ass-kicking, although I imagine those boots could do some damage."

"The boots can come off, and the jeans too," Debbie teased, "if you play your cards right." She winked and headed down the balcony.

As on cue, Phillip returned with a couple of cold beers, icy cold, Arctic-Tundra-cold. Beer just does not get any better than that. "How did you ever find a beer this cold?" I inquired.

"Brian, Brian, Brian. How many times do I have to tell you? You've got to have connections wherever you go. Thought you would have learned that by now."

We clanked the frosty bottles together and tipped the ales down the hatch while perusing the crowd below. After a few moments of silence and a couple of deep swigs of beer, our task was abruptly interrupted by a crack resembling a horsewhip.

"What the hell?" Phillip squealed like a child.

Debbie stood behind, her hand firmly planted on Phillip's ass.

"You boys were looking a little dry. I thought you might be in need of a refill."

Phillip flashed a wolfish smile even though his ass had to be on fire. "Why that's mighty thoughtful of you, ma'am. Tell me, do you offer up beer refills with such enthusiasm to all of your customers?"

"Only when I see a couple of boys I'd like to get to know better, after I get off," she said, turning the provocative charm on full throttle.

Sensing a potential financial landfall, Debbie was going to milk this for all it was worth. Phillip's Armani golf shirt and khaki pants screamed preppy pushover. She was accustomed to dealing with his type. Without breaking eye contact with Phillip or letting go of his ass, she sat her tray down on the stool next to us, removing a shot and downing it without a flinch. From past experience, a lesson learned all too well: woman drinking tequila like water, run away.

She eyeballed the two remaining shots and then looked back at the both of us. "Bottoms up, girls." Grabbing the shots, I handed one to Phillip and we fired them back. Phillip groaned and winced as the cheap tequila burned all the way down. He chased the shot with beer as quickly as possible.

Drink up, bitch, I thought.

"Holy shit, Brian, do you believe that? She's jonesin' for me, big time." Phillip's enthusiasm was of a sixteen-year-old virgin in a Vegas strip club.

"Too bad you will have to wait until tomorrow to hear all about her," I boasted, stoking the fire. "There is no way we are going to share."

"Bullshit!" Phillip, incensed, protested loudly. "She wants me. I didn't see her feeling up your ass."

"By the time she gets off, she will be so over you and ready for an upgrade." I egged him on, knowing Phillip's ego was about to best him again. "Want to put a little cash behind that bear trap mouth of yours, buddy?" Phillip grabbed some cash out of his pocket.

"Last I checked, you were on the short side to the tune of thirty-five K. And speaking of that bet, here comes your next girlfriend." Phillip pointed out another woman, this one kind of mousy, goody two-shoes looking, a cross between Mary Ann of *Gilligan's Island* and June Cleaver. She was with a guy that looked like he came straight out of the cornfields of Iowa. His Farmer Bob ensemble was complete with overalls and a John Deere trucker hat.

"I don't even want to waste the beads." Phillip had chosen exceptionally well, again. "However, I don't want to give you the instant satisfaction of getting more of my money without a fight." I tossed the beads in her direction, hitting Farmer Bob instead. Could be her brother, if they were from West Virginia I thought. He picked up the beads and looked up to the balcony to see who had thrown them. By his irritated expression I figured Bobby was pissed.

Surprisingly, and much to Phillip's dismay, he screamed out, "Ya'll wants to see her titties?"

Before I could respond, about ten other guys and one really drunk woman all screamed out in approval. "It's gonna take more beads than that," he bellowed. Within the blink of an eye, beads came raining down on the pair like a rainforest monsoon. I could actually hear Phillip next to me, gritting his teeth. "Don't do it, don't do it," he uttered under his breath.

"Go head, baby, show 'em your rack!" On cue, she lifted the shirt and bra and set her bodacious, dairy-farm-size breasts free. As a bonus, she shook them wildly side to side. A howl of jubilation erupted out from the balcony instantaneously. Farmer Bob was obviously quite proud of "her rack." Missing a front tooth, he grinned ear to ear with pleasure knowing his girl was the cause of all the jubilation.

I do not know who enjoyed the show more, the balcony crowd, Bob, or me. All that mattered was Phillip's luck just ran out. Time to deliver the house of pain.

Smack! Like the sound of a leather belt on a naked ass, Debbie's return was announced. "Dammit!" Phillip cried out like a girl scout who just spilled ten boxes of cookies on the sidewalk.

"You boys miss me yet?" On her tray were two more shots. "I know I missed you," she purred, directing a sultry gaze at Phillip who was rubbing his ass.

"Damn, girl, you keep smacking my ass like that and I won't be able to sit down tonight."

"And who said that's a bad thing." Debbie cut a wink in my direction. "I saw you boys getting all riled up over those girls down there. I hope it won't be necessary to remind the two of you who owns your asses tonight. Now drink up!"

Phillip continued rubbing his ass while I removed the shots from her tray. "You are right, Debbie. He was getting all worked up, but this should help him settle a bit." I handed Phillip one of the shots. "Bottoms up, bitch."

Between Debbie and the booze, my losses had nearly evaporated. Surveying the crowd milling about, I nearly choked on the night air. A little more than a block away, I was relatively certain Samantha was approaching, accompanied by an equally attractive woman.

"Double shot, double the bet," I proposed. "Two girls at the same time for ten grand."

Phillip nodded in agreement. At this juncture, he would have agreed to a swift kick in the nuts.

"Two blondes, four doors down past the intersection on the far side of the street, heading this way." Phillip followed the directions until he locked in, like a lioness tracking prey. Almost instantly, he regained a semblance of sobriety for about ten seconds.

"Hell, yes! Damn if don' they look smokin' from here."

"They both have to go. If they do, ten grand your way. If you only get one or neither, then the ten grand goes my way. After you strike out, I get a crack at them. When I succeed, ten grand my way."

"So potentially, downside is twenty Gs on this bet, if I be righteous." Phillip sought to clarify, although his speech was anything but clear.

I could not help but smile at my drunk friend. I was truly a bastard. "Potentially yes. Are you in or out, Alice?"

"All in."

We watched the women draw closer. I took a position out of Samantha's line of sight, peeking over Phillip's shoulder like some kind of frightened child. My pulse slowly accelerated until it was pounding like cannibal drums at dinnertime. Something was definitely wrong with me, and the sooner I could get the hell away from this city, the better. I contemplated a pit stop by the local voodoo shop on the way out of town to ensure there was not some wicked sort of love curse placed on me. And just to be extra safe, not one foot would be placed in southern California for at least three years.

"Get chur ass re deee to pay, and no whiner-in about it der res of da night. Dese babes are mine!" Phillip declared as he tossed the first volley of beads in the direction of the girls. Amazingly, his pitch was relatively accurate.

I reached into my jacket pocket and slid on my shades. I remained behind Phillip, turned slightly, acting completely disinterested in his activities in hopes of appearing not to be with him. The beads landed in the path of Samantha's sister, skidding right into her cheetah pumps. I slid back to the threshold toward the bar, putting additional distance between me and Phillip.

The sister bent over and picked up the beads without glancing up. She uttered to Samantha, probably explaining the tradition or relating a personal story about the beads, which caused Samantha to cover her mouth and laugh. Her face glowed like a summer sunset. She placed the beads around Samantha's neck as they waved in the direction of the balcony without looking, not remotely concerned with who had thrown them. Their expression said, "Thanks, but no thanks."

They continued passing, now directly in front of the balcony. "Cha-ching," I roared. Phillip shrugged. In desperation, he hurled a handful of beads that managed to find Samantha's leg.

"Ladies, don' leave!" he implored frantically. The financial downfall about to beset him had a sobering effect. This time, Samantha picked up the beads as they turned to see the source of desperation. Now locked in eye contact, Phillip explained, "Thaz not how it works. You can't juss wear my beads without earning dem. Dat would make you like ... a poser or somethin' worse."

"I'm sorry. I did not know the rules. My sister did not explain them," Samantha apologized while pointing to the guilty party. Her smile was so inviting, every man on the balcony appeared entranced. She walked closer to the balcony. "Do you want your beads back?" she asked, beginning to remove her souvenirs.

The sound of her voice sent waves of heat coursing through my body. Debbie was looking in our direction, and I signaled for a shot desperately needed. Maybe Samantha *was* a voodoo queen, witch, or some kind of enchantress. Whichever the case, she was here, right now, right under the balcony, and nothing else mattered. Edging closer to Phillip, from the improved vantage point, I now saw her face clearly. I wanted to say something, but refrained. She took Phillip's beads and threw them back at him, hitting him squarely in the chest. "What an arm," I mumbled.

"Ahh, now don' go and do all dat!"

"Thanks, but no thanks." Samantha smiled and turned back to her sister.

Samantha's sister turned, took two steps toward the balcony, took off her beads, and hurled them at Phillip. "Show us yours, big boy."

"Hey, beautiful, what's your name?" Phillip laughed as he watched the beads sail through the air

"I'm Dana. This is my sister, Samantha," she replied above the disapproving cries of Cro-Magnon's seeking another flesh show.

Showtime, I decided, moving closer to the railing. "Hey, Dana. If I jump off the balcony, will you and your sister show my friend what he's dying to see?" I moved into Dana's eyesight, shielding Samantha's view with Phillip's body.

"If you're dumb enough, what the hell? Sure," Dana agreed boldly, wanting to see the feat performed but not believing anyone was stupid enough to do it.

Samantha jabbed her sister in the ribs, hard. She was saying something to Dana I could not hear. It looked as though Samantha was not on board with the wager. Samantha was too occupied giving her sister an earful to look up.

I handed my shades to Phillip. "I am out of here. Have my cash ready when I get back."

"You don't have to do this," Phillip insisted.

I surveyed below for a landing sight, put two fingers to my lips, and blew the crowd a kiss. Without another thought, I grabbed the rail, flipped up and over, dropping quickly to the ground. Hitting the ground on two feet, I dropped into a crouch and quickly popped back up on my feet. Lacking time for any pre-flight fanfare, immediately upon sticking the landing a voracious cheer rang out. Samantha was to my back, but the instant I turned we made eye contact. I felt a lump in my throat and a sudden rush of adrenaline that failed to exist seconds before. Samantha looked as though she had seen a ghost, her mouth gaping in disbelief or shock

"I think you owe my friend on the balcony a little performance," I said, smiling slyly at Dana, not acknowledging Samantha.

Without saying a word, Dana reached over and grabbed

Samantha by the arm and jerked her close. Facing Phillip on the balcony, "Sorry, sis," is all she could say, shocked by the stupidity of my stunt. Samantha kept her head turned to me, a queer expression on her face. I was not sure how to interpret it, but whatever the meaning, it certainly was not, "Hey, Brian, I'm so very glad to see you again."

"Dee!" Samantha hissed at her sister while her eyes grew venomous.

"Come on, Sam, this will only take a second and we'll be done. Try to think of it as a liberating expression of letting yourself go, after years of wasting your life on an asshole. Just think how pissed he'd be if he could see you right now."

"Yeah, Sam, just let yourself go." I taunted with my best boy scout smile.

"Brian! You asshole, I can't believe you did that."

"Hey, I never said I did not enjoy a good party," I said, defending my honor. "Besides, you were the only reason I did it."

"Sam, please don't tell me this guy is your secret agent buddy from the flight."

"Disappointingly so. Dee, meet Brian the asshole. Brian the ass hole, this is my sister, Dee."

"It's a pleasure to meet you, Dana." Preferring to keep things proper for the time being, I dusted off my hand then extended it. Dee did not offer her hand in return but looked back at her sister with a most irritated glare. "I told my sister you were full of shit," she explained without breaking eye contact with Samantha.

"Hey, what the hell is going on down there? It's showtime, baby," Phillip cried out impatiently. "My boy almost killed himself for God's sake. Time to pay up."

The vast majority of eyes were on Dee and Samantha. The girls looked at each other. Only hours earlier, Samantha had confessed personal, intimate details to a complete stranger, one she believed was unique and trustworthy. Her eyes now sharp enough to cut steel, she grabbed her shirt and began to lift it.

"Wait a minute! I really do not need to see this." Grabbing Samantha's hand, a spark of exhilaration charged through my body. "I am going to go back inside. Dana it was a pleasure to meet you. Samantha ..."

"Oh no you don't, mister! You most certainly are not going any-where." The seductress who placed her hand on my leg hours earlier returned with a vengeance. "I want you to see what you will never see again."

Dee's jaw dislodged, almost resting on her chest, broadsided by her sister's brashness. She stared at Sam in disbelief as Samantha flashed a smile. "You said it, Dee. Time to cut loose."

"Ladies, thank you, but this whole bead chucking ritual really is not my bag. But my buddy up there, as well as the rest of the guys, will surely appreciate what you have to offer." I repositioned myself directly behind the girls. Dee and Samantha turned to Phillip and the rest of the balcony audience. Grabbing their shirts, working up to their bras, Samantha let out a nervous sigh.

Phillip called out jovially, "Showtime, baby," even though the end result was about to increase his debt by twenty thousand. Through his glassy eyes, the battle lost was worth the cost.

As they fidgeted in preparation, I leaned in between their heads. By this time the catcalls were beckoning for a performance. "Excuse me, I would like to offer an alternative solution." With my face close enough between the two to kiss either, they both backed away a safe distance. "Come inside, have a drink with us, and we will call it even."

The women scanned each other's reaction. "Just a drink, noth-ing more." Dee laid down her terms with an unjustified accusatory finger.

"I don't know, Dee. We can just do this and it's over. I'm sure we will find better company elsewhere." Samantha's demeanor glistened with irritation.

"Just a drink," I beckoned, not ready for the encounter to end, "unless you really have somewhere better to be,"

"Bed," Samantha replied sarcastically.

"Slow down, girl. I might look easy, but down deep I am quite old-fashioned. You will have to get me drunk before you get any-where near my pants," I teased.

Dee nodded her head toward the door, instructing Sam to relent.

"What's going on down there?" Phillip whined.

"Come on. One small drink."

We approached the door with a roar of pathetic cries from above. "No, no, no."

"Your friend is upset," Dee proudly observed, unaware of the full extent of Phillip's disappointment.

"Believe me, he will get over it. He gets his heart broken five or six times a day. It usually takes five minutes or so for him to totally forget who upset him and why."

CHAPTER 8

Upon entering the bar, the band had just returned from a break, affording an ample supply of tables. Just as I was about to sit, Phillip came staggering our way. "Excuse me, ladies. I need to find the bathroom," I said.

I grabbed Phillip by the arm and led him away. Eyes glassy as waxed marbles, I had to accept responsibility for the drunk before me. "Phillip, go easy on the bullshit. This one is different."

Phillip tugged at my ears as if to pull a mask off. "You fucking impostor, what did you do with my best friend?"

"Phillip," I said firmly, "this time is different. I want more out of life. Something down deep has changed."

"I know what you need. You need to take a piss, have another drink, and get laid. Am I wrong?"

"That is what I love about you, Phillip. You can completely blow off anyone's coherent thoughts and flip the scenario to fit your needs without stressing a single brain cell."

"You say that like it's a bad thing." Phillip slapped my back and ushered me into the john.

Phillip and I finished our business in the men's room. As we walked back to the table, the mere sight of Samantha put a fresh lump in my throat. I suddenly worried that she might not have appreciated my peculiar sense of humor. When had I ever been concerned about a woman's impression of me? N-E-V-E-R. Phillip was right, I was completely off my game, big time.

Although he had to be trashed, his swagger had virtually returned to normal. Phillip, eager to impress, had screwed on his best game face. Despite the tequila-induced glossy eyes, his moderately charming mannerisms were in full throttle.

For the next hour, the conversation consisted of Phillip and Dee immersed in the art of impressing each other. The effort was entirely unnecessary. It was evident from the outset they were mutually enamored. It did not take a rocket scientist to see where they were headed. We worked through several rounds of drinks. I smiled often, laughed at all the appropriate points and used as few words as possible, avoiding any words with more than four letters. The entire affair appeared somewhat awkward for Sam as well. By the third round of drinks, Sam's irritated demeanor had softened. She was smiling and interacting with Romeo and Juliet. I, on the other hand, continued to critique every word I contemplated speaking, deciding nothing was right, and resolved to play the role of mute geek to perfection.

Mercifully, the band continued ripping out one great song after another, affording me the opportunity to bob my head to the beat, assuring my friends I had not died at the table. The intensity of inebriated party people had ramped up to a fever-pitched frenzy. Packed tighter than imaginable, they resembled a giant coral anemone whipping rhythmically to storm-driven ocean currents.

"I like the band." Samantha labored to strike up a conversation in absence of any from my end of the table. "Are you feeling alright?" Samantha asked, disappointed with my lack of involvement. "You seem like you want to be somewhere else."

"As a matter of fact, I am not alright and would much rather be somewhere else." I stood up abruptly. The three stared intently, my words piercing the deafening beat of the music. "I would much rather be over there," I pointed to the crowded dance floor, "dancing with you," now directing my words to Sam, "rather than listening to these two carry on." Extending my hand, Samantha eagerly took hold, leaving Ken and Barbie in her wake.

Not to be insulted without response, Phillip shouted out, "Watch out for him, Sam, he's a real scumbag on the dance floor. He's been known to cop a feel while pretending to dance."

Samantha's smile turned devilish. "I certainly hope so."

Sam and I worked our way over to the jam-packed dance floor. For almost an hour, with hardly room to maneuver, the cramped quarters forced us to dance exceptionally close. "So which one?" Sam asked, scanning the crowd.

"Which one what?"

"If we had not come along, who would you be with right now?"

"I would be back in my hotel room working on the job, had you not come along."

"Brian, do you honestly expect me to believe with all of these hot young women in here, you would not have tried to take one back to your hotel?" Sam surveyed the crowd as a smirk curled up her lip. "I don't recognize anybody from our flight, no golden rule BS."

I could not help but smile at her insightfulness.

Grinding her glistening body seductively against mine, her expression told of undeniable desire.

As if on some karmic cue, the band geared down to Jonny Lang's *Touch* as the vocalist soulfully belted out the lyrics. With decisively sensual rhythm, Sam backed her body against mine, arching the back of her head on my shoulder as she began mesmerizingly gyrating her ass against me. I placed my left arm around her taut waist and ran my other hand through her silky hair, pulling it back tightly, drawing her face even closer.

Okay, I would love to have blamed my lack of self-control on the alcohol at this juncture, but it was pointless. The truth be told, I was absolutely into the moment. I was totally into Sam and not about to let her stop taking advantage of me. I turned my head and lightly brushed the side of her face with my lips. The mere contact electrified my entire body, pulsing shock waves of uncontrollable passion throughout. Out of control? Hell yes!

"765-233-0947." I recited the cell number she had given me at the airport. "I cannot tell you how many times I fought calling your number all day." Her sweet fragrance filled every molecule of my existence. "I have not been able to stop thinking about you." She pivoted in my arms, now facing me. With my arm still around her neck, I pulled her face to mine and our lips together. We kissed. It lingered an hour, or was it only a minute? For one brief moment the world evaporated around us. Isolated amongst the crowd, an inferno of passion made the surrounding air frigid and lifeless.

"Can we leave?" Abruptly ending the kiss, Sam's eyes ignited with hunger and anticipation.

"I don't know if I can make it out the door."

She took my hand and jerked me from the dance floor, leaving years of shattered excuses behind.

"Let's go tell Dee and Phillip we are leaving," she suggested, voice trembling.

I nodded, not that my opinion mattered. Phillip and Dee had abandoned the post and were nowhere in plain sight. "They must be upstairs," I observed, but knowing Phillip they were most likely somewhere else. "We could call—"

"They'll just have to wonder what happened to us." Sam had no interest in calling or organizing a search party. She fired up her twin diesels and with the force of a tugboat, towed me out the door.

I was not accustomed to this treatment, being led around like a little bitch poodle on a leash.

Bow wow. We cleared the doors and blew out onto Bourbon Street, not wasting a precious second.

"Which way?" Sam eagerly awaited direction, face aglow with anticipation.

I pointed left in the direction of Toulouse. Once again in tow, Sam forged through the crowded street. Moving less than a block away, she halted abruptly and pulled me close for another volley. We kissed, this time longer and harder. She was beaming and giggling in jubilation. I felt after all of the years of abstinence from airplane relationships I should resist this on principle alone or at least put on a facade of intention of such.

Frankly, for once in my life it would be nice not to analyze every damn detail and just go with it. "My hotel is this way." I took her hand, but did not enjoy the opportunity to lead as she took my cue and pulled ahead. Grinning like nuns in the wine cellar, anticipating imminent passion, our pace accelerated.

It was well after three in the morning as we discreetly entered the empty hotel lobby. There was no trace of the night manager as we moved briskly to the elevators. I pushed the up button as Sam fell against me with a chuckle. The elevator door opened and we tumbled into the back wall with a muffled thud, rocking the car as we attempted to contain our laughter. Sam stared into my eyes once again with famished desire. We frantically embraced and kissed, as if the moment would pass forever if we did lay siege immediately. I looked out of the corner of my eye, leaned, and then stumbled. Sam refused to loosen her grip or be interrupted as we fell into the control panel, mashing all the buttons, including the alarm. The door closed and the gravitational momentum of the elevator lifting apparently created a similar reaction of items much more personal.

The elevator door opened as if rusted gears were being cranked by a one-armed field mouse. *Come on.* Key card in hand, I led Sam to the door, heart pounding wildly as if I were sixteen and *this* was the first time I ... screw that, *this* was far worse. In the heat of a gun fight in the jungles of Colombia, I had never experienced such palpitations. Having key card issues in my frantic state, I was unable to manage the door.

"What's the matter, Mr. Smooth? Having trouble getting it in? I can come back later, maybe in the morning," Sam taunted with a coy smile.

"Thanks for the offer, but no, that will not be necessary. Just step back and let a seasoned professional do his job."

"Seasoned professional?" She began poking her fingers in my ribs, attempting to locate an area to tickle. "I hope you won't mind, Mister Seasoned Professional, if I reserve judgment until the morning."

With a joyful click, the sound of success, the door swung open, banging into the wall from my impatient thrust. The faint street lights below cast long shadows barely illuminating the bed in the dim quarters. We catapulted onto the bed, kicking the door shut as I passed. The kissing and caressing accelerated, becoming increasingly intimate as lips and hands explored uncharted territory. Sam attempted to unbutton my shirt as she straddled on top. I brushed her hair back, revealing a face filled with anticipation. I caressed her face, exploring the definition of her cheeks and jaw, then the texture of her lips.

Impatient with her progress, Sam ripped my shirt open. "Sorry," she said with an unsympathetic devilish smile.

"No you're not." At the moment, I was not remotely concerned with the welfare of a relatively new Armani shirt either. Being stupid drunk, the words rolled out as if someone else planted them. "Alcohol-induced frenzied sex followed by regretful awkwardness in the morning is no way to start a relationship."

Sam studied my face, digesting my reasoning. The frown turned to an expression of understanding and quite possibly a touch of admiration. In the heat of passion, I had stopped the sex freight train in its tracks and rejected her advances, all for the sake of virtue.

"Start a relationship? Kind of egotistical to imply anything beyond tonight, don't you think? "

"I hope so." Without a trace of internal deliberation, I had unintentionally confessed to aspirations beyond a one-night stand.

The intense stare down was on. Who would crack?

"Are you quite certain it's not fear holding you back? If it is, you can still search me for weapons."

"If your offer remains on the table in the morning, you will not have to ask twice. Meanwhile, park your ass in the bed and get some sleep. I have a few business-related details requiring my attention." I glanced at my laptop, alluding to the nature of work. "I would suggest you get plenty of rest. You are going to need all of your energy in the morning."

"Are you absolutely sure I can't change your mind?" Sam unbuttoned the top button of her blouse.

"You could, rather easily I fear, but I would prefer you not. In the morning you might decide this was all wrong, and I want no part of that." Having voiced my objection a second time, I rolled her off the top, laid her beside me, and continued to gaze into her wanting eyes, avoiding the new, dangerously lowered button line. "We have the morning ... and all day if you want."

"All day?"

"As long as you desire." At this point, I was saying all the wrong lines, wrong by a set of standards held in highest regard ... once upon a time.

"You'd better be very careful, Brian Denman. If word of your behavior tonight leaks out, people will say you've lost your edge."

She was absolutely right. Men are from Mars. We are pigs. Men have a one-track mind. Little head always rules the big one. Suddenly, struck upside the head by the realization of emotional attachment, I needed her to understand my twisted, conflicted predicament.

Sensing a stalemate, Sam sighed heavily. "Brian, if this is how you honestly feel, I suggest we both get some sleep." She slid out of the bed, walked to the bathroom, and turned once inside. "Men your age require a lot more rest before expending the energy you'll be needing." She winked and closed the door.

A squeak of the faucet and a rush of water announced I had just enough time to get on my laptop and send a few e-mails. For this job, the specific skills of a few select associates were needed. My fingers blitzed the keyboard, typing encrypted e-mails, attempting to finish the task before Sam emerged. The water stopped, the towel rack rattled, and the bathroom door creaked slowly open. Positioned with my back to the door typing frantically, Sam inched out and placed her warm soft hands on my neck.

"I thought you might want *certain* reassurances before we go to sleep," Sam purred.

"I do not need any, Sam. Besides, I really do not sleep much at all." Typing feverishly, the mental image of lying beside her proved most distracting. I stopped typing while feasting on the slideshow playing in my head.

"Nonetheless, your fears are not unfounded." She leaned in tight, placing her lips close enough to gently brush against my ear. "You should conduct a thorough search to ensure I have no concealed weapons." The heat of her breath and softness of her whisper ran chills up my spine. Did I dare to turn around?

I rubbed my hair and straightened my back, popping a few vertebrae in the process. I turned to find her standing naked, except for those black heels. There is an instinct that seldom occurs in a life, where instantaneously you know you have just witnessed the absolute vision of your deepest desires. For some, maybe it's a car, a job, new home, or simply a naked woman standing directly in front of you. So beautiful. The uncontrollable heat of passion swelled up inside. Drunk or not, this was a defining moment in life that would no longer be contained or denied. I jumped from my chair, swept her up in my arms and eagerly into the bed.

The experience that followed was nothing short of a phenomenal spiritual journey unlike anything I knew could exist. As our passion rose, then ultimately descended to its conclusion, we collapsed tightly into each other's arms. Watching Sam fade into serene slumber, a blissful fatigue washed over, transporting me to a peacefulness unlike any experienced. In Sam's arms, I found sleep no longer my long lost friend.

CHAPTER 9

SAM AND I awoke physically spent and hungry, our naked bodies clinging and sticky. We both needed showers and food. We left the hotel arm in arm and out into the midday heat. Conversation over lunch was light. I loved being with this woman; in fact, I loved her and wanted her to know, but crossing that bridge could be treacherous. As the coffee and food revived me, my thoughts segued from passion and lust to my career and the reason I came to New Orleans. The two were on a collision course. *Think like a CIA man, not a love-struck wimp,* I admonished. *Sam's going to get hurt. Someone always does.* That's what the CIA taught me.

I never got over the fact the CIA just let me retire and walk away. Guys in my position never made it to retirement. By all rights, with a bullet in the head, neither should I. The more knowledge possessed, the more dangerous each successive assignment. My knowledge could send high-ranking individuals to prison for a very long time. It was entirely feasible my airplane buddy was a would-be assassin. The vigil I had maintained throughout the subsequent years, which kept me alive, suddenly collapsed in the presence of Sam.

Sam headed back to Dee's just before dinner, and I to my room. I fired up my laptop and took a couple deep swigs of Abita. Other than the periodic slamming of a hallway door, muted sounds from the street below, and the humming of my laptop, the room was soothingly quiet.

With Sam temporarily out of the picture, it was time to send details to my compadres. Rob was a diehard surveillance geek who could identify the sex of a tick on a dog from two miles away. He also claimed the ability to hear an earthworm fart a mile underground. If something needed to be seen or heard, Rob was the man with the magic ears and eyes. Jimmy B could crack the alarms at Fort Knox. He was a key player in several big jewelry heists in his younger days after being discharged from the Navy. Eventually, after several years of profitable thieving, he found the Lord, kind of, vowing to break the law as little as possible. Chuck was just a badass Marine, executing commands as instructed, without exception. If the job got dirty, Chuck got dirtier. As an ornery child, he would pull the wings off of flies. As an ornery adult, he pulled the appendages off his adversaries. The random assignments, which brought the team together over the years, proved their worth individually and as a crew. By sunrise, I would have confirmation of their commitment.

My cell phone began vibrating as I worked. I had turned the ringer off last night and left it in the room all day. Glancing at the screen, I stuck in my Bluetooth and barked out, "P dog!"

"Where the hell have you been? I've been trying to get in touch with your ass all day," Phillip was growling, unaccustomed to being ignored.

"Number one, my cell phone is for my convenience, not yours. Number two, I took the day off."

"Excuse the hell out of me. I just wanted to make sure you were okay." There was a momentary silence as Phillip digested the news. "What the hell do you mean, you took the day off? Are you fucking kidding me? You've never taken a day off!"

"Well if you had not left my ass in the bar last night, you would have known exactly where and how I was."

"Hey, I came out on the dance floor looking for you and almost died of a heart attack. You guys looked like two fornicating cobras, all twisted and wrapped up all over each other. My God, I got so hot and bothered I nearly soiled my pants. So I figured I had better take

Dee back to my place for your protection. If she had seen the way you were taking advantage of her little sister, it would have been lights out for you, buddy boy."

"So by taking Dee back to your place, you were doing me a favor?"

"Well, yeah. What the hell are good friends for anyhow? Even though you never appreciate me, as usual I had your back. Last night was just another on the long list."

"Damn, Phillip. I guess I owe you." My sarcasm flowed thick and sticky like maple syrup.

"Gratitude accepted."

"Lying sack of shit." I laughed at Phillip's efforts. "Do you want to hook up for a beer tonight, before I get started?"

"Kiss-and-tell session. That might be worth my time."

"There is nothing to tell. She passed out on the bed after throwing up on the way back to my place. I sat up and worked all night on the job. We ate a late lunch, made a little small talk, and I sent her packing. Not a very exciting chapter for your fantasy sexcapades novel."

"Damn, dude, sorry to hear that. It sure looked like you were on the road to Scoresville. Are you going to try to see her again? You know, take another run at it."

"I do not think so, at least not in New Orleans. Maybe next time I am back in LA." Lying through my teeth and enjoying every minute of it, I knew Phillip would be seeking to collect on a wager never made.

"Dee was a total firecracker. In fact, I'm thinking about hooking up with her tomorrow. She was more fun than my last ten girlfriends combined. I already offered to fly her up to New York for Phillipalouza."

"Damn, Phillip, who sounds like a lovesick puppy now? New York's most eligible bachelor has finally been bitten. The tabloids will have a field day with this."

"Let them as long as my paper gets it on page one first."

Phillip hung up the phone without a goodbye, kiss my ass, nothing. Getting in the last word was just his way of being alpha dog.

I shut down my laptop just as abruptly and headed out, intent on finding the coldest beer in New Orleans. Drifting down Toulouse, I absorbed all the night had to offer. Rocking blues and sizzling-hot women grew from the balconies like kudzu vines. My attention was straying.

Renaldo and the tour guide had both mentioned the Chamber and its anointed queen of the damned, Isabelle. I wanted a crash course about this culture, and queen of the proverbial bloodsucking losers was obviously the one to seek concerning the convent.

The truth about the convent was my sole objective tonight, and Isabelle was the means to an end. Like it or not, she would damn well denounce the existence of vampires, then potentially provide insight as to the content of the third floor. Waiting until midnight for it to open irritated me beyond reason, as the place I really wanted to be was sure as hell not the Chamber. Focused concentration was at best marginal, and if advising a trainee on such matters, I would insist they abort. But not me. Above trivial distractions, it was time to get a grasp on the freak show.

Walking down Toulouse at twelve-forty, an hour since my last beer, my game face was on. I crossed crowded Bourbon Street and looked to the right, reminiscing where memories lingered hard from the night before. Those vivid images were abruptly interrupted by a haunting melody echoing out, like that of a child's voice singing. There was no warmth, no scents, no other sounds. All sensory details were derailed by the single shallow voice crying out, deploring me to turn away. As I fought to detach from the song, it ended abruptly as it began.

Placing my hands on my knees, I bent over and ferociously shook my head side to side. "Shit," I called out. "What in the hell?" Had I been doing 'shrooms I would have been okay with the entire episode. Was somebody fucking with me? I raised my head, scanning for anyone who might be watching. Nobody. My focus immediately snapped back to full attention upon discovering the Chamber directly before me. I crossed the street and approached the entrance, an unusually narrow door, unlike any other in the Quarter—an appropriate prop for Alice in Wonderland. A small crowd of eight young idiots, in full gothic attire, gathered at the entrance. Edward Scissorhands guarded the door, not the most intimidating bouncer I had ever crossed paths with.

"Hey, freak, what's going on tonight?"

He cut his eyes to me and gave a half-sneer without responding.

Obviously, I did not fit in with the crowd and did not warrant a response.

"Mind if I go in?"

"That's the line." He spoke blandly while pointing to the oddballs awaiting entrance. "You might want to try the back of it."

"Do I look like I should be waiting in line ... with them?"

He looked me over—jeans, black shirt, and a black sport coat. While some might consider my attire stylishly vampish, I certainly did not resemble any of the inked-up, pierced-to-the-max freak shows standing in line. "To be perfectly honest, you really don't look like someone who needs to go in at all."

I reached in my pocket, pulled out my Chrome Hearts shades, and popped them on. "How's this?"

He rolled his eyes and scoffed.

"What is your name, freak?"

"Royce," he replied, with a sneer of superiority.

I grabbed him by the arm and led him away from the line, all one hundred forty pounds. Turning my back to the crowd, to shelter my actions, I applied sufficient pressure to create moderate discomfort. He looked down at my hand, constricting his thin toneless arm in a vise-grip lock. "Royce, I think we can agree I do not fit in with this crowd. The fact I need immediate entrance should be alerting you I have urgent business inside. Is it fair to say you understand?"

Royce nodded.

"Now, I would love to tell you the nature of my business, but I cannot. So there is no need to discuss the matter any further. Still with me?"

He nodded again, discomfort becoming obvious.

I pulled a little grease money out and stuck it in his hand. He looked down and then back to me, pain easing via gratuity.

"If the person I am meeting finds out you gave me any shit, they will wipe up the sidewalk with your wormy pale ass. So would you like to profit or should I make a call?" Completely releasing his arm, I reached for my phone. "Either way, I go in and sure as hell will not be waiting in the freak show line."

"Naw man, we're cool. Go right on in." He ushered me to the door and cordially opened it. A crooked sidewalk wound through a narrow alley to a second door, this one manned by a gorilla-sized bouncer. His neck and arms were as thick as a fire hydrant, a breathing endorsement for steroids. His face was dark and weathered with deep circles under his eyes. His chin was a shadow of stubble.

"ID."

"For real?"

"Everyone," he responded in a forceful monotone bark.

"Do you run with this crowd?" I flipped open my wallet, producing identification.

"Do I look like I would hang with this crowd?" He glanced at my license, then back to me. "Little old to be hanging out here, eh pops?"

"Part of my ten-step plan. Counselor says I have to face my addictions. You know?" I snatched back my identification. *Living Dead Girls* rebounded harshly off the dimly lit walls. Between the music and the dungeon ambiance, Rob Zombie would be proud to call this dump home. "I have an appointment with Isabelle, Queen of the Damned. She here?"

"Go past the bar and down the stairs. She's got a table on the left side, towards the back."

"Thanks." I sliced my way through the crowd, receiving stares ranging from hostile suspicion to a desire to consume. Fucking freaks! I would venture to guess most of these pathetic misfits knew each other by name and blood type. To them I was an obvious outsider.

I forged through the crowd to a stairwell splitting in two directions—one up and the other straight down into hell. The passage down was excessively dark in a feeble attempt to be forbidding, while music thundered at decibels sure to cause auditory hemorrhaging. The lights radiating from the dance floor below gave just enough illumination to see the way. I decided it would be prudent to scope out upstairs before descending into the basement where the opportunity of escape would be at best, limited. I headed up, into another darkened hallway, which led to another bar. It was nice to know these people did not waste money on trivial expenses such as lighting.

The atmosphere of the loft was subdued and darkly sinister, compared to the audible assault from the floors below. And the music? Try to imagine dance music to the rhythm of a lava light. The only illumination flickered from randomly placed candles and a bar sandwiched between two dirt-streaked windows. Couples, or in several instances, threesomes, with no particular gender prefer-ence,   occupied the room on various mismatched couches. They were doing what I suppose any drunken horny vampire would. Ap-parently, I had drifted into some kind of "vampire" love lounge. How fucking lovely. They were all just busy getting busy and my intrusion went mostly unnoticed.

I crossed the room to a window. Straining to see through the grime, I found a fire escape to the alley below. Secure in the knowl-edge a secondary exit existed, I wandered purposefully, studying all that encompassed the darkened room. Observing the night crawlers, I detected most were drinking a wine-colored beverage. Deep inside, I knew it was not wine.

Our tour guide had professed the existence of a blood drink-ing culture and though I was skeptical from the outset, now I was absolutely confident Merlot was not the spirit of choice. Having seen plenty of blood in my day, I never once thought about drinking it.

I navigated the stairs to the basement, wondering if this could get any worse. Drug dealers, warlords, and dictators all seemed like a better class of humans now. The sizable basement was packed with people seemingly fused together as they gyrated in a flowing motion. It appeared to be some type of ritualistic, erotic sex dance. Although I possessed abnormally keen night vision, the motion and shadows made it difficult to focus on intricate details of my surroundings. I moved counterclockwise around the perimeter of the sinuous masses until reaching the far side of the bar.

Through the darkness I could discern a square table, set into a recessed area of the wall, scarcely making out the details of a woman seated in the rear. She was flanked by a small entourage at the table. Posted by the side of the recessed cube was a meathead, obviously the Queen's imperial guard. Seemingly, I would not be granted an audience without minimal interference. I meandered up to the right of the table and looked around the henchman. Isabelle appeared un-naturally pale, skin taut to her soft but prominent cheeks, a slender pointed nose sweeping gently up to her deep-cobalt eyes. She had an utterly flawless face, framed by long, tightly curled black hair, which draped down just past her shoulders. Although her body was slender, she appeared quite fit. Dressed entirely in black, her lacy top was tight and cut low enough to partially expose her well-rounded breasts. Victorian attire. What a surprise. She took notice of my attention; her intensely penetrating eye contact blew a shock wave through my body. "Sam who," a bedeviled voice chirped out.

"Can I help you?" The bodyguard stepped between, terminating eye contact.

"Why yes, Igor, I am here to see the queen."

"My name is Butch. And nobody sees Isabelle unless she chooses." Insistently impolite, he began sizing me up. I was probably spotting Butch a good three inches and about sixty pounds. Most men would find Butch quite intimidating. To me he was an oversized nuisance.

"Well, Butch, why don't we ask Isabelle what she has to say."

Butch rolled his eyes as if he had something better to do, then begrudgingly turned to Isabelle and pointed his open hand toward me. Her lips were rosy red and glistened in the dim candlelight. She studied my features. A haughty expression adorned her face. Without any commentary, she simply shook her head "no."

"Well there you have it, chief, better luck next time." Butch attempted to usher me in the direction of the stairs.

"I should ask her myself." Resisting, I sidestepped his oak tree body and moved toward the table. Butch swiftly positioned his body in front and put both hands on my chest to halt my advance.

"She already said she does not want to see you. End of story. Now you should leave before it gets painful."

I took a half-step back. "Did you say *painful*?"

"Very painful. This is my turf and I am the law."

I could not restrain my inborn smart ass, knowing full well the consequences. "Well then, can I see your badge, Sheriff?"

"I am a regional MMA champ. That's all the badge I need to kick the living shit out of you if you insist on pissing me off."

"Mixed martial arts champ? Butch, I am impressed. That would make you like half Kung Fu and half Muhammad Ali." I took another half-step back.

Butchie's shit-eating grin acknowledged confidence, believing my retreat was inspired via intimidation.

"Butch, I am here to see Isabelle. You need to understand if you interfere in my business, I will lay your Kung Fu ass down."

Butch looked at me like I was a total idiot. He shoved me

backward, annoyed by my audacious lack of respect. Due to the darkness and deafening music, nobody appeared to notice the escalation. "Wait just a minute, I will be right back." I walked to another table and returned with a chair. Even though it was not raised into a striking position, Butch raised his arms, prepared for defense. "Easy Daddio, I am not going to hit you with the chair." I set it down against the wall next to him and backed away.

Butch eased slightly from his posture. He looked at the chair out of the corner of his eye and then back to me. "I thought you might appreciate resting in the chair as opposed to being sprawled out on the floor."

Butch's benign amusement instantly vanished, irritated by my peculiar arrogance. "You know, when they do your autopsy they're gonna wonder why you got teeth coming out your ass. I hope you enjoy pain."

I glanced past Butch to Isabelle and her party. They were oblivious, confident Butch was completely in charge of the situation. I looked back at Butch. "No hard feelings, right?"

At this point, Butch was beyond pissed, his veins bulging as his arms grew taut. "Last chance, Bozo."

I extended my jaw and tucked my arms behind my back. "I suggest you take a shot so nobody will say I sucker-punched you."

Jackpot! Butch took a direct swing at my face. I blocked it with speed unlike any he had ever witnessed. I returned a devastating blow to the center of his forehead, before he realized his punch never landed. Cold-cocked, his knees buckled, and as he fell back, I grabbed his shirt, guided him down into the chair, and turned my attention to my original target.

"Good evening. Mind if I join you?" I politely greeted everyone seated at the table and without waiting for a reply, forced my way with a hip nudge into the bench seat. Gawking at an unconscious Butch, their focus returned to me. "How is everybody besides Butch doing tonight?" As a speechless collective group, their stone-cold expression spoke volumes. I would venture to guess they were accustomed to Butch handling outsiders in his usual abrasive style.

"Okay, I apologize for knocking Butchie out, but he was quite disagreeable." Still lacking any reaction, I continued on. "Generally, I am a pretty nice guy. I was just curious about this place and wanted to get to know you, specifically Isabelle, better." I aimed a demanding eye at the sultry vixen.

Listening intently, no one flinched. Isabelle appeared shell shocked. Stella's deadly warning echoing in her mind, her quiet confidence was rocked by Butch's inability to protect.

"Come on you guys, lighten up." I might as well have been talking to cardboard cutouts, which at this moment certainly would have made better company.

I decided it would be better to strike up a one-sided conversation as opposed to no conversation.

"I am thinking I would like a minute alone with Isabelle, if you people would not mind excusing yourselves." The continued lack of any response proved to spark a flicker of irritation. "Come on people, it is not like I am going to bite her. Although I cannot say the same for her or any of you for that matter. Go on ... y'all get your asses over there and ooze around on the dance floor for a minute or two while I keep Isabelle company. Before you know it, I will be out of here, and you can go back to your Red Cross meeting."

They all looked to Isabelle for direction. I stood up to make way for the mass exodus. Without a word, she nodded in accordance and one by one, they begrudgingly moved away from the booth and headed to the dance floor. As the last female began to pass, I grabbed her arm and handed her some cash.

"Do me a huge favor, doll. Please bring me a cold beer, any type will do, and another of whatever it is Isabelle drinks. Get your buddies whatever they want with the change." She flashed a contemptuous smile, telegraphing strong vibes of animosity.

I slid back into the booth and cozied right up to Isabelle, probably closer than she preferred. What better way to instantly establish dominance in the relationship than to invade her personal space? She turned and looked at the proximity of our bodies and glared in disapproval without moving.

"So what would you like to talk about?" I opened with a whimsically absurd icebreaker, considering present circumstances. And believe me, the ice was Antarctica thick.

She did not have to answer. "You are so much sexier in person." I offered up a lame compliment as a peace offering.

"And you felt it necessary to knock Butch out just to share that?"

"For some reason he was unable to understand the magnitude of my desire. Then he got rude. So yes, I did. You did have the opportunity to spare him the pain."

Isabelle looked as if she were replaying the memory in her mind. "I know why you are here," she announced in a tempered tone.

"Do you now?"

"The gypsy has foreseen it."

"What exactly did the gypsy foresee?" I was doubtful anyone could possibly have any insight as to my purpose, but curious to hear the explanation.

"She prophesied your arrival—that you would come to destroy me." Isabelle recounted the old woman's words without emotion.

"Sorry to disappoint you Isabelle, wrong guy, wrong night. I just have a few questions. Call it an encapsulated historical education. And as long as I am here, nobody will harm you. I promise."

"Your arrogance may prove to be the undoing of us both."

"Unless the gypsy told you, there is no way for you to know this, but I have been in enough shitstorms in my life to know what I can and cannot do. I can absolutely promise you, outside of this building blowing up, you are safe from any harm tonight as long as I am sitting here. So if you honestly fear for your life, please consider my services tonight in exchange for a little information."

Sliding away, just enough to turn without our heads colliding, her expression transformed from unpleasantly irate to seductively appreciative. Instantly, her sex appeal ignited hot enough to melt a brick. She brushed her hair back and touched my arm. Her neck was long and white as bleached flour, contrasting against her black dress. Damn, if I were a bloodsucker I would not mind nibbling on that, I thought.

"So you will protect me ... all night, if I ask you to?"

"It looks like you have plenty of eager and loyal subjects that would trip all over each other for the honor. It certainly does not appear you will need my services all night."

"Them?" Isabelle gazed out at the swarming masses. "Please do not get me started. Besides, what I have and what I need are not necessarily one and the same. Tonight I might desire something, or someone, different."

The young girl returned with my beer and exchanged a silent

look of collaboration as she set Isabelle's drink down. She nodded her head in affirmation and briskly departed to join the others.

"I normally would have a hard time turning down such an enticing offer from a beautiful woman, such as yourself. But tonight I must. I am here on business and surely you know what they say about mixing business and pleasure." I watched the girl as she disappeared into the crowd. "Interesting dancing, kind of combines drunken salsa and Roman orgy." I took a deep swig of the icy brew. "Do you dance?"

"No, I do not know anything about what they say, and know nothing of business. On the other hand, you will find I am a connoisseur of dark pleasure. And yes, I would love to dance."

"Well, in honor of your ignorance of modern catchphrases, I suppose we should just see where tonight leads. After all, the night is young." Putting my best provocative foot forward, I clinked my beer bottle to her glass.

"Nothing is as young as it appears."

She took a drink from the newly acquired cut-crystal glass. The liquid was a dark-crimson color.

"'Type O?' I could not pass up on the opportunity to remain a wise-ass.

Isabelle flashed a crooked devilish smile. "I prefer A negative."

The thought had me drinking my beer down hard. I watched, repulsed as she poured the glistening ruby liquid past her full moist lips, extracting a deep sensual pleasure as it glided over her inviting tongue. Running her tongue across her lips, tauntingly, she gently bit down on the lower one and gazed ever so seductively. I quivered at the notion. Vile, yet sexually intriguing, unbeknownst, my ability to resist temptation eroded in her transcendent presence. Isabelle, quite confident in her ability to seduce, sensed a nick in my shield.

"How about that dance?" I whipped my head away from her performance in an effort to regain my composure.

Leading her by the hand, we fused ourselves into the throngs of sweaty sub-human creatures inhabiting the dance floor. Between this and the room upstairs, the only item missing, short of a good porno movie, was the camera. Sexual energy was being discharged in every direction to the point I felt it clinging to my entire body. Forcefully, I diverted uninvited, random, twisted thoughts to the passion that transpired over the last day with Sam. The mental images helped restrain me from spiraling into the abyss of this rabbit hole. Needing to play her game, I pulled Isabelle tightly, entangling our bodies to the slow-grinding music. Her body filled every void of space between creating a sensation of oneness. A sudden weakness swooned over as I studied her almost indescribable beauty, flawless and fragile, yet morbid, but desirable to the point of unrelenting anguish.

The brazen nature of my public display of affection was met with evil stares of disapproval from the surrounding freaks. Obviously, dancing so personally with the queen was not appreciated. Isabelle offered no resistance, so the hell with them. Taking the liberty of exploring her inviting body, she surrendered to my advances with pleasurable groans. I would use this advantage to ascertain the information needed and then get the hell out before becoming physically unable to.

I slid my hand behind her shoulders and slowly traced the root of her neck up into her thick hair. I guided her face close enough to kiss, her lips parting, awaiting contact. The heat of her breath blew gently across my face in feverish anticipation. I hesitated, almost failing, before moving my lips past her alluring mouth then next to her ear.

"Tell me, what is it like … to be the leader of all of these people?"

"I am not their leader." She seized the opportunity to kiss my neck. Moaning as she tasted flesh, her lips explored without prejudice.

Without doubt, this definitely did not help matters of fending off my caveman instincts. I forced myself back to the task.

"Everything I have heard and read says you are."

"You don't impress me as a man who believes everything he reads." She attempted to pull away, frustrated with my inattention to her efforts.

I refused to let her.

"You are right. I do not. Yet, you do have bodyguards. Somebody believes you are important enough to protect."

"I'm not," Isabelle replied softly as she positioned her face dangerously close to mine.

Seductive beyond logical explanation, unlike any woman I had encountered, including Sam, my guard dropped without intention. Isabelle was a woman worth exploring for pure reasons of intrigue, minus her obvious drinking problem. I allowed my lips to brush against her cheek.

"If I were to ask if you're a vampire, what would you say?"

"I wouldn't say." Her tone was somewhat saddened for reasons yet to be discovered.

"What are you? Who are they?" Isabelle looked at the crowd surrounding us. "People crave definition. What they do not understand creates discomfort. I don't like labels. I am nothing more than Isabelle." She pulled her face away, exposing an inexplicable purity in her eyes.

"But you are aware of the stories," I insisted. "Surely they would not have been written if they did not contain some essence of truth."

"I know the stories," she said, her frustration evident. "Truth is all about perception. What you want to believe is all that matters concerning truth. How many innocent people have been put to death because they were perceived guilty?"

I allowed an expression of understanding to roll across my face.

"So I guess the myth of your age, what was it, over one hundred years, all fantasy? Because honestly I had you pegged for about thirty." With no response, I tried to read into those glistening cobalt eyes.

"And what is the story with the blood drinking? Sounds kind of crazy, you must admit."

"I don't believe we know each other well enough for me to answer those questions." Her smile was taunting. "Why do you ask such questions? Are you a reporter?"

"No, not even close."

"So why are you here? Why are you seducing me so?"

"Seducing you? Is that what you think I am doing?" Happy she figured it out, I was ready to press the issue and get the hell out of Dodge.

"Do you deny this?"

"I am in New Orleans conducting research on a project. I stumbled across an article about you and was fascinated. There is no grand scheme of seduction, as you put it."

"Yet here we are," she said in a sultry tone while observing the congruency of our heated bodies. "Do you customarily get this intimate with your research, or am I an exception?"

"I do not believe in wasting time, if that is what you are asking.

Life is way short too not to go after the things you want."

"A little early to be confessing your intentions, don't you think?"

How in the hell could one woman express infinite sadness, seduction, innocence, and confidence all at one time. It was as if I was
looking into the mind of a multiple-personality disorder, only what
should not be seen was not only visible, but stood before me in the
flesh. At this point, I should have sensed something was terribly
amiss.

"And if I choose to end this now, where would that leave you?"

"Well, I suppose this moment would have to be enough." I
paused, awaiting her reaction. "I have been around the block enough
to know the only guarantee in life you get is right now. Your next
breath could be entirely somebody else's decision. Tell me, exactly
when did you choose this lifestyle?"

"I honestly do not remember any other way. Time passes and
with each day it just passes me by."

I thought I detected a hint of remorse. "So your age? The
rumors?"

"Does it matter? Believe whatever you want. I am young but old.
Good yet evil."

Feeling more unbalanced as we danced, I began to consciously
recount the beers consumed, seeking a reason for this sensation.
Needing to return to my seat before my lack of balance became obvious, I took Isabelle's hand and led her back to the table. "I need a
drink." With my equilibrium in peril, I knew something was wrong
and getting worse by the minute. Losing control, it was time to exit
with all haste. After all, if Butch were to wake up, I would be suscep-
tible to a major ass-kicking. I took one last swallow of beer. "I have
somewhere I need to be."

"I thought we might spend a little more time together, alone," she
purred while caressing my arm.

"Later." Disorientation overwhelmed me as I turned and headed
in the direction of the stairs, thoughts of panic rearing an uninvited
head. I staggered, making my way through the crowd, many laughing
as if they had seen this before. I pushed my way through, stum-
bling to the top of the stairs, swaying side to side, bouncing off the
walls, through the bar, colliding with people and bar stools clumsily
making my way out. My flesh turned white and clammy.

"I see you found Isabelle," the bouncer crowed as I sped past. "Sweet dreams, ass-wipe," he said with a chuckle as I disappeared up the alley.

"Wait!" Isabelle beckoned from behind, rushing to catch me.

Head spinning, pounding violently, I could not afford to stop. *Must reach the street!* A warm rush of blood rose to my head, the loss of consciousness waiting to collect me. Sounds of Toulouse Street just ahead reverberated, guiding me as I crashed through the outer door. The sanctuary of the streets offered no relief. I blindly moved in any direction away from the Chamber. Poisoned? Thoughts of Sam flashed past my glazed eyes. Was life's end drawing near? God I hoped not.

I turned up a dark and deserted alleyway. Ramming my finger deep inside my throat, I violently heaved most of the contents from my stomach. I did it again. Hunched over, wondering if this solitary alley would be the last stop, I had no trepidation of dying or what may lie ahead. I had been down that road before. But why now?

"There you are," Isabelle called anxiously as she turned into the alley. "What is wrong with you?"

"I should ask you," I accused, still hunched over, feeling I had not regained a shred of control.

"The vampire's curse," she replied harshly, her facade of innocence no longer needed. "Now you will do as I command." She marched up close, grabbed my shoulders, and forcefully stood me straight up. "Nobody leaves without permission."

As my eyes rolled back in my head, I caught a glimpse of her daunting stare. I was helpless to defend myself. Instincts dictated to knock the bitch out and get the hell away from this place, but my body was paralyzed.

Isabelle drew closer. Once again, I could feel the heat of her moist breath against my skin. "After tonight, you will be mine forever."

She began to kiss me slowly, biting at my lip. With every shred of strength, I fought her advances but to no avail. My conscious thoughts were overtaken by a force the likes of which I had never encountered.

Isabelle's passionate kisses escalated to a feverous pitch. I tried to focus on Sam, but could not maintain the thought of her or anything. I desperately searched my survival skills for any trace of strength to force my arms up and push her away. Nothing. Regretfully, I succumbed to her desires, kissing her wildly. Echoes of the streets grew faint, and darkness from the night sky drew down upon me. Light faded from perception. Futilely fighting with what little hope remained, darkness moved in and swept me away. Surrendering to the crushing defeat of the abyss, the battle was lost.

CHAPTER 10

MY BODY WAS still and void of sensation. Painfully, my eyes cracked open, bearing witness to the first glimpse of daylight, wearily processing fuzzy details of an unfamiliar room. Over my head were large chunks of missing plaster and weathered peach walls with peeling paint. I was alive, but somehow had been deposited in this shithole.

Unable to focus, I heard the faint sounds of birds and what sounded like a lawnmower outside the window. The sun seeped in scattered rays through holes in the weathered, dust-encrusted curtains. Having no recollection beyond staggering out the Chamber, I struggled to lift my head, which collapsed back with a thump on a surprisingly soft pillow bearing a familiar sweet fragrance. "Isabelle, you bitch," I muttered. I drifted in and out of consciousness, abstractly piecing together the events of the previous night.

Just as I began drifting back into the unconscious realm, the bouncer's final words came screaming back into my head, "Sweet dreams, ass-wipe." He knew I had been drugged. I turned my head and surveyed the room, the ability to focus gradually returning. This was definitely not my hotel room. Alone in the room, I rolled to the side and began to pry my body away from the mattress. The fresh white linen sheets stuck to my sweaty body as if they were made of Saran Wrap. The floor was a minefield of candles, indiscriminately scattered about, various shapes and sizes, a few still burning.

My clothes were strewn, and suddenly it occurred to me—I was naked. I had no recollection of how I got this way. As I bent over to pick up my jeans off the dirty wooden floor next to the bed, my head pounded as if jackhammers were chiseling away the inner layers of my dura matter. I checked the pockets, wallet, and cash—happily in place. My jeans looked as though they had been used to mop the filth. Worse yet, they smelled and appeared to have vomit spattered on them. I spotted my jacket in a dusty, ragged chair across the room. I pulled my pants over my trembling legs and hobbled over to retrieve it. My shirt was ripped and torn with only two buttons remaining. Sadly, it looked as though my shirt had been to the same puke festival as my jeans. I lifted my jacket, and contrary to all of the current disappointing circumstances, Loretta was there. I inspected the jacket, hoping to cover the grotesque display of stupidity that decorated my shirt, but this was not my lucky day. My new black linen Etro jacket bore the same fate as its perfectly paired ensemble.

I checked Loretta, ensuring she had not been fired. A bittersweet consolation to an otherwise disastrous night, finding a full clip assured me I had not shot anybody during my lack of consciousness.

Splashing my face with the cold water from the bathroom sink helped clear my vision and my head. I dried my face best as possible with my hands and shook off the excess water. There was no trace anyone else had been in the room with me, other than Isabelle's scent on the pillow. Whoever brought me here was gone. But where was *here*? Not knowing what, or who might await outside the door, I reached for Loretta, ensuring no mortal would impede my exit.

Pathetically, this predicament was another first in what was turning out to be a peculiar set of circumstantial screw-ups. Drugged and kidnapped. Before Samantha, this shit never happened. Obviously, this vampire clan played their games far more seriously than anticipated. This had to be my last miscalculation.

I turned the crystal doorknob slowly and tugged firmly. Squeaking loudly, announcing my departure, the door popped open just enough for me to check the hallway. All was clear in my immediate vicinity. Although the bedroom had been scarcely furnished with secondhand antiques, the hallway was void of any furnishings. Sunlight penetrated the hall from a broken window to the left, near the stairs, glare on the dusty floor exposing two sets of tracks. Apparently one mine, the other most likely Isabelle's. The bitch drugged me and brought me here to do God knows what.

Scanning the empty hall again, I left the confines of Isabelle's little pleasure chamber. By all appearances, this house had been neglected and deserted for many years. A thick, silky matting of cobwebs hung from the chandelier over the stairs. I used the wall to steady my descent, as a large section of handrail was missing. With each step down, I continued to scan ahead and behind, Loretta leading the way. The first floor was neglected much as the second. Just off the base of the stairs, to the left, was an impenetrable guardian in the form of a solid-weathered oak door. I peered through a crack in the adjacent boarded-up vertical transom. Through the smudgy pane, it appeared as though I was still in the French Quarter. A couple passed on the sidewalk as a solitary car drove by. I tried the knob, but it was locked. The skeleton key to the tarnished brass deadbolt had been removed. The remaining windows appeared to be boarded, accounting for the lack of sunlight throughout the lower floor. Two choices presented themselves: find another way out or bust down the door. I bent low and studied the floor. Sure enough, you could see a trail leading from a door down the darkened hall, toward the rear of the house. An ajar knobless door led to a darkened basement. I flipped the switch by the top of the stairs. Big surprise: no lights. The rickety, narrow wooden stairway sagged and moaned with every measured step into utter darkness. Most basements have transom windows or doors, so precariously I shuffled to the left inch by inch, waving my arm about slowly. About six feet from the stairs, I acquired my target—a damp and gritty wall. Using my hand to guide, I probed the wall searching blindly, in the process running my hand through countless tacky spider webs. Finally, locating what felt like a window, I groped for, then wrestled with the rusty latch until it flipped open. Once unlocked, a couple of good tugs partially opened the window. Sunlight steamed into the basement.

"What the hell?" I uttered softly. The faint vision I witnessed rocked my foundation of beliefs to the core. Maybe I should have been expecting it, but how do you expect something so absurd? In the middle of the room were three caskets set neatly about. It would be an omission of truth to deny the existence of chills that suddenly crept up my spine. Instantly, the gray area between fact and fiction blurred into one. I was waste deep in a river of shit.

Candles were placed in similar fashion to Isabelle's love nest above. Looking as though it had been used recently, an antique cast-iron bed seemed awkwardly out of place against the farthest wall. I could only imagine the freakish rituals that transpired in this soulless void.

Just to the left of the bed was the cellar door, which I unlocked and quietly swung open. I quickly moved about the room, opening all of the transom windows, filling the basement with glistening sunlight. The moment of truth had arrived. Time to expose the freak show or battle the undead. I surveyed the three caskets, deciding which to open first. Latching the two on the right, I moved to the casket on the left, closest to the exit. Golden trim and floral ornamentation cloaked the dark-cherry box. "I do not believe in vampires," I reminded myself while sucking in one last deep breath. "Three, two, one." I flipped the lid off and as it crashed to the floor, the occupant awoke in terror. My eyes popped in anger, discovering one of the boys from Isabelle's table. The complete panic in his eyes assured me I had nothing to fear. Grabbing him by the shirt, I yanked his scrawny ass out, sending the casket tumbling from the pedestal it rested upon.

"What the fuck?" he screamed out. Having been rudely awakened, totally unprepared, he looked around frantically, attempting to gauge his predicament.

I dragged him by his shirt over to the sunlight. I lifted him off the floor and slammed his back against the wall. Basking in the warm glow of the sunlight without reaction, I shoved Loretta against his temple.

"No!" he screamed frantically. "Please don't!"

I pressed her cool steel tightly in place while waiting for the sunlight to singe his flesh. No smoke, no flames, no surprise. "Hey, why aren't you writhing in agony? Aren't you supposed to ignite or explode in sunlight?" I yelled mockingly.

He whimpered, looking at the sunlight illuminating his trembling hands.

"Where's Isabelle?" I demanded.

"I don't know." His parted lips displayed a relatively expensive set of cosmetic fangs.

"Well, obviously you're no vampire." I released my grip, lowered Loretta, and took a step back. He sighed, his body slumping in relief. "Not so fast, freak." I pointed Loretta right between his eyes, gangsta style. "Should I test the theory of immortality here?" Shaking his head briskly side to side, he objected. "Pretty damn sure if I pull this trigger, your brains will splatter all over the wall, thus concluding your pathetic existence." He could not muster the courage to look me in the eye. "What do you think, Drac?"

He shook his head.

"Who is in the other boxes?"

"Friends," he stuttered.

"Isabelle?" He shook his head "no." "Let me guess, more faux Vamps?"

"Hey, we're not posers, just because—"

"Shut up! I swear to God I will shoot you right this second if you insist on spewing any of that annoying bullshit." He swallowed hard. "What did they do to me last night?" A muffled voice from one of the caskets expressed displeasure with the locked lid.

He cut his eyes to the casket and then back to me. "It was Isabelle. She cast her spell on you."

"What did they give me?" I grabbed his chin, forcing his eyes to mine.

Squirming and trembling, he whined, "I don't know!"

"Too bad." I pressed the Beretta squarely on the bridge of his nose. He attempted to swallow, beads of sweat forming on his forehead.

"What's your name, freak?

"Ja ... s ... s ... son."

"Well, Jason, what's it going to be?" There was a moment of silence as he struggled with his options. "Have it your way." Slow and with much deliberation, I began to squeeze the trigger. "Look at my finger," I demanded. "It is the last thing you will see."

"Stop, stop, stop," he pleaded desperately. "It might have been the sacrificial elixir."

"Sacrificial what?"

"I'm not exactly sure, but I think they mix peyote and E ... you know, Ecstasy."

"They?" I lifted my finger from the trigger.

"When we party, we drink a little, and then, it's like anything goes. You wake up a couple of days later and don't remember a damn thing. It's pretty wild. Isabelle's into it big time. But I didn't have nothin' to do with what happened to you."

I knew all about peyote cocktails, administered it years ago for various situations—very effective tool against the enemy. The bitter taste made perfect sense now. "What day is it?" Suddenly and acutely aware, I feared several days may have passed into oblivion.

"It's Saturday." Jason took in a deep sigh of relief as I withdrew Loretta. Brushing down the front of his shirt, I smoothed out the wrinkles, relieved to only have lost about fifteen hours.

"Dude, you need to get a new life. This game will get you killed."

"No doubt." He dusted imaginary dirt off his shirt to conceal the angst of nearly crapping his pants.

"Here is the deal, Jason. You people think I intend to harm Isabelle, but if that were so she would already be wearing a toe tag. Nevertheless , I do not appreciate getting knocked on my ass by the cactus juice last night. I am going back to the Chamber tonight. If I get the slightest suspicion you have ratted me out, I swear your ass will be needing this casket for real. Understood?"

The intermittent knocking on the casket lid had turned into an impatient banging. He nodded in affirmation as he looked to the source. "Sounds like your friend might be a little claustrophobic." I turned to leave via the cellar door. "I suggest you think really hard about getting out of this whole vampire career thing."

Jason nodded.

"It is bad for your health. There is no future in it." With my closing words of wisdom, I headed out into the neglected, overgrown yard where the ragged hedges obscured all view of the surrounding houses. Still unstable on my legs, I trudged through the thick knee-deep grass. I made my way over a ramshackle fence, across the front yard, and out into the street. Using the sun to get my bearings, my head still reeling from the effects of the hallucinogenic cocktail, I promptly headed back to the hotel. Fucking vampires!

CHAPTER 11

SWEAT EMANATED FROM every pore as the lingering toxins executed a mass exodus, or was it a result of anxiety? I assured myself this was nothing more than an aftershock, lingering paranoid hallucinations associated with peyote use.

Upon arriving at the Maison Dupuy, I sped through the lobby, hoping to go unnoticed.

"Mr. Denman."

I twisted my head further away, hoping to remain anonymous.

"Mr. Denman," Renaldo persisted.

I stopped, sucked in a deep breath and let it out slowly, looking down at my grimy, puke-stained shoes. Brushing my hair back, I turned my head to the side and cut an ornery glare.

"People have been asking for you—Mrs. D and another couple. They've come through several times. Are you okay? You don't look so good."

"Yes I am. And thank you for your concern." Fatigue laced my reply. Navigating toward the elevator, admittedly looking and smelling like shit, at this juncture I did not give a rat's ass. Even on my worst of days in Colombia, I never looked this bad. Fucking vampires!

Rarely does time cooperate or give a damn about the arrogant and careless idiots of this world. Waiting for what seemed like hours, guests approached the elevator and sneered at my appearance. I would not beg time for mercy. I did not deserve it.

Finally returning to the solitude of my room, I checked my phone, which I had left behind last night. Yep, ten calls from Phillip. Better call before the shower or Phillip the Impatient might ring another ten times.

"Where the hell have you been? You have not answered your phone and you haven't been at your hotel all day." His bark was agitated.

"Hey, buddy, good to talk to you too. In case you forgot, I came down here to do a job. So fill in the blanks." I surveyed the remnants of what had once been a damn nice outfit as I paced in front of the mirror.

"I don't want to hear any whiney-ass excuses. My ass got dragged all over town by two shopaholics." Phillip's voice cried through the phone, revealing the nature of his angst. "I thought we would have hooked up for lunch. Where the fuck have you been?"

"Rough night. I'll tell you about it later. I am going to catch a quick shower, get dressed, and then catch up with you. I am hours past hungry."

"What are you in the mood for?"

"Food!" I yelled loud enough to pierce his eardrums, then hung up the phone.

The cold water delivered a stinging, much needed shock to my body, and more importantly, my brain. I grabbed the washcloth and began scouring, working down toward my legs. At the top inner part of my thigh, I felt a dull ache. Finishing quickly, I proceeded to dry off, once again hitting the area of irritation. I slung my leg on the cold marble counter and caught a glimpse of the source. "Oh, hell no! She did not!" I yelled loudly, infuriated by the sight. "That bitch." A black and purple bruise encompassed two puncture wounds, spaced far enough to be a bite. "That bitch has carried this vampire shit way too far." If I had to yank Isabelle out by the hair and beat the truth out of her tonight, I would have my answers.

Before heading out, I checked my e-mails. The boys indicated they were on board and headed for the Big Easy. Tomorrow would bring familiar faces and a work ethic that was sorely missed up to this point. Tomorrow, order would be restored.

But this evening, I would enjoy the company of Phillip and the girls until it was time for the trek back to the Chamber. My anticipation of seeing Sam was dampened by what transpired last night. Until I had some answers, no sex with Sam. Who in the hell knows what that vamp bitch infected me with. Returning to the sweltering outdoors, I phoned Phillip. "Dushea's," he barked without as much as hello. "I'm having drinks with the girls. Better hurry before I take them both home."

Thankfully, Dushea's was only seven blocks away, but I was still in no condition to hoof it.

Just as I stepped outside, a cab rambled up the street. Jumping in front, I bellowed, "Yo, taxi." He leaned on his horn while slowing to a stop. I remained in his path of travel.

"I already got a fare, you crazy asshole!" His head popped out the window like a prairie dog. "You trying to get yourself killed or something?"

"Hang on! Wait just a minute," I pleaded. "Tell your passenger I will give her one hundred dollars if she shares the cab. I only need a ride to Dushea's, but I need to get there like five minutes ago."

"One hundred dollars for my fare? Whatcha got for me, money man?" Suddenly concerned for my quest, his demeanor changed.

I pulled out two one-hundred-dollar bills, enticing him with the bait. "I need to be there five minutes ago."

"Get your crazy white ass in." He reached over and flipped open the front passenger door without consent of the fare in the rear.

The cab squealed away and in less than two minutes he stomped on the brake as the cab screeched up in front of Dushea's, sending the shell-shocked lady passenger and myself lunging forward.

"Fast enough, mista?" An air of satisfaction filled his voice.

"Good enough for Daytona."

"No, better than Daytona!" A virtually toothless grin broadcast his pride.

My original intentions were to put a little distance between Sam and me, cool things down just a bit for the next couple of days, and remove my head out of my ass. "If you are headed back the other way, do me one last favor. Hang a u-ey and pull up to the flower shop we passed two blocks back." With the door still open, he yanked the gear shift into reverse, nailed the accelerator, which caused the door to lunge forward then slam shut as he raced backward two blocks. "Good enough, Captain?"

"Perfect." I exited quickly, for fear he would take off with one of my legs remaining in the cab. Initially, I had been feeling rather blasé about dinner, but somewhere between the hotel and the restaurant the love genie lit a voracious fire under my ass. Turning the brass knob, I forced the heat-swollen door to open as the attached bell announced my arrival. Sadly, I could not remember taking the time to enjoy the scent of a rose or any flower, but today the sweet fragrance inundated my senses. I afforded myself a moment to gaze upon the brilliantly contrasting exquisite designs of floral art, studying the intricate details of the various blossoms inhabiting the shop. Walking back toward Dushea's, I glanced down at my purchase. First time for many things.

Away from the haunts of tourists, Dushea's was one of the swankiest eateries I had seen in the city thus far. Fine hardwood tables with linen tablecloths and deep-red-velvet-covered chairs accented the dining area of deep, rich mahogany woodwork and polished brass. The tables were appointed with fine crystal and sterling silver cutlery appropriately placed, awaiting diners who would appreciate the obvious attention to detail. Each table had a unique fresh-cut floral creation, most likely from my previous stop, adding to the romantic ambiance. Numerous candles dimly lit the dining area, giving it a warm, unpretentious radiant glow.

The maître d' greeted me at the door. "Good evening, sir. Welcome to Dushea's. Might you be Mr. Denman?" Relatively confident I matched the description given to him prior to my arrival, he sported an air of confidence.

"Yes, I would."

"Right this way. We have been expecting you."

He led me through the main dining room toward the rear, where a candlelit corridor led to private rooms adorned with red velvet curtains for privacy. "The last room on the left." He gestured ahead, then trailed as I proceeded.

Making my way down the swanky hallway, embellished with modern works of local art, my heartbeat accelerated. I stood in the archway of the last room, Sam's back to me. Phillip rose immediately, grinning broadly. Sam turned and eagerly launched from her chair before Phillip could get a word out. Dressed in formfitting black capris and a white sleeveless shirt, unbuttoned just enough to make you look, my heart pounded like an African tribal drum. Her hair lightly brushed her shoulders and glistened in the candlelight. I could not waste this moment of overwhelming desire for the sake of continuing to snowball Phillip and Dee. The wild lust in Sam's eyes confirmed my emotions. She took two steps forward as I rushed toward her. We embraced and launched into a deep, intimate kiss, ignoring the presence of our stunned companions.

"What the hell," Phillip protested after being snowed for the better part of the day by Sam. Meanwhile, a shocked sister began choking on her vintage Merlot.

"I'll tell your waiter you need a few minutes," the maître d' said, raising an eyebrow as he turned and departed.

Dee's gagging went from unintentional to a deliberate volley of throat-clearing coughs in an attempt to interrupt our enthusiastic reunion.

"All right already. Come up for air for God's sake," Phillip protested.

We ended our kiss, but stayed face to face, reacquainting the confirmation in each other's eyes. "I missed you."

"I'm glad to hear that. After you played Houdini all day, I was afraid you changed your mind and ran away."

Sam glowed in gratitude, growing ever more confident. "You already had me with the roses, Mr. Romantic. Are you sure seducing women is not your second occupation?" Speaking loudly, Sam winked at Dee.

"I could do this for a living ... with you." My voice remained hushed.

"Hey, hey, no whispering. It's rude," Phillip protested.

Sam and I sat down. Dee continued staring, mouth agape. "My God, this is more serious than I thought."

"I'd call it obscene," Phillip added

"Congratulations are in order for breaking the icecap off Brian Denman, a feat tried by many and up until now, always resulting in failure," Phillip said as he raised his wine glass.

I retrieved the roses from the empty chair. "These are for you." Sam received the first dozen with a blush, and then leaned over to kiss me.

"They are so beautiful. Thank you."

"And these are for you, darling." I stretched the bouquet out in Phillip's direction, and just as he reached out to receive them, I redirected them. "Actually, for the pain and anguish of putting up with Phillip for almost two days and keeping him out of my hair, these are for you, Dee. You deserve so much more, but they will have to do for now."

Phillip sneered, signaling a desire for revenge for sucking up to his date.

"Brian, that's so nice of you. It's been a while since anyone has brought me roses."

Phillip scowled as he mimicked her words while flipping me off every opportunity the girls were not looking in his direction.

Spending the next few hours eating and drinking, I gained better insight into Dee. She was in many ways just like Sam, but also quite different. Dee was career oriented and driven by success, while Sam was driven by a zest for life. Both were playful, but Sam excelled in laying on the BS at any given opportunity. They both had a propensity to be intense and change demeanor at the drop of a hat.

By the end of dinner, the girls excused themselves for the ceremonial tandem bathroom break, leaving Phillip and me a minute to chat.

"You are such a kiss ass," he accused as he shook his head in disapproval. "But aside from that, straight up, no bullshit, I've got to know if you really think you are in love?"

"Straight up and in over my head."

"Then I'm really happy for you. No shit. You know I've been trying to set you up for years."

"Believe me, I know."

"So, what's up with the job?" Phillip had an annoying habit of starting a discussion on one topic, then suddenly, without cause, completely changing subjects.

"It's on. That is all you need to know."

Phillip contemplated his next words briefly. "I was thinking, Brian, maybe I want in this time. Something in my life is missing. I want to experience what it's like on the edge, to feel the exhilaration."

"Phillip, if you want the thrill, go drive a Formula One or try sky diving. You don't need my kind of excitement—it's dirty. Screwups could land you in jail for the better part of your life or worse, you could die. Although the upside to dying is you are not locked up the rest of your life being Phillip the Bitch," I lectured sternly, as a father would a restless child.

"There you go again, refusing to let me screw up. I'll bet I could not pay you enough to change your mind on this one."

I agreed, nodding my head. "You do not have enough money for that."

Phillip looked at his watch. "What the hell? They've been gone a long time. You think they're talking about us?"

"Most likely talking about you. Then they came to their senses and hauled ass."

"I hope so. Then we could finally get down to some serious fun."

"Serious fun? Like getting shit-faced and coercing young ladies to show their tatas? Don't get me wrong, Phillip, but I quite prefer tonight's company over whatever we might have come into last night."

Our departure was looming uncomfortably near. Before any additional intimacy would take place, it was imperative to find out exactly what went down last night. Painstakingly, I would have to find a way to end tonight and part ways. Four empty bottles of wine told the tale of the evening. With no clear solution before me, there was no motivation to leave. Casting random stares of uncertain implications, I interpreted reservations from Phillip concerning ability to execute this job effectively, considering current circumstances. Undoubtedly, tomorrow he would return to busting my chops with his trademark sarcastic banter, the humbled love kitten long forgotten.

I was preparing to order one last bottle of vino when Phillip tossed the proverbial monkey wrench into my ... well-orchestrated plan. "Anyone up for dancing, or maybe a little balcony mischief?"

The girls chimed simultaneously, "I am."

"Well, all righty then," Phillip chirped giddily at the thought. "I'll treat for the beads."

Time for modifications, pronto. This new wrinkle would have me out well past midnight, Phillip and girls in tow. Possibly, I could find an excuse to slip away long enough to return to the Chamber, find Isabelle and wring her neck. If the interrogation revealed good news, then an overnight with Sam was back on the table. If it was bad ... I did not even want to think of the consequences.

Almost on cue, our waiter brought the check. There was no discussion over the bill. Phillip paid unbegrudgingly as he was eager to embark on our new adventure and waste not a minute more in the restaurant.

I visualized my explanation of the teeth marks on my ass to Sam, followed by the confession of committing *out-of-my-frigging-mind sex with a vampire*, which honestly was not my fault. Yep, I was sure that conversation would have a happy ending. Run. Run away and never look back. Only problem was, I could never hide from myself.

CHAPTER 12

PHILLIP AND DEE led the way back to Bourbon Street while Sam and I lagged comfortably behind. My motive for lagging was decisively different from Sam's.

"You know," Sam purred, "eventually I'm going to get you alone, and then you'll pay for being MIA all day."

Missing in action. Yep, that about summed up where I needed to be now. But her smile and attitude melted the anxiety like wax on the back burner.

"Hey, how about when you get me alone, not only will I make you forget I was missing, but render you absolutely speechless for...," I paused to gauge time on my watch, "at least a minute and seven seconds."

"I can hardly wait." She leaned into me, wrapping her arm in mine.

"I need to leave the bar at one o'clock for a short period."

"Wow, you've got it nailed down to a precise time. I am impressed. Usually, I like my sex a little more spontaneous, but if you think it's one or you'll explode, then one it is."

"I am sorry. I was not referring to that." Obviously, my previous proposal was still looming in her thoughts. "That will have to wait just a little longer."

Sam's befuddled expression beckoned explanation.

"It is the job. I have to see a contact, around one. It should not take more than fifteen minutes."

"Can I come?"

"No," I said abruptly. "I do not want you anywhere near these people. Trust me, they are not your kind of people or mine either. Just a means to an end."

Sam's expression registered disappointment.

With a borrowed cliché move, I turned her chin up, forcing her eyes to mine. "After this job, I will be at your disposal, twenty-four-seven."

"Twenty-four-seven? Getting a little ahead of ourselves, aren't we?"

I put my arm around her shoulder. "I certainly hope so."

We meandered our way to the scene of the crime two nights prior. Phillip made a brief pit stop en route to pick up beads. I placed a few strands around Sam's neck. She raised her eyebrows

"If you think this means you're getting any preferential treatment or some kind of bawdy show later, you are sadly mistaken, mister."

"A guy can always hope."

Doug, standing vigil at the door, spotted me and waved us in ahead of the Saturday night crowd. I passed him an Uncle Bensky in appreciation. Once inside, we ventured to the balcony and joined in the drinking festivities while tossing the occasional strands. Sam's and Dee's enthusiasm for the tradition surprisingly dwarfed Phillip's.

In the usual manner of proper protocol, the girls decided it was time for the tandem pit stop.

I took the opportunity to question Phillip. "What's up, Phil? What is the deal? Two days straight of Dee. Time to move on?"

"No," he said with a raised edgy reply.

"So, are you going to keep me in the dark?"

"I like her too much."

"What did you just say? Do my ears deceive me? Could it be you see her as more than just a playmate? Or what did you call it? Beaver fever?"

"Asshole." Phillip could not hold the irritated gaze but a second.

"How the hell do you think this makes me feel? I'm going to come across as some kind of pathetic copycat. My bro falls in love, and I go and do the same?"

"And if my math skills are correct," I said, "she is almost eight years older than you. That makes her old enough to be the mom of the majority of your other girlfriends."

"Fine, let's all kick Phillip while he's down."

"I'll save the ass-kicking for later. But for now, in about a half an hour, I need to haul ass for about thirty minutes for the job. I have already told Sam. Do me a solid and keep the party going till I return."

"Only because it's for the job, otherwise I'd hang you out to dry, buddy boy."

As one o'clock neared, I reminded Sam, and she pouted just enough to express disappointment but not enough to be a nuisance. I kissed her goodbye and headed out into the street. Before leaving, I put a fresh bottle of beer in my jacket, not wanting to rely on the beverage service at the Chamber a second time. Doug was still doing his thing by the door, mainly shooting the shit with the more attractive ladies in line.

"Hey, Doug, are you tight with the bouncer down at the Chamber?"

"Kirk? Just enough." Doug's attention strayed only a fraction from the redhead before him.

"Does he hang with that crowd?"

"A little I think, just for the trim." Doug turned, a growing curiosity warranting attention.

"If things get out of hand?"

"I wouldn't want him watching my back if that's what you mean. What's up with all the questions. You got a beef down there?"

"Just a minor situation."

"Look, bro. They don't play nice down there and they don't like outsiders. People go missing from that place. Don't nobody down there ever talk about it though. They're tight," Doug warned. "You need somebody to watch your back?"

"Tell you what. If I am not back in thirty minutes, my buddy up there will pay you five grand to come in with the cavalry. No need to ask, just do it. You have my word." We bumped fists and I took off.

Never before had I asked an outsider to watch my back, but with three separate warnings, plus last night—and unfortunately, Chuck and the boys were not here and I could not wait for them—I had to make an exception.

I hustled down Bourbon, made a right, and within a minute I was at the Chamber. The line was longer tonight, Royce again manning the door. I was positive his instructions were to bar my entrance, or at a minimum, give warning if I arrived. I wasted no time. Walking behind him, I called out, "Yo, Royce." Acting as if we were old friends, I slung my arm around his shoulders, spun his back to the crowd, and led him away. "What's that down there?" I asked as I pointed below with my free hand. As he looked down, I stuck his brachial plexus with a precision blow that turned his lights out. His knees buckled, but I continued to hold him up by the shoulders. I kept my arm around him as if we were talking with our back to the crowd.

I turned to the freaks. "Royce said for everyone to go on in," I announced loudly. None questioned the opportunity. They all piled through the door and down the alley. As the last one cleared the door, I sat him on the ground against the wall and placed his head on his knees as if he were sleeping. I headed down the alley, quickly rejoining the crowd. Kirk, the bouncer, was consumed with the mad rush, shouting at the crowd while futilely attempting to reach Royce on his cell. I stayed relatively low, shielding my face from his view.

"All of you wait here!" he barked out angrily as he sped up the alley to check on "Sleeping Beauty." He was an imposing mass of man flesh and the entire group of would-be gate crashers obeyed.

Once he was out of sight, I announced loudly, "The hell with him. I'm going in." As I rushed in, the majority followed.

"Hey, wait a minute!" Kirk screamed as he looked back to see his orders being completely ignored. I wasted no time heading for the stairs, plunging down into the darkness. The basement was packed, even more than last night, making it easy to mix right in. I immediately glimpsed the bartender from last night, remembering his chuckle as I staggered up the stairs on my previous excursion.

I worked my way into an opening at the bar and flagged his attention. By his reaction, I knew he did not recognize me. The driving reverberation of the music enabled our conversation to remain private.

"What can I get you?" he asked as he wiped down the bar.

"How about some more of that magic juice from last night."

"I don't know what you're talking about, Sport." Instantly, his expression changed. He remembered.

"The name's not 'Sport,' and I want one of those psychedelic love cocktails. You know, the same peyote shit you served me last night, Sport."

"Peyote? We don't have anything like that around here. That stuff is illegal."

"I tell you what, Sport. Did you happen to hear about Butch's misfortunes last night?"

"Yeah, and just so you know, if he sees you in here tonight, you won't get another chance to sucker-punch him again. In fact, you might want to consider leaving now before he finds you."

"Don't concern yourself with what will happen five minutes from now. Your immediate concern is what will happen to you if you insist on playing stupid. I want some of that juice, and I want it now." I pulled back my jacket, exposing Loretta. "Peyote, or I will blow your head off. You fucked with the wrong person last night."

He studied my face for any sign of a bluff. "Time's running out. I will put a bullet right in the middle of your head, and then I will get it myself." I began to unholster Loretta.

"Okay, okay. I'll get it." Begrudgingly, he walked to the refrigerator and retrieved a small glass vial. "It don't matter none. Your ass will never make it out of here alive," he threatened with a glare in his eye.

"Sport, I know you're pissed off, but I'm only going to be here for ten minutes. If I see you out from behind this bar, if the bounce crew, cops, or a mob of these freaks come anywhere near me before I leave, I promise you explicitly, I will blow your head off from across the room. Understood?"

He nodded, a fiery rage lighting his face.

"Thanks for understanding." Again, circling counterclockwise around the perimeter, I approached Isabelle's table from the right. Nestled in the back, surrounded by her loyal subjects, she appeared quite relaxed. I sauntered directly up to Butch. "What's up, bro? I hope you are not mad at me." Butch sported a look of disbelief crossed with rage. "Ready for round two, or would you rather do the smart thing and tell the lady I wish to speak with her."

"I was kind of hoping you would show up. You left before I had the opportunity to pay you proper thanks."

"Thanks? For knocking your ass out? I waited as long as I could, but you just would not wake up. Obviously, you were tired." I was taunting, increasing his agitation to a boil.

Out of the corner of my eye, I saw a second goon tracing my path. "So what is it going to be, Butch?" I watched as his eyes cut to his buddy moving into position. I sensed he was very close as Butch tensed up, then a hand grabbed my shoulder. The moment was now. "No hard feelings," I said. My elbow blew backward into his buddy's face, taking him down. Butch did not have the opportunity to launch a jab, as he received the same complimentary blow to the forehead as the night before, only not as devastating. He crumbled. Unlike last night, with two guys on the floor, the conflict was not entirely inconspicuous. About a half-dozen people caught the skirmish. I quickly moved in on Isabelle and her entourage.

"Baby, where on earth did you go this morning? I looked all over for you." Looking as if they were seeing a ghost, quite possibly they had expected my death. "Time for everybody to dance. NOW!" I demanded. Just over my shoulder, the freaks were inching closer. "Izzi, do us a huge favor and tell all of your buddies to mind their own fucking business."

A sickened expression consumed Isabelle's once serene face. "Go," she said loudly as she waved them away. One by one, they backed away, staring, glares of contempt meant to intimidate. Surely seeing stars, Butch and company remained down on their knees, attempting to figure out how they got to the planetarium.

My little friend who brought me the loaded beer last night was about to leave the table when I grabbed her by the arm. I walked her to the side. "What is your name, peaches?"

"Cindy," she replied coldly.

"Well, Cindy, the next time I ask you to bring me a beer, if it tastes anything like the one you brought me last night, I will smash your pretty little mouth right down your throat. Understand?"

The fear in her eyes made me happy. I hoped the little brat peed in her panties as she left.

I pulled my beer from my pocket and opened it. I took a long hard swallow and then set it on the table. "Brought my own tonight. I did not care for the house brand." I winked at Isabelle. "Mind if I sit?"

"Please do."

I slid into the table while pulling the vial from my pocket and uncapping it discretely. Sliding up against Isabelle, I turned my face to hers, blocking her view, and kissed her. With the palm of my hand concealing the vial, I poured it into her glass. While her lips were cold and hardened, she did not resist my advance. I kept the kiss relatively short. "Did you miss me, love? You almost look surprised to see me ... alive."

"No, I'm very happy to see you again." Her smile was tense.

"So tell me about last night. I really do not remember much at all. Was I sensational?"

Surprisingly, Cindy returned with an exaggerated sneer, set a beer on the table, and turned to leave.

"Wait," I ordered. I poured a small portion of the beer into an empty glass on the table and pushed it in front of Isabelle. "I do apologize, but after last night I hope you will understand, I no longer trust your friends. Drink up."

"I do not drink beer," Isabelle insisted.

"I understand, but I don't drink that shit you served up last night either." I pushed the glass close while watching Cindy's reaction.

"I really don't care for beer," Isabelle insisted.

"You will have to forgive me if I seem a little indifferent to your preferences, but after last night, I really do not give a damn if you like it or not. Drink it, or I slap you around like Butch," I thumbed toward Butch, who was just getting back on his feet, "and then pour it down your throat."

"You have no idea how much trouble you're in, do you?" Isabelle looked at Cindy, who offered a reassuring nod. She raised the glass to her lips and was about to drink when I grabbed her hand and pulled the glass away.

"After last night, I just wanted assurance." I directed my attention to Cindy. "You can leave now." She obeyed without a response. I picked up Isabelle's wine glass and handed it to her. "Let's hope tonight offers at least a few pleasant memories ... for me." Isabelle took a deep swallow of the wine, a trembling hand broadcasting her rattled nerves. I watched as the tainted wine transferred from the glass to her ruby-red lips. The clock was ticking. "About last night, exactly what happened?"

"Sadly, there's not much to tell. We went to the house. You ripped your clothes off like they were on fire, then literally tore mine off as well, like some kind of wild animal. You threw me on the bed. Then you just passed out. That was the full extent of it."

"You expect me to believe we were naked and did not have sex?"

"It's not like I didn't try, but you were most uncooperative." A hint of disappointment was present. "I wanted you, more than you know, but I've never seen anyone have such a bad reaction."

"I'm surprised you expected anything. You drugged me up pretty hard." I watched as she took another drink, knowing the drug would not take long.

"That was Cindy's doing. Sometimes she's a little heavy-handed."

"So if we did not have sex, at what precise moment did you decide to bite my leg."

"I wanted you, Brian, as I do now, and I *always* drink of my lovers' blood." Her tone grew seductive as she began caressing my hair. "I was extremely disappointed."

I ignored her enticing advances. "But we weren't lovers, and yet you drank my blood?" I recapitulated.

"No, we were not, and yes I did."

"I do not see any fangs in your mouth. How did you make those punctures in my leg?"

"They come out when I'm sexually aroused," she purred as the peyote's venom began to course through her veins.

"You were aroused, but other than biting my leg, nothing happened?"

"We may not have consummated the act, but we were very, very intimate."

I was relieved on one hand, but frustrated by a culture I did not understand and certainly loathed beyond explanation on the other. "So you see a naked man passed out, and he ... I could not deliver, so you what? Decide just to make a snack of me instead? I do not see how arousal comes into play at this point."

"It just does. I feed when my addiction beckons. Not every day, sometimes not for weeks." She stated her confession rather simply, as if it was as natural as breathing.

"And how about now?" I pushed my sleeve up to expose my arm and extended it to her face. "Go ahead, have a snack." Being ninety-nine and a half percent sure fangs would not magically grow out of her pearly whites, I taunted. The other half percent? I reserved the right to crap in my pants if they did.

The effects of the drugs were taking their toll as her eyes began to glaze. "I told you it's not like that. For me, it's very private. I never feed in front of the others." Although her speech was noticeably slowing, she still managed a tone of indignation.

I knew I needed to move on quickly. It would not be long before she was gone to Peyoteville. "I'm sorry. I did not mean to offend you. It's just ... I am a little angry over the whole getting drugged thing last night." I retracted my arm and pulled my sleeve back down. An intense sexual tension was building, and had it not been for Sam, how easily would I have allowed this twisted game to run its course? I needed to refocus.

"Tell me about the convent. What's the deal with the sisterhood that lives on the third floor? Do you live there?" Leading on, as if I actually believed the tales, I drilled down the bullet points of my inquisition.

"They are locked away, prisoners forever," she explained sadly. "Victims of times past, when our race was feared and loathed."

"You are not feared and loathed. It looks like society has pretty much become accustomed to your ways," I reasoned. "So why not just set them free, like everyone else in here? Seems like they would be right at home with this crowd."

"They are not like us. They are of the old way. A time when our race took whatever it wanted. Man has a way of killing whatever he fears or doesn't understand. Terrified by my ancestors, they hunted them, one by one, until virtually all were eliminated. We who survived had to learn a new way, one in which we could coexist. Now we only take the blood of the willing." Her eyes rolled backward with an impending head rush. "Brian, what have you done to me?"

I ignored her question. "Why not go, and teach them how the world has changed?"

"They are from a time when vampires were the masters. Released today, they would strike back with just vengeance and reclaim their rightful throne in today's society. They would conquer you, all of you." Isabelle spoke of her beliefs clearly, but her speech was becoming more indistinct. Though she spoke with passionate conviction, I did not believe her. This was the only world she knew, and without it, her life had no meaning. I looked out at all of her disciples. For the most part they had gone back to minding their own business. It was sad to see so many hapless people wasting their lives in this sick fantasy world.

It was time for me to get the hell out of the Chamber. Isabelle's head swayed back and then rolled side to side. Doug would be showing up soon with the cavalry looking to collect five grand. Butch eventually would be looking for reinforcements. The information I had hoped for, unfortunately, took an extra day and a pint of my blood, only to get a fantasyland story. I would have to go to the convent for the truth.

Isabelle had begun caressing my chest with one hand while pleasurably stroking herself with the other. I looked into Isabelle's impassioned but glazed eyes and saw she was mine for the taking. "You have been a bad boy, Brian. I know what you've done. Take me from here. Take me now."

"I'm sorry, that's not going to happen." Yes, I found her physically desirable, but I had changed. Yet somewhere buried deep within, I instinctively yearned for her in a manner I did not understand.

"Stay with me," she beseeched, her eyes so inviting. Momentarily, I lost myself as she leaned forward and kissed me. Her lips were soft, like a feather pillow. She took my hand and placed it on her waist.

Instinctively, I snapped back. "I have to go." I took her hand and kissed it and slid out of the booth. Butch and his buddy were back on their feet licking their wounds. As they watched me prepare to leave, they looked stupid enough to consider round three. I raised my hand as I approached them.

"Do not kid yourself into thinking the two of you are in my league." Butch leered, fuming with anger. "I hope you learned it does not pay to fuck with the wrong people, particularly me. I am the wrong people."

Delighted to be heading out of this place with my head on my shoulder and not up my ass like it was last night, I looked over at the bartender who was firing evil-eye daggers at me. I pointed my finger at him and pulled the trigger. He flipped me the bird.

I had hoped Isabelle would have yielded me some fathomable story about the convent. Unfortunately, she did not. No matter, in a couple of days the legend of the convent would be exposed.

Although it was not fresh and crisp, it was a welcome relief to breathe the outside air. Having returned back to reality land, like flicking the light switch on, my thoughts immediately dialed in on Sam. Despite the momentary lapse in judgment, allowing Isabelle's kiss, I could now put her and the rest of this shithole behind me. But if ever the opportunity to examine the events of the last few days and jump off the runaway train existed, this would be it.

CHAPTER 13

MY PHONE PULSED to life, rambling across the nightstand with its annoying vibration. Whoever it was, they could wait. It was only eleven in the morning for God's sake, and I was in no hurry to stir Sam. Whether it was Phillip or one of the crew, they would have to go to the rear of my attention line, for now. The vibrations made just enough commotion to rouse Sam. She rolled to her side facing me, her satin hair obscuring the beauty of her face. I brushed her hair back, as she peacefully opened her eyes.

With a smile of absolute contentment, she studied our naked bodies. "You did it again, didn't you?"

"Yes I did," I confessed proudly.

Gently and deliberately, I guided my hand down the side of her face, tracing her neck, then shoulders, over her firm breasts, continuing slowly to her trim abdomen.

"Stop that, or I'll, I'll ..."

"You will what?" My hand cruised lower.

"I'll tell my sister. She'll kick your butt." Reaching my target, her objection instantly ceased to exist.

"I quiver at the thought."

Sam brought her hands around my neck, pulled me close, and kissed me. "This all feels so awkward."

"How so?" Puzzled by her words, I paused the hand safari.

"I have been with only one guy in the last fifteen years. I don't know if I should trust what I think I am feeling because of this." She pointed and wiggled her index finger back and forth at our naked bodies.

"And tell me, Samantha, in simple words, precisely how do I make you feel?"

"Well, I love how I feel when I'm with you, and not just now, but dinner, walking around, talki..." Her words were interrupted as I resumed with the finger safari. Her eyes rolled backward and lips quivered; her intended words became lost in a rush of pleasure.

"You seem to enjoy a good tap dance. Would it kill you to say *I love everything about being with you*, or would that be too much of a concession?"

"Well, okay. I do love all of that," Sam purred, "and you."

I had been in this situation before, and the arrival of those words meant I had overstayed the relationship. In the past there was the often unappreciated "Thank you" or evasive small talk. Not this time.

"I love you too," I whispered. Never before had I uttered those words to anyone. I never had a mother, father, or high school girl-friend, and by the time the CIA was done with me, those words had no place in my life.

We searched each other's eyes for some mystical secret that would make sense of the moment. Sam's smile was tender and un-assuming. What do you say now? In three days we had ascended the summit and reached the pinnacle of relationships. This was so unfamiliar. It was downright scary in a comical sort of way.

A mountain climber once told me reaching the summit of K2 was not his goal, only a piece of it. Although a great accomplishment, his goal was to do what many did not: return to the base alive. In accomplishing this, he could relive the experience for the rest of his days.

If falling in love was the summit, never to be experienced again, the next step was surviving the treacherous descent. I bore witness to so many failures over the years. The key to surviving love would be finding happiness in the descent, exploring the crags and crevices, and climbing again and again, carving out new paths, never being satisfied with the previous ascent.

My cell phone vibrated a second time. The hour had arrived. There would be no prolonged affair today, although I would be willing to compromise on old standards. There was no logical reason to not see Sam after meeting the crew and reviewing our strategic plans.

"Sounds like you're in high demand."

"Unfortunately, I am. It's time to meet with my associates and get this job rolling. The good news: I will be done early and have the rest of the night free, if that works for you."

"Well I don't know, Brian. Dee and I are going shopping all day, and I might be too exhausted." Sam attempted to maintain a serious bluff.

"We can meet for a late dinner, say around nine. Then I will attempt to invent some mystical way to rejuvenate your tired body."

"Can we skip the dinner part?" Groaning, her body contorted via my playful exploration.

"That, my dear, I will leave entirely up to you." I suddenly stopped my probing and jumped out of bed. "In the meantime, you have shopping and I have work to do."

"Hey!" Sam objected to my sudden departure.

I fired up my laptop while grabbing my clothes.

While typing, the sounds of Sam dressing provided temptation to turn and cop a peek. I did not have the chance. The clicking of her heels on the hardwood floor alerted me the shoes were back on, a little too quick to be fully dressed. It would be pointless to ignore her advance, having failed at that already. Wearing only my shirt, barely buttoned I might add, and those damn shoes again, in short order, she possessed intimate knowledge of my weaknesses.

"I do not recall giving you permission to wear my shirt." The sunlight illuminated her naked silhouette through my shirt, wreaking havoc on my intentions of brushing her off until tonight.

"I'm sorry. I can take it off." With a teasing frown she started to undo the only button she bothered to fasten.

I grabbed her hands and halted the process. "Oh no you don't. I know what you are trying to do, and it is not going to work."

I called down to Renaldo for a cab. While waiting, I typed my instructions to the boys. Sam, being ever mindful of my need for privacy and concentration, sat playfully in my lap, kissing and doing everything possible to distract me from the task at hand.

Characteristically, I loathed distractions, but in this instance I was willing to make an exception.

"I know what you do can be dangerous. I suppose I'm a little worried something bad might happen."

"Don't worry, this job is a cakewalk. There is absolutely no way anything bad will happen."

Yes, I was being dishonest. I was fully aware just one night ago my careless actions could have meant the death of me, but those mistakes would not be repeated. There was no need to worry Sam over the trivial miscalculations, which resulted in some psycho bitch sucking off a pint from my inner thigh.

Sam startled as the hotel phone broke the calming silence of the room, Renaldo calling to announce the arrival of the cab. "Time to shop." I swept Sam up, cradling her in my arms, and carried her to the door, grabbing her purse off the bed as we passed.

"You know, just because you might be big and bad, it doesn't mean you can ultimately stop anything that comes your way."

"Sam, I will take care of myself like never before." I set her down gently. "Besides, there is no need to worry right now. We will only be planning for the next several days, so my biggest danger might be a paper cut or ingesting bad oysters."

With no aspirations to expedite Sam's departure, our goodbyes were pleasantly prolonged, leaving me uncharacteristically behind schedule. I hustled back inside, knowing the boys would be sure to let me know if I had kept them waiting. And in regards to them, that was never a good thing.

I set out down the balmy streets in the midday sauna. The heat permeated the scent of Sam still fresh on my clothes, illuminating vivid memories of hours past. The notion to call Aunt Rena crossed my mind, to let her know I had finally met someone. Throughout my adult life she always let it be known to me, and all the neighbors, how much I needed a good woman in my life. Aunt Rena would be a priority detour before disappearing off the map with Sam.

I arrived at Crawdad Pete's, which was off the beaten path, just beyond the outskirts of the French Quarter. Renaldo told me the food was exceptional here. I thought it would be a great place to meet with the crew. I had a reliable network of guys who knew how to get the tough jobs done, but Chuck, Rob, and Jimmy were the ones I preferred working with. I found it slightly disheartening to realize the end of our adventures was at hand. After this job, our paths were never to cross again.

We made the best of our assignments during our years of service for Uncle Sam. Regardless of danger, there was never a time we did not find a way to laugh our way home, never knowing when the breath you just took might be your last. I trusted these guys with my life, and they trusted me. Anything less was not an option.

I knew the guys would be expecting me to feed them, so I decided to have a few beers while awaiting their arrival. Crawdad's was an out of the way dump on the edge of the Quarter. It was not very busy, and four guys having a few beers could go largely unnoticed. Across the restaurant, the bartender acknowledged my arrival. "Dos Equis, please," I ordered a decibel below a shout, just enough to be heard, choosing a table which had seen its better days, near the open air doorway. Wobbly, with burn marks, food stains, and carvings, it looked as if it had seen over a century of service. Feeling at home, not that my furniture looked anything remotely similar, I pulled a chair across the cement floor.

Phillip would have loved to hang with the crew, but they knew nothing of him, and like Sam, I had every intention of keeping it that way. I thought of Phillip like a little brother who often needed my protection. It was in his best interest to remain as far away from the action as possible. Unlike myself, he could not just disappear.

A beer-bellied, bandana-wearing, scruffy-faced waiter in a dirty white T-shirt brought me my beer. I settled back into a creaky wooden chair. The joint was wide open to the breezeless afternoon heat, making everything sticky and damp. A rusty ceiling fan creaked overhead as it swiveled like a clock pendulum. There was some great blues playing on the jukebox, the likes of which I'd not heard in years. It was actually filled with 45s. The atmosphere of this dive brought back memories of weeks entrenched in Third World shitholes I had the ill pleasure of sojourning. Sam would find this joint grotesquely cozy. I found it oddly amusing how she continued to filter into so many of my random thoughts. There was a time, like just last week, where no woman would have been allowed remotely this close.

A cold sensation pressed against the back of my neck, like the barrel of a gun. Only judging by the diameter, it felt more like a Budweiser than a revolver. "In Colombia, in a dump like this, self-centered carelessness could get you a nice necktie." The voice was familiar, even though it was masked with a bad Colombian accent. "I know you would not dream of starting without me."

"Rob, you snake. You should know better, sneaking up like that. I could have blown your ass away by accident." His shit-eating grin boasted of a successful sneak attack. Rob was of Celtic descent, possessing just a touch of the family accent. Typical to his clan, Rob had receding salt-and-pepper hair, sharp facial features accentuated by deep, penetrating dark-sienna eyes set beneath heavy brows that broadcast his mood. When angered, his brows turned down and his eyes appeared to sink further into their sockets. Just under six feet, he was lean and muscular. The ability to produce an intense scowl, combined with his strong physique, was enough to back down even the most serious challengers. This afternoon, he sported a half-lit smile, indicating his consumption of ale had already begun.

The cold barrel of the gun—a beer bottle. Big surprise there. "Who started without who?"

"I knew if I was the last to show, chances were you guys would drink the place dry. Figured I'd better get a head start."

"Have a seat." Back in the day, this was more than merely an invitation. It was code for "all is clear." Until "have a seat" was offered, we always presumed the potential for hostility.

"It has been too long, Rob."

"Too damn long," he echoed. "I was beginning to think you either retired or got yourself killed by one of those high-class psycho bitches you date."

"Nothing so exciting. I have been laying low trying to enjoy some of the cash we made. How is life treating you?"

"I started a surveillance company out in LA. The money is phenomenal. Corporate crime and infidelity, it's nonstop. Fucking unbelievable how much takes place out there on the Left Coast. I've already made over two million this year. Check this out: I actually have employees, a bookkeeper, and a secretary. Nothing like the old days you know, but it'll do. I sure was glad you called. I've been needing to get away from all of that LA bullshit, get a little excitement back in my life." Rob drained the remaining beer. "It's been too damn long."

"Yes it has." I looked over Rob's shoulder to see Chuck and Jimmy B. walking into Crawdad's together. "Look what the dingo dug up." I loudly pointed out our arriving comrades.

"Shit, Jimmy, it's just like I told you. I knew those conniving bastards would already be meeting, figuring out a way to screw us out of our cut." Chuck was two hundred and thirty pounds of nothing but badass Marine. His body was thick and coarse, as was his temperament. His face, mounted on a tree trunk for a neck, looked as if it was chiseled out of granite. He maintained the high and tight hair from his days in the Corps. Through and through, Chuck was all leatherneck.

"Up yours, Chuck, you psycho jarhead," Rob retaliated.

"Hey, if it ain't 'perverted peephole Bobby.' Want to sell me some of your dirty porno-spy videos," Chuck jested.

"Damn, Jarhead, don't you ever get tired of watching those videos of your mom?" Rob retaliated.

"I would, except I get off watching you lick the corn out of—"

"Foul, low blow," I interrupted. "I am getting ready to eat here. If you boys need to continue, how about taking it down the street so I can enjoy lunch."

Maintaining poker faces, exchanging glances around the table, Jimmy cracked first, then we all burst out laughing. None of us had changed a bit over the years. Nothing was sacred, nothing off limits.

"What's up, Jimmy?" I asked. Jimmy sometimes needed a prompt to actually engage, preferring the silent observer role. An obsessively meticulous working machine, he was moderately thin with dark-brown skin and short thick hair. Like Rob, he was just under six feet, and not remotely intimidating by Chuck standards. In a pinch, Jimmy could pass off as a younger Denzel Washington, and when the occasion arose, that's exactly what he did. What he lacked in physical demeanor he made up with lethal intellectual precision. He executed every mission exactly on time without hitches, always. A perfectionist, he was the voice of reason in the eye of the storm.

"Life is good. What's the job?" Right to the point, as expected, Jimmy was never one to wait to learn the details of a gig.

"Have a seat. You are going to need a couple of beers to catch up with Roberto." I motioned to our sweaty waiter to bring over a round of Dos Equis. The scratchy blues playing on the jukebox was more than loud enough to mask our conversation. At the moment, we were the only adventurous souls in the establishment. I gave Pig Pen a crisp Benjamin. "Keep them coming till it runs out please."

"You got it, boss."

"So what's this job?" Jimmy inquired again impatiently.

I raised my bottle in a toast, ignoring his persistence. "Damn, it's good to be back together. To one last gig, my friends."

My unexpected declaration did not slip by unnoticed. Shocked would barely begin to described the expressions before me.

"What the hell is that supposed to mean?" Rob never appreciated decisions made without his opinion or consent and was duly incensed.

"Just what I said. I am retiring after this one."

Starting with a chuckle, then a snort, the silence was replaced with a barrage of laughter as their puzzled appearance changed collectively to one of amused disbelief.

"Bullshitter," Chuck called out.

"Believe what you want. This is the last dance for me."

"Are you for real?" Jimmy leaned in to the table, sensing this was no joke.

"On your mother's grave, after this one, I'm out."

"Dammit, Brian. What the hell?" Stunned, Rob was not enjoying the feeling of being out of the loop.

Jimmy leaned further in with an air of indifference. "Sorry to see you go, mate. Now, if you don't mind sharing with us, what's the job?" Jimmy had a unique gift of insight, able to spot a flaw in the simple mannerism of a smile. A misplaced quiver, tensing of an appendage— an almost undetectable deviation others would miss—would set off his internal alarms. You never played poker with Jimmy. It was better to just hand him your money rather than have him dismantle your confidence one dollar at a time. He read me like a book and knew the pages had been altered.

Stone-cold Jimmy was his MO, never showing a sliver of emotion, but just like the other guys, he would take a bullet for one or for all.

I looked around just to ensure nobody had wandered within earshot. "There is a convent down the street. It is Vatican property. No outsider has been allowed on the third floor for over two centuries. Your employer thinks there are items of great value stored there. He wants it, or at least wants video proof of what it is." As I laid out the job, I intentionally omitted a few key details.

"Wait a minute, let me see if I got this straight. You want us to break into a church and either steal or video what's on the third floor?" Chuck asked, puzzled by my abbreviated job description which did not sound complicated, considering the crew assembled. "Forgive my doubting your judgment, but this doesn't really sound like the type of work that requires my skills. These other guys for sure, but what the hell do you need me for?"

Okay, time for the hard sell. I was hoping to at least get five or six beers in them before they received the full briefing.

"Well, exactly what is up there may be more than any one of us is prepared for."

"Shit, don't tell me you want us to believe they are hiding the Holy Grail or something like that." Rob's rhetoric signaled he had not one shred of belief in the probability.

"I don't know, it could be. But it does not matter. Your employer wants to know, and more importantly, is paying good money to find out. What is certain, no one, not the local law, FBI, no outsider, has been allowed on the third floor for over two hundred years. On top of that, there is this local legend, which I am not completely comfortable with."

"Legend?" Jimmy perked up. "Do tell."

"Although it is completely outrageous, we cannot entirely discount it either. Local legend says the priests and nuns have imprisoned vampires on the third floor since the seventeen hundreds." I attempted to maintain a professional temperament, knowing all too well the response about to follow. "Personally, I do not believe the legend, but I would consider it foolish to ignore the realm of possible encounters."

Rob and Chuck stared at each other, waiting for the other to react. After a delayed emotionless stalemate, they simultaneously started laughing. Chuck, who had not moved his beer bottle from his lips, almost choked, then abruptly spit the beer out on the floor.

Jimmy found nothing about the tale remotely amusing, concern etched across his face.

"Come on, Jimmy, this shit's funny, you've got to admit," Chuck snorted as he attempted to get Jimmy to join in on what he believed was an obvious hoax.

"Damn, Brian, you got to come up with something better. First the retirement and now blood suckers in a convent." Rob scanned my face, looking for some signal I was kidding.

"No guys, he is serious," Jimmy said with a stone face.

Rob and Chuck cut their eyes to Jimmy and then back to me. The laughter stopped as they studied my expression. "I am two-hundred-and-fifty-thousand per man serious."

"Holy hell," Rob jumped in. "Fuck the dumb shit, I'm in."

"For two hundred and fifty Gs, wipe my ass with garlic and call me Chucky the Vampire Slayer," Chuck jested. "Count me in."

We all looked to Jimmy, awaiting his response. He was obviously disturbed by the proposition as a sickened expression registered on his face.

"I don't like it. I've got a bad feeling about this you guys."

"Shit, Jimmy, who's got your back?" Chuck boasted.

"You do, big guy. But it's not my back I'm worried about. Vampires? I highly doubt it. Whatever is up there apparently they've felt the need to keep locked away all this time. If priests and nuns believe whatever they possess deserves to be kept that way, I don't know if I want any part of disturbing these things. I can't see what possible good could come out of this."

"Two-hundred-and-fifty-thousand pieces of good." Chuck, sporting a greedy smile, reiterated the payoff.

Bagging the job before we started would not have hurt my feelings, but for unexplained reasons I felt compelled to give it a shot.

"Look, let's walk through this thing. We can start the job and check out all of the angles, and if at any time it gets too thick or any of you feels unrighteous, we can pull back and get the hell out. We are getting paid a premium for our time, whether we come out with anything or not."

"Some idiot is willing to pay a million bucks or a little less just for us to try?" Rob asked. "What's the worst that could happen? We get in there, the nuns wake up, and we have to smack them around long enough to shoot some video? Not my idea of fun, but I've done much worse in my life."

"If they possess any items of significant value, they will be well prepared to protect it. Better plan to smack something a little heavier than a nun," I cautioned.

"You mean like a monk?" Chuck asked with a devilish grin. "I spank the monkey all of the time. You might say I'm an expert at it." Chuck never missed the opportunity to insert his perverted humor, regardless of the subject.

Jimmy sighed and rolled his eyes. He turned his head and looked out to the street at the few passing souls and lost himself briefly in thought. Turning back, he looked at each of us individually with the utmost apprehension.

"Guys, I think you need to take a harder look. If you go in with this half-ass jokester attitude, we will wind up having our dicks served to us on a platter. I believe this will be much more difficult than you are considering. Get your heads out of your asses and on straight and I'm in. But if I call it off, it's off for all of us. Job over, agreed?"

"I can live with that, Jimmy. You've got a point on this one." I knew putting the final go in Jimmy's hands was the best choice to be made. His head was always in the right place. "Guys, let's make my last dance our finest one."

"Here's to slow and dirty," Chuck said.

"Let's tango," chimed in Rob. "But I still think you're full of shit about retirement."

"Here's to no fuckups!" Jimmy chimed in.

We raised our beers, then drained them.

"Anyone hungry?" I asked. "I'm buying."

"Damn right. If you're buying, bring on the pig. I'm eating two of everything on the menu," Chuck boasted.

The afternoon drifted away as did most of the kick-ass food, as Chuck had promised. Buck, our waiter, turned out to be the owner. His "like I give a shit" attitude went from initially annoying to lovable by the end of our meals, all of which were his personal recipes. I decided if the food did not kill me, I would definitely return before leaving town.

Patrons drifted in and departed throughout the afternoon

without paying much attention to four old friends reminiscing down memory lane. From time to time, Buck would pull up a chair and join in for a beer. He arrived in New Orleans straight out of the Army to take over for his cousin Pete, who was killed in Korea. He shared dark stories from his past, painful tales we shared from similar experience. Buck and Chuck hit it off immediately, other than the obvious Army-Marine pissing contest. Buck killed more than his share of enemy soldiers, many by hand, making him royalty in our eyes. Mercenaries, soldiers, assassins, we were all killers of the same breed, sharing an unspoken camaraderie and a mutual admiration. It takes a damn good man to take another man's life and a better man to find a way to live with the anguish and nightmares as the years pass.

At some point in time, I realized the money I had given Buck had most likely run out. He refused to take anymore.

"'Bout half of the people in here don't pay for shit," he said proudly as he pushed my money away. "You know we all fall on hard times every now and then, but as long as you got some food in the gut, you've got half a chance to beat the bastards back. I know you boys ain't got no problem payin', but shit, Semper Fi, motherfucker."

Buck, the guy who did not give a fuck, as he was often overheard saying, had a heart bigger than the four of us combined, and his generosity would not go unrewarded. Dinner passed, as did the sunlight. The joint eventually filled to the rafters with locals who knew the common tourist would not consider setting foot in this place. Crawdad's was a dump by design and Buck the mastermind was indeed smarter than he appeared. He loved the locals and they loved him. Crawdad's was not quite what I had envisioned while scouting for a hole in the wall for our meeting, but the boys loved it, so we made due. We rolled on well beyond our second dinner, although it never really seemed like a single dinner thanks to Chuck and Buck. Buck continued delivering dish after dish, and Chuck kept disposing of all the food remnants on the table.

Unlike the food on our table, the dinner crowd never dissipated. The patrons did transform from food to mostly alcohol consumption. As the sun faded, the natural light was replaced by many dimly lit hurricane lamps. By nine o'clock the crowd had spilled over to tables and chairs Buck had placed outside. I looked at my watch and thought of Sam waiting on my call.

"I hate to bust the party up guys, but we need to take a walk." Without any doubt, removing Sam from the equation, our party would have gone on all night.

"Why?" Rob asked sharply, inspiring snickers from Chuck and Jimmy.

"Job," I replied bluntly.

"Oh hell, there you go again. Always busting up another good party." Rob served up the reminder it had always been my duty to corral the cattle.

"Tell you what. We will take a short walk. Then you guys can come back here, drink yourselves into oblivion, and close the place down," I suggested.

"You guys?" Chuck questioned, raising a brow.

"Yes, I have a deal up the street which requires my attention."

"Brian's getting laid," Rob sung badly out of tune.

"No, nothing that interesting. I have business to attend to, that is if you want to get paid."

"Getting paid so we can get laid," Rob continued to serenade out of key.

Buck returned to the table. "Mr. Buck, my buddy here informs me we must leave for a short time, but we will be returning ASAP," Chuck alerted.

"Like I give a shit," Buck snorted.

The four of us headed out the open doorway, feeling bloated and downright uncomfortable from all of the food and beer. The evening light had faded, giving way to night made hazy from the humidity and the glow of the gas lanterns. We meandered down and across several quiet streets in the direction of the convent. Our pace was intentionally casual, attempting to walk off the discomfort of the gorge fest. Over the years, our work was high speed and danger-ous. On the occasional "off-duty" night, we slowed the pace enough to breathe a little fun into what normally were very intense times. Tonight was definitely one of those nights.

Our conversation volleyed between travels, future plans, and girls, mostly pertaining to the guys. I avoided any discussion of my imminent retirement and especially Sam. The less these guys knew of Sam, the better for her—and me.

As we closed in and caught first glimpse of the convent, I stopped the crew. "This will do." The haze created an altogether ominous, intimidating aura. Cloaked in a mist of dense haze, the lights encompassing the building produced a foreboding glow. I gestured toward the historical landmark.

"Gentlemen, I give you the Old Ursuline Convent."

The guys looked down the street. "Piece of cake," Chuck piped in with overriding confidence.

"I hope so. With a little luck, it is just a victim of overstimulated imagination of people with nothing better to do than to prey on the fears of misfits looking for unnatural phenomena to give purpose to their meaningless lives."

"Unnatural?" Detailing every word as was his character, Jimmy desired deeper clarification.

I blew off his inquisition and addressed the concerns of the job.

"If the Vatican is truly guarding an item of great value, then it is a safe bet they will have a sophisticated alarm system and guards ready to respond to intrusion. Jimmy, naturally the alarm is all yours. Once you have identified the system, we will have a better understanding as to the level of importance. Until we know, we proceed as if we were breaking into the Pentagon. But remember, this is Vatican property. What happens in there is not U.S. soil. If anything goes wrong, there will be no help of any kind. Just like Iraq."

"Just like Colombia too, eh Brian?" Rob reminded.

"Yes, but there should be no need for any of that intensity here."

"Hey, it's a convent. Just a bunch of nuns, right?" Chuck was looking for reassurance to relieve any premonitions which might stand in the way of a quick payday.

"I still want to hear about the unnatural," Jimmy repeated.

"We need to keep all options open." I was looking for a temporary excuse to increase concern without diminishing validity, which any discussion of vampire chicks would instantly accomplish. "There could be a platoon of badass albinos guarding the place, you know, like in *The Da Vinci Code*."

"Bring 'em on, bitch," Chuck bragged. "I'll show them the true meaning of badass hombre, courtesy of the United States Marine Corps."

"The plan is to slip in, then slip out. No conflict, no ass-kicking, and definitely no guns. So, Chuck, you will have to keep your badass guns holstered," I ordered.

"Killjoy," Chuck objected with a bark of disapproval.

"Rob, I want to know who and how many people come and go out of this place over the next couple of days. How much food goes in, what kind of deliveries they receive. Keep an eye on the amount of garbage they generate. Get me some heat signature readings so we know where the bulk of the staff is at various times of day and night. I want to know electricity and water usage, cable or DSL, whatever they are using, everything and anything. Jimmy, we need building schematics, entry, exit, and alternate strategies. Hack their phones and network. Anything of interest, forward to me ASAP. You guys keep Chuck busy and out of trouble. Any questions?"

Chuck, Jimmy, and Rob nodded in unison.

"I will be in touch in a couple of days. If you need anything, get it. Expenses will be reimbursed. Let's make this go down in three days, unless there is a damn good reason to extend the window. Okay?"

"Where are you going, bossman?" Chuck pried.

"I am working a tangent; there are some peripheral acquisitions which need my attention. One thing you must remember: Besides your employer, nobody wants us on the third floor. Not the locals, our government, and especially the Vatican. If this thing blows up, there will not be many places to run. The Vatican's arm extends almost everywhere, so unlike Colombia, where you could count on rival drug cartels, there is no backup on this one."

"Geez, Brian, you need to chill down, dude. You make it sound like we're going to steal the remains of JC himself. We're not going to need any backup for this one, boss," Chuck promised. "We'll slip in and out, like a visit to Ho town. They won't feel a thing."

"Guys, have fun tonight, but not too much. Keep a low profile. When this goes down, they will be looking for us. Do not leave a footprint."

My steely expression and lack of humor accentuated my concerns. In the past, we would march into the gates of Hell, my face blanketed with a half-ripped jackass smile of delight, joking all the way. My change in demeanor caught Jimmy's attention.

"I don't think so, Brian. Something stinks."

Having hardly spoken a half-a-dozen sentences all night, Jimmy objected to my departure. But he was like that. He usually only spoke when spoken to or when something was gnawing at him. Otherwise, the remainder of the time was spent in deep contemplation.

"I'm not going in anywhere until I know what gives. I've known you for over twenty-five years, and we've been through a lot of crap. You are not right, my friend. You haven't been all night. You are concealing something from us."

It is always the quiet ones, like Jimmy, who are so keenly aware of even the most minuscule changes in their environment.

"No shit," Rob agreed. "You are not one hundred percent on board with this job. Jimmy's right, something else is going on here. Give it up or we walk."

"This is why I hate working with you guys. I should have known better," I confessed.

"I knew it," Jimmy proclaimed proudly.

"Dog, what's the deal?" Chuck demanded. "I know there's more to this job than what you're giving up. I mean, come on, you don't need guys like us to break into a convent."

"Yes, I do need guys like you, and I really wanted to get through this without having to deal with a non-job related issue."

"Too late for that," Rob interrupted.

"Like I told you earlier, after this job my ass is retiring."

I paused to consider how to tell the complete truth without setting myself up for a royal-ass reaming. With the exception of Phillip, these guys were my best friends, but I was not in the mood to wade through the bucket of shit that was about to follow.

"What the hell, there is no other way to say this. I have met someone."

"Girl or guy?" Rob interrupted.

And it started. "Whatever. When the job is done I plan to be spending a lot of time with her. "

"Define a lot of time. Two weeks or so?" Chuck knew me all too well. "We all know for you a week might as well be eternity. Come on, dude, think of all your other relationships. Two weeks was like what? Ten days too long?"

"Yeah I know, guilty as charged." I confessed to the crimes of a personality disorder previously worn like a badge of honor. "But this is different. I have changed."

"You've changed? You don't even change your underwear," Rob continued.

"Up yours, Rob." I turned my attention to Jimmy and Chuck. "I knew you guys would give me a ration of shit, which is why I chose to keep it dark."

"Brian, guys like us don't settle down," Jimmy began to lecture. "It's not in our blood. It's not in our DNA. We live for the adrenaline rush. We're junkies. You won't, you can't get that in a relationship with a woman, at least not for more than about fifteen seconds. Think about it, B," Jimmy pointed to the convent, "this is the shit we live for, the game you love. Guys like us don't fall in love with women. You can't just turn off the addiction for the game just because you met an exceptional piece of trim."

"You know, that is exactly where the root of my problem lies. Maybe my need for the thrill is gone. Maybe I need something else. Maybe my life's feeling pathetic." Never, in all our years, had the three been collectively so silent.

"I thought about it the other day, on the way here, about life in general. How many times have we come close to biting it?" I illustrated with my thumb and forefinger almost pinching together. "And a month, or even just a day later, come right back and do it all again? Adrenaline junkie? Nah. I just did not have anything meaningful enough to make me give a damn about myself."

I told the guys how I met Sam and how I struggled. They looked disgusted and concerned.

"So this woman is the reason why you're not hanging with us tonight," Rob surmised.

"Something like that."

"Not if I float her first," Chuck jumped back in.

"Dammit, nobody floats her. There will be no capping of her ass. In two nights, when everybody has their shit together, we will meet back at Crawdad's and get hammered. In the meantime, this town is full of freaks who like to play pretty sick games. Trust me, I know. Stay away from a bar called the Chamber. It is trouble we do not need."

"The Chamber sounds like a great place to go kick some freaky ass," Chuck boasted.

"I said, low-profile, Animal, very low profile." I finger thumped Chuck in the chest. "That does not mean mixing it up with the local freak show."

"I'm just screwing with you man."

"Crawdad's in two nights at twenty-two hundred."

"Roger that," Rob confirmed.

As I started to move away, Jimmy followed me and grabbed my arm. "Brian, this relationship, it's a good thing. I wish you the best."

"Yeah, glad one of us is getting some poon tonight," Rob bellowed.

"Thanks, JB." I headed away from the convent and the hecklers. I would make several shoulder checks to ensure they did not follow. Inasmuch as they were soldiers, more so they were pranksters. I did not need any middle-of-the-night uninvited visitors.

"Don't forget your rubber ducky," Rob broadcasted as I headed further away.

From a hundred yards away, Chuck yelled, "Hey, old man, if you can't perform, give me a ring. I'll be on deck, and I don't require stinking Viagra like you older guys."

Shoe on the other foot. If it were one of them I would be busting balls exactly in the same manner, I mused as I continued away.

"Are we really going to let him get away with this?" Chuck asked Rob and Jimmy.

"Not this easy, not in a million years. No bimbo gets our friend before we say so," Rob replied slyly, his mind off to the races. "Not while we still call ourselves his bro."

CHAPTER 14

Attempting to maintain a relatively low profile over the past two days, I had purposely avoided areas where any chance meeting might occur, thus delaying a confrontation with my envious, horny mercenary buddies.

Since tonight's dinner date with the boys was already prearranged, Sam and I were enjoying what might be our last meal until the conclusion of the job. Customary to discipline, I was seated with my back to the rear of the café, facing the front, maintaining a watchful eye on all that moved. While some habits will never die, I had not contemplated the possibility of any covert assault from the kitchen in the rear. After all, this was New Orleans, not South America, and other than the night crawlers, I had not pissed anybody off enough to warrant concern. "Excuse me?" Sam spoke with an appalling glare in her eye to a mystery person standing behind me.

I turned and much to my dismay it was Rob. He did not acknowledge me, as if I was a complete stranger. He continued to stare at Sam intently. I could only imagine what he must have gestured while my back was turned.

"So what do you say, Blondie?"

Sam took one look at my suppressed smile and the cat was loose.

"Brian Denman! Please don't tell me you know these guys?"

"As excruciatingly painful as it is to admit, yes I do."

Sam had a wildly perturbed gaze in her eyes.

"I would personally like to apologize for my associates' behavior. I am Jimmy, and these two assholes are Chuck and Robert. I personally did not approve of Robert's tactics, but he insisted we couldn't let Brian run off and retire without us approving of the bimbo first, you being the said bimbo."

"So that gesture was your lame idea to what—see if I'd throw a knife at you?" Sam pointed the accusatory finger of shame directly at Rob.

Suddenly timid, Rob had no response. Chuck came to the rescue with his own half-baked explanation.

"Yeah, we followed Brian back to his hotel and kind of staked out the joint. We decided today was as good as any time to check you out."

"And then you followed us here?" Sam asked.

"Alright then," I said, intentionally interrupting any explanation. "You have met her, so now you can go back to work."

"We bugged the room," Chuck replied proudly. "By the way, did you guys know how much noise you make when you're having—"

"Thanks for coming by," I said loudly, cutting off Chuck's words as I rose to usher them out the back door.

"No. Wait, Brian," Sam intervened. "I'd like them to stay, so we can get to know each other."

The guys smiled and pushed their way past me. "Seriously? Don't you guys have work you need to be getting done?"

"Nah, it's lunchtime," Chuck replied as he pulled a chair across the floor to the table.

"So, exactly how did you bug Brian's room?" Sam's attitude shifted from aggressive to curious.

The boys all looked at each other sheepishly, forcing concealed grins. "Just an audio bug," Chuck responded unconvincingly.

"Yes, just audio. At no time did we see any video images," Jimmy chimed in.

The boys rounded up chairs from surrounding tables and crowded in. Ordering beers and food, they made themselves right at home, settling in for the long haul. Not quite what I had in mind for lunch, but with Sam having met the crew, it was time to make the best of it. About the time they had finished their food and a second beer, almost on cue, Jimmy rose with Chuck and Rob following his lead.

"We are sorry for putting you through the meat grinder, Samantha, but Brian is a true friend. There is not one of us who wouldn't take a bullet for him. We just wanted to be sure you were worthy of the same."

"And?" Sam asked.

"You are," Jimmy claimed with a smile and nod of approval. "Brian said you were exceptional, and I could not agree more. I apologize for interrupting your lunch."

With the most uncharacteristic polite manners, Jimmy and Chuck bid Sam goodbye and in turn gave hugs. "Do us both a favor, Rob," Sam said softly.

"Just name it."

"Take care of him, for me."

Rob nodded and followed the boys out the door.

"Promise me one thing," Sam said as she placed her hand on my shoulder.

"What would that be?"

"Before we go too far this afternoon, you'll get that spy stuff out of your room." Unabashed, her eyes sparked with mischief.

"Well, that would depend. If there is a camera, I think we might want to review the films, for training purposes mind you."

In short order we were back in the hotel, headed for the elevator. An unfamiliar male voice called out from the lobby.

"Samantha, wait."

Sam's face cringed with angst. She recognized the voice. Grimacing as she turned, drawing a deep breath, she lashed out in a curt tone. "Mike, what in the hell are you doing here?"

"I came here to keep you from making a huge mistake."

Her ex-husband was tall and trim, with tight, curly blond hair, sporting a polo shirt a size too small, attempting to flaunt his physique. He was tanned and well-groomed, the epitome of the classic Hollywood "playa."

"Well, if anyone would know what big mistakes are all about, you would be the expert," Sam proclaimed. "How in the hell did you find me? Why did you even bother?"

"It does not matter."

"Look, Mike, you need to leave now. Go back to LA. Go back to little Miss Fisher Price what's her name."

"Cindy and I are done. I ended it two weeks ago. I realized she was never right for me. It just took some time for me to figure it all out. I've been searching my soul and I came to this major revelation ... I still love you."

The moment Sam had rehearsed in her mind for the better part of two years was staring down her face. "Why?" Looking as though she had received an uppercut to the jaw, the only word she could conjure had stumbled from her lips.

"I had already made up my mind several weeks ago. I wanted to make things right between us. A couple of days ago, I spoke to Dee, who told me what's going on with you."

"So that's what this is all about—you're jealous?" Sam's voice cracked slightly, struggling to maintain composure.

"Jealous of what, him?"

Mike pointed an offensive finger in my direction, which I briefly considered snapping off. But this was Sam's battle to finish, so I remained neutral and calm, like Switzerland.

"Are you serious? He can't possibly offer you the things I can or replace the great memories we've made. He won't understand you like I do. Nobody can. You know this is true, Sam."

Never had I met a person I so quickly wanted to kill.

"You are so right, Mike. Brian can't replace the heartbreak, embarrassment, and general misery you caused. But in one short week he has breathed life back into me, a life that you managed to suffocate, and helped me discover what love actually feels like. I can't even begin to tell you how great that feels. So I suggest you get back on whatever horse you rode into town on and never bother me again." Sam turned her back on Mike, took my arm, and led me to the elevator.

I shrugged my shoulders at Mike and gave him a major shit-eating grin. "Sorry, dude, have a safe flight back home."

As we approached the elevator, I felt the presence of Mike following us. He grabbed Sam by the arm and pleaded, "Wait, Sam, let me talk to you ... alone."

"Mike, there is nothing you can say to me, ever again. Now let go of my arm," Sam demanded.

"No, I'm not finished. I need to talk with you."

I had already surveyed our immediate surroundings. We were alone. "This is over. Take your hands off of her ... NOW," I demanded.

"Back off, asshole, this isn't your business." Smile intact, he served up his best glare of intimidation.

"Sorry, counselor, the judge has issued her verdict." I instantly clamped my hand down with a crushing vice-like force. He winced in discomfort. With his arm extended, I immediately launched a bone-crushing blow. His forearm snapped with a chilling crack. He doubled over, grasping his arm. From there I shoved him into the wall and elevated him by the neck four inches off the floor.

Although Sam appeared shocked, I thought I caught a glint of long overdue satisfaction in her eye. Mike had employed psychological intimidation as a means of manipulation over the years. This moment of utter humiliation would break the remaining bondage.

"Mike, you are a truly lucky man today. Normally I would have snapped your neck." Any scream he might have made was muffled by my chokehold across his throat. His face turned azure and lilac from the lack of oxygen. Finding pleasure in the moment, the way an artist admires his work on canvas after days of labor, it occurred to me he was about to pass out. "I am going to let you down now, but if I hear as much as a whimper out of you, I will knock your ass out cold. Understand?"

Releasing my grip, he dropped to his knees, doubled over, and gasped for air as the color streamed back into his face.

"Asshole, you broke my arm."

"Like I said, you are lucky I stopped with your arm. Now, it is time for you to get the hell out of New Orleans and forget about Sam. I promise you emphatically if you do not, I will make you regret life in measures you cannot begin to fathom."

We watched as Mike hobbled out to the street. Sam was trembling ever so slightly.

"Are you alright?" I touched her shoulder where Mike had forcefully grabbed her.

"Okay, so after meeting your friends I thought I knew what kind of guy you were, but I never imagined what you were capable of. Holy crap! It was like bam, fight over. If I had blinked, I would have missed it." Sam appeared giddy as she recapped her feelings

"Double O Seven, licensed to kill." I smiled, attempting to make light of the event. "Does this change anything?"

"Well, I certainly know not to piss you off. I wouldn't want you to break anything of mine." With trembling hands and a nervous smile, she pushed the elevator button.

CHAPTER 15

NEWLY LIBERATED, SAM'S passion was like a Texas twister, uncontained, leaving me utterly demolished. Grateful for a much needed reprieve, she left for her sister's, and I attempted to reassemble my agenda. I casually strolled back to Crawdad's, taking in newly discovered details of the city: abstract patterns created by peeling paint, web-like designs created in the fractured sidewalks, images of the shadows cast by buildings, their shutters hanging crooked on their rusty hinges awaiting the day they would tumble to the earth. The Crescent City had an unspoken charm, only to be discovered by eyes blinded to the daily toils of everyday life. I was experiencing a world of obscure treasures ignored for sixty years. My senses embraced the air of new life.

The savory carte du jour of Crawdad's, specifically the Cajun fried oysters, had me salivating long before the aroma reached my nose. From a block away I could see, then hear, the boys seated at the table in the corner. They had not waited.

"There was a time when you were always the first one here," Rob called out as he eyed my approach. "I can tell this thing, this temporary madness, is getting the better of you. Aren't you over her yet?"

"Thanks for all of the concern over my personal life, gentlemen. So, let's dispense with the bullshit and get to work. Can we get this thing done tomorrow night?"

Rob began to lay out the details.

"It's not clear when or how, but probably during or before the Civil War there was an escape tunnel built from the convent to the Beauregard-Keyes House." Rob passed a picture of the yellow stucco house. "It may have been built to help soldiers, and maybe slaves escape or hide out." Chuck handed over a copy of a crudely sketched blueprint and a newly taken picture of the Keyes House courtyard where the tunnel originated. "No one has come or gone by this tunnel over the last forty-eight hours. According to the diagram, the garden fountain is on casters and should roll away exposing the tunnel. As you can see from the close-up, the foliage around the fountain is undisturbed. There are no visible signs of any recent activity, so we are assuming the tunnel may be abandoned or inaccessible. This is our Alpha entry. If it fails, we abort and execute Beta plan the night after. Assuming Alpha goes as planned, the tunnel emerges in what appears to be a closet. According to the diagram, the floors and ceilings are hinged, like a trapdoor. So we can climb from the first floor all the way to the third floor. Not knowing the content of the third floor, Jimmy suggests we exit on one and advance from a conservative approach."

Rob paused for questions. There were none.

"With the original convent floor plans, I have sketched out several routes to the target. From best estimates, there are about twenty overnight subjects, although we could only identify sixteen bogeys exiting the building over the last few days. My thermals show the place settles down nicely in the evening. After twenty-three hundred hours the only movement was from the racks to the loo, with the exception of these two. Their location and lack of movement suggest they might be sentries. All of the photos, specs, and diagrams are here on the flash drive." Rob slid an IronKey flash drive across the table.

"So to the novice eye, all appears to be quite ordinary. But here's where it gets juicy," Rob continued. "Jimmy found several red-flag abnormalities, the first being an ultrahigh-frequency security system. It's state of the art. We crossed-referenced it with the

French manufacturer's specs and it's a sure bet this system includes some form of laser security. With no outside assistance and such an elaborate system, it made us wonder who responds in the instance of intruders. We considered the possibility of the unaccounted bogeys in the convent potentially being a hostile security detachment.

"The second item is a little more bizarre. The thermal heat sensor scan showed the first two floors significantly warmer than the top floor, which is inconsistent with virtually all Southern multi-floor structures of this era and construction. The top floor should be warmer by a good eight degrees. It's not. Secondly, the heat image scan, which normally reveals subject movement, did not reveal subjects on the third floor, minus the sentry, but did show aberrations in the temperature patterns not consistent with anything identifiable. The aberrations appeared only slightly warmer than the surrounding air and moved around in no apparent pattern or sequence. And here's the kicker. Everything on the right side of the third floor is almost thirty degrees colder than the rest of the structure. Check it out," Rob instructed as Jimmy slid the image across the table.

"So, it is a sure bet something is up there." I studied the images while rubbing my temples. "So, potentially a bulkhead here," I fingered the diagram, "and no signs of life."

"Actually, several times a day, one or two bogeys would trek up there via the stairs on the northeast wing. The scan showed they moved about a third of the way down the corridor, spent only a minute or two, and then turned back," Jimmy reported.

"Maybe a routine security check or changing of a guard?" I guessed.

"Not a change. The heat patterns remained consistent. The person that arrived was the same that departed," Jimmy confirmed.

I surveyed the images spread before me.

My finger froze on the image of the fountain. In the past the decision would have already been made. Cowboy up—just a matter of execution. This was slightly different, well, actually, it was grossly different. I had a bad vibe: the history, the legends, and those fucking freaks. I continued to weigh all the options as I resumed tapping the images.

"Tomorrow night?" I hoped to hear just one voice of dissent.

"I'm in," Rob said without hesitation.

"In," affirmed Jimmy. "But with one caveat. If any one of us decides to pull the plug, the job is done, no questions, no debate. We are all in or all out."

"Let's kick ass." Never one for much in the way of planning, Jarhead sealed the deal.

"All right, we are on."

I had already made several photographic passes of the area and knew every alley and vacant building near the convent. Unbeknownst to Sam, I canvassed the blocks surrounding the convent, playing tourist, photographing her with pertinent areas of interest in the background. I pulled the pictures from my pocket and thumbed through the stack. I tossed the picture of a vacant house on the table. "1111 Royal Street, about a block and a half from the convent. We will meet there at zero-one-hundred hours. Chuck, lights out for five minutes prior, with a duration of thirty. That should be sufficient to get us in the tunnel."

"Got it covered. I just got these new micro imploders. They are da bomb, literally. Remotely detonated, no explosions, nobody sees a thing. They send a spike through the power line strong enough to blow a transformer. I will place one on the meter box at the rendezvous and let it rip five minutes before showtime. That will keep the lights out for a while. I'll set one on the convent's generator later tonight and a few other locations on the grid, just in case things get dicey. I can blow half the freakin' town and put 'em all in the dark if needed."

Chuck's face bubbled, excited over the opportunity to show off his new toys.

"Then we are set. One last thing, guys. This is a non-lethal job, unless there is absolutely no alternative. I will bring tranquilizer guns for everyone."

I paused to contemplate my last words carefully.

"I am not sure what we will find, but we absolutely need to be prepared for anything: Holy Grail, vampires, anything, and everything. I know it is a convent, but be mentally prepped for shit like we have never seen."

We ordered up a table of food and spent the next hour reliving more memories of the good old days. It was a welcome way to kill an hour, avoiding the inescapable thoughts of a job that weighed heavily like no other. After we polished off enough food to fill a caravan of gypsies, I said my goodbyes and headed toward the convent.

The feeling of solitude stalked me as a lazy breeze nudged a lifeless wind chime into melodic song. Staring at the convent several blocks ahead, it loomed dauntingly, as if it were aware of my presence for the first time. A strange glow reflected off the humid night sky and cast a foreboding shadow on the convent's third-floor dormers. Those very same dormers which had been sealed for centuries now appeared as though they were wide awake, studying my every move.

As I circled the block around the convent, I could not escape the sensation of being caressed by a multitude of bygone spirits. Pressing on, passing the historic house where the assault would begin, I felt like I was being watched by something not of this world.

I forced my way in the direction of Jackson Square. The nightly ritualistic carnival was in full swing. Crowds of unwitting tourists watched the various street urchins lined against the wrought-iron fence, performing their theatrical crafts. Evenly spaced, effectively allowing small groups to surround the various performers, the curious and gullible crowded into each performer's imaginary territorial venue.

I could not help but notice one gypsy intensely staring at me. As we made mutual eye contact, she became tense, rose from her rickety chair, and backed away. She crossed herself feverishly, crying out loudly, "Lord help us, he has descended. Lord, deliver us from this evil."

The old lady singled me out with a mangled arthritic finger, continuing to wail out her warning. Turning away, I decided to ignore her melodramatic rants and continued toward Toulouse. The other gypsies followed her lead, making the sign of the cross as I passed. Drawing more attention than I cared for, I pressed on quickly, singing, "Psycho, everyone's a psycho." There was no way an old hag with more wrinkles than an elephant's ass was going to derail my resolve.

CHAPTER 16

"THREE, TWO, ONE," Chuck whispered, then snapped his fingers. "Lights out, motherfuckers."

On cue, all lights for several blocks silently popped out. The immediate neighborhood became dark and blind to the ensuing approach of four men on a mission.

Immediately, scanning outside, Rob commanded, "Showtime!" Exiting the side door of the vacant house, we arrived at our destination within minutes, passing by unsuspecting civilians who emerged to seek out the source of darkness. With a quick heave, Chuck and Rob pushed me to the top of the eight-foot stone wall surrounding the Keyes House courtyard. Silently, pulling them up one by one, and in a matter of seconds, we were over the wall. Jimmy and I waited, as Chuck and Rob moved to the fountain in the back of the garden. Without fail, we were in position in less than five minutes, just as scripted.

According to the diagram, the fountain rested on a set of rollers hidden beneath the thick marble. The base was covered with ivy thick enough to hide the locks securing the entrance. Chuck produced a pair of bolt cutters while Rob groped through the vine.

"Got it," Rob reported in a hushed tone. Chuck mechanically sliced through the bolt like butter. Rob had already moved into position with a crowbar and began to apply enough leverage to set the slab in motion. With the slab displaced a mere two feet, Rob disappeared underground as Chuck pulled back to our position.

"I've got nothing," Jimmy reported as he scanned for any wireless signal or silent alarms that would indicate our presence. With no word from Rob, a moderate level of anxiety began to surface.

Chuck pulled his gun, patience waning. "I'm gonna go check on the boy."

"Give him thirty more seconds," I ordered.

"That's all he's got. We need to be in the convent in less than five minutes," Jimmy stated.

"All clear," Rob reported over the Bluetooth.

One by one, we moved through the garden and dropped below. Once inside, Rob and Chuck forced the marble slab shut, concealing our presence. The room was black, requiring the assistance of night goggles. Three marble caskets on elevated slabs, appearing undisturbed for a great many years, practically filled the chamber. The padlocked casket on the right was our gateway to the unknown.

"Game on, gentlemen." Chuck produced his bolt cutters and cut the lock, while Rob cautiously raised the lid with his pry bar.

"It's wired," Jimmy reported softly

Sliding in place, he analyzed the configuration, then attached a series of jumper wires. "This system is ancient. I doubt if it even works. But give me five more seconds ... done." Not knowing if any audio listening devices were in place, we continued to whisper through our Bluetooths.

Chuck and Rob struggled to remove the marble lid, taking care not to dislodge the jumper wires. The casket was empty. I groped around the bottom until I located a seam in the base. Chuck and Rob pulled their tranquilizer guns and trained them on whatever might exist on the other side. I pried at the seam until the base popped open revealing a stone staircase to the black underground. "After you, bossman," Rob whispered.

I looked down the dust-covered narrow steps. Judging by the amount of undisturbed soil, it looked as though the stairs had not been used in a hundred years. All was clear from this point. I checked

my right hip for the tranquilizer gun and my shoulder harness for
Loretta. For the most part, the tunnel was only about five feet tall
and three feet wide. We remained hunched as we scurried along,
scanning for any form of advanced security. The walls were brick
and mortar and from my best guess, we were about fourteen feet
underground. The tunnel abruptly ended at a second set of stairs
leading down into a large chamber. The size and depth of the void
amazed me, considering much of New Orleans is below sea level.
The catacomb was filled with at least two hundred caskets, the majority recessed in the walls.

"Are you getting this?" I wanted to ensure Rob had switched on
his head cam.

"Yeah, all of it. You know, given the legend of this place, I gotta
tell you this is freaking me out just a little. All of these dead people
down here and nobody knows this place exists."

I turned to the guys. "My thoughts, exactly. Anyone want to turn
back?"

"Hell, no! Bring on the zombies. I've got something special for
them too." Chuck's ego never allowed thoughts of failure. Guns
ablaze, he could always blast himself out of any predicament.

Jimmy and Rob nodded their heads, concurring with Chuck.

We reached the bottom of the stairway, at which point the ceiling was about twenty-five feet above. The floor was a maze of crudely
constructed cypress boxes in various phases of assembly, stacked
high atop one another. Cobweb-covered oil lamps were scattered
about alongside antiquated wood-working tools abandoned by car-
penters more than a century ago. We snaked our way to the far side
of the catacomb, locating the ascending staircase.

"Why in the hell would these guys need a secret graveyard?"

"Million-dollar question, James," I replied.

The tunnel began to narrow as we pressed ahead through the
dark passage. Brushing against the damp bricks, the condensation
moistened my clothing as we began to ascend. The masonry ceiling
was now replaced by exposed joist and tongue-in-groove planking.
Apparently, we were now under the convent.

Jimmy squeezed by and silently drilled a minute hole in the
planking overhead at the top of the steps. Through the hole, he
threaded a fiber optic camera and studied the image briefly. "Brooms,

mops, and a bucket on the floor—looks like the closet. He pulled the camera back and surveyed the structure overhead. Two thick steel slide bolts on the furthest joist secured the trapdoor. Jimmy quietly pried the rusted pins open. Applying sufficient upward pressure, he dislodged the secret hatch. Raising the door in fractional increments, the cleaning supplies shifted silently to the side. With the hatch opened enough to slide his torso into the darkened closet, he began handing down the cleaning items until he could fully open the hatch.

After thoroughly inspecting the closet for any additional alarms, Jimmy signaled all was clear. Sliding the camera under the exterior closet door, he scanned the outside hallway.

"Gentlemen, we are green."

"COM check," I instructed.

"Check" whispered Chuck, Rob, and finally, Jimmy.

"Showtime." I moved past Jimmy and cautiously opened the closet door. The hallway was dimly lit, as the emergency generator had kicked in. Chances were, the sleeping inhabitants were unaware the power had gone out.

We moved swiftly and quietly to the stairway. As we came to the second-floor landing, Jimmy looked around the corner with the fiber optic camera. He hand signaled: one guard, armed. He passed me the hand monitor so I could get a fix on the guard's position. The sentinel sat in a wingback chair on the left, thirty feet out, reading a book. A clean neck shot would be challenging from this angle but imperative for the quickest dispersion of drugs. I signaled below for the guys to hold their position as Jimmy and I traded vantage points. With tranquilizer gun ready, I moved into position at the top of the landing. Stepping around the corner, the guard caught sight of my silhouette in his peripheral view, but before he had time to react, I fired a clean shot into his neck. He slumped in his chair. Immediately moving down the hall, I removed the dart and repositioned his limp body.

"Double up," I ordered quietly. We needed to move faster and cover our rear. If "Sleeping Beauty" were discovered, all hell would break loose. We moved past several closed doors before reaching the stairs to the third floor. Moving to the top of the stairs, I did not wait for Jimmy and the camera. I turned the corner, acquired my target, and fired immediately. My aim was true, and just like the previous guard, he was out before he knew what hit him. We moved swiftly down the hall, the temperature plummeting with each step.

"Shit, would you look at this," Chuck said as he passed the downed guard. He nudged the body to expose his weapon. "This guy's got a Mac just like mine. That's some heavy shit for guarding a bunch of Catholics."

Returning the guard to his chair, we inched forward.

"Step aside. Let the professionals take it from here," Jimmy ordered. At this point, Jimmy took the lead wearing his infrared goggles. He moved quickly to the end of the hall where it doglegged left. He slipped his head around the corner for a quick glance.

"No guards, but I've got a laser intrusion system," he reported. "Watch our ass, I'll have it down in a minute."

The alarm was not a concern. If it was made anywhere on the planet, chances were Jimmy probably had a hand in designing it. He was a foremost authority on alarms, and many security companies, unaware of his supplemental income, consulted with him on designs. Within a minute he called back, "Green."

The dimly lit hallway looked as though it was right out of a Vatican museum. The ceiling, walls, and heavy-wooden door all appeared to have come from a medieval castle, crucifixes of all shapes and sizes displayed everywhere. Even the carpet had crosses woven into its fabric. An intricate network of exposed copper piping lined the walls and ceiling and stalks of garlic were strategically placed around the entrance. As we moved through this most occult gauntlet, our shoes sloshed through the carpet, wet to the point of saturation. An access port large enough to allow items to be passed through the door was bolted from the outside.

"Is the door hot?" I asked.

"Already disabled," Jimmy said.

"What the fuck is all this about?" Rob asked.

"Hell if I have ever seen anything like this. I'm guessing the floor might be wired, add a hundred and ten volts and stop a charging bull. The piping, some type of nerve gas, maybe. Anything else, I sure as hell don't have a clue."

"You know I don't buy into any of this voodoo shit, but what's up with all the crosses and garlic?" Chuck asked.

"Probably meant to spook the hell out of anybody that might stray this way," I guessed as I slid the latch and opened the port. Frigid air smacked me in the face. The icy blast, combined with a healthy dose of apprehension, sent a shiver down my spine unlike anything I had ever experienced. I pulled back to the crew.

"Jimmy, check it out." We waited anxiously while he scanned the room."

"Infrared, thermals, and audio all clear. If there's anything in there, it isn't alive," he reported.

"Post up the rear. Watch our backs," I instructed.

"Don't have to ask me twice," Jimmy said with a half-hearted smile.

I mentally inventoried exit Plan B. Blow a rear dormer window, toss smoke grenades, and rappel down the back of the convent. "Chuck, got the Plan B package?"

"Little late to ask now, don't you think?"

"Let's do this and get the hell out," Rob said as he headed toward the door.

The thick, heavy door was bolted from outside, but surprisingly not locked. I pulled the bolts back and opened the door. The frosty air rushed out, howling as it passed. Cobwebs hung heavily on the antique chandeliers and what little lighting existed appeared to be emanating from the last room on the right at the end of the hall.

The central hallway cut the third floor in half. To the left, I saw an open door. I stuck my head in the room and, seeing no sign of life, I clicked my flashlight on to get a better look. The flashlight glowed in a mist of unknown origins. The room ran about half of the length of the hallway, a vast space where crates and furniture were randomly stacked. I gave a hand signal to Rob and Chuck to hold their position as I entered the room and inspected the numbered crates. Without a manifest, if the Grail were here, every crate would have to be opened. Although many appeared to have been undisturbed and stored for decades, or longer, a few appeared more recently deposited.

I returned to the hallway where Rob and Chuck were standing watch. The right side of the hallway was lined with a series of six doors, all closed. I hesitated as I surveyed the situation: six doors on the right, one more on the left. Fuck, it was too quiet. In the jungles and deserts, there were always reassuring earthly sounds. In this

frigid vacuum where shadows were feared, the silence was eerily
unnerving.

"Chuck, take the first two doors, Rob, the middle two. I'll take
the last. Let's do this quick and get the hell out. Rob, take a quick
pass through there and get the crates on video."

I pulled my tranquilizer gun out, as did Rob and Chuck. I traveled the length of the hall and turned to ensure we were set. Rob gave
a nod of his head as he and Chuck entered the room. I placed my
hand on the frigid crystal knob. Instantly, something felt very wrong.
I looked down the hall. Chuck and Rob had disappeared into the
dormitory room containing the crates. I tentatively crept in. On first
glance, I observed a furnished room, much like a Victorian parlor,
appearing as though it was currently in use. The room smelled odd,
an unfamiliar odor, which I could only describe as sickly sweet. I
tentatively treaded deeper into the room. There was a large Louis
the Fifteenth wingback chair facing the boarded up dormer, its back
to the door. Moving closer, I could make out the details of a head or
something shaped like a head.

"Chuck, Rob, pull back! Pull back now and hold by the main door,"
I ordered. A sickening dread welled up inside of me as though a terrible
truth was about to be revealed and I had no choice but to confront it.

"Roger that," Rob replied.

"Secure the door. Nothing goes out."

"What's the deal?" Rob asked.

"Just pull back and hold the door," I repeated sharply.

I approached from the left and then moved cautiously in front
of the chair. I could not believe, or want to believe, the sight before
me: a beautiful woman, wearing only a sheer, white garment, speechless and expressionless gazing back at me. Her hair was silky, dark,
tightly curled, and flowing down past shoulders of the whitest, most
flawless skin I had ever encountered. Her face was delicate, almost
fragile-looking, while steely, blackened eyes followed me intently as
I continued to circle. Moving to her right side, I began to consider
if this might be one of Phillip's elaborate hoaxes. Although he loved
a good prank, I could not fathom him executing such a complex
charade. The other nauseating possibility confronting me: I was face
to face with a vampire.

Continuing in her silence, she scrutinized every detail of my face, her own lending a concealed distress.

Now directly in front, I knew something had to be said. "Who are you?" Knowing the cavalry would be hearing at least my side of the conversation, I felt a wisp of relief.

"My name is Angelique." She spoke with a soft French accent.

"My name is Brian. If you do not mind me asking, why are you sitting here all by yourself, barely dressed in this freezing room at two in the morning?"

"I do this every night, as I have for years ... waiting for you, Brian."

"I apologize for my tardiness." A hint of sarcasm laced my reply. "Why me?"

"To deliver us from this prison." Her voice remained placid, as did her demeanor.

"So you are not alone?" Emphatically, I repeated her claim, hoping to escalate the boy's state of alert.

"Can you tell me, are your captors hiding anything else up here? Are there any important artifacts, documents?"

A crooked smile crossed her face.

"Is this why you have come?" Her smile was strained as she considered the possibility that I was not her knight in shining armor. "Are you some kind of treasure hunter?"

"No, I am no treasure hunter. But I have heard stories."

"I will put your wonderings at ease. No, there is no treasure, it is only us."

I was not ready to admit to the absurdity of the moment. I could visualize Phillip buying an abandoned building and setting up this whole elaborate hoax, Sam and all. Everything had fallen so neatly into place. I bore witness to some of his pranks in the past, but never on this magnitude. Could he have gotten to the boys? If so, they would be laughing their asses off right about now. Without warning, I pulled Loretta and pressed her firmly to Angelique's forehead. "No more screwing around, doll. Did Phillip hire you?"

Without a flinch or any sign of anxiety, she calmly asked, "Who is Phillip?"

Regardless of acting experience, with the barrel of a Beretta against her forehead, she should have demonstrated some fearful reaction. Instantaneously, all I held to be true in this world vanished. If she were a vampire, I was defenseless. Shit. She sensed my vulnerability.

"Brian, you know in your heart what I am." Placing her hand on Loretta, she pushed her aside. "Now, allow yourself to believe what you thought incomprehensible. At long last, you will now fulfill your destiny."

Instinctively, I withdrew Loretta and took two steps back. Angelique rose, floating effortlessly from her chair, retracing my retreat. Drawing near, I felt the icy chill of her breath. Silently, she held my eyes with a gaze so powerful, it rendered me defenseless. Placing her cold right hand gently behind my head, she began chanting: "Spiritul de întuneric, Te implor. Posedă această ființă indisciplinat. Forja cuvintele mele asupra sufletului lor. Viața lor să fie a mea, sângele nostru să fie una." She repeated the verse until I was physically incapable of resistance. She kissed me, then backed away just enough to examine my condition.

"Like the years that have passed, this too has been too long." Her voice overflowed with deep fulfillment from the stolen pleasure. "Mmm, your lips are soft and warm." She kissed me again, this time passionately, caressing my face with fingers so cold, I quivered.

I could offer no resistance, though I desperately craved my lost freedom. This imprisonment was unlike Isabelle's potion-induced intoxication. I was fully cognizant, but unable to move my thoughts against her. I experienced her unbelievably strong and paralyzing willpower as it gradually filled my every thought. How could I have been so arrogant?

"No," I muttered helplessly. If only I had allowed myself to believe in what might have been. A cross, a stake, anything. I had to stop this now. With every shred of strength and primal instinct to survive I possessed, I called out, "Red Dog!" Whatever was to become of me no longer mattered. I could not allow this evil to escape.

Angelique grabbed me by the throat with incredible force, strangling my ability to speak. She shoved me violently backward to the wall, chanting more intently until my world fell into darkness. I saw and felt nothing, as if I was floating with no sense of direction, light, or meaning. Jimmy called back, uncertain of my perilous condition, "Come back, Brian. Did you say *Red Dog*?" Red Dog; terminate all ops, lethal force authorized.

"Come again, Brian?" he repeated. "Did you call *Red Dog*? Chuck, what the hell is going on in there? Rob? Somebody respond!"

CHAPTER 17

REGAINING CONSCIOUSNESS, MY first cognizant sensation was of falling. In reality, Angelique, her silhouette assimilating before my eyes, was driving me backward by a sheer invisible force. Any attempt to regain self-control was met by her dominating, impenetrable will. My body turned without thought. Halfway down the hall stood Chuck and Jimmy, motionless, surrounded by nine creatures. An immediate wave of doom washed over me as I helplessly observed my companions. "Tell them you need their help," Angelique ordered.

Do not do it, a faint voice whispered from within.

"Your will is strong, Brian, but you will submit." She began softly, yet firmly chanting her spell, peering menacingly into my eyes.

Again my willpower vaporized with each line she recited. "Jimmy. Chuck," I said flatly, "I need your help."

Jimmy, still holding his gun, dropped his weapon to the floor. The creatures moved in closer, rabid hunger consuming their once enticing, yet ghostly expressions.

Angelique smiled euphorically, knowing their centuries of imprisonment were nearing an end.

"Brian, you and your friends will carry us through the arches of the hall. Once we are safely on the other side, you will set us free. You will make no effort to detain or harm us. Do you understand?"

My mind raced with the primal instinct. If we resisted, they would kill us and possibly still manage escape. It was of no consequence. As much as I wanted to refuse, I could not deny her. My body answered involuntarily to her unspoken commands.

"Tell them what to do. Tell them now," Angelique ordered. Her instructions encroached my mind, forcing my body into action.

"Jimmy, Chuck, carry them out to the main hall and around the corner. We must free them now." Angelique's instructions resonated so clearly in my mind, her thoughts bridging some paranormal connection and vocalizing through my mouth. In concentrating on this phenomenon, not resisting it, I began to perceive her thoughts. Her fears, so acute. Holy water saturating the carpet, crosses, and garlic adorning the walls. All powerful Christian weapons used in the war against vampirism. The depth of her fear became mine as I bore witness to visions of destruction centuries ago. They were powerless to pass this gauntlet without assistance.

Chuck and Jimmy had begun ferrying the vampires out until only Angelique remained. "Take me now." I swept her up in my arms as a groom would cradle his bride. Wrapping her arms around my neck, her eyes recounted some deeper soulful connection that bridged the centuries.

With each step taken, I attempted to deviate my path. Even the slightest variation would be indicative of a hard-fought victory. It was not to be. If only I could muster the will to drop her onto the carpet sanctified with holy water.

"I know the thoughts you desire. But you cannot destroy me as you dare to dream. Our fates are now one forever. To kill me would end both our lives." She looked into my eyes as a lover would, not some vile creature worthy of death. "Do not hate what you do not understand. In time I will return to you and reveal all that you seek."

She closed her eyes and held her breath, the strength in her body fading as we passed the gauntlet designed to maintain their captivity. Evil, which had been kept locked away for centuries, was now free. The diligent work of many unsung protectors of the innocent was now undone. I set Angelique down gently, her arms remaining around my neck, her lips finding mine for a final kiss.

Fixated on the anguish kindled in my eyes, she spoke softly, "Brian, please do not be angry. This has been your destiny from the day you were conceived, so it shall be when you return to me, willingly, without prejudice or anger. Until that night arrives, it is time for us to part ways." Without trepidation of obstacles ahead, they gracefully glided to the stairs and disappeared into the welcoming darkness.

As the distance between us grew, Angelique's dominance slowly began to fade. I struggled to raise my hand to my face, taking one step forward in the direction of Chuck and Jimmy. As Angelique's presence disappeared, her veil lifted, allowing me to return to my spellbound comrades.

"Where is Rob?" I snapped. Our time was up and we needed to find Rob and get the hell out of Dodge. Lacking response, I slapped them both in the face. "Where is Rob?"

Chuck's face remained catatonic; he struggled to point in the direction of the third room on the right. I bolted toward the room, Jimmy and Chuck staggering behind.

The sight of Rob on the floor slammed into me like a cement truck. Lifeless and gray, his eyes agape with fear and pain, he lay on the floor. As an agent of death throughout my life, I was all too familiar with its face. It was pointless to check for a pulse. Rob's neck and arms were grotesquely littered with a multitude of punctures. Those bitches had feasted on my brother and cruelly bled him until he was the lifeless corpse before me. Chuck and Jimmy arrived behind me, silently beholding the horrific image.

"Motherfuckers." The only words forged ignited an uncontrollable rage I would not try to contain. I dropped to my knees.

"Sweet Jesus," Jimmy said.

Surreal, far beyond any fathomable nightmare, I refused to believe after all the shitdigs we had survived this was the end of the line for Rob. "Chuck, what the hell happened here?"

"I don't know. One minute we were getting the fuck out and then she appeared. After that, I don't remember a damn thing. Where in the hell is that bitch now? She's a dead woman."

"Guys, keep it down." Jimmy reminded us of our precarious situation.

"We escorted them, all ten, right out the door." Not wanting to believe, the realization of my responsibility hammered me in the gut.

"Shit, man, those bitches got to die," Chuck demanded.

The conversation was broken by an earsplitting alarm. "Cats out the bag. Time to go," Jimmy said without hesitation.

"Grab Rob's gear," I ordered. Jimmy and Chuck gathered all of Rob's equipment, including his camera. "Jimmy, what's the plan?"

"From here, Plan C. The closet we came through on the first floor had a latch in the ceiling. I unfastened the bolts and placed a wedge to keep it closed. The third floor access trunk should be in that closet, right over there." Jimmy pointed toward the corner. "It's probably bolted from below, but if we can get it open, we should be able to drop down the trunk quickly with minimal exposure."

"Let's do it, otherwise we will just have to blast our way out. We cool with that?"

They both confirmed. "Chuck, you have thirty seconds to get that trapdoor open. Jimmy, watch the door."

Chuck dashed to the closet, flung open the door, and began hurling objects to gain access to the hidden hatch. Once cleared, he drove his crowbar through the old timber floor and applied enough leverage that the old bolts snapped effortlessly. The screaming alarm provided a much needed audio mask, helping conceal our intended escape route. Chuck then plowed the crowbar through the ceiling and busted out two large holes that allowed him to loop his rope over the joist above. Dropping the rope to the floor below, in less than thirty seconds he had secured our escape route.

"Time to go," Chuck announced.

I rose from Rob's side. "I'm sorry, bro."

"Peace be with you, my brother," Jimmy added solemnly.

"I got your payback covered, bro," added Chuck. "This will not go down without extreme punishment."

Moving into position to evacuate, we bid silent farewells to our fallen friend one last time. The sounds of panicked voices drew near. "We needed to be gone two minutes ago," Jimmy warned.

As I looked back, it suddenly occurred to me that, quite possibly, Rob might be condemned to the same fate as the vampires. This would be no life Rob or any of us would choose. I hustled across the room, grabbed a wooden chair, and violently smashed it on the floor. Void of emotion, I took the shattered leg, approached Rob's body, and after taking a cleansing breath, thrust the wooden spike deep into his heart. Expecting a graphic explosion of blood, I was astonished by the complete lack of it.

"Holy shit, Brian, what the hell did you do that for?" Chuck howled.

"He would not want to be like them, none of us would."

The voices were close, but apparently proceeding with caution, unsure of what lay before them. "We need to be gone, NOW!" Jimmy yanked a ski mask out of his pocket and pulled it over his face, then grabbed the rope and rapelled straight down to the tunnel.

I trained Loretta on the door as the voices drew nearer. Chuck and I pulled our masks down as well. "You are next," I ordered. Chuck rapelled down the trunk and was out of sight in a matter of seconds. I holstered Loretta and grabbed the rope. Pulling the closet door behind me, I couldn't help but look back one last time.

Just as I started to descend, I heard a distraught voice cry out, "My God, they are gone." Lowering myself through the second floor, I heard frantic voices, one in Italian, just outside the door. I could make out enough words to know he was frantically calling for reinforcements. "Find Daniel, immediately," were the instructions.

Passing through the first floor, I dropped into the tunnel and began to pull the hatch, attempting to conceal our escape route. Jimmy and Chuck were already in the tunnel, their night vision goggles on, preparing to flee upon my arrival. As I climbed onto the stairs and began to pull the hatch, the closet door suddenly swung open. An older man, grim and wrinkled, dressed entirely in black, stared at me. A brief instant elapsed, and then he flinched. I was in no position to beat him to the draw. I grabbed the broom we had left propped against the wall and thrust it into his face, striking his nose. Falling back with the gun he had drawn, he fired wildly.

"Gunshot," Chuck warned from below.

I threw the broom, this time striking him squarely in the forehead. He fired again as I dropped into the tunnel.

"Go, go, go!" I ordered. Chuck and Jimmy moved away quickly.

"They are here, under the convent!" the man screamed.

Hastily, I backed deeper into the tunnel. Upon reaching the stairs, dropping to the lower catacombs, I turned my back and quickly caught up with Chuck and Jimmy. "If they know about the tunnel, they might know about the exit across the street. We've got to get the hell out of here now!" Concerned our only exit might be compromised, I turned on my halogen torch, flooding the burial chamber with painfully bright light. "There's no time to be feeling our way around in the dark. We have got to bust ass out of here."

In less than half the time it took us to make the trip in, we were back at the chamber under the courtyard. Chuck, garnishing his Mac, stormed the stairs, burst through the lid of the casket and into the vault room with no regard to danger. Ready to storm the court-yard wall without concern for consequences, I held him back. "Let me check it out first."

Distant sounds of the chase echoed from the tunnel below, beams of approaching lights signaled their pursuit. "We've got company down below," Jimmy warned.

"Gas 'em," I ordered Chuck.

Jimmy wasted no time taking up the lead as I diverted my attention below. "I'll check the front," Jimmy offered. He rolled the heavy slab back enough for our escape, cautiously extending his head. "We're clear."

"Hold the gas till the last minute," I instructed Chuck as I moved in behind Jimmy.

Jimmy's last foot had not cleared the hatch when I heard a familiar sizzle cut the air above. I knew the sound all too well, but before I could verbalize a warning, a dull thud ensued, sending Jimmy crashing down to the ground.

"Oh, fuck! I'm hit, I'm hit!" he cried out.

"Dammit!" Frustrated by the complete debacle, I struggled to assimilate our options.

"What the hell's going on, Brian?" Chuck growled, close to abandoning his composure. I had witnessed that frenzy before: guns blazing, shooting everything in his path. The consequences of those actions here would be grave.

"Jimmy's down. We have a sniper. Gas 'em now!" I listened as the canisters tumbled down into the tunnel, muffled explosions signaling detonation. Our backside would be temporarily covered. From our location below I could not see Jimmy or the convent. "Jimmy, where are you?"

"I'm ten yards out, just short of the hedges. I think the shot came from the convent."

"Are you okay?"

"Are you fucking kidding me? I've been shot. It hurts like hell and I'm bleeding all over myself."

"Stay down. Make them think you're dead."

"What's the plan?" Chuck asked impatiently.

"Jimmy says we have a sniper in the convent. It's pretty simple. I am going to pop up, acquire the target and take him out." I reached in my backpack and retrieved my tricked-out sniper pistol. "Jimmy, can you give me a target?"

"Second floor, third window from the far right."

"Are you fucking crazy?" Chuck grabbed my shoulder as I prepared to take my shot. "That is a two-hundred-yard shot in the dark. He'll nail your ass before you even see the convent."

"Any better plans? Time is running out."

"Yeah, let's put some ass behind it and tip the fountain slab over. That will give you the cover you need to take the sniper out."

I was pretty sure the slab and fountain weighed over six hundred pounds, but Chuck's plan beat the alternative of getting my head blown off. Chuck, the guy that usually went full tilt, guns a blazing, was uncharacteristically the voice of reason. After several failed attempts, Chuck grabbed my arm. "Momentum. Let's close it and then roll it forward, fast. When it hits the stop, we've got to shove up with all we've got." Following the plan, as the slab rolled into the end stop, the fountain rocked. "Up now," Chuck screamed. "Come on you wimp, put some ass into it." With one last heave, the stone slab tipped forward and crashed over to its side.

I wasted not a second. I grabbed the pistol, leaned out to the left, and acquired the bogey. The single shot echoed across the courtyard as my target went down.

"Get Jimmy out. I will cover."

Chuck sprinted out and over to Jimmy. Assisting him to his feet, they scrambled through the hedge. Muzzled shots rang out, bullets ricocheting off the brick wall. Making out the silhouettes of multiple hostiles at the southeast garden wall, I fired in their direction, forcing them to take cover as I sprinted to the wall. Chuck had already boosted Jimmy over the wall. Giving Chuck a leg up, in return he pulled me to the top.

The streets remained eclipsed in darkness thanks to Chuck's power outage. "Get him out of here, now," I ordered Chuck. "I will cover." Chuck and Jimmy ran down Ursuline, turned on Royal Street, and disappeared. I ducked into an alley between two houses halfway up Ursuline, keeping a vigilant eye to the corner of Chartres for any signs of a posse. Weaving between buildings, I made my way to the corner of Governor Nicholls and Royal where I had chained a bike to a street light.

Peddling swiftly, several blocks farther away I turned into a narrow alley. Quickly stripping off my black attire and stuffing it in my backpack, I cautiously returned to the street, checking for any signs of pursuit. Multiple sirens shattered this once quiet part of town, all heading toward the convent. The shots fired did not go unnoticed.

I continued at a casual pace down Governor Nicholls, turning left on Burgundy, then left again on Bienville Avenue. In the relative certainty of potential employment, I had leased a vacant office, a safe house, prior to arrival. Riding down the alley, I pulled up to the back door of the office, unlocked it, and pulled inside. Once inside, I stashed my backpack in the drop ceiling, removed my gloves, and slumped to the floor. The unforgiving image of Rob, lying brutalized, seared my mind. Having no idea how severe Jimmy's injury was, I pulled the phone from my pocket and pressed the speed dial.

"Yo," Chuck answered.

"What is the word?"

"Everything's cool. As cool as it can get, all things considered. We'll be back at the watering hole in a day. We both need a drink."

In times of crisis, daily time frames were always divided by two. If anyone was eavesdropping, they would have a hard time pegging our plans. Hours were clicks and minutes were ticks.

"We need to go over the proposal. I'll see you on the flip," I said. "On the flip" was code for "as soon as possible." "Keep low." The last thing I wanted was for Chuck to seek retaliation for any of tonight's events.

"Roger that." His tone was sharp and bitter as he hung up. I had known Chuck long enough to gauge his pissed-off meter. This one soared in the stratosphere.

I sat against the wall contemplating the epic fuckup of a lifetime. What was I going to do to make it right? This legend, so absurd, so fucking impossible, had instantly become explicit reality. We had liberated an ancient evil on an unprotected city. I had no choice. I had to make things right.

The sun would be rising soon. I had until dusk. Checking my watch, it was four a.m. I called Phillip.

"What the hell are you thinking?" he asked wearily.

"Are you alone?"

"Thanks to you being alone, yes," he mumbled, still half-asleep.

"Get up. I will be right over."

"Call me back in a few hours. I was out late—"

"Ten minutes," I snapped.

Retrieving my backpack from the ceiling, I pulled the video camera out and stuffed it into a smaller messenger bag. The streets remained hauntingly quiet and empty. I scouted around anxiously for any signs of the undead. I had no method of protection from creatures who did not fear guns or physical intimidation. Creatures? It was time to deal with reality. Fucking vampires. I kicked a picket from the fence behind the office, creating a makeshift spear. So much for sophisticated modern-day weaponry. Oddly enough, the addition of this crudely procured primitive weapon fortified my fragile sense of security.

I walked out of the dark, sullen alley, and headed down to Bourbon Street. There was a maligned sensation in the night air. I had been instrumental in its creation, and now it was up to me to undo the evil I had set free.

CHAPTER 18

I SLIPPED THROUGH the lobby of Phillip's hotel unnoticed. A multitude of late-night revelers remained outside the hotel on Bourbon Street, so there was nothing unusual about guests returning at this hour. Phillip answered his door promptly. "How did you know where to find me?"

"Come on, Phillip. It's me."

"You've been there, haven't you?" Instantly, Phillip recognized my strained expression.

Without invitation, I brushed by. "Until a few hours ago, I thought I had everything in life figured out. Turn your laptop on."

Phillip fired up his Mac while I pulled the digital recorder from my shoulder bag. I studied the camera, the secrets it contained so much larger than its insignificant size.

"I suppose this is so hot it couldn't wait until morning?" Phillip quipped.

"No, it could not. A good friend died tonight to bring you this." I unraveled the USB cable and handed one end to Phillip.

"Jesus, Brian, what the hell?" Phillip held out his hand for the camera.

I placed the tiny recorder in his hand but did not release it. "I am not sure; I do not know if you will be able to do anything with this." I released the camera to him. Phillip took one look at my grim expression and it rattled his nerves. "It is true, you know, the legend." I spoke in a defeated tone. "And what you're about to see on the tape is just the beginning."

Hands shaking, Phillip fidgeted with the cable, struggling to plug it in. Finally succeeding, he pressed play. The grainy image of the quiet courtyard came to life in black and white. "Skip this part; you can watch the whole thing later."

We fast forwarded until the video showed me disappearing into Angelique's room. Rob turned the camera on Chuck. "Let's get this done, Jarhead." Just as Chuck and Rob split up, my orders to pull back were heard on the tape.

"Did you see anything?" Chuck asked.

"No. Secure the main door. I'll look in here," Rob said.

I turned my head and grimaced, knowing the outcome. With the darkness of the room blinding the camera, Rob had switched to infrared. The dimly cast image of ten caskets, five on the right and five on the left, appeared out of the shadows.

"Please tell me you did not make this shit up." Awestruck, Phillip adjusted the screen for a better view.

"At this point, I wish I had."

The camera swung wildly back to the door as Rob called Chuck. "Get your ass in here."

Chuck appeared instantly in the video. "Holy shit, this can't be real. No fucking way." Chuck made a beeline to the first casket. "Get your ass over here, Rob." The video followed Chuck, Rob moving beside the casket. "I'll open the lid, you get the picture." Chuck raised the lid on the first casket without hesitation. Sleeping serenely, then suddenly startled, a beautiful young woman immediately opened her eyes. Rob backed away instinctively and the camera captured Chuck's reaction as he pulled his gun. The video revealed a pale, delicate hand with long fingernails grasping the side of the casket, pulling the young woman up. Climbing gracefully from the casket, a ghostly glow shrouded her body.

"Back off, lady. I ain't playing around," Chuck ordered. The sound of his deep masculine voice, though hushed, stirred the occupants in the remaining caskets. The woman stopped her advance, looked back to her rising companions, then smiled devilishly at Rob. Just as quickly as she had risen, so too her eight companions now filled the video.

"Chuck, we need to get the hell out of here," Rob said, panic peppering his voice.

"Roger that." Chuck began to back away from the approaching vixens.

Once again, I heard the familiar words Angelique had spoken, this time from the mouth of a vampire out of the camera shot. "Spiritul de întuneric, Te implor. Posedă această ființă indisciplinat. Forja cuvintele mele asupra sufletului lor. Viața lor să fie a mea, sângele nostru să fie una." I muted the computer, not knowing what effect the recorded words might possess, not hearing my final warning, *"Red Dog!"*

From that instant, Rob and Chuck stopped talking. Another vampire, not the first to rise, stalked Rob as the camera captured every detail of her assault. Appearing fully in the lens, her lips uttered in unison the ancient spell. Rob's arm remained extended and his fist clamped onto the palm sized camera, which he instinctively pointed toward himself. The wide-angle lens captured the gruesome scene, a vampire plunging her pointed canines into Rob's neck. His body contorted, writhing in torment until he collapsed to the floor. One by one, the other demons converged, draining blood from his arms and legs until Rob was dead.

With only a grainy image of the ceiling before us, Phillip finally spoke. "Shit, Brian, I don't know what to say."

His words bounced off my musing without response. Minutes continued to pass, as we stood ensnared by the picture on the computer. Eventually, words began to fall. "His name was Rob. He was a damn good friend and a brave man," Numbed by the experience, I confessed, "That should have been me."

"Don't say that, Brian." Phillip pressed stop and unplugged the camera. "You know we all go when it's our time. It's not yours."

"Yeah, you are right, but knowing and living with it does not make it ..." I stared at the blank screen. "And as I said earlier, this is only the tip of the iceberg. It gets a lot worse."

"Worse?" Phillip was fearful of how anything could possibly be worse than the massacre he had just witnessed. Particularly anything he was directly responsible for.

"They are gone, they are all out."

"Gone?"

"The vampires, they forced us ... we helped them to escape."

"How?" Phillip's voice registered alarm, knowing full well his part in this plot had exceeded the reasonable boundaries of capturing a story.

"Just like you saw on the video, they used some type of hypnosis to control us. Angelique, who you did not see, used the spell on me. I do not have a fucking clue what she did while I was out. From the point she initiated the spell until we set them free, I do not remember a damn thing."

"Shit, so what do we do now?"

"We? We do nothing. I have to get those bitches back inside the convent or make them disappear permanently. Honestly, I would just as soon wipe them off the face of the planet for what they did to Rob." I paused and considered if returning one or all of them was even an option.

"What do you need from me?" Phillip asked.

"Get me some vampire stuff. The stuff you see in movies. I am not sure what will actually work, but the convent was loaded with crosses, garlic, and holy water, whatever you can get your hands on. Get me two-by-two pickets, twenty of them, and something to sharpen them with. I need all the stuff ASAP, like before lunch. I have one day to hunt them down."

Realizing the daunting task had to be completed before nightfall, I reached for my phone and called Chuck. Two rings, and he picked up.

"How is our boy?"

"He'll make it."

"Keep your head on straight. We have much to accomplish today. The job has to be wrapped up by tonight, with or without the gimp."

"Meet me for breakfast in four clicks, the usual," I instructed. "The usual" was the last location where we had previously met, Crawdad's in two hours.

CHAPTER 19

MITCH O'REILLY HAD been one of New York City's finest until investigating the grisly slaughter of a family and their infant children in Manhattan led to a psychological breakdown and ensuing drinking binge.

On the advice of the department shrink, he took a short leave of absence. Not knowing where to go or what he would do, he followed the advice of a few good friends: head south and check out the New Orleans Jazz Festival. He never returned to New York.

O'Reilly was single and a savvy investor. With money in the bank, disability checks on the horizon, and not much desire for a job, he stayed in New Orleans listening to jazz and blues, feasting on the local cuisine and fishing.

After five years of doing as little as possible, he happened upon two detectives rehashing a recent murder investigation over lunch. At a dead end and beating their frustrated heads together, they searched for a fresh angle, anything that would deliver a break. So intent on their mission, they overlooked the eavesdropper seated next to them. O'Reilly considered the alibi of one suspect too iron-clad and took it upon himself to tell them so.

At first, the two younger detectives were skeptical of this odd-looking man. His hair was a gray-faded blond, looking as if trimmed by a chainsaw. His eyes were a youthful, brilliant blue, yet his lean, weathered face revealed years of stress and hard work. His dialect was quirky, accentuating words at all the wrong places, making his New York accent difficult to confirm. Initially, his interjections were a minor annoyance for the detectives, but the more he forged on with his theories, the more plausible they became.

"Nine out of ten times, the most obvious innocent is guilty of something." O'Reilly then introduced and invited himself to sit in. O'Reilly's theories bordered on criminally brilliant. The befuddled young detectives decided to give him a crack at their suspect's alibi. Within two days, an arrest was made and his involvement did not go unnoticed by the New Orleans Police Department. A week later, he was offered a job.

The phone on O'Reilly's desk rang just after five in the morning. "This had better be good. You must know I'm extremely busy at this hour." *The New York Times* crossword puzzle was O'Reilly's one true passion. Once he started, if left undisturbed, he could usually knock it out in less than an hour.

Most cops knew better than to disturb him in the midst of his passion, only life or death being a viable excuse. "A dumpster? Get out!" O'Reilly replied. He listened to the voice on the other end explain. "Today's not white trash day, is it?" O'Reilly tapped his pencil on the crossword clue he had been working on as he listened to the incoming information. "No, no. I want it. Don't touch anything, and I mean anything."

Barely fifteen minutes had passed before O'Reilly arrived. "Damn, either that's a really bad shrimp jambalaya or it's a cracker á la corpse."

"This guy's been dead about two hours. He's missing most of his blood," Walt Dekker, the medical examiner said.

"Note the multiple puncture wounds on the neck. Classic vampire bullshit," Dekker said bluntly as he spit some chaw just over O'Reilly's shoe. Dekker had seen this before, usually one every two years or so. "Those goddamn kids again."

Mitch had never worked one of the bloodsucker cases before, but he had heard sufficient stories. "So what we have is one dead guy. Somebody wants us and the general public to believe we have a vampire roaming the French Quarter. Or maybe they don't care if anyone knows." O'Reilly scratched his head. "Possibly, his fatal blood loss was one of those freaky rituals gone wrong. Either way, it's a shame to waste our time on this crap. These idiots don't deserve our efforts or the taxpayer's money."

"Yup, just like the rest," Dekker agreed.

O'Reilly looked puzzled by the odd wounds. Something was different about this victim. In a random visit to the morgue, he had examined a corpse involved in a blood-drinking ritual several years ago and found the puncture wounds to be suspiciously dissimilar. "Make him bleed, Doc."

"What?" Dekker was surprised and annoyed by the bizarre request. Dekker, like everyone else, knew O'Reilly was sort of an oddball. He was not accustomed to performing any procedure on one of his corpses initiated by a second party.

"Just do it. I don't care how. Just get him to bleed somewhere on his body."

Dekker pulled a scalpel from his workbag, lacerated the victim's finger, and gave a squeeze. "Damn, will you look at that?" Dekker was surprised the laceration did not produce even a drop. He moved to the victim's leg, pulled up the pants, and made a longer incision across the greater saphenous vein on the front of the shin. Again, not a drop. "Son of a bitch," Dekker grumbled. Now determined, Dekker targeted the carotid artery in the neck, on the opposite side of the puncture, and sliced it open. No blood. He laid the artery open wide and examined it. "This beats the shit out of me. There's not a drop, almost like the son of a bitch was embalmed, except there's no embalming fluid either."

Dekker stared at the artery, contemplating deeply. "You know, I've had maybe a dozen or so of these types of killings over the last twenty years. It always turns out to be some lunatic trying to make people believe he's Dracula. But this stiff beats them all. It's the first time I've ever seen a corpse like this. You're going to be looking for someone with extraordinary knowledge of embalming techniques. Might want to check the archives for the case of those NYU students back in the eighties."

"Did you guys find any blood in the dumpster?" O'Reilly called out.

"Not a drop yet," a detective replied. "But we'll need to sift through it for several hours before I can give you a definite yes or no."

"Get this guy gift wrapped quickly and out of here," O'Reilly instructed Dekker. "I don't want anyone besides us to know the cause of death or any of the details until after I've talked to the captain." Mitch paced back to his car.

"What's up, O'Reilly?" a detective asked, leaning against the car.

"Some lunatic wannabe vampire bit our vic on the neck to impress his peeps. I want you guys to find Lady Isabelle—*today*. Bring her in. Have me paged when you've got her. Secondly, keep your mouth shut about this. We don't need the public with their panties in a wad or any vampire-envy copycats running around."

O'Reilly's phone rang. It was Dekker, who had returned to his car across the alley waiting for the wagon to show up. "I just got a call from another crime scene. Seems they've got a dead guy with puncture wounds in his neck."

O'Reilly climbed into his car. "How utterly fucking original."

CHAPTER 20

I WAITED AT Crawdad's for almost an hour. It was not like Chuck and Jimmy to be late unless something was wrong. I ordered breakfast after considering they might not show. My job would be decidedly more difficult without their support. I broke out the maps and listings of the city cemeteries and spread them across the table. It would be impossible to cover them all before sunset, and there was no guarantee the vampires would even be in a cemetery. They could be in an abandoned home, warehouse, anywhere. I tried Chuck's cell again. Still no answer.

I finished my breakfast and considered enlisting Phillip's help. I needed an extra body, but Phillip had no training that would be remotely useful. I needed an experienced killer. If I had to hazard a guess, a larger and more neglected cemetery would be the logical place to start, far enough from the convent, but not too far. I recapped the list and the descriptions before making the final call.

I threw my money down, folded my paperwork, and headed out the door. Walking briskly, deeply unsettled over Chuck's and Jimmy's absence, I speculated on their circumstances.

"Yo," a familiar voice called from behind.

Relieved, I turned to see the boys closing the distance behind. "Damn, I am glad to see you."

"I always knew you loved me." In the thick of death and destruction, or even the loss of a good friend, Chuck maintained his sense of humor.

"I hope you assholes know you missed breakfast."

"Sorry, girly boy had to have something for pain. And then Dipshit had the audacity to drop my cell off the hotel balcony this morning. Needless to say, that phone is FUBAR."

"How are you holding up?" I asked Jimmy.

"Percocet does the trick." Jimmy replied with a strained smile.

Walking over to an unoccupied street corner, I pulled out the maps. "We need to split up." I handed the list to Jimmy. "You guys start with these two. Most of the vaults are single-serving size, but a few mausoleums do exist. Look for signs of being disturbed. If you have any doubts, jackhammer the shit, quietly. We cannot afford to miss anything. If you find something, call me. I will let you know how to proceed from there."

"Call! On what? You want me to send smoke signals or something?" Chuck sarcastically knocked on his head. "Were you not paying attention? Sir James nuked my phone."

"Then go to a payphone. Go buy a new TracFone when the stores open, but just get going. We have to locate and destroy them before nightfall, for Rob and the rest of the people in this town."

"Why don't you take Gimpy? He'll only slow me down," Chuck suggested.

"You take him, for now. Keep a sharp eye. Those guys who shot Jimmy will likely be out today, hunting the same game, or maybe us. Watch your back. By now the local law might be involved as well."

"Yeah, we got it covered." Jimmy, sounding a bit fatigued, winked.

"Are you sure you are up to this, Jimmy?"

"Yeah, got no choice. We gotta make this right."

"One more thing." I deliberated the possibilities before issuing my final request. "If things go south, if something happens to me, get the local cops involved, then get the hell out of Dodge. Way out. Understood? Neither one of you are to go down for my screwup, and I sure as hell do not want you joining Rob any time soon."

"Damn, you'd think he almost cares about us, Jimbo."

I cut a stern look at Chuck. "I will see you guys in a couple of hours, with some tactical gear. Until then, we are just trying to get a fix on our targets. Understood?"

They both nodded. I flagged a cab.

The morning sun was already cooking up a humidity stew. It was going to be a long sweltering day indeed. I dialed Phillip. "Are you on top of things?"

"I'll have everything you asked for by noon."

"Good. Be ready to deliver when I call." I hung up and stared out the window.

Saint Joseph Cemetery lacked any trace of impending tour groups. Pacing off the steps to the entrance, the city of the dead stood before me. Entering the cemeteries alone was considered dangerous, even in broad daylight, due to the assortment of unscrupulous individuals that found the habitat to be a safe haven. Now they could add vampires to the list. Intrepidly entering through the archway, I trekked to the far side and worked my way forward, crypt by crypt, with the sun bearing down heavily. Laboring to breathe in the dense air, after just a few rows I began to measure the daunting task which stood before me. To cover all of the graveyards in one day would be impossible. If the vampires had spread out, tonight would deliver an unsolicited taste of misery not seen in two centuries.

Two hours passed before I completed my sweep of Saint Joseph. It was just after eleven-thirty. Once back at the hotel, I called Phillip. "The Alpine, be there in thirty minutes."

"Hey, wait. Sam wants to see you. She knows something is up. What do you want me to tell her?"

"Not today, no way. I will call her on the way." I hung up. Finishing Saint Joseph, I was discouraged. Coming up completely empty was a far cry from my expectations. I headed back to my hotel, needing to change my sweat-soaked shirt. Not that it would matter for long. Shortly after lunch, the new shirt would be as disgusting as the old one, but a clean shirt and a splash of cold water might help change my perspective. I called Sam as I headed back.

"Hey, I miss you," Sam said in a lonely voice. "Where are you?"

"An unexpected complication arose which will require a little more time to wrap up than originally planned. But as soon as this is over, we are going to fly to an isolated island and lock ourselves in some remote bamboo hut for weeks. You can let your imagination fill in the details."

"I'm ready now," Sam purred.

"Sam, I am going to be running like a Tasmanian devil today and probably all night trying to wrap this up."

"Are you sure everything's alright?" Interrupting, she could not mask the concern in her voice. "You don't sound so great."

"Yes, I am sure." Unintentionally, a wisp of a sigh passed through the phone. The lies proved to be an uncomfortable burden. "I will call you later." My obvious displeasure over the circumstances seeped through the phone.

A brief moment of silence ensued. "I love you."

In silent emptiness, I pulled the phone away from my mouth and struck my forehead repeatedly. With the phone remaining against the top of my head, I could hear Sam speaking. "It's okay, Brian."

I took a breath to recompose myself. "No, Sam, it is not okay. I just need you to understand ..."

"I do." The angst in my voice forced Sam to temper her reply. "So I'll see you soon."

I knew in my gut the possibility existed: I might never see her again. "Not soon enough."

Showering quickly and changing, I headed back to The Alpine. Phillip was already in the restaurant having a beer, with one waiting.

"Brian ..." Phillip stood to greet me and looked me over. "You look like shit."

"Thanks, bro. You look like shit too."

"Do I?" Phillip was incensed by the revelation he might look less than perfect. Through any adversity in his life, Phillip always managed to remain dapper, even a crisis of this magnitude.

"Don't crap your pants. You look beautiful as always. You got my stuff?"

"Yeah, I've got you a couple of genuine Van Helsing the Vampire Slayer starter kits." He slung one of the black duffel bags stuffed with equipment on the table. "Want to see?" His adolescent enthusiasm was not befitting the nature of the crisis. But after all, this was Phillip.

"No, I will check it later." I removed the bag from the table and set it beside me. The waiter appeared with two bowls of steaming jambalaya, noting the bag's change of possession.

"Coke," Phillip deadpanned.

"Guess that bodes well for my tip," the waiter jested before leaving.

"I didn't know if you would be hungry or not, but you should never hunt on an empty stomach. A growling stomach might wake the dead."

"I appreciate that." It had only been four hours, but I was unnaturally hungry. "Look, Phillip, there are several details I need you to remember." Shoving a spoonful in my mouth, the jambalaya roasted my lips. "I know I have already told you, but it is imperative to keep off the streets after dusk until I tell you otherwise. This may take several days, but if I do not check in with you an hour before sunset, get Sam and Dee out of the city immediately. I don't care how you accomplish it, just make sure it happens."

"You think those two dead guys this morning are related to our mess?"

"What two dead guys?" This was the last thing I wanted to hear. If they had begun reproducing, my task could grow beyond my control.

"Police found two dead guys, not together, but in close proximity. New Orleans cops are beyond tightlipped with the details."

"I need the details, like an hour ago. If something should happen to me, you make sure Sam is well taken care of. Aunt Rena knows how to access my financials. Tell her to keep what she needs, and Sam gets the rest."

"What if Aunt Rena wants it all?" Trying to lighten the burden, Phillip maintained his humor.

"Then you will have to take care of Sam for me. Understand?"

Phillip nodded, his mind ready to deliver another volley of offbeat commentary, the door of opportunity ajar.

"Do not even think of going there. Additionally, if I get killed, you need to get the story out immediately. People need to know before the morgue fills up."

"No worries. Consider it done," Phillip guaranteed. "But I know things will work out."

My phone rang: Chuck calling to report the only thing found this morning was a new phone.

"Keep at it. Supplies will be at the house in a few." Two cemeteries and not one vampire. I hung up the phone, feeling downhearted.

"Brian, I am so sorry I got you into this."

"Not your fault. I made my choice."

"Before you go, I want you to take this." Phillip pulled his sterling crucifix from around his neck. He had worn it for as long as I had known him. "Go on, take it. You need it more than I do."

Although I was never a huge fan of jewelry, I had always admired this particular piece, a serpent intertwining the intricate Celtic design. "I can't take that." I pushed his hand away. "I do not know if I will ever see you again, and I can't promise it will not get destroyed."

"It's not for you to take care of. It's for taking care of you, to protect you. And I won't take no for an answer." Phillip placed the cross in my hand and turned it over.

I took the crucifix and hung it around my neck, tucking it into my shirt.

After dropping off one of the bags at the safe house, I returned to the northwest side of town to begin searching Saint Louis Number One Cemetery. While similar to Saint Joseph, there was one critical difference: Hordes of tourists filled the graveyard. While several tour buses were parked out front, Number One was a short walk from the Quarter, and as such, many tourists made the journey there on foot as well.

In the stifling heat, I forged on with no success. Completing the second row, I became aware of an odd fellow lurking in the distance. Odd, not only by means of appearance but by his actions as well. Dressed entirely in black, in this heat I might add, his hair was a fine snow white, receding and long. He appeared to be in his sixties. Keeping him in the corner of my eye, I searched on. Mimicking my actions, either to decipher my purpose or to annoy the shit out of me, he studied my every move. Not remotely on top of my game, had I somehow missed him this morning or did he just pick up my trail this afternoon? If he had followed me all day, Phillip and the girls could possibly be in harm's way.

It was time to take action. At the end of the second row, I turned the corner and immediately disappeared behind a tomb. It should have been no more than two minutes, but as time passed there was no trace of him. Maybe I was just being paranoid. Maybe he was just another one of the Crescent City lunatics, hanging out in a ghetto cemetery, dressed entirely in black, chilling out in one-hundred-degree heat because he had nothing better to do.

Preparing to resume my search, a high-pitched Italian accent called out from behind. "You will never find what you are searching for."

Damn, this guy was good. Other than Rob, no one had ever been able to sneak up on me.

"What makes you think I am looking for anything?" I turned to gaze upon the gaunt, grisly man who trailed me so efficiently.

"We all are looking for something: love, the mysteries of life and death. But you, my friend, will never find what you are seeking." His skin was pure white, beyond albino, and his eyes were hidden by small and dark vintage glasses. His suit looked to be Armani.

"What makes you so sure?"

"Because you lack the necessary faith." He pointed a single finger to the sky.

"I have faith," I insisted. My faith was anchored to childhood beliefs, hand in tow with Aunt Rena to church every Sunday. Never dissipating, but never developing, I loosely held on to the notions I had grown up with.

"Hardly. What you consider faith and that which is the true essence of faith, let us call it unconditional faith, are two completely different beliefs. My faith makes all things possible. Yours has limitations, to the point that impossibility is allowed to exist. It is the very reason you failed."

Assuming he was from the convent, I decided to turn the table. "Unconditional faith? It seems to me your unconditional faith, as you put it, has failed you as well. Otherwise, you and I would not be having this conversation."

His stoic expression cracked as a smile slipped across his lips. "Your lack of faith caused you to fail. Faith in God tells us all things are possible. Thus vampires are possible, and therein lays the foundation of your failure. Likewise, unconditional faith demands we succeed in our endeavors, not to our means, but to His."

"So, let me see if I have got this straight," I replied. "Faith in God will give me the mystical powers to locate vampires, have strength, and more importantly, the righteousness to drive a wooden stake through their hearts?"

"God gives us strength to accomplish many tasks, even the most unpleasant," the man countered. "The purpose and righteousness is His alone to determine."

The old man spoke with a passion and confidence I sorely lacked at the moment. "You will never find what you are seeking until you quit searching with your eyes. Free yourself of your physical body and allow your spiritual being to take over. Sit a minute. Close your eyes, silence your mind, confess your deeds, and then simply ask for what you seek."

As I was getting nowhere fast, I did as he instructed. I slumped down against a sunbaked tombstone. The only connection I experienced was the sweat running down my back pressed up against the heated marble. "Nothing yet."

"There are other forces far greater than you could ever imagine, constantly aligning against you. Rooted in evil which has festered for centuries, you must learn, and rather quickly I might add, to gain a faith not of your own being, but from above, if you are to conquer what you seek. It is the only way you will survive."

I leaned back and attempted to shut down the flow of pictures broadcasting like a movie reel. Everything which had transpired from the moment I set foot on that plane, pieces of a puzzle fitting together, forces I had no control over moving continuously, plotting, creating this masterful disaster. For the first time in my life, I understood the magnitude of my limitations. I never possessed control—it possessed me. As I surrendered to the revelation, a refreshing, cool breeze, which existed only in my mind, lifted my spirit. Unaware I had cascaded into a deep slumber, my thoughts faded to blank pages of an unbound book. Transformed to a formless substance, drifting on the gentle currents above, I gazed down on my weary body, hearing the words whispered from my lips below, "Help me."

CHAPTER 21

"YOU KNOW WHERE they are. Yes?" A familiar voice called me from a destination I could no longer see.

My eyes gradually awoke to the realization the sun had dropped significantly, the majority of tourists gone. Checking my watch, I had been out for nearly two hours. I jumped to my feet with renewed vigor. Without a word to my spiritual guru, I cut across the cemetery toward the west, instinct driving me like a bloodhound.

We arrived at what appeared to be the largest mausoleum in the cemetery. Unlike any I had come across as of yet, this one had an iron gate on the backside leading underground. Beyond any doubt, this was the tomb of a bloodsucker.

"You know what needs to be done," the old man admonished.

"The bitches must die," I said.

"And you have the necessary equipment?"

"Buddy, I was born to kill. I am sure pounding a stake through a woman's heart is just like riding a bike." I removed the padlock, which hung freely on the unsecured iron gate.

"Is there anything you would like to know before proceeding?" he asked softly while peering over my shoulder.

I turned back to find him uncomfortably close. "What's your name?"

"Daniel."

"Daniel, I have seen *Dracula* at least twenty times. Can I pretty much expect the same type of action?"

"Well, the simple answer would be yes. But these creatures are more vicious, stronger, and faster. Otherwise, they are pretty much the same."

"Great, then we should have no trouble." I turned and treaded down the steps cautiously. Once below, I discovered six elevated freestanding caskets, all trimmed with intricate appointments of a wealthier class. The first casket showed signs of activity. There was an uncharacteristic tremble present in my hands as I opened the duffel bag, withdrawing the stake and mallet, clutching them tightly. For additional protection, I pulled Phillip's crucifix from under my shirt. I looked to Daniel, who had followed me down, and drew a final cleansing breath. Hoping to hear him say "Let me do this," he merely offered a reassuring nod. The golden rays of the setting sun partially illuminated the passage down, but no direct sunlight shined in this musty space. Quietly and slowly, I raised the heavy lid, fearful of waking the sleeping dead. Relieved but disappointed, I gazed upon a decomposed corpse. I instantly began to doubt my newfound senses.

I stepped back beside Daniel, masking my surging emotions. "Just a quick question: the sunlight thing, fact or fiction?"

"It is a fact, to be sure."

"So if things get out of hand, running is a good option?"

"Though I've never seen the theory tested in real life, it is my honest belief sunlight will kill them. But I should warn you, be prepared for an extremely violent reaction. One theory is on your side: When sleeping in a casket, they do not wake easily," Daniel said as he patted me on the back. "Before you proceed, I have a final question for you, my young friend. Can you look into the beautiful face of a sleeping woman and without hesitation drive a stake through her heart?"

"Did you see my friend Rob?"

"Assuming it was you who placed the stake in him, you should know, there is no mistaking the process of extinguishing the immortal. If someone appears dead, rest assured, they are."

"I was afraid he might become one of them." Embarrassed, I justified my actions.

"I have spent a lifetime with these women, learning their ways," Daniel continued. "One fact I know for certain, they are not in a hurry to repopulate. Centuries ago, by mistake they created too many, with no respect for authority or the discipline necessary to maintain secrecy. This ultimately led to their demise. But make no mistake, they will feast. They have craved the blood of the living for centuries. Living blood will give them the power and strength they brandished centuries ago. What you encountered was but a glimpse of their true power."

"If they were so powerful, how were they trapped in the convent?" I asked.

"According to the legend as it was passed down, only Angelique and Monique arrived at the convent as vampires. Only Monique, as it was told, feasted frequently upon the inhabitants of our city. Subsequently the death rate almost doubled after the arrival of the 'Casket Girls,' as they would become known. Accusing the priest for the evil misfortunes befalling the city, the citizens blamed the Church and demanded resolution.

"Believing all to be guilty of this evil, whispers of fear within the convent only stroked the flames of misfortune. It is believed, when they came to seal the third floor, eight innocent women were condemned to a fate more vile than death. Locked away in a convent, where surely no evil could survive, it was believed they would starve to death.

"Eventually, the two began to feed on the eight. The screams heard inside the confines of the third floor were unbearable, but not knowing what to do, the priest did nothing. Eventually a portal was cut in the door, allowing food to pass to the other side. In time, the desire for worldly nutrition vanquished, replaced by incessant cries for blood."

Daniel looked over the caskets with sadness in his eyes. "And in the convent, they existed for centuries, waiting for the one who would free them."

"Great, so my destiny was a screwup of historical proportions," I said.

"Don't be hard on yourself. It took great skill and courage to accomplish your feat. Many fools have tried over the years, only to receive the same harsh fate as your friend. My family has stood vigil for over two centuries and now, after years of duty, my task draws to its conclusion. Like the vampires, my day of freedom has come."

"You are welcome," I said sharply. "But if your freedom was earned by their death, why did you not kill them yourself years ago?"

"I am seventy-two years old. For fifty years it has been my charge to protect, never my duty or obligation to destroy." Daniel directed the accusatory finger at my chest. "That would be your task."

"What if I choose not to? Where would that leave you?"

Daniel produced a pistol from his jacket, pointing it in my direction. "I am sure you will do the right thing." His smile was sly, showing confidence that armed intervention would not be necessary.

I returned to my duffel bag and studied the contents. The second casket appeared undisturbed. Daniel inched closer to observe my progress. I moved in position, hovering beside the third. The seal, like the first, had been dislodged. Again I raised the lid back cautiously, revealing another decayed corpse. The fourth casket offered an unexpected surprise. "What the hell?" I mouthed. Apparently, somebody had taken the liberty of stacking three decayed corpses into one casket.

"Quit looking for what you seek," Daniel whispered.

Observing what appeared to be small shoe prints in the dusty floor, I knew the fifth casket was the one. My adrenaline surged, realizing the first of the ten was before me. Standing over the mahogany and brass box, I took a deep breath and laid my hands upon the cool wooden lid.

"Good," I heard Daniel whisper.

I froze for an instant, not wanting to raise the top, doubting my ability to deliver the lethal blow.

"Do it," he coached softly.

Raising the lid back ever so gently, my heart pounded as though it was about to catapult straight up my throat. There, resting peacefully, was one of Rob's assassins. Her skin was soft and pale. Pale enough to be dead, but her lips were full and rosy. Her long blond hair draped softly over her shoulders and breast. In sleep, she appeared beautiful and innocent. But I had witnessed her savagery and knew her appearance was far from reality. I gripped the stake and mallet firmly, a resolve for vengeance leading me forward. With my heart pounding wildly, I took another deep breath and placed the stake above her chest and raised the mallet high.

"Do it," Daniel implored in a whisper while taking several steps back.

I froze, backed away from the casket, and walked over to him. "How do I know she is really a vampire?

"I saw it in your face when you looked down on her. You know in your heart what she is."

"Yes ... I do."

"Then for God's sake, do it. You must strike her down. Her true nature will be revealed."

I had never killed a woman before, much less one in her sleep. Moving back into position, I steadied the stake less than one inch above her chest and raised the mallet high. Once I committed this act, there would be no turning back. I would have to kill them all, or they would hunt me down. My hand struck down, forcefully driving the stake with a heavy thrust deep into her heart. Blood splattered across our bodies. Gasping for air, her throat filled with blood, rendering her unable to scream. Her eyes filled with terror as she witnessed my rage. I raised the mallet a second time and pounded the stake violently through her chest just as she brought her hand up in a feeble attempt to stop the savage assault. She moaned deeply and gasped her final breath. Death was instantaneous. Her mouth gaped open, revealing a pair of blood-covered, razor-sharp fangs— the same fangs which had drained the life from Rob.

The symphony of death, although relatively quiet, must have been just enough to stir the second vampire; the remaining casket lid set in motion. I quickly grabbed another stake and set up just behind the casket. Watching in anticipation, a delicate white hand slowly maneuvered the lid. The slow, methodical movement was not an instinctive reaction of a creature in fear for her life. Raising the top just enough, her head appeared from within. The golden glare of the setting sun directed a beam of light into her corner of the mausoleum, blinding her eyes. Immediately retreating into the casket, she shielded her face from the fading sunlight.

"Sophia? What is happening?" Her French accent sounded

alarmed.

Sophia found it hard to answer with my bigass stake pounded through her heart, I mused.

"Sophia's not here, Annabelle," Daniel replied.

"Daniel!" Scorned anger welled in her voice. "What have you done with Sophia?"

"Sophia no longer walks the path we share."

An evil hiss emitted from within the casket. "Daniel, you will pay for this outrage. I will make you suffer eternally for this."

I remained silent, poised directly behind the casket.

"My dear Annabelle, I have warned you for years not to leave the convent. You knew the consequences. Now, like Sophia, you must suffer the penalty." Daniel baited her further. "If you are experiencing an uncontrollable desire to kill me, I invite you to come out and strike me down."

At that, she screamed in rage, knowing the predicament she faced.

"Tell me, Annabelle, where are the others? I would very much like to visit them." Daniel listened as the sound of her heated breath escalated from within. "If you tell me, I promise you may return to the convent, unharmed."

"I would die before that happens."

"I knew this would be your choice, my beauty. Why don't you come out and let us dance one final time."

Her breathing grew louder with each rage-filled breath. Much faster than I anticipated, she flipped the lid and leaped out, lunging for Daniel. "Daniel, you will pay for this with your life," she shrieked. Her unnatural speed took us both by surprise. In the blink of an eye, she was on him before he could retreat to the safety of sunlight. With her hands around his throat, she sank her fangs into his neck. He gurgled and moaned as she began to drink his life away. I sprang from behind and thrust a stake through her back, into her heart. Unlike Sophia, who went rather quietly, Annabelle screamed out in agony. Abandoning her assault, Daniel collapsed to the dusty floor as she turned her attention to me. Soulless, black eyes, engorged with hatred and agony, Daniel's blood dripping from her mouth, Annabelle staggered toward me. In retreat, not taking an eye off her advance, I groped around my bag for another stake. Annabelle's pace had slowed, unable to summon the strength for another assault.

I grabbed two stakes from the bag, formed a makeshift cross, and waited for her reaction. She hissed and retreated toward the darkest corner. As I traced her path, in a final act of desperation, cornered and dying, she lunged forward. With not a second to spare, I turned one of the stakes into her body, piercing her heart. She arched her head back as her entire body stiffened, impaled by the oak spear. I reached around her back and grabbed her narrow shoulders, pulled her close, and drove the stake further into her body. With her fangs inches from my face, I could smell Daniel's blood on her chilled breath. "That is for Rob," I proclaimed defiantly.

Her body surrendered to death and collapsed. I rushed over to Daniel, his attention focused on the blood spewing from his neck. "You must leave now. If anyone heard her scream, the police will come to investigate."

"Are you alright?" Daniel's ability to focus on necessities while nursing a near mortal wound was nothing short of amazing. Clearly underestimating his resolve, I discovered a deep-rooted appreciation for the old goat's fortitude.

"I'll be fine. She only got a pint or two." He pulled his hand away from the wound and studied his blood-covered fingers. "You must go now. I'll take care of this. Go quickly. You have much more to accomplish."

I watched the blood continue to stream down his neck. I took my knife and cut a portion of Sophia's shirt to use as a bandage. "Let me help you. Then we can both get out of here."

"Better get on with it, minutes are crucial."

I tied the fabric around his neck, securing additional fabric over the wound. Without delay, I scooped up Annabelle's blood-covered body and returned her to the casket. I sealed up all of the coffins as Daniel slung handfuls of dirt over the blood-spattered floor. We inspected the mausoleum to ensure we had covered our presence.

"Time to go." I grabbed my duffel bag and ushered Daniel to the stairs.

"You leave. It would not be wise for us to be seen leaving this place together."

"Are you sure you will be alright? You look unnaturally pale." Concerned for his survival, I hesitated leaving him.

"I always look unnaturally pale. Go now."

Reaching the outer gate of the mausoleum, I surveyed the surrounding tombs for signs of life. The day was nearly gone—the cemetery left only to the dead. Initially, I hoped to have found all of the vampires in one location. In retrospect, I was relieved there were only two. Had there been more I probably would have been killed.

I removed my bloodstained shirt and headed out of the cemetery. Wandering in a stupor, I reached the street beyond the main gate. A deathly chill overwhelmed my body in the sweltering heat. The ghosts had returned, a seemingly endless parade of the dead, all vanquished by my deeds, screaming the pangs of deathly thralls, their names wailing out above the echoes of gunfire and explosions. Abruptly, for the first time in my life, the brutality of my actions rained down on me. Never had a kill been so intimate, so passionate. I witnessed the sadness in Annabelle's eyes and a desire for life as her soul faded into eternity. Fully cognizant of her crimes, I was suddenly besieged with the guilt of my own wickedness.

CHAPTER 22

I HEADED DOWN Bienville Avenue for the safe house, considering the possibilities: irreparable brain damage from Isabelle's potion? Dead? Dante's Inferno? It certainly was a plausible explanation for this fantasy world. Brian in Wonderland, wake the fuck up!

I needed help. I dialed up Chuck. "Meet me at the house."

"We are already here."

Patches of blood decorated my pants like a Rorschach test. My dark denim Diesels camouflaged the evidence of my crime, leaving me thankful I had left the khakis on the hanger.

Chuck and Jimmy were eagerly awaiting my arrival. "Damn, Stud. I didn't get the memo we were supposed to do this shirtless. Do naked man breasts render the vampire bitches defenseless?" Chuck teased.

Silently, I unzipped the duffel and tossed my bloodstained shirt to Chuck. "While you two guys were jerking each other off, I was busy taking out two of our friends from the convent."

"Oh yeah, well jerk this off," Chuck said as he handed me his new cell phone. "Push that button right there."

Opening the file, the first picture was a third vampire sleeping in a casket. "You were supposed to call me before you did anything," I lectured.

"It was just one scrawny French chick. I believe Jimmy and I were qualified enough to handle her without interrupting your busy day."

"Yeah, like we handled them last night." I scrolled forward. The next picture: Chuck standing over the woman with a stake over her chest and mallet raised high, smiling like a guy who had just caught a twenty-pound bass.

I scrolled on. The next picture: The stake submerged deep in her chest, blood splattered everywhere, and her face contorted in agony. I was all too familiar with this scene. I began to hand the phone back.

"Wait, B, there's more," Chuck said anxiously.

In the next picture, Chuck was in the casket simulating a sex act. "Oh, you are a sick bitch." I tossed the phone back.

"Rob would have liked that one," Chuck said proudly as he grabbed a Bud from a ripped open twelve-pack. "Sure looks like you need one of these." He tossed me one and grabbed another for himself. "So you got two? Got any proof ... like pictures?"

"No, sicko. I do not have any pictures. But I have a witness."

"Who might that be?" Jimmy inquired.

"The guy who put the bullet in your arm."

Chuck nearly choked on his beer. "Got a picture of his dead body?"

"Not yet." Maybe I had lost my edge. In the past, if you took a shot at the crew, you were a dead man, regardless of circumstance. "Apparently he knows practically everything about these women, so he could be an asset. Besides, we broke into his turf."

"Like you ever cared about assets before." Chuck's sarcasm was his methodology for riding my ass whenever the situation called for strapping on the saddle.

While explaining the events of my afternoon, with both remaining uncharacteristically silent, I noticed something missing. "Where are your crosses?"

They looked to each other with, "Who, me?" expressions.

"You want to end up like Rob?" I searched their duffel bags and found several necklaces in the bottom. "Wear these at all times. Make sure it can readily be seen. After today, the seven left will probably be hunting us."

"Hey, I like yours better." Chuck pointed, his hand extended. "Wanna trade?"

"Mine was a gift. Get over it. You guys should head back and get some rack time."

Defiantly breaking away from his usual quiet demeanor, Jimmy held out his necklace. "Got our crosses, we are good to go. Crawdad's is calling."

"In an hour, Crawdad's it is."

Chuck and Jimmy wasted not a second bolting out the back door. Under no circumstances could I go back to the hotel looking like this. Civilians and vampires had been murdered. In my current state, I was sure to fit the profile for potential suspects. I cleaned up just enough to make it back to the hotel without raising any red flags. Once there I would check in with Renaldo, get his perspective on the events of the day, shower off the invisible death which adhered to my skin like tree sap, and think about calling Sam.

I completed my task at the hotel in a timely fashion, including a well-rounded internal debate concerning Sam. I chose to abstain.

Unlike our morning rendezvous, Chuck and Jimmy were punctual. The tall order at dinner was attempting to put the shit of the last two days behind us. Strained laughter, prolonged periods of silence, and an obvious exclusion of any topic including Rob, were all pathetic attempts to avoid the painful truth—we had all failed our friend.

Feigning to enjoy an otherwise delicious meal, we forged on until Buck wandered over with a look of dismay. "Hope you boys are enjoying the meal." Buck's voice aired a genuine tone of displeasure. "Anything look out of sorts to you boys tonight?"

"Well, not having eaten here enough to say what's normal, it's hard to say. But it does seem a little quiet, unlike the last couple of nights," Chuck guessed.

"Bingo, you're goddamn right. The place is a ghost town."

"So what's up?" Jimmy asked.

"I was hoping you boys might be able to shed a little light," Buck said emphatically. "First thing I know, you guys show up, all ex-military and whatnot, and bodies start popping up all over town. And if that's not enough, stories start cropping up about vampires and some sort of break-in at the convent."

"Shit, Buck, we don't know anything about that. We're just here for beer drinking and hell raising," Chuck responded.

"Bullshit! I ain't never seen no church-sponsored poontang parties. I see what you're wearing."

It was going to take some lightning-fast bullshit to bluff our way out of this one. Chuck and Jimmy looked to me, the Bishop of Bullshit, to get the job done. "Yeah, Buck, we heard the rumors." Borrowing a line out of Phillip's skeezbag playbook of pickup angles, I said, "We thought these crosses would help us capitalize on all of this vampire fear with the babes. Fear, my friend, is a great aphrodisiac."

Buck scratched his bearded face as he mulled over my explanation. "Sorry boys, I just get pissed when those dumbasses get everyone all riled up. It happens every five years or so. You'd think by now the law would have busted up their little playland down the street."

Buck stared out to the street, an expression of deeper concern set in his eyes. He had lived here long enough to know the difference between the past and current circumstances. Possibly all he wanted was a bullshit story rather than the truth, but nevertheless I felt a cloak of dishonor tightening. I knew the truth and felt obligated to warn the feisty old soldier. "You know, if you are going to be here by yourself tonight, you might want one yourself. Cross, that is. A little extra faith never hurt anyone."

Buck produced a cross from under his greasy food-stained T-shirt. "Never leave home without it," he said with a smirk. "'Round these parts you never know." He walked away. "Sorry I interrupted your conversation. You boys enjoy your dinner."

Chuck raised his beer bottle, "To the Bishop, always on your 'A' game."

"The Bishop," Jimmy chimed in.

Keeping a watchful eye for whoever might pass the doorways, Buck was right about one thing: The streets were nearly empty.

"Gentlemen, I suppose we are done tonight. There is no reason to take unnecessary risks when we have a decided advantage in the daylight. I think we should rest up for another run in the morning."

The boys agreed without debate. "One last thing," I said, grabbing Jimmy and Chuck by the shoulders as they prepared to leave. "Do not let them use that hypnotic spell on you. It sounded Romanian.

Yell, scream, run like hell. If they use it on you, you will wind up like Rob."

"Better like Rob than to end up like Chuck," Jimmy joked.

"Damn right." I finished my beer and muffled a guttural belch.

Chuck flipped us the finger, accompanied by his trademark unpleasant sneer.

I stood to leave. "You need us to walk you home?" Jimmy asked, adding his dry but welcome humor to my departure.

"No thanks, 'Dad.' I will be just fine." I headed toward the door, leaving the boys behind. "I will buzz you at oh-six hundred hours."

I stepped out onto the sidewalk, the night firmly in control. The street was dark, the gas-glow lights seemingly dimmer than previous nights. Too late, I reconsidered Jimmy's offer. I would not suggest either one of those guys travel alone, but here I was, alone. Trekking on the cobblestone into the hazy lights, several blocks ahead, I spotted the silhouette of a solitary person on the corner. I checked my crucifix, ensuring it remained securely attached. The unidentifiable subject remained stationary as the distance between narrowed. My heartbeat accelerated, Buck's words resonating, "It's a goddamn ghost town." If it were one of them it would be futile to turn and run. I tensed as I continued drawing nearer, slowing my pace. Close enough to begin carving out details, I recognized the familiar lines. Although it was well into the evening, Daniel continued sporting his retro shades.

"Did Buck treat you well?" he asked.

"You know Buck?"

"Indeed. All the locals know Buck."

"Did you get yourself patched up alright? You are still looking pretty pale."

"I always look pale. But thank you for inquiring. It is amazing what a fresh pint of blood will do for you."

"Well, Daniel, since you were following me, you should have joined us for dinner."

"I have already eaten. Do you mind if I ask your plans?"

"Well, I plan on resting until sunrise, as it seems I would forfeit a decisive advantage in the darkness."

"You may be a little smarter than I initially gave you credit for." One smile for all occasions, Daniel's smile was a carbon copy from earlier.

"Hey, Daniel, in case you had not noticed, it is dark now. Assuming you are trying to remain somewhat inconspicuous, you might want to lose the shades." I motioned toward my temple and duplicated his plastic smile.

"Once more, thank you for your concern, but I am fine."

I rolled my eyes at his obstinacy. "In case you would like to know, we capped another one of your girls today. Seven more and you can take that overdue trip to Jamaica, you know. Little fun in the sun."

"Assuming they have not reproduced yet." Daniel offered nothing in the way of congratulations or reassurance, his demeanor remaining as even-keeled as when he was attacked.

"Damn, Danny, you sure know how to make a guy feel good." My tone registered dismay with his pessimism. "I am going to catch a little shuteye and would suggest you do the same if you plan on hanging with me tomorrow. Besides, in case you have not heard, the streets are not safe."

"So I have heard."

I walked toward the brightening lights of Bourbon Street and the company of the uninformed or unintelligent flesh bags. A shallow air of security followed me knowing Daniel was nearby, lurking in the shadows. On the flip side, it disturbed my sense of professionalism knowing he was having little trouble tracking me. Actually, the ease in which he accomplished it pissed me off. Either I was slipping or he was better than me. I peered through the hazy sky to witness a blood-red moon rising. How ridiculously appropriate, I thought. As a mercenary, I had developed an unnaturally keen awareness of my environment. I was being watched. I glanced around. No one in particular stood out as I became acutely aware of a focused energy. My cross dangled from my neck, the weight of it reassuring as I bent down and laced my already tied shoe. I continued to scout out my surroundings. A few foolish revelers passed, but Daniel was long gone, or so I thought.

"You look as though you are lost." The delicate French accent spoke from directly behind me. Angelique's voice immediately sent a piercing chill up my spine. "Do not turn around, please. I know what you wear on your neck."

I thought of turning, but other than the cross, I was defenseless. Her scent had changed, no longer displeasing but somehow enticing.

"You have no need to fear me. If I wanted to kill you, I would have already done so."

"What do you want, Angelique?" Her frigid presence pressed closer.

"All I want is for you to leave this place and never return. Your task is complete." She spoke in a sultry whisper, the chill of her breath imminently close to my ear.

Her words were soft and convincing. I desperately wanted to turn, to behold the beauty of her face, but resisted. Doing so would have been most unpleasant for each of us. "No, Angelique, my task is not complete. I can't leave you and the others here to feast on these people as you please."

"Feast? Like the men of this world feast on whatever they deem to be their domain?" she scolded defensively. "When we feed, we do not take the life of the one that provides our nourishment."

"Then I suppose you had nothing to do with the two dead bodies relieved of their necessary allotment of blood last night?"

"I know nothing of this accusation."

"Then I suggest you check with your friends, because some-body's diet was rather deadly for the boys they found this morning."

"I will do this for you. But you must agree to leave," she insisted.

"I am sorry, Angelique. I cannot do that—not yet."

"Then I cannot protect you."

"Why do you feel as though you need to protect me, Angelique?"

Her lips resided dangerously close to my ear, brushing tenderly against my skin. The heat and humidity of the night air evaporated in the coolness of her presence. "We have a destiny which lies beyond the boundaries of this city." Her lips glided against my ears, then turned down my neck, forming delicate kisses as she explored the carotid artery pulsating beneath my skin. Then, as suddenly as she appeared, she vanished.

Longing for a glimpse, I turned, knowing full well she had with-drawn. The heat of the night returned. Downhearted, my face turned to the ground. A single rose lay on the sidewalk where she had stood. I picked it up and inhaled its fragrance.

Wandering inside the hotel in a stupor, fatigue forced its

unrelenting hand. Resting my head on the pillow, I placed the rose on my chest and drifted into subconscious realms where events unfurled with lifelike clarity. In the depths of unquiet slumbers, I spiraled into a world of dark affliction.

CHAPTER 23

SENSATIONAL MEDIEVAL DREAMS ferried me into the night. Great battles of men raging against armies of the unholy, my life perilously hanging in the balance. I witnessed a great one, appearing not unlike myself—dead, yet so vibrant, his will set against the scores of thousands. Shunning the bitter visions of the lives lost on the battlefield, I soared between realms, erotic dreams of Angelique's glistening white fangs inching ever so close, encompassed by enticing ruby-red lips. Fully cognizant this was merely a dream, I was unable to stir from the fantasy. "Take me," spoken aloud, my words stirred me from slumber.

A ruckus in the street below jarred me unwillingly back to reality. So compelling was my vision, I craved the outcome like an addiction. The faint smell of Angelique's rose on my chest aroused my senses. How long had I been asleep? Rolling to the right to check the nightstand clock, my attention instantly locked onto the pillow beside me. A second rose greeted my awakening.

"Holy shit!" I immediately catapulted from the bed in a panic. Frantically, I scrambled to the bathroom mirror, prepared for the worst. A thorough inspection of my arms and legs revealed not one bite. The reflection of my cross dangling from beneath my shirt provided comfort, perhaps its very presence accounting for my survival. Not only had she been in my room, but apparently, she had laid beside me during the night.

I turned on the cold water and splashed my face. Maybe a dream? I looked back to the nightstand—no such luck. With the windows and door remaining locked, apparently Angelique could come and go as she pleased. Obviously, Daniel had omitted a few details I deemed critical for survival. If we were to live long enough to purge New Orleans of its unwanted residents, Daniel would have to come clean.

Even though I only slept about three hours, I was fully alert with a burning desire to bring this to an end. Contemplating the possibility of Angelique's buddies frequenting the Chamber, birds of a feather so to speak, the theory provoked me to action. I threw my clothes on and grabbed only a few items for the trip. I could hardly tote a bag of stakes through the door, but a few vials of holy water should do the trick. Becoming somewhat obsessed about its presence, I stroked my hand across my shirt to verify my cross remained securely fastened. I grabbed Loretta, not that she would be of any assistance with vampires, but I was in no mood to fuck around with the rest of those derelicts. I pulled the cross out from under my shirt. Traveling through the Quarter, I had no intentions of becoming anyone's late night snack.

I glanced in the mirror one last time, then headed out the door. The four blocks to the Chamber passed like one. It was three thirty-five in the morning and oddly there was no line or doorman. I tucked the crucifix inside my shirt and entered the narrow alleyway. A generous description of my disposition would be agitated and confrontational. I would work swiftly and act with extreme prejudice in dealing with these clowns. I was prepared for a confrontation with the inside bouncer, but by luck of the draw, it was a new guy. I showed my ID and entered without incident. The bar was packed beyond reason. Surely the fire marshal would not approve. Scanning the crowd, I pushed my way through the sea of posers.

With luck, Isabelle and her posse would be in the basement giving me ample opportunity to scope out the top floor without incident. Upstairs, the love lounge—a likely location for a lonely vampire to find a two-hundred-year past-due hookup. Failing to find a vampire worthy of a good staking, I turned my attention to the den of hell and another rendezvous with Isabelle. After my first two visits, vampires or not, the expectation of an unpleasant experience was high.

Worming my way through the multitude, I perused the masses, searching for any of Rob's killers. For the moment, none were nearby. Circling my target, I took a visual inventory of Isabelle's companion.

"Son of a bitch," I hissed. Tenderly stroking Isabelle's hair with seductive intent was another vampire. Her facial features were thin, a well-defined tapered jaw, and lips of Botoxian proportions. Long, thick eyelashes sheltered a pair of beautiful iridescent eyes Her skin, like the others, was flawless. Apparently, altering her appearance from last night, her shoulder-length, sandy-blond hair was now short, cinnamon, and parted to the side, tucked behind one ear. Looking like a fashion model, there was no mistaking her lethal identity.

Enraged, I cut straight through the crowd and up to the table.

Intercepting my approach, a new bodyguard stepped in quickly. I grabbed him by the neck and shoved him down on Isabelle's table. "Tell him to back off, or I swear to God, I will break his fucking neck."

As I squeezed his throat tighter, he gurgled for help.

"I don't take orders from any man," Isabelle snapped back sternly.

"You're next. I am in no mood for games tonight."

A dozen or so people were now watching, awaiting their queen's command. She looked at the bodyguard and then back at me. "You already had your little payback. What else do you want?"

I flashed malevolent eyes. No words were needed.

Waving her subjects away, disagreeably, she ordered loudly, "Leave us."

I released the bodyguard and shoved him away. "Who is your new friend, Isabelle?"

"This is Monique." She placed her arm affectionately around the vampire's shoulder.

Monique looked at me with a gleam of distaste. "We have already met."

"I know." I returned the glare. "I just wanted to know your name—kind of a personal inventory thing." I connected with Isabelle's eyes.

"Isabelle, whatever it is you think you know, believe me, you do not want her as a friend. She is a bonafide flesh-and-blood killer."

My warning brought an end to Monique's seduction. Leaning back with a twisted smile and arms crossed, she listened as I reeled off my warning.

"She will live the life of a killer, always on the run, hunted until the day somebody drives a stake through her coldblooded heart. If this is the life you desire, then you are in the right company. But I do not believe for a minute it is a life you would choose."

Monique's smile was short lived, transforming to an aggravated sneer. "Perhaps, Brian, you should mind your own business before you get hurt."

Isabelle intervened, attempting to defuse the aggression. "Brian, I am fully capable of choosing my friends, but I appreciate your concern."

"I'm growing weary of your disobedience," Monique interrupted. "Leave now, Brian, or so help me, I will forsake Angelique's bidding and deal with you personally." In an effort to intimidate, Monique flashed her fangs. With my attention directed to the evil before me, three of Isabelle's followers grabbed my arms and attempted to subdue me. Without discrimination, I put all three on the deck with forceful head shots. The one-sided melee instantly attracted additional mutants, all closing in on my position.

Showtime! Brandishing Loretta, I made damn sure everyone knew I was wielding a gun. The growing mob immediately began to scatter and flee amidst the screams and cries of, "He's got a gun!" More screams, then the music stopped. I moved to the wall to cover my back. "Hey, who wants to play a game called 'are you immortal?'" I yelled, fanning the gun in the crowd's direction. Panic ensued, the multitude rushed the stairs in a mad dash, screaming, shoving, and trampling their fellow freaks.

I watched with pleasure as the cowards scattered in fear. "Monique, I am not leaving here without you." Time was of the essence, knowing it would be a short matter of minutes before the cops showed up.

"I knew it was a mistake to let you live," she snarled.

"Isabelle, you truly do not want this bitch in your life."

"What is so wrong with her life?" Isabelle had to be completely unaware of the true nature of the beast beside her.

"Because she is dead."

"Brian, this has gone far enough. You really should go now," Isabelle insisted.

"Not convinced? Try this on for size." Without warning, I took aim and fired at Monique. The impact jolted Monique's head back violently against the wall. Blood splattered indiscriminately about.

"Oh my God!" Isabelle screamed. "Brian, what have you done?"

I studied Monique's posture. Her head was contorted and rolled back as if the impact from the bullet had snapped her neck. I did not pause to consider the ramifications of my actions—after all, she killed Rob, and I had sworn my vengeance. Daniel had not covered blowing a vampire's head apart so I was unsure of what to expect next. "Isabelle, you need to leave—now!"

She stared in shock. "Go now! All of you!" I yelled and pointed Loretta at her remaining friends.

As Isabelle began to rise from the table, Monique's hand jumped back to life and grabbed her with unnatural strength. "Isabelle is not going anywhere. She is mine." Monique lifted her disfigured head and peered at me through blood-covered eyes.

Terrified, Isabelle frantically tried to pull away—to no avail. Monique began to recite her deadly incantation.

"Spiritul de întuneric, Te implor. Posedă această ființă indisciplinat."

"No," I screamed, as I covered my ears. The words penetrated my hands, suffocated my thoughts, and corroded my resistance.

"Forja cuvintele mele asupra sufletului lor."

"No," I repeated as my will faded.

"Viața lor să fie a mea, sângele nostru să fie una." Monique chanted, the rage in her voice accentuated with venomous vexation.

The ancient spell once again gripped my consciousness and eroded my strength. With what little resistance remained, I extracted my cross from beneath my shirt and fumbled for the bottle of holy water. With the force of a middle linebacker, Monique shoved the table into the air and out of her path, her eyes smoldering in wrathful fury. She continued the chant. With hardly the will to complete the task, I removed the cap and poured it over my head, then splashed the remaining water in the direction of Isabelle. Already deeply entranced, she did not flinch as the water rained down upon her. As Monique closed in, sharply accentuating the conjuration, a strange phenomenon occurred. I began to murmur the spell as if the words were my own.

Moving behind me, shielding herself from my crucifix, Monique placed her deathly cold hand on my shoulder. She winced in pain as the holy water burned her hand. Infuriated with my interference, she backed away, and in a tirade she randomly grabbed a male and viciously sank her teeth into his neck until he collapsed to the floor. She returned behind me and arrogantly boasted, "His blood is on your hands."

Trapped in some odd subconscious void, I continued to mutter the spell.

"You will suffer a thousand deaths and beg me to end your miserable life, but I will show you no mercy. This is the price you will pay for your insolence. I hope she was worth it." Monique turned and stormed from the room, leaving behind the pestilence and stench of her anger.

Police sirens wailed from above. Monique's departure allowed me to awaken from the trance before the others.

"New Orleans police. Is anybody down there?" a voice called out.

I could have answered, but chose not to. Decisions had to be made, and quickly. Pleasantly surprised, all my faculties had returned. If this was anything like my first encounter under the spell, the others would not be going anywhere for a few more minutes. I quickly moved to the bar and stashed my Beretta behind the ice cooler, wedging her amongst the wires and beverage lines. I considered returning to my previous position and playing catatonic like the others, but too many people witnessed me pull the trigger. It would not be worth the effort to play the victim. I grabbed a beer from the fridge, popped the top, and drank it halfway down. I went back over to the booth, sat next to Isabelle, and put my arm around her. The cops were inching down the stairs.

"O'Reilly called, said to wait for him," a voice reported from the top of the stairs to the cops nearing the basement.

"Everything is cool, guys," I called out. "Come on down. I am unarmed."

"We're coming in. Place your hands on your head where we can see them," a voice demanded.

"Hey, I have my hands on a beer, and I am not letting go. Not after all of this shit."

The first cop poked his head around the corner.

"I am over here," I called out.

The first cop, followed by a second and then a third, arrived with their guns drawn, aimed in my direction. "I told you I am unarmed, and these guys, well they are not going anywhere soon." Not lowering their weapons, they moved, tentatively, to the first vertical victim and studied him curiously. "What's wrong with him?" an overweight cop asked.

"Him? You mean all of them, except for the dead guy on the floor." I pointed out the stiff. "They are under some kind of hypnotic spell, except for the dead guy. I honestly believe none of them have a clue what in the hell is going on right now."

Just about the time tensions eased, a distinctly agitated voice came rambling down the stairs. "Yeah, I'll show you who he is. That asshole has been coming around for a couple of nights making trouble."

I should have known Butch was returning for revenge, cowering behind a badge. I loathe cowards. "That's him, right over there, drinking a damn beer. Motherfucker." O'Reilly, attempting to restrain Butch, pulled him by the shirt to no avail. "We all seen him shoot that girl."

With O'Reilly in tow, he waded past two of the victims, oblivious to their condition, and stepped over the corpse just to get in my face. "They got your punk ass now, bitch. Ain't so bad now, are you?"

Without warning, I rose and nailed Butch with an unmerciful blow to the forehead. The cops all jumped to attention before he hit the floor. "Easy guys. I am done." I raised my hands in surrender. The detective who attempted to slow Butch's progress was still clutching the oversized oaf's shirt as he stared at me, mouth agape. Then another cop, "Heavy Duty," drew his sidearm.

"Why isn't this man in handcuffs?" O'Reilly steamed. "And what the hell is going on with these people?"

I ignored the detective's inquisition. "You know, a simple 'that's him' would have sufficed." Amused by my actions, the older cop began to reach for his cuffs.

I directed my conversation to O'Reilly, who we had been waiting for. "If you want me to cooperate, you had better forget about the cuffs."

O'Reilly studied the marbelized victims as he contemplated my offer.

"They will be fine in a few more minutes. What is your name, detective?"

"O'Reilly, Detective O'Reilly."

"Well, O'Reilly, how about getting one of your guys to grab a couple of fresh beers, and I will tell you exactly what transpired. It will save you hours of uncooperative bullshit at the precinct."

He continued to process the crime scene. "What are you waiting for, Rogers? You heard the man, grab him a beer." He stepped over Butch and pulled a chair up in front of Isabelle and myself. O'Reilly scanned the name badge of the younger cop. "Dawson, get this guy out of here," he said, referring to Butch.

He looked back at Isabelle's friends, then the dead guy sprawled on the floor. "Nice work. Want to tell me about them first?" He gestured toward the spellbound victims.

"Hypnotized. But at least they are better off than the guy on the floor. He is just dead. Now Isabelle here, what little I do know, I suspect you probably already know."

"Okay, let's start with something a little more basic. What is your name?"

I reached in my jacket. Cops, just being cops, reached for their weapons. "Relax guys. Don't be so cliché. It's just my wallet."

O'Reilly did not seem to share my sense of humor—at least not at the moment.

"My name is Brian." I tossed him my ID. "You got a name other than O'Reilly?"

"Yeah, it's Mitch." Scrutinizing my ID, he tossed it back.

"Do you have any ID, Mitch?"

"No," he said tersely, but with a smirk. "I don't."

"So tell me, Brian, unless you want to put the bracelets on, what's the story here? What am I looking at."

"Well, Mitch, why don't you have these guys sit at the bar while we talk."

"Guys, go have a drink," O'Reilly ordered.

I waited until they were out of earshot. "Up front, I consider myself a relatively sane guy, but what I am about to tell you is going to sound like utter lunacy. Without going into petty details, that's blood, skull, and brain matter all over the wall, table, and chair." I pointed to where Monique had been sitting.

"It sure looks to be so," O'Reilly agreed.

"The woman that was sitting here, her name is Monique. Here is where it gets kind of crazy. She is an honest-to-God real-life vampire. Now, I know the difference between reality and the idiots that frequent this place. To prove my point to the morons, I put a bullet in Monique's skull, right here." I pointed to the center of my forehead. "It kind of pissed her off."

"I can see where it might do that," O'Reilly agreed.

"Isabelle, who you know, and these five other idiots ... well, Monique used some type of hypnosis on them, which is why they are not moving. Then she killed the guy on the floor. The bite marks in his neck and blood loss will confirm COD. I am pretty confident you have already seen this type of murder. With a belly full of blood, bullet hole in her head, Monique bolted out of the place. Then you guys showed up."

"Wow, that's quite the nutshell. Problem is, Brian, I kind of like the story of the nut, not just the shell, so if you don't mind I have a few more questions."

"Fire away, Mitch."

"First, where's your gun? It would make me feel so much better if I could hold on to it."

"You're going to have to get that from Monique. She took it."

"Why aren't you in a trance? How is it you shot her, and then what? Just handed her your gun?"

"I shot her before she could do her spell thing. I am not entirely sure why I came out of it first. I just did." I glanced at Isabelle. The expression on her face was softening from the horror-induced panic of Monique's resurrection. "Looks like they are waking up, except of course for the dead guy."

"Hey, guys, seeing as how you're not too busy, how about start looking around for a gun," O'Reilly instructed the cops at the bar. "Sorry, Brian, if I seem skeptical. I just have a hard time believing a vampire would have any desire to keep your gun." O'Reilly's face contorted, a quirky expression displayed his doubt. "So you shot her. It appears you hit her, but nobody upstairs mentioned a dead woman covered in blood running out the door. So I gotta ask, where's her body?"

"You ought to know how these vampire tales go, stake in the heart, chop off their head, that kind of stuff. I will bet you have never heard of anyone claiming to kill a vampire with a gun. It's like I told you—I just wanted to prove a point, and I did. She survived, then waltzed right out the door unseen."

"Why do you think after you shot her, which would piss anybody off, and she put you under her spell, didn't she kill you instead of that guy?" O'Reilly thumbed in the direction of the corpse.

I pulled my cross up and dangled it in front of him. I pointed to the empty water bottle on the floor. "Holy water. I only had enough for myself and Isabelle."

"Got a gun," one of the cops called out.

"Bring it here," O'Reilly ordered with a broad smile of satisfaction as the officer made his way across the bar. "Are you ready to amend any part of your statement, Brian?" Triumphantly postulating he had cracked my disclosure, he sat erect and held his hand out to receive the evidence.

I glanced at the unfamiliar weapon. "Nope, but I can save you some work. If you check the embedded slug in the wall, it clearly does not come close to matching the caliber of that gun. That little peashooter would not penetrate a roll of paper towels."

"Brian, you sound like you might know a thing or two about police work."

"In today's world, it pays to know a little bit about everything." I knew what he wanted, but chose to remain vaguely obstinate.

"Brian, I'm afraid I've got some bad news for you. Even though we don't have ... what did you say her name was ... Monique?"

I nodded in confirmation.

"Monique's body. Even without her body, the evidence confirms a crime has been committed, which by the way, you confessed to. I do have a dead guy on the floor, which is another whole can of worms. I've got a bar full of witnesses, and these people down here, if they ever wake up." O'Reilly looked at the woeful assortment and shook his head. "These fine officers are going to escort you for processing.

I've got a lot more questions, but that will have to wait until we've processed the crime scene, and of course, find Monique's body."

"Mitch," I said firmly, "I have a deal for you. Have them take me to a holding cell. Lord knows I need a little rest. But let's agree to postpone the processing. We will talk more when you get back to the station. I promise, there are some twisted details that nobody here will be able to fill in except me. Deal?"

O'Reilly deliberated my proposal while staring at Monique's bloody fragments.

"Process me, and my lawyer will have me out on bail before you return to the precinct. Work with me and who knows, we might even go out later and share a few laughs over a beer or two."

"Somehow, I kind of doubt it." O'Reilly motioned the two cops to take me away. "Keep a tight eye on him. I wouldn't put it past him to walk away if the opportunity presents itself."

"Hey, Mitch, try not to be too long. I have a very busy day today. Got a vampire to catch. And by the way, my gun's behind the ice chest."

Glaring at me, O'Reilly suddenly changed demeanor and winked, then instantly returned to his best evil-eye scowl.

Minutes later, as I peered through a crack in the front door, I saw reporters and camera crews hastily preparing the story for the morning news.

"Wait, guys." I planted my feet like an anchor and turned my back to the gate. "I can't be seen like this. You need to do one of two things. Preferably, uncuff me and we can walk out to the car like three cops, or take my jacket and cover my head. Vampires, the CIA, and all of the people I have pissed off over the years might see me and most likely not wait in line for a piece of my ass. I will promise you, if my face is on the morning news, in less than twenty-four hours a world of shit will rain down on New Orleans like you have never seen."

Rogers and Howard looked blankly at each other. "No way I am uncuffing him," Howard said.

Heavy Duty said nothing, but chose to stare at the rookie in a disgusted manner.

"Guys! Do you see the blood on my shirt?"

"Yeah," Howard replied.

"I'm telling you right now, I put a bullet point-blank into a woman's skull. The back of her head exploded all over the wall. You want to know where she went?" I pointed beyond the door. "She and six of her friends are out there, somewhere." The boys continued their facial tango of indecision.

"Think about it. There's a dead guy down there with bite marks, missing enough blood to guarantee he will not be at work next week."

Rogers reached for the keys and uncuffed me. "After the shit I've seen the last two nights, you are the least of my worries."

"You have no clue how right you are, my friend." I straightened my jacket and shirt, preparing for the onslaught of reporters. "Rogers, when they start asking questions, tell them O'Reilly will be out momentarily with a statement. While they are focused on you, Howard and I will head to the car."

With the sickly scent of the undead hanging heavily in the air, we reached the cruiser and climbed in. As we made our way back to the precinct, I began to postulate my next series of steps. Once inside the holding cell, I blew out a long, exaggerated sigh.

I saw the cot and was grateful for the opportunity to rest and the fact that I was still alive.

Several hours later, a familiar voice called out, "Get up, Brian. You've got some explaining to do."

I opened my eyes to see O'Reilly staring at me from inside the cell. "What time is it?"

"Seven o'clock. Are you hungry?"

"I could eat."

"Good. Get used to being hungry. Until I get some straight answers there will be no food or drinks. Let's start with your real name."

"Ouch." I sat up and looked at O'Reilly, who appeared exhausted. "Long night? You seem a little crabby."

"Just answer the question."

"Sorry, that is one question I can't answer. Next question."

"Okay, let's get one thing straight, right now. We are not in the club anymore. You are in my house, and in my house we play by my rules. Got it?"

"Mitch, I don't mind playing by your rules, but I am going to tell you straight up, there are some questions you are not going to get the answers to. My name is one of them. And in case you are thinking of printing me, I promise, it will be a waste of time."

O'Reilly studied my face for any hint of a bluff. "Okay, I've got at least twenty-four people that will swear they saw you cap Monique in the club. I have your gun, the slug, and your confession. I've got blood, bones, and brains all over that back wall. The only thing I don't have is a body. But we will disassemble that club wall by wall until we find her." O'Reilly sat back and awaited some response, but none arrived.

"Let's cut the crap. I know you claim Monique just walked away. Problem is, Brian, I don't believe in ghost stories or vampires. Let's not waste time with any more of that bullshit. I've got three dead people all missing more than eighty percent of their blood, and I'm damn sure you are connected somehow."

"Let me ask you something, Mitch."

O'Reilly's eyebrow furrowed, incensed by my complete disregard for his interrogation techniques. "By all means, ask away."

"How many beliefs do you suppose humans have held to be impossible throughout the course of history? What would a caveman have said about computers, planes, or brain surgery?"

O'Reilly cocked his head oddly, as if the logic of my argument had burdened the load on his neck.

"Before I came to New Orleans, I was like you. Believe in vampires? That is just absolute lunacy. I allowed my doubts to interfere with my responsibility. I can't share the graphic details, but my lack of foresight is directly responsible for what transpired at the Chamber. And make no mistake, Mitch, if you fail to believe me, your skepticism will lead to the death of many more innocent people."

O'Reilly snapped his head back and his eyes popped open wide. "Brian, I wish I could believe you. Really I do. But I've been dealing with these whack jobs for years. I know they routinely drug outsiders like you. I know Isabelle drugged you a few nights ago. You might still be suffering from hallucinogenic fantasies, or maybe you are just looking for payback. Who knows? But I promise you, vampires do not exist."

O'Reilly stood up, signaling the interview had concluded. "What I do know is you shot and killed a woman—Monique—tonight. So here's what's going to happen. I'm going to grab some breakfast and give you a little more time to think about your statement. Later, I'll come back and formally arrest you. Then we'll go through the entire booking procedure. Eventually I will go home and get some sleep. When I come back in tonight, we will talk some more and see if we can't straighten out some of your confusion. How does that sound?"

"Hey, Mitch." Ignoring his plans, I needed to stall his departure. "Did you like my gun?"

He looked puzzled. "Yeah, it's a nice piece."

"Do you have it somewhere safe?"

"Yes, it's locked in my desk. But you don't need to worry yourself about it. It's going to be quite some time before you will need that gun again. Guard!" O'Reilly called out.

A guard appeared at the interrogation room door and unlocked it. "Hey, Mitch, have you got a card on you with your number? You know, just in case I remember any details I might have overlooked."

"Just tell one of these guys. They'll know how to reach me."

"Humor me, Mitch, I collect business cards."

Continually amused by my oddities, O'Reilly backed away thinking I might seize the opportunity to draw him near, subdue him, and attempt an escape. He reached out with his left hand and set a card on the table, his right hand on his gun. "In case you need to call." He was indeed insightful, as that was precisely my intended course of action.

As I weighed my few remaining options, a subconscious instinctive course of action seized control. "Spiritul de întuneric, Te implor. Posedă această ființă indisciplinat." The words of Angelique and Monique rolled off my lips in fluent Romanian. "Forja cuvintele mele asupra sufletului lor." The words came softly in the beginning, O'Reilly moving closer, attempting to decipher the unfamiliar tongue. I repeated the phrases louder, now clearly audible and distinct to O'Reilly and the guard. First O'Reilly, followed by the guard, became catatonic, frozen motionless in their shadows. Astounded by my accomplishment, I was clueless to the meaning, the mechanics, or how I recited the phrases without flaw. I rose from the table, continuing the dialogue, and made my way out of the cell. I picked up Mitch's card and relieved him of his keys as he stood helpless.

I headed down the hall, my words echoing ahead of my arrival. Every cop and bystander became paralyzed, immobilized by the ancient words I chanted. I looked around until I located Mitch's desk. Unlocking the drawer, I was delighted to find Loretta resting securely in an evidence bag. Removing my trusted friend, I kissed her on the barrel and headed toward the exit, continuing to chant with every step of my flight from justice.

Outside the precinct I was alone, free again to continue the hunt. And hunt I would. My arsenal of weapons had improved twofold. Yet I had to wonder how I came to recognize a scent so previously faint I barely sensed its existence, and how, in merely a night, I unconsciously developed the ability to use their incantation. Should it matter? Maybe. But it was sunrise and I was free. Free to resume, then complete my task, collect Sam, and get the hell out of this God-forsaken city, before I, too, became a part of the legend.

CHAPTER 24

OUT IN THE morning air, I gained an appreciation for the radiance of the sun, warming my frostbitten body, courtesy of the precinct's turbo polar AC unit. Moving like a man on a mission, I traveled as expeditiously as possible, knowing Mitch and the boys were going to be some pissed off hombres when they awoke.

Back in the safety of my hotel room, knowing Chuck and Jimmy would already be hard on the hunt, I scanned the list of remaining cemeteries. Saint Louis Number Two appeared to be my next logical choice. Checking in with Phillip, I asked him to pick up a fresh supply of holy water and inquired about the girls. Thankfully, they had stayed indoors watching movies all night. Indicating Sam's demeanor, Phillip suggested a call might improve her disposition. I flipped my phone on and punched in her number. The phone rang twice before she picked up. "Hi, Sam."

There was an awkward silence before she replied. "I was worried when you did not call. Some boys were found murdered not far from your hotel, and I just didn't know if—"

"I'm sorry. Things got complicated. It was impossible to call."

"Those dead boys ... are you involved?"

Dammit, I mouthed silently, annoyed with my predicament. "No." This was truth from a twisted perspective, but truth nevertheless. "I have to run. I just wanted to let you know I am alright, and in a day or two, this will be over."

"I love you."

Her reply was solemn. She deserved a better man. I would strive to be that guy. "Just give me these next few days, and I'll show you just how much I love you."

I knew the New Orleans police would be after me as soon as they thawed from the vamp hex. I grabbed my emergency kit and headed to the shower. Forty-five minutes later, I inspected the finished results—newly dyed blond hair, cut and spiked, sideburns gone, and my eyes were a lovely shade of green, thanks to opaque contact lenses. I swapped driver's license and credit cards to match my new look, complete with new name. Brian Denman was officially deceased. Hello, Carlisle Dietrick. I grabbed an Affliction T-shirt, a shredded pair of True Religion denims, and a worn pair of boots. I picked an oversized pair of Chrome Hearts shades and inspected the finished product. "Rock star," I said aloud. Completely satisfied with my craftsmanship, I headed out the door, prepared for another round of search and destroy.

Standing at the gate of Saint Louis Number Two, much larger than its previous namesake, I was relieved by the lack of tourists. Nestled firmly in the projects, the isolation of this cemetery demanded an extra layer of vigilance. The few souls wandering this graveyard were not of a sociable nature. If only they knew what rested amidst the tombs, certainly they would leave this city of the dead. I closed my eyes and inhaled deeply through my nose. The pungency of death thickened as I waded deeper into the cemetery. Somehow, Angelique had found a method to conceal the offensive fragrance of rotting flesh emanating from her walking-dead sisters. I followed it to a tomb, barely discernibly disturbed. Although there were many tombs, none were as vast. A rusty, unfastened lock hung from the iron door of the all-brick tomb. I circled the structure, inspecting its details. A small crescent window on the back was the only portal, but it had been covered from the inside with a plank. Somebody had taken strides to camouflage a trespass.

I removed the lock and lifted the iron gate, opening it ever so slowly, barely making a sound. A tattered plank door behind the gate creaked as I pushed it gently open. Unfortunately, the sun glared blindingly from the rear, delaying my acclimation to the darkness.

Within seconds, I could make out a crudely built wooden box pressed up against the boards, blocking the rear window. A trail on the dusty floor indicated the casket had recently been dragged in. The vamp surely knew by now that they were hunted. If she were awake, and waiting, game over.

I could call Chuck, but I did not want to pull him off his mission, or involve Phillip, who was busy protecting Sam and Dee. With no sign of Daniel, there really was only one logical choice. I stepped out of the tomb, pulled the wooden door closed, and walked a safe distance. I pulled the card from my pocket and dialed.

"Hello." A gruff voice on the other end announced an ill-tempered man.

"Mitch, you sound pissed."

"Brian? You're damn right I'm pissed. And when I find you, you're gonna know up-close and personal what pissed feels like. I got my ass chewed up one side and down the other."

"Don't be mad, Mitch. There was nothing you could have done to stop me." Silence never sounded so intimidating. "Tell you what. I am about to give you the opportunity to either believe me or arrest me. Does that sound like a fair deal?"

"I'll settle for the arrest part. Does that work for you?"

"Well ... I hope not, but here is the deal. If you follow my instructions, I will go quietly after we are done. But you must follow them explicitly. Okay?"

"Within reason. What do you want?"

"I need you to bring me a mirror, something in a medium size. Come to the Saint Louis Number Two. Play by my rules and then we can play by yours. Deal?"

"I'll be there in thirty minutes. How do I find you?"

"Don't worry, I will find you. And by the way, if you bring any backup, this will be the last conversation we ever have."

"Yeah, yeah, yeah. Just be there," he snapped and hung up.

I hurried out of the cemetery, crossed the deserted street, and headed into the projects. There were several boarded-up vacancies facing the cemetery. Not wasting a second, I broke into the first one with an advantageous view. I peered out the crack in the door, awaiting Mitch's arrival.

The thirty minutes dragged on excruciatingly. Occasionally, I checked out the boarded-up rear windows, not fully trusting Mitch to uphold his end of the bargain. With no suspicious activity thus far, it appeared as if Mitch would be flying solo. The late morning air had grown dense, a lingering haze hanging on, a vampire needing to die. Tick-tock.

In the distance, I finally heard the soft thud of a car door. I quickly returned to the front of the dilapidated apartment. Cracking the door to get a better view, I spotted Mitch standing at the center of the cemetery archway, holding a framed mirror. He appeared anxious and irritated, unlike his demeanor of last night when he was smooth as a twenty-year-old single malt. He immediately detected the motion of the apartment door. "It's showtime," I said, exiting the apartment and walking directly toward him. As I drew nearer, his eyes darted around anxiously as he reached for his gun. "Relax, Mitch, everything is cool. Glad to see you got the mirror."

Mitch looked bewildered. The voice he recognized, but that was the extent of it. "Brian? Obviously you've got skills we took for granted last night." His stern expression eased off a notch. "Don't count on that happening again."

"As long as you do not assume I will go down that easily again."

"Yeah, last night," Mitch shook his head disapprovingly. "Blond is not your color. And any guy with half a brain would be three states out of Dodge by now."

"In a few minutes, you will understand why I'm still here," I retorted. "Come on. Time is a luxury we cannot waste."

I turned my back without responding and headed into the cemetery. "We had better hurry up and get this over with," I spoke over my shoulder, not wanting to stop. Walking at a brisk pace in silence, we stopped about twenty yards short of the crypt. "Here it is," I said quietly.

"What?"

"Shhh. This is one of those defining moments in life; things you believed, whoosh," I flung my arm, "right out the window. You will no longer walk the streets of doubt, as I once did. Do not say another word, and you must do as I say." Mitch rolled his eyes and snapped a salute.

I slowly entered the crypt, Mitch in tow, pointing to the casket. Mitch shook his head in disgusted amusement. I gently pushed him back toward the door. "Inside that casket should be a sleeping vampire," I whispered. I reached into my sack and pulled out a stake and mallet. "This is where you need to do it." I placed the stake and mallet in his hand and guided the tip to my chest, indicating the precise target. "Right here. I will open the casket and then you must drive the stake deep into her heart without hesitation. Failure to completely pierce her heart will not be a good thing for either of us."

"Why me and not you? After all, aren't you the vampire hunter?" he whispered.

"I have done this before. Should something happen to me, there will be nobody to teach you. You have to make your first kill now. There are still six more remaining, somewhere out there. And Mitch, just so we are crystal clear, if you hesitate and she wakes up, all hell will break loose. As a last resort, grab the mirror and reflect the sunlight on her."

"Why not do that now?"

"If we shine the light in now, the minute that lid comes off she will be like a Tasmanian devil. With a little luck, I can get the lid off in the darkness without waking her."

Mitch looked at the stake and mallet in his hands. "Brian, I've got to tell you—I have no doubt somebody's in that box. No doubt in my mind whatsoever. But she is no more a real vampire than Isabelle. You might believe it, and 'Sleeping Beauty' over there might as well, but I do not. As such, I don't have time for this nonsense." Mitch's voice elevated.

"Okay then, if that's how you feel, let's do this differently. Why don't you just go in there and wake her up. But I warn you, she is *not* going to be happy. In fact, I would expect her to be downright nasty."

Mitch scoffed and rolled his head back in dismay. "Fine, I'll try to be gentle." Brazenly parading over to the casket, he pointed mockingly. "In here?" His cavalier attitude and decibel level were all the ingredients needed for a major ass-whooping.

I grabbed the mirror and retreated into position, visualizing his imminently rude reality check. I stepped away from the door, ensuring whoever was in the casket would think Mitch was alone. He wiggled the lid lightly to make sure it was loose and then flipped the lid back violently, sending it rattling to the floor. "Get up, darling. This game is over," he said abrasively.

Immediately, her eyes exploded open as she vaulted from the casket, pinning Mitch on the dusty floor. Her lips parted, exposing her razor-sharp fangs.

Shocked by the strength and speed of her assault, Mitch had yet to assimilate the severity of his predicament.

"Oh damn, Mitch, I thought you had things under control! Looks like somebody needs to spend a little more time at the gym," I taunted, deservedly so, as he wallowed in helplessness. Startled by my presence, she cut her eyes at me and hissed like a viper.

"Dammit, get her off of me!" Mitch yelled as he thrashed about.

I ignored his pleas, wanting to study her reaction. Her foreboding sneer alluded to her arrogant newborn confidence as she turned back to a now-frantic victim. Targeting his neck, indifferent to my presence, she inched closer, feasting on the scent of excreted fear.

"That is about enough fun for you two." I angled the mirror to catch the reflection of the sun's burning rays and shined the blistering reflection on the struggling pair. The sunlight caused an instant singeing of her flesh as it illuminated her skin. She howled in agony and retreated to the darkest corner, out of range of the reflected light. The smell of seared flesh filled the tomb. Mitch, completely out of breath, scrambled off the floor.

"Enough of the fucking games, you two," he said in a prepubescent squeal as he jumped to his feet. Reaching for his phone, preparing to call for backup, he rotated visual contact between the two of us.

As he looked back at the cowering vampire, I set the mirror beside me and pulled Loretta. Mitch recognized the distinctive sound of racking back a Beretta, and turned in my direction, ignoring the true danger behind. "I was wondering where that got off to."

"Mitch, this is not a fucking game." She withdrew cautiously from the corner, her flesh still smoldering. With catlike movements, she prowled in O'Reilly's direction.

I flashed reflected sunlight in her direction, pressing her back. "Tell him what you are!"

Through the darkness of the corner, the festering rage in her eyes forewarned an imminent charge. I angled the rays menacingly close.

"My name is Claire De Garr. I am a vampire."

"Yeah, whatever," Mitch scoffed.

"Damn, Mitch, still not a believer? Give me your gun."

"Are you out of your mind? No way."

"It is not a request, Mitch. I already pulled the trigger last night. You have three choices: I can kill you, she can kill you," I yelled, interlacing a theatrical dose of hysteria, "or you can give me your damn gun right this fucking minute." I trained Loretta at his head. "You know my gun is real."

"I hope you know when this little game is over you're going to beg me to take you into the precinct. You are so fucked now, my friend." Begrudgingly, he un-holstered his gun, stepped in my direction, and set it on the ground.

"It is loaded, right?"

"Yeah."

"Don't worry, Mitch, I have done this before. Do me a huge favor and take a big step to the left." As he complied, I fired at Claire without warning, striking her forehead dead center. She vaulted back into the wall and fell to the ground.

"Goddammit, you psychotic asshole!" Mitch screamed. He lunged forward, swung the mallet wildly, and struck me in the head, knocking me to the ground. Dazed by the vicious blow, I fought to remain conscious. "Son of a bitch, I can't believe you murdered her right in front of me."

I was not out cold, but was stunned beyond the ability to react. He took both guns as I lay helpless.

Mitch moved to the corner where Claire lay, slumped against the wall. "Dammit, I can't believe I let that shit happen. Shit!" In anger and disgust, he looked at the catastrophic damage to Claire's forehead. He checked for a pulse. Oddly, he thought he felt one. In an instant, Claire's enraged eyes sprang open as she grabbed him by the throat in a stranglehold. Terrified, Mitch struggled, striking Claire once in the chest and then in the face. Her face snapped back from the blow, blood splattering from the gaping wound. Unrelentingly, she tightened her suffocating grip.

"Wait!" Mitch was barely able to vocalize his protest through Claire's constrictive grip. "I didn't shoot you. He did."

With a crazed smile, Claire gazed over my still body. "You are right. I owe you my sincere apology." She loosened her grip around Mitch's neck and rose to her feet. "I am sorry."

O'Reilly gasped for air, free from a grip unlike any he had experienced. Having but a split second to contemplate her supernatural strength and the fact she had a gaping bullet hole square in the middle of her head, Claire yanked Mitch up by the arms. She spun him around, raised him high off the floor, and pinned him to the wall. "You should have heeded your friend's advice, monsieur."

There was no cop training O'Reilly had received that taught how to deal with this situation. The dire consequences glared angrily before his eyes.

"Foolish man. I told you what I am, as did he. As such, you know what fate awaits you."

O'Reilly fought with all of the adrenalized strength he could muster, but he was no match for Claire's unnatural strength. "It will be easier if you do not resist as you pass into eternal darkness. But fear not, your blood will live on, nourishing me, keeping me strong. For that I am eternally grateful."

As Claire parted her rosy lips, Mitch stared in terror at her glistening fangs. Fighting for his life, he headbutted Claire, the blow knocking O'Reilly senseless. She laughed at his feeble attempts. "Heed my words, simple man, let your life pass willingly into mine."

O'Reilly's struggle had ended as his body went limp; he prepared to draw his final breath. Claire rolled her head to the side, Mitch's jugular pulsating as if answering to its master's call. Mitch rolled his eyes upward to the heavens as the wetness of Claire's teeth brushed his flesh. Imagining the excruciating pain of her penetration, an abrupt violent thrust shoved Claire against him, driving them both harshly into the wall. Claire snapped her head back in agony, screaming out all of the evil she possessed. O'Reilly, saturated from the blood of the beast, shoved her away.

I drove the stake deeply into her heart from behind, piercing her lifeline and releasing the evil which had been trapped for centuries. Releasing Mitch, she fell backwards into me. I drove the sharp wooden stake deeper as I felt her strength waning.

I thrusted and twisted the stake until it protruded from the front of her chest. She collapsed into my arms. I cradled her body and whispered into her ears, "Claire De Garr, your time has ended. I have delivered you from the endless life of the undead. Leave now and find true peace, bitch." I allowed her limp body to slump to the floor.

I stood before Mitch, covered in blood with an untamed, ferocious expression. Mitch was at a complete loss for words, his jaw hanging near dislocation. "You know, Mitch, for a minute I considered allowing her to have you. My head is bleeding for God's sake." O'Reilly remained speechless. "A simple 'thank you' will suffice."

He remained silent and paralyzed by fear. "Dammit , would you look at this?" I said, inspecting my blood-soaked clothes. "You know, that is one thing that sucks about this vampire business—I have found it virtually impossible to kill one without ruining a perfectly good set of clothes."

As Mitch began to regain his composure, I collected the guns, putting Mitch's back in his holster and Loretta in mine.

"You weren't bullshitting," Mitch said in a muted, stoic voice.

"And thanks to me, you are not one of the damned ... just yet."

"I've got to call this in." Mitch fumbled for his phone, which was nowhere to be found.

"I have already thought about calling in the troops, but follow my logic for a minute. Once the word gets out we have vampires down here, what do you think will happen? You will have hundreds of crazed vampire hunters, probably killing all those idiots down at the Chamber and a media circus to boot. The whole town will blow up into one big stinky mess. On top of that, the real vampires will probably haul ass."

O'Reilly deliberated briefly. "What would you suggest?"

"The same thing I have been doing for two days. Kill them one at a time. With your assistance, I should be able to get to the remaining six much faster."

Mitch looked at the gruesome flesh heap which was Claire. "You should just let us handle this," Mitch said, implying the New Orleans PD.

"Well, for starters, do you honestly believe you can capture and detain a vampire when you could not even detain me? And even if you could, do you seriously expect to put two hundred-year-old vamps on trial?"

"Yeah, speaking of detaining, how did you—"

"I wish I knew. But it worked for Monique, and it worked for me too."

"Are you sure it's not because you are one of them?"

I glared at him as I gathered the rest of my belongings. "If I was one of them, you would be dead and Miss Claire and I would be rocking the casket over there in a post-feast love fest."

Mitch considered the scenario. "She was rather attractive, I guess. I wouldn't blame you." Needing the sanity break of a laugh, we both chuckled at Claire's expense. "So assuming I agree with you, where do we go from here?"

"You get to stay here and do something with this mess. I am going back to my hotel and clean up. After you get done, I suggest you do the same. I will call you after lunch."

O'Reilly nodded in affirmation. I scooped up my mallet from the floor and replaced it in the duffel bag. Grateful to survive a hard-fought battle, I headed toward the door.

"Hey, Brian, I'm sorry I whacked you on the head," Mitch called out.

Without turning, I raised my hand and waved. "Apology accepted."

"Hey, Brian," he called a little louder as I disappeared from sight. "Thanks for not letting her kill me."

"Don't worry about it, Mitch." I stuck my head back in the door. "Just another day at the office, eh?" It hurt to smile, but I did so anyway. "Do me a favor before we meet later."

"What's that?"

"Get yourself a crucifix and ... change your pants. I think you crapped them, dude."

Alone in the room, O'Reilly sniffed the air, "Damn, I think I did," he confessed. "Things could be worse," he quipped as he nudged Claire's lifeless body with his foot. "I could look like you. Hope it was good for you too, sweetheart."

CHAPTER 25

PACING THE LENGTH of the cemetery, having forgotten to change my shirt, I ducked behind a tomb and quickly stripped. Damn if that would not have raised a few eyeballs, even in New Orleans. Once changed, I headed for the exit, calling Chuck in route.

"What is the word?"

"One less night crawler," Chuck reported. "And let me tell you one thing buddy—if this wasn't personal, you'd be getting one hell of an extermination bill."

"Yeah, I got that. I will see if the boss will come up with some overtime compensation for all of the pest control."

"Don't worry about it. Like I said, it's fucking personal." Chuck's voice aired an unusually humorless hostility. And though he would never confess it, the fatigue was evident.

"How are your supplies holding out?"

"We are good to go for the rest of the day."

"Good. If nothing has changed, it looks like five down, five to go. I will check in later." I stood at the gate of the cemetery for a moment and tried to shake off the heat and exhaustion. The weight of the long course and gruesome task of the past forty-eight hours had literally sucked the life out of me as well. Revenge is a soulless quest, and I was taking no pleasure in the pursuit of avenging Rob's death. It felt as though every encounter with these women forced me down another rung of a ladder, deeper into a lifeless pool of despair. Without thought, I slumped down on the dirty curbside, put my head in my hands, and stared down at my blood-soaked shoes.

Even with half of my goal achieved, I felt defeated, lost in the ironies of the situation. Even with the best possible scenario, this place, these vampires, would haunt me forever. My shoes were an appropriate reflection of this entire fiasco. I took my phone out and called Sam.

"What's wrong?" She knew something was dreadfully out of sorts from the tone of my voice.

"It's nothing. I guess the heat and the long hours are catching up with me." In this instance a lie sure beat the hell out of the truth, but the pieces were adding up to a precarious weight.

"Brian, I wish I could believe you. I think it's more complicated. This thing between us, although you might not want to admit it, I think it's got you trapped in a corner with nowhere to run."

"Stop, Sam," I said wearily. "It is nothing like that. It is nothing like you could ever imagine in your most twisted dreams. I just need a little more time."

There was no answer on the other end. "Sam, are you there?"

"Yes," she replied softly. "You sound exhausted. Instead of meeting us for lunch, why don't you get some sleep. When this job is over, we can decide where we go from here. Okay?"

"I know where I want to be." Disappointed, but relieved, I knew it was for the best. "Do me a favor. Let Phillip know I will catch up with him later."

"I'll tell Phil."

During a prolonged silence, I postulated on her thoughts.

"I want you to know, this has been the best week of my life. And for that, I thank you."

Unintentionally, Sam's words gutted my soul. This was in no way what I had envisioned for us. The pain swelled like a wave, and I wiped away a small trail of sweat that trickled from the corner of my eye. Now it was me who was speechless.

"Brian, tell me what's going on with you," Sam begged.

"I have to go. I will talk with you soon." I hung up, wanting to
smash my phone onto the sidewalk. I pressed my hands forcefully
against the blistering concrete, sighed deeply, and pushed myself up
off the curb.

Once back at the safe house, I burned everything stained with
blood then washed up in the sink. I resupplied my backpack, studied the maps of the remaining cemeteries, and checked my watch.
My instincts were guiding me in the direction of Saint Vincent's. I
reached into the fridge for an apple and a beer, then sat on the tattered sofa, a surviving refugee from the previous tenants. The cold
beer soothed my parched throat. In the course of the day, I had not
taken the opportunity to hydrate. In a matter of minutes, I passed
out, Mitch's blow to my head finally taking its toll.

Startled awake by ringing, I fumbled for my phone, struggling
to see in the dimly lit room. Shadows played on the streets as the
sunlight departed from view.

"Brian, where the fuck are you?" Chuck's voice was adrenalized, more so than I ever remembered throughout the course of our
friendship.

"The office."

"Jimmy and I have been compromised. We found two of them
together. But it was late, and the sun was going down. They woke up.
Holy shit, they're some crazy bitches! We had to use the crosses and
the holy water. Damn, it was like fighting some kind of rabid animal.
Jimmy finally doused them with the water, but I don't know man. I
think they might be on our ass. We don't see them anywhere, but it
sure feels like someone is tracking us."

"How close are you to Jackson Square?"

"About three blocks."

"Get to the Saint Louis Cathedral. If the door is locked, bust it
down, do whatever you need to do to get in. Stay on crowded streets.
I do not think they will attack in public. Once you are inside the
church, stay there."

I tossed my phone down and rubbed the residual lump on my
head. A beer sounded like the perfect solution for the aching noggin.
Night had fallen, which would make any hunt virtually impossible
and ill-advised. Their strength, speed, and ability to control the
mortal mind were unmatched, but I knew I could not remain idle

until dawn. Sleep was not an option, knowing any blood shed tonight would be on my hands. Reflecting back on last night, I botched the perfect opportunity to remove Monique from the equation. I should have staked her during that five-second window between the shot and her recovery. I may not get another chance.

The nap had partially restored my focus. The situation was unraveling, so I called Phillip for help and to check on Sam. "What's up, Brian?" Phillip answered, the tone of his voice revealing an elevated level of stress.

"Is Sam nearby?"

"Not at the minute. I gather things are a little edgy between you two."

"You think? This situation ... I never imagined things could go so far south. Guess it is starting to wear on us all."

"I'm sorry I ever got you involved. I have looked at that video over a dozen times. I can't believe this shit is really happening. I should have listened to you from the get-go."

"Hey, what is done is done."

"Look, Brian, if there's anything I can do to make this right, let me know—manpower, money, whatever, just ask."

A trained crew of a dozen guys could cover all the cemeteries and half the vacant houses in a day. But one extra person might be one additional mouth I could not afford. "I appreciate the offer, but I'm good for now. Look, when I talked with Sam earlier in the afternoon, it did not end well. How is she holding up?"

"I could tell something was wrong, but she's not saying. She's been uncharacteristically quiet since you two parted."

Uncharacteristically quiet, I could live with that—things could have been much worse. "What is she doing now?"

"She and Dee are in the bathroom."

There was a hitch to Phillip's reply, which historically indicates something amiss. "The bathroom? Together? Where are you?"

"Dee and Sam insisted we go out. I tried everything short of telling them the truth, but there was no stopping them. It came down to either I go with them, or they were going without me."

If only I had a handful of shit and a fan. "Dammit, Phillip, you should have hogtied, drugged ,or even duct taped them to the bed. You know what is out here." I slung my beer across the room. The can exploded against the wall.

"Don't think I don't know, Brian. I've spent the past several days going as hard as possible to wear them out. I don't want to be out here anymore than you want us out here, but tonight, they would not take no for an answer."

"Where are you now?" I made no effort to hide my misguided anger.

"Joe's on Bourbon Street."

"Stay there. I'll be there in five minutes. If you hear any young women speaking with a French accent, get the hell out of there. They have the ability to hypnotize."

I hung up my phone, threw on some shoes, and sprinted out the door. Rounding the corner into a moderately crowded Boubon Street, I dodged pedestrians as if they were slalom gates.

Scuttling into Joe's, I spotted Phillip and Dee sitting at a table in the back. I hustled over, pushing the drunks out of my path.

Dee observed my bulldozing approach, her eyes locked in, but like O'Reilly, she did not recognize my altered appearance.

I barged up to the table. "Where's Sam?" My eyes flashed panic.

"Brian?" Stupefied by my appearance, Dee looked to Phillip. "You look like—"

"She left," Phillip interrupted, staring at my new guise. "She told Dee while they were in the bathroom. She was worried and wanted to go see if you were at your hotel."

I cut my eyes to Phillip, who swallowed hard, sensing my anger blanket him. "Phillip!"

"Damn, Brian, Dee just got back to the table when you came charging in. I thought Sam was still in the bathroom."

"Phillip, I can't deal with this, not now. Call your driver, have him pick the two of you up as close to the door as possible and get your asses to the airport. I want all three of you on your plane to New York within the hour. Dee and Sam can stay at my place or a hotel. Do not go back to Dee's. Buy whatever they need in New York. Just get on your jet and get the hell out of New Orleans."

Phillip nodded without a word, but Dee barked back.

"Brian, what in the hell is going on?"

"Phillip, make the calls now," I bluntly ordered. It was time for the Bishop to step in once again. I took Dee by the hand and led her away to an isolated corner. "There are terrorists in town. The threat has been growing steadily every day and now my identity may have been compromised, which is why I look this way. But it also means it is no longer safe for you and Sam. Realistically, it is not safe for anybody to be here now."

"But what about—"

"Please, I just need you, Phillip, and Sam to get the hell out of here. I will find your sister and have an escort bring her to the airport."

"What about you?"

"I have to stay here and deal with this. This is what I do. But I cannot do my job effectively worrying about the three of you. Phillip will see that you get everything you need when you arrive in New York. Can you please do this for me?"

"I will." Dee said. Phillip had just hung up his phone and was walking toward us. "Phillip does not know any of the details. He only knew a big story was about to break, and I knew he would want it. But if he knows the full truth, he will never leave. So please keep our conversation between us for now. Things have gotten far worse than our initial assessments."

Dee nodded as Phillip rejoined us. "It's done. The car is on the way. The plane will be waiting."

I kissed Dee on the cheek and hugged Phillip. "Don't let me down, Phillip."

"Be safe," Phillip pleaded.

I sprinted in the direction of my hotel, dread shadowing my footsteps. At this point, I could only pray Sam was safe. As Daniel had said, I must have faith.

With only three blocks to go, rounding the corner, I spotted Sam. Sprinting harder, I closed on her rapidly as she approached my hotel. Loitering by the entrance were a pair women, two of the remaining five vampires. Apparently, Angelique had become aware of my role in the eradication of her companions and sold me out. I cut over to the shadowed sidewalk and slowed my pace.

"Sam," I called out softly, hoping to catch her attention without alerting the watchful killers. She did not respond, so I ducked into a doorway and called louder: "Sam!"

Recognizing my voice, she turned and searched the street for the source. I peeked out from the shadows and called her name again, hoping the vampires had not been aware of my rapid approach. Sam edged to the shadows, attempting to pair the face with the voice. "Brian?" Initially she walked closer, but as my details became clear she began to back away. "Is that you? What is going on?"

"Long story, but we need to go right now." I took her by the arm and began to lead her back toward Bourbon Street. Unfortunately, we were spotted, and one of the vamps called out from behind.

"Brian?"

I tried to ignore her call, but Sam turned, looking at the two bodacious young women literally dressed to kill.

"You know them?"

Sam looked like she was ready to throw my ass under the train. "Believe me, right now is really a bad time to explain." I tugged harder, attempting to lead her away.

Sam was not budging without an explanation. The other vampire called out as they began to strut with intentions of creating conflict. Vampire or not, all women understood how to ratchet up the jealousy factor.

"Brian? I hardly recognized you. We have been looking all over for you. Where have you been?" Their smiles' singular purpose was to drive a wedge between Sam and myself. "And who is your cute little friend?"

Nail in the coffin, so to speak. They managed to push enough hot buttons to nullify any chance I had to convince Sam a hasty departure was in our best interest.

"No," Sam voiced her objection firmly, stubbornly resisting my attempts to lead her away. "I would like to know where you have been as well."

"Sam, I told you we would talk, and we will. But right now we are in danger. Trust me." My words were hushed, not wanting to be overheard.

"Brian, if you need to leave, then leave. I can handle myself with these two young girls."

At this point, it was too late. I conceded to Sam's obstinacy, fully cognizant how this had to appear.

"Brian, what did you do to your hair?" The one with the black hair spoke first.

Delivering the most ill-tempered look I could conjure, I remained silent.

"You did not tell us you had such a pretty girlfriend. Won't you introduce us?" The wavy-haired brunette gave Sam the once over, then rolled her eyes as to say the compliment was only out of courtesy.

"Monique will be quite surprised. She was most upset after you left last night. We have all been looking for you. Monique wants you back," the black-haired vamp added.

Sam looked at me, Molotov cocktails in her eyes. "Who's Monique?"

Before I could reply, the brunette interrupted, "He didn't tell you? Brian, you are such a bad boy indeed." She harrumphed just to increase the effect. "Monique is his mistress."

Sam jerked her arm from me and took several steps back, tears welling in her eyes.

"Sam, do not believe this bullshit."

"Sam, come with us. You will learn the truth from Monique," Black Hair offered.

"Sam, they are not what you think they are."

Pleased with their efforts, they smiled and flanked Sam on each side.

"Maybe it's you, Brian. Maybe you are not who I thought you were." Sam's voice cracked as she backed away, tears visibly cascading down her cheek.

Wedging herself between Sam and me, the brunette replied, "I promise you, Sam, he is not who you think he is." As she turned toward me, the other took hold of Sam's arm, leaned into her ear, and began to whisper.

Shit! In my haste to get to Phillip and the girls, I had left my backpack and holy water at the safe house. I had to do something, now!

I punched the brunette in the face with a thunderous blow, knocking her to the ground. I pulled my cross from under my shirt and shoved it against the face of the other. Searing her skin, she reeled away in anguish. Having witnessed my assault, two men began to approach. Second Amendment, Loretta style. "Everybody back the fuck off!"

Halting their approach, one implored, "Easy, buddy."

The brunette was rising as I took Sam forcefully by the arm. Appalled by my attack, Sam protested, "Brian, you're hurting me."

I ignored her complaint and yanked her away. "You can hate me later, but right now we are leaving."

The two vampires now stalked while shielding their view of my cross. "Brian, your insolence is intolerable. Monique will be most displeased." Wiping the blood from her mouth, the brunette inspected and licked each digit clean with deep satisfaction. "She will have you."

I continued to pull Sam toward the door of the hotel. Fending off the vampires with my cross, I pushed Sam inside the hotel lobby, handing her O'Reilly's card. "Go to the desk and call this man. Tell him to get here right now!" I shoved her deeper into the lobby. "Do it now!" I yelled.

Sam leapt toward the desk, handing the card to a clerk at the counter. "Please call this man," Sam implored. "Tell him it's an emergency."

Wielding Loretta like a madman, the two bystanders maintained their distance. "You guys get the hell out of here. She's gone inside to call the cops." They stared without compliance. Racking back the Beretta and pointing at them, they moved quickly up the street. Alone with the evil duo, I clutched my crucifix and stepped brazenly close. "Tell Monique I will see her."

"Come to the Chamber tonight," the black-haired one commanded.

"No, thank you. I have been to that freak show and I am not going back. Tell her if she wants to see me, I will be at Utopia in about two hours."

"You had better be there, otherwise I fear Sam will not live to see the sunrise," the brunette threatened.

I lunged forward and grabbed the brunette by the throat, surprising her with the magnitude of my speed and strength while holding the other one at bay with my cross. "If you touch her, I will—"

"You will what, kill me?" The brunette interrupted, her voice constricted. "After tonight you will not be killing anyone ever again."

"It's a date then." Before releasing my grip, I squeezed even tighter, wanting to snap her neck, but I knew it was pointless. I shoved her away like a rag doll. Turning to go inside, I did not bother to see if they followed.

Inside the lobby, I found Sam isolated, facing the wall and sobbing. "Sam," I began, tempering my tone. The sight of her tears instantly extinguished my anger.

"Has this all been a lie?" she asked.

At this point there were no remaining options, the Bishop could no longer save me, and frankly I was ready to bury him with all the others. "No. It was not." Not able to look her in the eye with my interpretative answer, I glanced down and saw O'Reilly's card crumpled in her hand. "Did you make the call?"

"Yes," she said, momentarily calming her tears. "Brian, what's been going on? Who are these women who seem to know you so well?"

I looked around. Although many eyes were on us, they remained a safe distance. "Sam, I will tell you everything, but it is so inconceivable, you're going to think I am crazy." I led her out to the courtyard, away from prying ears, and sat her down on the edge of the fountain. The cascading water made it difficult to be overheard. "Sam, I swear to you, everything I am about to tell you is true."

Sam looked into my eyes, desperately seeking a semblance of the truth.

"You know about the tours they do around here at night, ghosts and vampires?" Sam nodded. "As the legend goes, vampires have been locked up on the third floor of the Old Ursuline Convent for over two hundred years. Phillip wanted the story for his paper, so he paid me to break in. He thought it would make a great church conspiracy article."

Sam stared intently, absorbing the details as fast as I could spill them.

"Me and the guys you met broke into the convent two nights ago. Not being one to believe in fairy tales, I thought all we would find was a bunch of crap, take a few pictures for Phillip, and then get the hell out. That was to be the end of it. Then you and I were supposed to run away to some tropical island till we were old and gray. But I was wrong. Dead wrong. My lack of conviction cost Rob his life." Sam's eyes popped as her jaw dropped open.

"Yes, Rob is dead, and those two lovely bitches you just met took part in killing him. Here comes the hardest part to swallow. Those two women are honest-to-God real-life vampires. They had been imprisoned in the convent since the seventeen hundreds and used some kind of hypnotism that forced us to release them."

Reacting to her expression of utter disbelief, I forged on. "Like I said, you would have to be completely certifiable to believe a word of it, but I swear to you Sam, it is all true. The detective you called will be here shortly. He will verify everything."

Sam's demeanor changed, comprehending the scope of the situation. The revelation which I had once found unfathomable, she readily accepted as a life-threatening reality.

"So you set them free two nights ago. Where have you been since? Why couldn't you have told me?"

"We have been hunting them."

Sam placed her arms on my shoulders, the mere contact lifting the burden of anger and frustration. "Brian, if these women are killers, why don't you just let the police handle it? If they killed Rob, then you should turn it over to them."

"Sam, I broke into Vatican property and freed ten vampires that have subsequently killed at least four people in the last couple of nights. I can't just walk away. The only way to stop them is to kill them. I know you have seen at least one vampire movie in your life. You must know what has to be done."

"You're killing them?"

"Yes, Sam. I drive a wooden stake with a mallet right through their evil hearts, just like in the movies."

"Brian, I don't know what to say, but I think I need to find Dee. I need to go home now."

"Sam, there is no going back home. You and Dee are flying to New York tonight with Phillip. He's tried to keep you home, away from all this, but now they know about you. They will either kill you or use you to get me and then kill us both."

Confused and flustered, Sam sighed, "I need to talk to Dee."

"Call her. She is on her way to the airport with Phillip as we speak, but I told her we were dealing with terrorists. She would have thought I was certifiable if I had told her the truth, and I had to get her to agree to leave. Phillip can show you all of the proof you want once you are on the plane." I scanned the surrounding area to ensure the vampires were not lurking in the shadows.

O'Reilly entered the lobby and glanced side-to-side until he spotted Sam and me in the courtyard. He acknowledged me with a wave and headed in our direction.

"How you doing, Mitch?"

"Well, considering the events of the last few days, I'm doing better than some of the people I've come in contact with lately." He looked Sam over, signaling his approval with a quirky smile. "It's a good thing she called. The dispatcher was sending about thirty cops your way. Some idiot was beating women up and waving a gun in public. I knew it had to be you, so I called off the offensive. Makes us almost even now."

"Pretty damn close." I gestured toward Sam, but looked above her gaze. "Mitch, this is my very good friend Samantha. Despite my best efforts, they found out about her tonight." Shooting the evil-eye of reprimand in her direction, I remained unable to gaze directly into her eyes. "It will only be a matter of time before they come for her. I need a big favor."

"You want me to lock her up at the precinct?" O'Reilly said with a mischievous smile.

"I need you to get her to the airport ASAP. I have a friend waiting with a private jet who is going to take her out of the city tonight."

"I can do that, although I like the precinct idea better. You know those private planes are not nearly as safe as police stations."

"Wait a minute," Sam said, with an unfamiliar scowl on her face. The emotional balance scale was tipping back toward angry. "I don't think I need the two of you deciding what's best for me." Sam pointed at Mitch. "You. I would like to see some identification. And you, Brian," Sam manipulated her head, finding the eye contact I had avoided. "You just admitted lying to my sister, and we already know your track record with me certainly is lacking. And look at you, with your blond hair!"

"Sam, please come with me, just for a minute. Hear me out and then do whatever you want." We moved away from O'Reilly, seeking the most isolated area behind the fountain, beside the foliage surrounding the pool. The expression of uncertainty in her eye convinced me more than anything that she desperately needed to hear something she could trust.

"Sam, however you feel about me right now, I can't change. I certainly would take it all back if I could, but I cannot undo any of this. Not the convent, not Rob, and especially falling madly in love with you. But whatever you think or feel, I am begging you, please go with Detective O'Reilly to the airport. Because of me, they will come for you. Please trust me on this one thing, and maybe when it is all over, hopefully you will find a way to fall in love with me again. If you do not want to go to New York, go wherever you want. Phillip will get you there, and I will make sure you have everything you need until it is safe to return. But please, just leave New Orleans tonight."

Sam took my hands in hers. "Come with me. Let's leave together. Leave this to the police."

"I can't leave. This is all my fault, and mine to fix."

"Then I won't leave you. If I leave, I feel like we'll never see each other again."

"Sam, you have to go. I can't do this knowing every minute you stay your life is in danger." Without a word, her eyes revealed her dissent. "If you refuse, I will have Mitch arrest you and haul you to the airport in cuffs."

I pushed Sam away, but maintained a firm grip on her shoulders, looking sternly in her eyes. "Get to that plane and do not waste a second getting the hell out of New Orleans."

I pulled the cross from my neck and placed it around hers. "Wear this. It will protect you."

"But you need it," Sam objected.

"I have more. You wear it, and never take it off." I looked over to O'Reilly. "You got yours?"

He pulled out an oversized, tacky gold cross resembling something from a wannabe rapper's garage sale. "Does this qualify?"

"That would definitely qualify. Listen, when you get in the car, lock the doors and drive like hell. Under no circumstance should you stop."

I kissed Sam one final time. "I love you, and I will see you in New York. I promise."

O'Reilly took Sam gently by the elbow and began leading her toward the street. "My car is right outside."

"Here is my number. Call me after you have dropped her off. We have a lot of work ahead of us tonight," I instructed.

Sam kept staring back. The disquiet in her eyes forewarned of infinite sadness. It was beyond my reach to lighten the burden and calm her spirit. "Call Dee so they know you are on the way. Make sure Phillip has the jet ready to fly the instant you arrive." I began trailing them to the street. "Sam, call me as soon as you get to New York. If I don't answer, leave me a message."

She nodded.

"Wait," I ordered, as I made sure the passage to O'Reilly's car, parked on the street adjacent to the side door entrance, was clear. I studied the street intently, sniffing the air for any trace scent or any premonition of their presence.

I turned to Sam and kissed her again. "Go now." O'Reilly and Sam scurried into the car. He fired up the Chevy and began to pull away. Sam stared blankly out the window, raising her hand to wave farewell, committing the image of this moment to memory.

CHAPTER 26

I LAID ON the bed and stared at the ceiling, cataloguing memories and formulating plans. The shower had served its purpose; the filth of my deeds were sufficiently, albeit temporarily, washed away. Not knowing my plans, Chuck and Jimmy were content staying put for the night. Preferring to have them alive and ready for action in the morning, I felt secure in knowing regardless of tonight's outcome, they would survive to continue the hunt.

O'Reilly had already returned from the airport and set up surveillance in and around Utopia. Monique and her sidekicks were in place, but there was no sign of Angelique or the unidentified fifth bloodsucker.

Leaving the hotel and heading to the office to grab another crucifix, I maintained an ultra-high vigilance, scanning for anything that did not feel exactly right. One peculiarity I observed: There was no trace of the foul funk that had permeated the air for the last several nights. Perhaps a fifty percent reduction in the vampire population had something to do with it.

Once back at the office, I grabbed what little gear I considered necessary and headed back to Bourbon Street. Walking briskly, I tugged repeatedly at the unfamiliar cross around my neck, ensuring it was secured beyond all measure.

Half a block from Bourbon Street, passing the scene of last night's crime, my thoughts turned to Isabelle. Was she safe? Had the reality of last night prompted her to consider a change in lifestyle?

As I reached the corner of Bourbon, a solitary rose intercepted my path. Fuck. Perhaps happenstance, but I doubted it. She was near. I inventoried the list of the traits which differentiated Angelique from the rest. One: She did not smell like the others. Two: She was not hellbent on killing me. Three: She had been in my bed without my knowledge or permission. Four: She laid claim to some sort of personal intertwined destiny. Yeah, I sure would like an answer to that before staking her.

Again, the sensation of being stalked prompted me to action. Ducking into the first tacky gift shop on the left, my adrenaline rose, my heart racing in anticipation. O'Reilly appeared suddenly from around the corner. I grabbed him by the shirt and yanked him in. "You know, it is not a good idea to follow me. I am a little jumpy these days."

Not anticipating the body snatch, the startled detective squealed, "Obviously." O'Reilly sighed deeply. "I thought you might appreciate somebody watching your back."

"Yes, I do." I released his shirt and smoothed the wrinkles. "Did you get the pictures I sent to your cell phone?"

"Yes. My men have them too. I've set up surveillance points with personnel and electronics, with strict instructions not to engage the subjects. We should be able to track them with the live bodies and cameras I have set up exiting Bourbon Street and the Quarter."

"Live bodies. That worries me."

"I issued crosses to my crew and ordered them to remain at least fifty yards from the suspects," O'Reilly explained.

"Issued crosses? Bet that raised a few eyebrows."

"They think it is so you can readily identify them. Otherwise, they were not afforded the opportunity to ask questions."

"Remind your team to keep their voices and conversations to a minimum. A vampire's audible sensitivity is about three times more acute than our own," I warned.

"You bet." O'Reilly looked blankly into the throngs of partiers traversing Bourbon Street. "It seems like your girl Monique is making herself right at home with all these bozos drinking and carrying on. Are you sure she is one of them?"

"Mitch, I blew a hole right through her skull from four feet. You tell me."

"Either she found a really good plastic surgeon or is very good with makeup. I saw her picture, and I gotta tell you."

"Neither." Not wanting to get sidetracked by O'Reilly's fascination over Monique's allure, I disclosed, "According to legend, a vampire's wound will heal itself in a day or two."

O'Reilly raised his eyebrows, "That would be a nice problem to have."

"Yes it would. As long as they drink the blood of the living, their body rejuvenates. It is one of the many myths which I now know to be true."

"So what happens between now and the time they leave the club?"

"Plan A is rather simple and boring. I will try to keep them in the club almost until sunrise. They will then go directly to their resting place, which your team will locate. After sunrise, you and I will politely gouge their hearts out. Plan B, should the need arise," I grabbed a plastic sword off a display, "is to smash a barstool, use the leg as a stake, and drive it through her heart." O'Reilly jumped back as I thrust the cheesy souvenir at his chest.

"That mighty fine shirt would be a terrible mess if you resort to plan B. For the sake of your shirt, we should focus on plan A. After all, can you imagine all my paperwork, a bloody execution with hundreds of witnesses?"

I looked at my relatively new Robert Graham shirt. "I know, but this was all I had left. Haven't had much time for shopping lately, you know?"

"Yeah, I have that problem myself. There's never enough time to accessorize my wardrobe." O'Reilly peered down at his clothes comically. "Could buy one of those off the rack." O'Reilly pointed to the stack of tacky tourist shirts.

"If the pendulum of fate should swing the other way tonight, there is no way I am checking out in one of those."

O'Reilly smiled at the notion. "What will you do if she decides to attack?"

"Well, this bottle of Dasani is actually filled with holy water. So if need be, I can always douse myself with it. Other than that, I have this." I produced a new cross from under my shirt. "And my last resort is this." I reached down to my ankle and produced a six-inch Cold Steel knife from my ankle. "If you know how, and yes I do, it is sharp enough to decapitate."

"Alright, let's hope I don't have to see that." The speed at which I deployed the glistening blade caused O'Reilly to raise an eyebrow.

"Cut the carotid left to right deeply, which, given the major loss of blood, should slow her substantially. Then, with most of the muscles and tendons out of the way, flip the head back and finish off the spinal column." I folded the knife back and replaced it.

"Hey, that cross looks like you got it from the Goodwill dumpster. Maybe you should wear mine." O'Reilly began to reach in his pocket for his tawdry cross.

Having seen it before, I quickly passed. "No thanks, Mitch. And you need to have that around your neck, not your pocket."

As he retrieved it from his pocket, I instantly recognized the intricate carvings. A Celtic cross, entwined by a snake with a braided black leather cord—the very one I had given to Sam—now lay in his extended palm. "What are you doing with that?"

"When Samantha was safely onboard, she told me you would need it more than her. She said it had protected you so far, so she thought it would be good for you to have until this was over."

Removing Phillip's gift-shop-purchased crucifix and shoving it in my pocket, I took the cross and hung it around my neck. Having never been superstitious, the comfort it provided was welcome beyond expectation. "I forgot to tell you, Mitch—thanks for taking care of Sam. I appreciate it more than you know."

"Hey, it doesn't take special detective skills to see she's exceptional. I was glad to do it for you. I owe you at least that much."

"So, are we ready to do this?" Armed with a renewed sense of confidence, I was ready to wrap this up.

"I've thought this through, and I don't see where we have a lot of choices. I'm sure when this is all over I'll be in jail, right beside you, but what the hell?

"You are a good man, Mitch."

"Hey, Brian, if that is your real name, one question before you go in."

"What would that be?"

"Who the hell are you? Why are you here?"

"I wish I could say I am simply here doing a job. But it has been said by someone apparently much wiser than me—I am fulfilling an unavoidable destiny, whose time has tracked me down."

"Good enough, so let's do this thing," O'Reilly said, a wild gleam in his eye.

CHAPTER 27

"WHERE IS HE?" Monique irately demanded of her companions, the bone-shaking music making it difficult to hear. Monique was in a particularly foul mood, having been unable to locate Isabelle and use her to provoke Brian into a careless mistake.

For his part in freeing the vampires from the convent, Angelique had declared Brian untouchable. Monique initially honored the request of the woman who made her immortal, but circumstances had changed. First, he had interfered in her affairs with Isabelle, then he shot her. Just to prove a point? Angelique or not, this man would suffer a painful death. Monique surmised Brian was a vampire hunter who had come to the convent to destroy them. Seeking out her fellow sisters, only to discover them slaughtered, Monique learned through Celine and Gabrielle that two other men were hunting them as well. Her accord with Angelique was now void as she declared Brian a threat to their very existence.

Sitting in the corner overlooking the dance floor, Celine and Gabrielle exchanged anxious glances. Neither wanted to answer, for neither had a suitable reply. Their mistress was growing increasingly impatient with each passing minute. "I will go back to his hotel if you like," Gabrielle offered, attempting to appease Monique.

"No, you will stay here. Should he arrive, I want the both of you with me. He is treacherous, and it may take all three of us to dispose of him. I hope you realize that every day he lives, more of our kind will pass into the shadows. He must be stopped tonight," Monique declared, scanning the crowd, seeking her prey.

"Monique, you should go dance," Celine suggested. "Find yourself a young boy to satisfy your thirst. We will watch for him."

Indeed, Monique had thirsted for a young man she had observed. He was tall and muscular, with dark, wavy, slicked-back hair that made him look Latino. Dancing sensuously, he had drawn Monique's hunger the moment she laid eyes on him. Considering her ability to dominate men who thought of themselves as superior, Monique knew she would extract immense pleasure taking this hunk down.

Celine was acutely connected to her mistress's desires, falling victim to Monique's insatiable hunger. "Maybe you should take him, make him one of us. It is time for you choose a mate."

"Fool, have you forgotten? It is not for me to choose who becomes one of us. Only Count Tepes has that authority. Have you forgotten the law? Only out of the need for survival did I make you, after enduring the cruelty of starvation."

"We are thousands of miles from our homeland and the Count's law. After two hundred years, we have been long forsaken. If he still lives, and word should reach him, our colony could be far too powerful, even for his law."

"But Angelique ...," Monique began to protest.

"Angelique?" Defiantly, Celine interrupted her mistress. "We have not felt her presence for two nights now. Surely she has passed to the darkness at the hands of those who hunt. It is time, Monique, to lead us to the power we rightfully deserve. Too long we remained in bondage at Angelique's insistence, waiting for a pardon the Count never intended to grant. My sisters and I were innocent of your treason, yet we all suffered your consequence. Set us free, lead us to a new glorious beginning. It must be now, before our nights come to an eternal end."

Celine's argument was forceful and convincing. Monique knew it was the only path to survival. Angelique had been in love with

Count Tepes, but despite his love for her, he chose to marry mortal royalty in an effort to unite Romania and Hungary. Infuriated the Count had not chosen her friend, Monique conspired to eliminate the new countess. Monique took the woman's mortal life and delivered her into the dark world of the vampire, forever possessing the ability to control her will. As punishment, the Count exiled an innocent Angelique and Monique to the New World. They would remain in exile until he granted a pardon.

Angelique accepted responsibility and punishment for her friend's deeds, waiting as the centuries passed for the opportunity to seek forgiveness from her one true love.

Monique knew Celine was right. Considering her options, a sinister smile crossed her face. "Let me know as soon as he arrives."

"How shall we deal with him?" Gabrielle asked. "You claim his mind is strong and cannot easily be controlled."

"His mind and body are strong. But once he ingests a single drop of my blood and it courses through his veins, he will prove completely powerless, a mere slave to my desires. Then I will drink all but the last drops of his blood. He will suffer greatly, helplessly bearing witness to the death of Isabelle and then to this other woman, Sam. He will rue the day he defied me with his dying breath."

Monique gleamed at the young, unsuspecting stud of a man commanding the dance floor. "Until then, I believe I shall dine Cuban style." She unfastened an additional button on her white satin shirt, adjusted her skin-tight, dark denim jeans, and set her path to the front of the stage. Monique, in her black leather pumps, towered over the many women in her path. Her shapely body and seductive beauty turned many a head as she prowled the floor. Ignoring all potential suitors in her path, the predator's eyes locked on her target.

The Cuban was dancing with a fiery redhead. Monique cut in, her hip shoving the redhead aside. Standing toe-to-toe, Monique looked directly into the Cuban's accepting eyes. Before Monique could speak, the redhead grabbed her by the shirt and yanked her around, tearing another button off.

"Beat it, bitch. Carlos is mine."

Monique grabbed her by the throat and glared at her. "He belongs to me. You will leave us now."

The redhead could not break the gravitational force of Monique's commanding stare. Her steely eyes of death overpowered the unsuspecting, suddenly defenseless girl. The redhead released Monique's shirt as her aggression lapsed into submission, then confusion. She babbled a few words, then aimlessly wandered away. Monique's conceited smile broadcast her arrogant superiority over humans. Without a word, she turned to Carlos, put her arms around him, and began gyrating her hips into his, grinding to the salsa inspired motions.

"She tore your blouse," Carlos observed as he gazed down eagerly.

Monique looked down to find the newly severed button missing. She pulled her blouse open, revealing her chest to Carlos. "So she did. Does it bother you?"

"No, ma'am, it's no problem for me." Carlos continued staring down, eagerly examining Monique's white, well-rounded breasts framed in a laced brassiere.

Monique pulled him closer, grinding firmly into his groin. Taking his large hand, she placed it on her breast. Although Carlos was brimming with anticipation, the seduction would be short-lived. Monique was hungry and ready to feed. She would feast at the very root of his soul, dominating both his physical and mental strengths, creating a subservient being that would live only to please his mistress. Tonight, Celine's prophetic advice would arise, bearing witness to the birth of a renewed vampire nation.

CHAPTER 28

LEAVING O'REILLY BEHIND, I traveled down the street pick-ing out his men along the way. If our plans were executed as detailed, Monique and her friends would be easy marks to trail back to their hideaway. Passing youthful groups of revelers, I imagined myself in the mix, briefly wishing to be among them, knowing full well that tonight would bring the biggest challenge of my life. Attempting to enter incognito, I donned a New Orleans Saints football cap and my Chrome Hearts shades. I pressed up to the bouncer policing the uncrowded entrance.

"What's up?"

"Don' know, Hollywood, but sumthins goin' down tonight. Lotso heat on the street ... and in here too." He thumbed in the direction of a pair of undercover cops across the street. "Dey think we don' know."

"Gonna get hot in here?"

"Always hot in 'ere. Ain' no oder place to be if you know whut I mean. We crankin' it out every night. Po-po or not."

"Thanks." I looked to the outside world one last time, then headed into the open-air courtyard. Needless to say, with hordes of drunks staggering about, it was easy picking for a vampire looking for meals on wheels. The techno Latin beat was erupting from the back as a mass of humans gyrated on and in front of an elevated stage. Knowing Monique was somewhere in the mix was all the motivation I needed to wade in. I steered toward the right, mixing in with the drink line, hoping to get a fix on them to formulate my approach.

From my concealed vantage point, out of the corner of my eye I spotted two foreboding women sitting at an elevated table on the left, toward the rear. The flashing strobe lights pulsating in various neon colors made it difficult to make a positive ID, but instinctively I knew it was them. More than instinct, I could sense their presence. Engaged in conversation, cuddled close, they appeared more concerned with each other than my arrival. "Why not?" I muttered. Their table was approachable from the back corner to the left of the dance floor. The cover I needed was seated right beside me: four women, all buttered up and toasted, bopping their heads to the beat, waiting for an invite to shake the moneymaker.

"Anyone care to dance?"

My unsolicited offer did not suffer the embarrassment of rejection or undo delay. The blonde with spiral curls, blue eyes, and a heavy hand in the makeup department, jumped to her feet.

"I'd love to."

I positioned her to my left, shielding their view while scouting for Monique as we moved into the dancing fracas. My shoes crackled, sticking to the beer-covered floor as we began to sway to the beat.

"I'm Brenda," my impromptu camouflage reported.

"Tom. Nice to meet you."

Thanks to my dance partner, my preoccupied vampires remained oblivious to my presence. As we moved toward the bar, I stood at the far end, my back turned, while inching closer. Checking the mirror behind the bar to confirm their location, a cold chill drove down my spine. They were gone! I quickly turned expecting to find them behind me, ready to attack. But as I turned, a phenomenon bore proof of more ancient folklore. They remained seated, alternately watching the dance floor, the entrance, and each other. I swiftly turned back to the bar, my pulse racing. I gazed into the mirror again. Poof, no vampires. I peeked over my shoulder and there they were. "Son of a bitch," I said softly.

As they panned back to the entrance, I seized the opportunity to slide to the end of the bar within twenty feet. From here, approaching from behind would be relatively simple. Formulating my plan on the fly, I ordered two bottles of water.

Unaware of my approach, their senses were not as keen as I had anticipated. Was it the abundance of perfumes, sweat, and the alcohol which permeated the air? Perhaps the drinks they were consuming? Could a vampire become intoxicated?

Removing the caps, I crept directly behind the oblivious pair. "Ladies, do not move, and if either of you utter one word in Romanian, I will add a new meaning to holy water wet T-shirt contest." I extended my arms enough to reach their peripheral sight. "Where is Monique?"

Wincing at the thought, it was apparent they understood the end result. "She is out there." The brunette pointed toward the dance floor.

"What are your names?"

I detected a quiver in the brunette's lips. Fear defeating arrogance, she replied. "I am Gabrielle, and this is Celine."

"Well, girls, I will offer you a choice which your companions did not receive." I parked my Saints cap on Celine's head and tucked my shades in my pocket. "Return to the convent tonight, right now, or I will hunt you down and put an end to your miserable lives and you can join your sisters in Hell."

"You display a great confidence, Brian, for one who has seen his last sunrise," Celine replied gleefully. "After tonight, we will claim our rightful return to power. And no mortal, particularly you, will hinder our destiny. You should consider how you will enjoy your final hours. Personally, I would seek out one final act of pleasure before your life is over."

"Join us, Brian. Forget this madness," Gabrielle suggested. "Celine and I can be most accommodating. Monique is quite occupied, and there is no reason why she should be the only one who enjoys the night."

Momentarily, I actually considered her proposition. To declare a vampire's power of seduction is overwhelming is an understatement.

Gabrielle's naturally bewitching appearance did not help matters.

Her wavy-brown hair draped over one shoulder and accentuated the cleavage tucked beneath her cheetah halter. Every man has his own kryptonite and cheetah is mine. Legs? Okay, two. Lacking any rational objections, I fantasized brushing my lips across her exposed porcelain shoulders and down her back.

The silhouette of Celine's glossy-red lips beckoned to be kissed deeply. Like Monique, she had fashioned her jet-black hair to taper down, following her sleek jawline. She sported a black tank top and jeans so tight that they appeared to be sprayed on. In the midst of the tantalizing duo, the tension in my arms relaxed as I gazed out over the dance floor. Perusing the masses, images of my first night with Sam flashed through my mind. That was all of the reality check I needed.

I snapped back. "I appreciate the offer, ladies, but I am afraid I must pass. My business tonight is with Monique."

"Such a shame," Gabrielle said with a sigh. "I have heard you are very talented in the ways of love."

Again with the innuendoes, but the inquisition would have to wait. "Believe me, ladies, the loss will be all mine," I said apologetically. "But to show you I am not an ingrate, I will offer you one final opportunity to go back to the convent. But do not confuse my generosity for kindness."

"It is understood," Celine said in her snappy French accent. " Go, find Monique. She has waited long enough. But do not plead to us for intervention."

"I would not drink this if I were you. It might give you heartburn," I suggested as I set the bottles on the table. "Ya'll hurry on back to the convent now. The nuns do go to bed early."

Remaining at the table with smug expressions, they watched my every move as I forced my way into the thick of the crowd searching for Monique. Looking left then right, it was hard to adjust my eyes in the pulsating lights. My first glimpse was her backside, a mighty fine backside. "Such a waste," I mumbled. Monique was indeed into the moment; grinding and kissing some ripped, dark-haired jock.

My body tensed as I prepared for the encounter, knowing Jocko was about to get his feelings hurt. I tapped him on the back.

He turned slowly and looked very annoyed at the sight of me. "Can I help you?" he sneered.

"Yes, I need to speak to my wife." Monique looked on pleasurably, sensing a confrontation of gladiator proportions about to erupt.

"Your wife is busy. Come back later, when I'm done with her."

Not wanting to attract any attention or turn this confrontation into a barroom brawl, I timed my assault, catching him squarely in the windpipe in an instant of darkness. The precise attack left him prone, down on his knees, gasping for air. Surely he was not the first drunk to fall tonight. "Darling, I have been looking all over for you. Where on earth have you been?" I took Monique's cold hand and forcefully pulled her away.

Monique peered back at Carlos, still on his knees gasping like a fish out of water. Not accustomed to being forced around, she resisted. I pulled harder, not to be deterred by her stubbornness. She smiled back at Carlos. "What a shame. I was just getting to know him."

"I think he will be much happier tomorrow, having missed out on your brand of intimacy." I pulled her through the courtyard and off to the side. Face to face, her flawlessness was incredible. Two hundred years old and she did not look a minute over twenty. Her facial features were delicate and inviting, as if a photographer had airbrushed her to perfection. Looking in her brilliant-teal eyes, it was difficult to imagine her as an evil killing creature.

We stared each other down in a moment of uncomfortable silence.

"You changed your hair. I liked the old Brian better."

What do you say when confronted with something so incredibly beautiful and yet so viciously evil? There was no imminent battle to be won, for the moment. I was indecisive, to say the least. "Your face healed nicely." I ran my finger across the precise point of Loretta's rage.

Tilting her head, she gently pressed against my touch, enjoying the sensation of warm flesh. My outstretched fingers raked into her silky hair. "Bastard," she whispered softly.

How could I stand here, caressing the face of a killer, in love with Sam, yet lusting for Monique with my every molecule? The involuntary attraction was mystifying and dangerous. I had to draw her in. My ability to terminate the duplicity at the precise moment of the kill was my only fear.

"So what do we do now, Brian? I assume you have come to kill me." Her eyes glistened, infusing sensual desires within mine.

"Unless you and the others are willing to go back to the convent ...yes."

"I have been in that forsaken place for over two hundred years. I will never go back." She backed her face away from my hand.

"Then your fate is sealed." My thoughts betrayed my words, for I had lost all desire to destroy her.

"Why must this be my fate, to live like a caged animal or perish?"

"You kill indiscriminately, and not out of necessity. You existed for over two hundred years without killing."

"You speak of what you do not know. Existing and living in our world are not one and the same. And yet you kill not out of survival, but pleasure, do you not?" Monique searched for any hint of my resolve weakening.

"No, I only killed with purpose, never out of pleasure. My kills were determined to be justified, never merely about getting a meal."

"You feed on many living creatures because you are superior. We do only the same. The difference is the number of legs our prey walks upon."

"But you could feed on the same blood as us. Instead, you choose to kill innocent humans, and in our society this is just not acceptable."

Contemplating my argument, her demeanor shifted. "If one of us is to die tonight, I think I would like a glass of wine." Monique's unexpected strategic shift caught me unawares.

"Sure, why not. Can I trust you to wait here until I get back ... and not kill anyone?"

She leaned in and pressed her moist, velvety lips against my cheek. "Tonight, I am here only for you and will not leave without you."

Her words resonated as I drifted to the bar. "Hot piece, bro," the bartender said. "Saw her come in solo. You two together, or did you just get lucky?"

"Her kind of fun is not worth the burn. Trust me, if there is one piece you should run away from, that would be the one."

"I find the pain is usually worth the pleasure," he replied, grinning. "What can I get you?"

"SoCo and lime and a glass of Merlot." Gawking at Monique, her hooks were deeply embedded into his psyche. "You know, before meeting her, I felt the same way. But I have to tell you, I have never met a woman so capable and equipped to destroy everything she touches."

"That bad, huh? In that case, boss, I'll make yours a double." I sympathized with his preoccupation as he made the drinks.

Monique's treacherous powers of seduction were far reaching as once again my focus regressed. Suddenly, feeling awkward and conflicted, I coveted this perfected vision, craving her more than any other woman in my life. And yet here I stood, plotting her death.

I returned to Monique feeling less confident than desired. "They did not have much in the way of selection. I hope you like it."

"As long as it's served at the proper temperature, it will suffice." She took the glass and sipped the burgundy libation. "Thank you."

She sampled a second time. "It is perfect." Monique glanced around the bar awkwardly and then hesitantly back at me. She remained silent as she looked away once more. It appeared to me as though she was troubled, possibly conflicted by her thoughts.

"What's on your mind?"

"You have killed the others, haven't you?" She looked away, awaiting my answer.

Could it be she believed Celine, Gabrielle, and herself to be the only survivors? If so, Angelique and the elusive tenth were unaccounted for by all concerned.

"Yes," I replied solemnly.

"So how will you kill me, Brian?" She turned, directing teary eyes to mine. "Will you drive a stake through my heart or cut off my head?

I opened my jacket, revealing one slightly sexy Beretta and a rather innocent looking bottle of Dasani. "No stakes or meat cleavers. I really did not come with a plan."

"You do not seem like a man without a plan. The great ones always have a plan. Van Helsing had a plan."

"Van Helsing? You have to be kidding me. I thought he was just a storybook character."

"Storybook? No, he was a very dangerous and evil man. Many were annihilated by his hand. If not for the Count, our race would have ceased to exist."

"So Count Tepes ... the Dracula and Van Helsing's legend were real?"

"Actually, it was the grandson son of Vlad, Levente Dracula."

Although fascinating, the history lesson needed to conclude. "So ... how are you planning to kill me?"

"I would start by sharing a few drinks to relax you." She looked to our libations and smiled. "Then I would gradually begin the seduction. As your defenses falter, eventually you would crave me more than the air you breathe. My touch would overpower your senses. Then we would make passionate love, unlike anything you have ever experienced. At the climax of our interlude, slowly I would begin to drain the life from you and you would gratefully pass into the darkness rather than end the experience."

Monique had a playful look of sincerity as she described what was to be the end of my life. She honestly believed that I would enjoy the entire process. I must admit it sounded pretty damn good ... right up to the passing into the darkness part.

"Why kill me? Why not make me like you?" Here was my subtle ploy to discover if she had already begun the process.

"We were forbidden. The Count maintained supreme authority in the decision." Her frustrated tone foretold of a deeper conflict. "Our race is bound to live by his law. In that respect, he was very much the same as mortal men, desiring domination over any creature deemed inferior. The dawn of our age is upon the world, and we will never again be confined to the demands of man, be he human or vampire."

"It sounds to me like you are afraid of men."

"Only of your insatiable desire to conquer all you see. You are no different, Brian. You would have the same aspirations as Dracula, and I will never again bow down to the will of any man."

"Then I guess there is not much hope for me." Feeding her growing confidence would ultimately serve susceptibility and eventually carelessness. But I had to admit, their plight was compelling. If they could learn to coexist, perhaps there could be a path for survival.

"There never was any hope. It was Angelique alone who kept you alive, and what did she receive for her pity? In sparing your life, she forfeited her own. It only goes to prove your own heartlessness." Monique's eyes gleamed with conflicted remorse. "It is most unfortunate seven of my sisters perished as a result of her miscalculations."

Monique's posture softened as she placed a hand on my cheek. "To-night I will know both Angelique's pleasure and revenge."

Apparently she believed Angelique and the others to be dead. But moreover, first Gabrielle and now Monique assumed Angelique and I had ... shit! There was no fucking way I was with her. A brief inadvertent expression of bewilderment flashed across my face.

Monique laughed politely as possible. "Oh, Brian, you do not remember?"

Suddenly, rampant thoughts were stampeding through my head. Did something happen that first night in the convent, more than just a kiss? Or the night Angelique left the rose on my bed? Monique was bluffing, attempting to collapse my defenses by inflicting confusion.

The suspicion, no matter how unlikely, was backing me into a dark corner. I needed to regain control. My intention was to allow her to believe she held an advantage and to an uncomfortable degree she did. "Would you like another glass of wine?" The time had come for an overdue change of topics, refusing to acknowledge any allegations of sexual mischief.

"What is it are you drinking?"

"It is SoCo and lime. Apparently it is the official drink of New Orleans."

"Mmm, well if it is the official drink of the South, then maybe I should try one. That is, if you are not in too much of a hurry to kill me. May I?" She held her hand out for a sample.

Obliging, I handed my drink over. Monique turned her head and looked away. Raking her fangs lightly over the inside of her lip, she pierced it and allowed a minute drop of her venomous blood to seep into the drink. Completely unaware of her intentions and the devastating effects of her actions, I paid no attention as she set her ultimate plan into motion. She handed the drink back.

"It is good. I think I would enjoy one, after my wine." She focused her attention on the dancing masses, playfully swaying to the rhythm. Lustfully, I watched her body gyrate to the beat. I swallowed my drink hard, attempting to divert thoughts I preferred not occur.

Even though it was but a drop, within minutes I began spiraling down to the depths of Monique's dark desires, the hammering rhythm coursing my body as I succumbed to an erotic pleasure from every note perceived. All comprehension of danger had been vanquished, replaced by a sense of euphoria and invincibility. All the while, a festering burning emerged deep within my gut. I was becoming intoxicated with the shapeliness of Monique's body: the skinny denims tightly following every contour of her legs, thighs, and ass, and the white cotton shirt gaping open, exposing her beguiling breasts. Her silky hair flowed as though an artist had debated with himself over how he would place each and every stand around her delicate, exquisitely-crafted face. Monique, with her deep-teal eyes beckoning my heart to submit, was the absolute vision of—well, every precise detail I could ever have fantasized in a woman. I ached to possess her, to consume her.

Her diabolically planned prophecy had begun to unfold.

"I like this song. Will you dance with me, Brian?"

The sultry voice only deepened my desires. I lacked any power or reason to refuse. Her blood permeated through my veins, creating a newborn servant to her aspirations.

It was Monique's turn to lead me back, where only moments ago I had been in complete command of the situation. We began to dance slowly, ignoring the upbeat tempo blaring out. Monique arched her body, pulling her hands though her hair as she thrust her hips into my groin, sliding her thighs slowly against mine. She was a sexual force of seductive dancing, and men crowded around, thirsting to be near this ravishing vixen. She smiled with deep equanimity at the obvious tension created by the lustful suitors. As we danced, she separated, allowing other men in between, touching her, fulfilling her hunger for masculine attention. That momentary break stirred me back to my senses. I was spellbound and the only defense I could conjure in that instant was to think about Sam, her voice, her touch, her words.

Turning my back, I began moving away, dancing with other women abandoned by Monique's gravitational effects on their men.

"Don't you dare turn your back on me," an enraged voice called from deep inside my head. At this point, my insolence was most unexpected. Monique shoved her way back to me.

"I am thirsty. Get me one of your drinks."

At that moment, I existed in some bizarre dimension. Her demands and feeble attempt to awaken jealousy within me stirred nothing. I submitted aimlessly, zigzagging my way to the bar.

Monique danced with whomever she pleased, enduring the ire of other women as their men gravitated to her seductive appeal. In this new euphoria the concerns of the past vanished, as had Celine and Gabrielle.

My perception of reality hung by a thread. My entire universe flowed into one continuous source of energy—music, lights, and people all fused into one creation. I stared blankly at the two drinks set down before me. Instinctively, I shot down a drink, attempting to douse the growing inferno, leaving the ice-filled glass behind.

I returned to Monique, finding her occupied with several men, all desperately vying for her pleasure. Without gratitude, she shot back the drink, then rubbed the chilled glass around her neck and down her breasts, quenching herself from the blissful orgy. With obvious pleasure, she taunted me, parting her moistened lips with her tongue. Her erotic performance engrossed the pack of wolves surrounding her, but the show was meant exclusively for me. Unmindful of her attention, I danced with women, abandoned in the wake of Monique's exhibit of self-indulgence. In a twist of unintended consequences, I became the dance floor whipping boy, quenching the jilted's jealousy.

Monique took exception to my blatant lack of interest. Shoving aside those in her path, again she pricked her lip, grabbed my face, and kissed me passionately. Indifferent to her intrusion, I merely submitted. The taste of her blood, the thought of her intent, the consequences to follow, never registered as she continued probing my mouth. She pulled away and licked the excess drops of blood from her lips.

Never before had a second offering been necessary, but as she had warned her companions, my will was strong. Within seconds, I doubled over, collapsing to the floor in excruciating pain. Without conscious awareness of my predicament, my body convulsed, heaving to vomit without result. Electricity seared from my core, burning every inch of my being, my chest incinerating one pore at a time. I begged to scream, but no words left my mouth. All the while a sadistic pleasure erupted from the immense pain, imploding every organ in my body. Monique sneered with great pleasure knowing my battle was lost.

Hallucinations of Daniel attempting to extinguish the inferno played like a hellborn nightmare. All the while, Monique's demonic laugh taunted his futility. How long had I suffered these visions? Trapped in a void of blackness and sound, fear and elation ceased to exist. As the pain subsided, I arose from the floor, no longer weakened by the onslaught. Reaching out, I experienced a previously unobtainable consciousness as if looking out through the eyes of a newborn being. Without the benefit of death and rebirth, the blood of the vampire devoured my resolve, leaving me naked to my master's bidding.

"Dance with me." Monique gloated, knowing the end was near.

Without hesitation, I engaged her with what could only be described as a fully clothed dance floor fuck, our bodies twisting and fusing as one. Our lips met, kissing wildly with no regard to the bystanders ogling intently.

Knowing my demise was at hand, Monique's attention turned to her desire. "It is time to leave." With eyes of a wild animal, she took my hand and led me through the crowd.

Departing Utopia hastily, anticipating what was to follow, I was completely intoxicated by the ancient venom coursing my veins. O'Reilly, stationed on the balcony across the street, caught sight of our flight. He radioed to the waiting officers positioned at every intersection. "Gator's in the swamp."

We entered a vacant house six blocks away. Making our way through the kitchen, Monique's silhouette was illuminated against the scintillating moonlight. Not waiting for permission, I grabbed her by the shoulders, spun her around, and ripped off her blouse, sending the remaining three buttons flying. She eagerly unfastened my belt and jerked frantically at my pants. Returning the gesture, clawing at her jeans and yanking them to the floor, I paused momentarily to consume the visual feast of her naked body. She kicked her feet until her heels flew across the room, then wriggled her legs until her denims fell free to the floor. Sweeping her up, I set her on the Formica countertop. Grappling at my jacket and shirt, I flung them across the room without regard. The intensity that followed could only be described as beyond animalistic; two crazed creatures clawing and ripping at each other through hours of extreme passion.

With sunrise looming, Monique knew it was time to be done with me. Laying on top, she pricked her tongue and blood began to flow. Her tongue danced in my mouth one final tango, the blood trickling down my throat. Just enough, she thought, to ensure the collapse of any remaining resistance.

Monique moved from my lips to my throat. She gently kissed my neck as my veins bulged, beckoning her to indulge. Her mouth was wet with anticipation as she blissfully began to penetrate my flesh. Feeling her razor-sharp fangs, I instantly awoke to the realization that whatever was left of my life would soon perish.

Instinctively, I grabbed her by the throat and shoved her away. The strength of my resistance took her unaware. Never in her unnatural long life had she encountered a mortal with such power to resist. Clawing to free my hands from her neck, she was unable to break my death grip. The constricted flow of blood distorted her face, her porcelain skin evolving into unnatural hues of red. Once again, she tried forcing her way to my neck. I rose to a sitting position with Monique straddling my thighs, our naked bodies pressed tightly together.

Struggling for survival, we stared into each other's eyes. Monique's were frantic and frightened, and she was no longer a seductive temptress. Much like shooting a vampire, it is impossible to kill one by strangulation. But lacking any conscious thought of what to do next, I stayed the course. Monique twisted and rocked sideways until our naked bodies fell off the countertop onto the dirty wooden floor. Hitting with a hard thud, I quickly moved on top, matching her speed and agility. Powerless underneath, Monique flailed wildly, thrashing back and forth. Moving inches from her face, seized in panic, those beautiful teal eyes, so enticing, witnessed the black void in mine, the proclamation of her fate. I attacked like a vicious wolf, biting and ripping the flesh from her neck. On such an assault, mindless of my actions, surely I had gone mad. The attack lasted only minutes ... or was it hours?

The abomination before my eyes, the first lucid perception assimilated in hours—Monique, laying lifeless on the floor, the room, my face and body covered in her blood. Not conscious of what I had done, I instinctively jumped to my feet in near panic, expecting the same of her. Grabbing a kitchen chair, I smashed it into the wall and broke off several legs. Brandishing the sharpest, I stood over Monique's ravaged body expecting her eyes to flash back to life, just as that night in the Chamber. My body twitched with the slightest peripheral sound, still not convinced by any means she was truly dead. "I'm sorry, dear, but I don't trust you." I raised the oak leg high and drove the makeshift stake completely through her chest and into the floor.

Committed into the true darkness she deserved, even in mangled death, her beauty enthralled. And what of this rage which led me to kill in such a savage gruesome manner? I could not fathom or begin to recreate the circumstances that led to the carnage before my eyes.

I drifted over to the porcelain kitchen sink and washed the blood from my hands. Once again, I thanked God for the small miracle of an operational faucet. The water rejuvenated and cleansed my face and mind, the blood streaming into the sink, then in a whirlpool down the drain. I took her shirt from the floor and dried myself. Her perfumed scent reeled in another dose of obscure images of the night. Jesus! Gathering my clothes and dressing, I tried to understand how I could have been capable of this. Meandering to the door, I looked back one final time at the horrific scene.

As I moved back to the street, I could sense O'Reilly's presence or maybe it was just my dire need for a face of reason and reassurance. "O'Reilly!" I called out, searching the shadows of the dimly lit street.

"Brian?" He appeared from around the corner of the house next door. "Damn, I thought for sure the way you two left the bar she had already gotten you. We were going to wait until sunrise to move in and stake the two of you."

"I appreciate that, buddy." The exhaustion in my voice was obvious. "She is in there, but will not be coming out without a body bag. What about the other two, Celine and Gabrielle?"

"We know which cemetery they are hiding in. After the sun comes up, you and I can pay our respects." O'Reilly's team began popping out from various observation points.

"I will get up with you in a couple of hours." My head was swimming like a five-day drunk. "I have got to get some rest. Do me a favor, Mitch. Somehow I lost my cross in there. Would you see if you can find it?"

"Absolutely. You'll probably be needing it again before this is finished." Mitch forced a strained smile.

I turned and looked down the street. "It is pretty ugly in there.

I would not let any of those guys in."

"That bad?"

"Nah. 'That bad' don't quite cut it."

As I trudged my way back to the hotel, I checked my phone. One phone call was all I asked for, but not a word. I decided as soon as I had cleaned up that Phillip was going to get his ass woken up.

Arriving back in the lobby of the Maison Dupuy, not a single image of the journey registered. Exhausted and dazed to the point of collapse, I let my clothes fall straight to the floor of my room, cranked on the faucet, and climbed in the shower, not waiting for the water to warm.

The soothing rain showered my weary body. I scoured my skin, desperately wanting to wash away the filth and misery, the complete loss of everything valued. Opening the shower curtain, I grabbed my toothpaste, squirting a dab in my mouth to help rinse away the surprisingly sweet taste of Monique's blood.

Finished with the shower, I stood, listening to the water drip against the cool tile floor. Monique had clawed and scratched my skin during the night, both in pleasure and ultimately in death. Not wanting to know the full extent, but needing to see, to begin piecing together the events of the night, I grabbed the towel and tried to wipe the condensation off the steamed mirror. Wiping it again, I did not comprehend my towel's inability to clear the mist. I grabbed the hand towel. I rubbed until I realized the towel rack behind me was visible—but I was not.

A lump welled in my throat, making it virtually impossible to breathe as panic encroached. Overcome with light-headedness, I staggered from the bathroom, the treachery of my eyes obviously blinded by shear psychological stress. I stumbled to the dresser mirror, my eyes sealed tight. Taking a deep breath, I swallowed deliberately and opened my eyes. There in the mirror, I beheld reflections. Reflections of my bed, diligently trimmed by room service, the breaking light of dawn streaming from the parted curtains, the faded pictures hanging on the paisley-papered walls, reflections of every appointment in the room. Reflections of everything—except me.

"Oh, God!" I cried out. Gone was my reflection, lost to a world where I did not belong. Knowing what I was to become, my reflection, my life, was forever lost, and so was I.

CANINE COMPANIONS
FOR INDEPENDENCE®

Spiritul de întuneric
Te implor
posedă această ființă indisciplinat
forja cuvintele mele asupra
sufletului lor
viața lor să fie a mea
sângele nostru să fie una

Spirit of the dark

I beseech thee

possess this unruly being

forge my words upon their soul

their life be mine

our blood be one